PROMISE OF PASSION

Gillian's voice dropped to an unsteady whisper. "I am yours and yours alone, Captain, for as long as our agreement endures."

"You have the face of an angel, did you know that, madam?" he said quietly. "But I've known too many 'angels' with hearts as black as pitch."

Lowering his head, he pressed his lips to hers, then drew back slowly before kissing her once more, his mouth searching and lingering . . .

Gillian was shuddering when he pulled away. She heard the deep ring of passion in his voice when he spoke again. "You've made me many promises, so I'll make you one in return. I promise that I will give to you as much as you give to me . . . and that I will make the nights sweet when we lie together . . . sweeter than you ever dreamed."

TODAY'S HOTTEST READS
ARE TOMORROW'S SUPERSTARS

VICTORY'S WOMAN   (4484, $4.50)
by Gretchen Genet

Andrew—the carefree soldier who sought glory on the battlefield, and returned a shattered man . . . Niall—the legendary frontiersman and a former Shawnee captive, tormented by his past . . . Roger—the troubled youth, who would rise up to claim a shocking legacy . . . and Clarice—the passionate beauty bound by one man, and hopelessly in love with another. Set against the backdrop of the American revolution, three men fight for their heritage—and one woman is destined to change all their lives forever!

FORBIDDEN   (4488, $4.99)
by Jo Beverley

While fleeing from her brothers, who are attempting to sell her into a loveless marriage, Serena Riverton accepts a carriage ride from a stranger—who is the handsomest man she has ever seen. Lord Middlethorpe, himself, is actually contemplating marriage to a dull daughter of the aristocracy, when he encounters the breathtaking Serena. She arouses him as no woman ever has. And after a night of thrilling intimacy—a forbidden liaison—Serena must choose between a lady's place and a woman's passion!

WINDS OF DESTINY   (4489, $4.99)
by Victoria Thompson

Becky Tate is a half-breed outcast—branded by her Comanche heritage. Then she meets a rugged stranger who awakens her heart to the magic and mystery of passion. Hiding a desperate past, Texas Ranger Clint Masterson has ridden into cattle country to bring peace to a divided land. But a greater battle rages inside him when he dares to desire the beautiful Becky!

WILDEST HEART   (4456, $4.99)
by Virginia Brown

Maggie Malone had come to cattle country to forge her future as a healer. Now she was faced by Devon Conrad, an outlaw wounded body and soul by his shadowy past . . . whose eyes blazed with fury even as his burning caress sent her spiraling with desire. They came together in a Texas town about to explode in sin and scandal. Danger was their destiny—and there was nothing they wouldn't dare for love!

ELAINE BARBIERI

Only for Love

ZEBRA BOOKS
KENSINGTON PUBLISHING CORP.

*To those who surround me with love and
make the meaning of the word clearer every day.
You are my inspiration.*

ZEBRA BOOKS are published by

Kensington Publishing Corp.
850 Third Avenue
New York, NY 10022

First Printing: August, 1994

Printed in the United States of America

One

The surrounding stench was breathtaking, the scene incredibly wretched as the wagons rumbled along the cobbled streets in the darkness before dawn. Ramshackle houses lined the narrow passageways, their overhanging upper stories creating dark tunnels of fetid odors from gutters filled with rotting garbage steeped in pools of human waste. Trash dumped without caution or care impeded progress through the malodorous thoroughfares as great brown rats moved freely in the shadows, seeking their preference in the rank heaps, and croaking ravens awaited the first light of dawn to pillage amongst them.

Dark, verminous, damp, and penetratingly cold—the silent misery and reek of the London slums was yet another agony for Gillian Haige to bear as the wagons continued their path toward the sea.

Fighting inner revulsion and tears close to falling, Gillian momentarily closed her eyes. The journey of a few miles had seemed incredibly long.

The journey had begun hours earlier, while brilliant stars and a great, full moon had still glowed in the dark sky overhead. Sighing with relief as she had emerged out onto the street and the barred door had slammed closed behind her,

Gillian had not protested as their group had been herded into the waiting wagons and the round of local prisons and goals had continued. But her relief had been short-lived. The swelling number of penal transportees at each stop had added a merciless degree of congestion even as a frigid winter wind had lambasted the ill-protected occupants of the wagons unrelentingly.

Mumbled curses, growing louder with each corner turned and each stop served, had halted abruptly, however, as the wagons had neared the swiftly flowing Thames and London Bridge had come within view. The gory spectacle of tall spikes bearing heads of executed criminals had temporarily stilled audible complaint.

Raising her chin, Gillian swallowed thickly, pressing her lips tightly shut against their quivering as a familiar anger soared. She would allow no sign of weakness to mar her composure! She was not a criminal like the rest of the passengers here, and she would not behave like one!

Turning at a whimper beside her, Gillian met the gaze of heavily laden, silver-blue eyes identical to hers. She assessed a face exactly mirroring her own, delicate features framed by hair so fair that it glowed almost white in the semilight. But the exquisitely sculpted cheeks duplicating hers were damp from tears and devoid of color despite the chafe of the frigid wind.

The knot in Gillian's chest tightened. Reaching for her sister's hand, she gripped it tightly. Her brief smile was forced.

"Don't be afraid, Adria. Remember what Papa always said. We must be above fear. Those heads we saw back there . . ." Indicating the grisly display recently passed, Gillian unconsciously raised her chin higher. ". . . they were just another symbol of the barbarity which has become a part of the human condition, the inhumanity of man toward man, the reality that Papa fought with every ounce of his strength, every day of his life. It's a symbol of all the things we've been brought up to detest. We can't turn away from it. We must face it down—show that we don't fear it. We must—"

"Oh, Gillian . . ." A sob escaped Adria's trembling lips. "I'm so afraid."

Gillian's soft tirade halted abruptly.

What else had their scholarly father always said?

My daughters are two exquisite felines . . . one content to purr while the other seeks to roar . . .

Oh, Papa . . .

As always, her sister's need renewing her strength, Gillian gripped Adria's hand more tightly than before. Her voice hushed, Gillian whispered familiar words that came straight from the heart.

"Don't worry, Adria, dear. I'll take care of you."

The soft echo of Gillian's promise lingering, the wagons rumbled on toward the sea.

The morning had grown colder, his disposition more vile. The wharf a short distance beyond teemed with early-morning traffic in anticipation of sailings on the tide, but prospect of the imminent departure of the *Colonial Dawn* held little appeal for Captain Derek Andrews.

Looking briefly at the somber sky as a hardy gust rocked the deck under his feet, Derek braced himself against the wind and turned toward the sea. His strong features were severely drawn and his gaze cold. His tall, powerful frame, strengthened by years of heavy physical labor, was clad totally in black, a color that was his sole concession to the obscure corner of his soul where a similar darkness lingered.

The tight lines of his expression growing as formidable as the day that was dawning, Derek assessed the horizon in the distance. The swiftly moving, leaden clouds he saw there allowed him no respite from his deepening mood as he turned back to the dock, brows furrowed over eyes as black as his disposition.

Damn! Even a long night spent with Peggy, his favorite whore, had not sweetened his humor. It wasn't as if she hadn't tried. The accommodating redhead had all but worn herself out in the attempt, but neither his heart nor his mind had been in it.

His expression unchanged, Derek recalled the warmth of Peggy's full lips against his, the expert manner of a kiss calculated to excite, the slow, determined descent of her skilled mouth, and its eventual capture of a vital part of his anatomy that had surged full and firm despite his distraction.

Peggy had been determined to please him. He had read a need in her pale eyes and an emotion there that had surpassed affection. He had had those thoughts confirmed by the slender whore's hesitant whisper when he had bid her farewell, but he had not allowed her trembling words to touch him. He had learned in the most difficult of ways that words uttered in passion were often forgotten when passion cooled, and that the most beautiful lips of all often spoke the cruelest lies. His understanding of the true nature of the fairer sex, however, had not affected his taste for it . . . and, in the end, Peggy had gotten her due.

Derek's mind snapped back to the present with a shout from the deck below. He had no taste for the voyage soon to commence. Were it not for the ill fortune that had caused his ship to be beset by two powerful storms on the voyage to England months earlier, striking so close in succession as to dispel any chance of accomplishing the necessary repairs, his cargo would have weathered the storm and arrived intact. Instead, the merchandise in the hold, the good Pennsylvania foodstuffs—wheat, flour, biscuit, butter, all manner of beef and hams, not to mention every last one of the barrels of Pennsylvania apple cider he had believed securely lashed below—had suffered from damage to the hull that had come perilously close to sinking his ship. His ship had eventually limped into port, its inauspicious arrival silent testimony to the stout heart of the vessel and the courage of his crew.

That victory notwithstanding, he had arrived in London a bankrupt man.

Derek's gaze narrowed into slits as he recalled the night long weeks later when he had sat alone in his cabin and faced the reality that although he had saved his ship from the sea, danger of losing it was still very real. With no manner of inducement or persuasion having been successful in raising the sum he had needed to make repairs and purchase cargo for the return voyage, he had solemnly vowed in that silent moment to secure the necessary funds . . . *any way he could.*

The next morning, he had encountered John Barrett.

As if summoned by his thoughts, a black carriage drew to a halt on the dock below. A short man, strongly built and stylishly dressed despite his corpulence, stepped down onto the dock, and Derek's expression hardened. There was something about John Barrett that went beyond his somewhat repulsive physical appearance—a shiftiness of the eye, a twist of the lips, a hint of perversion that bespoke enjoyment of the trade he practiced and the power it wielded.

Watching as the man turned toward the open wagons

drawing up behind the carriage, Derek saw him shout a command that was lost to him in a furious blast of wind that rocked the ship more heartily than before. Reaction to the man's words was immediate as the rear gates of the wagons were released and the human cargo within began filing down onto the dock.

Derek surveyed the occupants of the wagons grimly as they were herded into uneven lines. Some shackled hand and foot, some bowed as if from the weight of years, all reflected in appearance and demeanor time spent behind prison bars. They were a sorry lot—convicts of the lowest degree, thieves, harlots of the most hardened moral tone, incorrigible criminals all . . . to be transported to the colonies to serve terms of indenture in payment of their crimes.

No stranger to the weight of shackles, however, Derek knew a surprising truth that those below did not. For some, those chains would prove preferable to an indenture more cruel than slavery could ever be.

Derek's expression grew more grim. But he had little sympathy for those in the ragged lines forming below him. Most were receiving their due. He had risen above the chains that had once bound him. He was captain of his own ship and master of his own fate, and he would not take a step backward . . . at any price.

That thought foremost in his mind, Derek turned slowly, deliberately, from the scene unfolding.

"Get in line there, all of ye, or ye'll feel the weight of my stick!"

Gillian turned sharply at the guard's coarse command, shooting him a contemptuous glance before picking up her small hand baggage and stepping down onto the dock.

Clutching her cloak tightly closed as a gust of wind dragged at her hood and set the voluminous folds to flapping wildly, Gillian glanced at the dock around her. The activity was briefly overwhelming. Vendors of all types and sizes loudly hawked their wares, as great carts loaded with towering supplies rumbled toward docked ships with little regard for pedestrian traffic. Merchant and beggar mingled with trollop and thief in an overall din of shouted curses and pleas, whinnied protests from horses pressed beyond endurance, and cries of joy, pain, and sheer frustration as the confusion mounted.

Shivering as another gust raised the folds of her cloak, Gillian turned as her sister stepped down onto the dock behind her. Adria's face was pinched and white, but her eyes were dry. Relieved, Gillian prepared to move forward as a rough hand shoved her unexpectedly.

"I told' ye to take yer place in line, wench!" The guard's rheumy eyes were suddenly close. His putrid breath set her stomach churning as he rasped more harshly than before, "And ye'll do best to keep yer eyes to yerself. Ye'll not get yer chance to sell yer wares here!"

Gillian's cheeks colored with heat. "Foul-mouthed brute! How dare you speak to me in such a way!"

"Aye . . . aye . . . 'how dare you speak to her in such a way' . . . ?" Gillian turned toward the mocking voice as a hard-faced woman continued harshly from her position in the line of transportees, ". . . 'cause she's a *lady,* can't you see? Not a poor, honest whore, like me."

Anger rising, Gillian snapped in return, "If you were as honest as you claim to be, whatever your trade, you wouldn't be here, would you?"

"Aye, that could be true . . ." The whore's expression grew gradually vicious, ". . . but then, if it was, what would bring a high-class *lady* like you down among the likes of us?"

"Indeed." Gillian paused for emphasis. "If it were any of your business—if I thought you were capable of understanding me in any way—I would explain." The fine line of Gillian's lips tightened as she continued more coldly than before, "But it *is* not . . . and you *are* not."

The whore's coarse features tightened. Silent rage glinted in her eyes the moment before she lunged unexpectedly, throwing the full weight of her body at Gillian. Knocking her off balance, the whore raked savagely at Gillian's face and hair, screeching shrill, vile curses that were interrupted by a sudden, harsh command from behind.

"Separate the bitches, damn you! I'll have no damage to my merchandise before we've even left shore!"

The raging whore turned furiously toward the voice only to halt abruptly, fear replacing wrath in her expression as she took a step back. Her heavy breasts heaving, her full frame blocking Gillian's view, the whore shuddered.

"I didn't do nothin'! It was her fault . . . actin' high and mighty, like she was the queen or somethin'!"

"Get this doxy out of my sight!"

The woman thrust from her path by a rough hand, Gillian froze at first glance of the man who had so shaken the frenzied harlot. Short, dark, and wide of girth, his features were thick and heavy, his complexion swarthy. His clothing was fashionable and meticulously pressed, but an impression of dishevelment, as if the man were personally unclean, overwhelmed. Perpetuating that impression was the perspiration that trickled in shiny paths down his jowled, heavily veined cheeks despite the cold that grew sharper with each successive gust of wind.

Instantly repulsed, Gillian watched as the unappealing fellow's gaze moved over her with discomfiting intensity. His slow smile raised the hackles on her spine as he spoke in a low, insidious tone.

"So, we have a rose amongst the thorns . . . a flower amongst the chaff . . ."

Reaching out unexpectedly, the fellow grasped a lock of Gillian's hair loosened by the angry harlot's attack. He held her fast as she attempted to draw back, his gaze intent until a soft voice interjected hesitantly from behind.

"Gillian, a—are you all right?"

Adria stepped into sight beside Gillian, and the fellow gasped aloud, his expression almost ludicrous with incredulity.

"Can it be? Two flowers, identically beautiful!" His expression grew florid as he laughed harshly. "Oh, how I will *enjoy* this unexpected garden during the long, lonely voyage . . ."

Turning away in abrupt dismissal, the offensive fellow addressed the guard. "Get them moving . . . all of them! Hold them over there until we're ready to board, and take care not to let anyone slip away!"

"Aye, Mr. Barrett!"

Turning to her sister as the fellow moved toward the ship, Gillian saw tears again glittering in Adria's eyes. Refusing to submit to the fear making slow inroads into her own mind as well, Gillian reached for her sister's hand and squeezed it reassuringly.

Still struggling to maintain her composure as the line of transportees began moving toward the ship, Gillian was struck by a sudden, violent push from behind. The breath knocked from her lungs, she stumbled helplessly forward, the hard surface of the dock rising rapidly up to meet her the moment before she was snatched back to safety by a strong arm.

Shaken, Gillian leaned heavily against the chest of the bearded, curly-haired fellow who had saved her from falling. Looking up, trembling words of gratitude freezing on her lips, she was startled to see the anger in the young man's pale eyes was directed *at her* as he grated, "Even a fool knows when he should watch his back!"

"Watch my back . . . ?" Uncertain, Gillian looked behind her. The whore snickered revealingly from her position in line a few feet away and realization dawned.

Restraining Gillian's angry surge toward the woman, the bearded fellow rebuked her sharply. "That would be a mistake. You've already stirred John Barrett's interest, which is something you'll regret. As for Maggie, you're no match for her. She's been on the streets since she was four. She'd slit your throat as soon as look at you, and not lose a minute's sleep over it. If you're smart, you'll just watch your tongue and keep out of her way."

Gillian's temper flared. "I don't recall asking your advice! I don't know who John Barrett is or who *you* are for that matter. Nor do I care! As for that woman . . . if *she's* smart, she'll stay away from *me!*"

The young man's gaze went abruptly cold. Releasing her, he slipped back into line without another word, leaving Gillian staring at his retreating back with the stunned realization that the strong hands which had prevented her fall were *shackled* . . . that the legs carrying her rescuer away without a backward look were *chained!*

A chill moved down Gillian's spine.

Her unexpected savior was a *convict.*

Adria's small, trembling hand slipped back into hers. Determinedly rejecting her burgeoning fear, Gillian gripped her sister's hand more tightly and moved into line.

"*I* am captain of this ship, Mr. Barrett. I suggest you remember that!"

The storm impending on the quarterdeck far outweighed the worsening threat overhead as Derek Andrews faced John Barrett's rabid countenance. His aversion to the short, unpleasant fellow moved rapidly toward contempt. Desperate circumstances had forced his participation in the transportation under way, but desperate circumstances could not force him to enjoy it. He was all too aware of the trickery and subterfuge common in transportations, as well as the kidnapping of adults and children that often swelled the lists of transportees. His position in this affair was heinous enough. He was determined not to allow his human cargo aboard until he was satisfied that there was not one among them who had not been duly sentenced by law to his fate.

Raising his voice so it might be heard over the screech of gulls soaring overhead and the harried shouts of seamen below, Derek repeated, "I'll tell you once more . . . in accordance with my direct order, my first mate will stand at the head of the gangplank so he may ascertain by individual questioning if the transportees have arrived here by legal means."

John Barrett's beefy chest heaved with barely suppressed fury as he gritted his yellowed teeth in a savage smile.

"Are you saying you doubt my integrity in this matter, Captain Andrews—indeed, that you suspect me of criminal conduct?"

Derek's dark eyes remained cold. "You may read whatever you like into it, Mr. Barrett, but my order stands."

His swarthy complexion flushing a darker hue, his rotund proportions appearing to plump with rage, Barrett hissed, "My, my . . . how righteous we are sounding, when a short time ago you were ready to agree to any offer made to you in order to save your ship, with no questions asked! But the London Transport Company was the only one ready to help you in your difficult position, wasn't it, Captain, the only one prepared to put up the money needed to finance the extensive repairs for your ship so it would be in condition to do any transporting at all?"

Derek's gaze turned to ice. "I sold you cargo space on my ship, Mr. Barrett. I did not sell you my soul."

John Barrett's responsive shout of laughter was unexpected. His complexion deepening to apoplectic color, he retorted, "Oh, did you not!" Barrett laughed again, the shrillness of the sound turning nearby seamen toward him with inquiring glances as he continued. "I suggest you read the terms of our contract again, sir! You are the captain of the *Colonial Dawn* . . . yes, but under the terms of our signed agreement, *I* hold the position of Supercargo for the duration of the voyage. In that position, *I* and *I* alone am responsible for the 'cargo.' All decisions made pertaining to each and every person included as a part of that cargo will be made by me—and *only* me. Acting with that authority, I tell you now as I have before, that every man and woman in that pathetic group on the dock below has been cleared for transportation by me, personally. With no little pride, I add that I have escorted similar groups across the sea many times before. Unlike you, I am well versed on the needs of people such as they. I have made provision for their voyage accordingly. I might also add that I have placed hundreds of these felons in positions in the colonies where they might make a positive contribution to society for the first time in their lives. For that monumental feat, I, as well as many others, feel I have made a contribution to society as well. I ask you to keep those facts in mind when you address me on this matter in the future!"

Not choosing to reply, Derek turned to shout out over the din below, "Mr. Cutter . . . Assume your position at the head of the gangplank."

A choking noise emerged from Barrett's throat as Derek turned back toward him once more. His voice icier than the wind that buffeted them, Derek continued. "As for the terms of the agreement I signed with the London Transport Company, I give you notice that I intend to abide by them fully. In your position as Supercargo, you will be responsible for all decisions made as to the 'cargo' and for its condition upon arrival at our destination. I am aware that interference by me will result in forfeiture of the compensation due me by the London Transport Company at the conclusion of the voyage. *However,* I ask you to remember that the 'cargo' does not come under your absolute authority until it is *on* this ship."

His dark eyes drilling into Barrett's florid countenance, Derek took a step forward, an unconscious act that heightened the import of his words as he stood towering over the shorter man to conclude, "I repeat, no member of that group will set foot on this ship until my first mate has personally ascertained that he has come here by legal means."

"All right!" Spittle spraying from his lips with the fury of his response, Barrett turned toward the steps in a quick movement that belied his obesity of form. Jerking back toward Derek again before he had taken a few steps, Barrett added hotly, "But I warn you now, Captain. I am not a man to be trifled with!"

Watching as Barrett made his way with surprising agility

down the narrow staircase to the crowded main deck, Derek silently acknowledged the truth of the despicable fellow's statement. John Barrett was not a man to be trifled with.

But neither was he.

His gaze frigid as it followed John Barrett's determined progress toward the gangplank where the first of the "cargo" prepared to board, Derek leaned forward, clasping the rail, watching intently.

A brief break in the solid banks of gray overhead allowed a shaft of light to shine down on the gangplank as the line of penal transportees surged toward it. No more than a narrow board with a rope railing strung along one side, it swayed and dipped with the motion of the ship and the steps of the uneasy column, providing footing that was insecure and slick.

Snatching up the small hand baggage containing all that was left of her personal belongings, Gillian moved silently forward, her heart pounding. Not daring to look behind where Adria followed in trembling silence, Gillian raised her chin in an outward display of courage that was as much for her sister's benefit as for her own.

Stepping up onto the board plank as the stinging wind continued its assault, Gillian looked up at the ship that was to deliver Adria and her to an unknown land far across the sea. The vessel was large and cheerless, forbidding and skeletal in appearance with its tall masts stripped of sail. The deck was crowded with sailors in all phases of work, each appearing to curse more loudly than the next in a jostling, dismal hubbub punctuated by shrill whistles and a loud hallooing from which there appeared no escape.

Gillian breathed deeply, her courage briefly waning. The

crew appeared to be of a considerable number. Their group of penal transportees numbered well over a hundred in size. She knew little of ships, but she knew that as large as the vessel was, it was not large enough.

Gillian's lips quivered briefly. She had heard rumors about these ships. She had heard that many of the transportees were not delivered there by legal means, and that legalities meant little to those who trafficked in such trade. She had also heard that the numbers of those being transported were often drastically reduced by the time destination was reached . . . and that no questions were ever asked about those who did not survive.

A shudder shook Gillian and her eyes brimmed unexpectedly. Suddenly ashamed, she forced her frightening thoughts to a halt and blinked away her tears.

What was wrong with her? Would she abandon everything her father had taught her at the first sign of adversity? Would she allow fear to make her forget who and what she was or ever hoped to be? She was Gillian Harcourt Haige, daughter of Morris Harcourt Haige, distinguished man of letters! Her father had been a brave man, an educator who had cared little for material wealth but who had schooled his daughters well. Of the many things he had taught them, one concept had been stressed above all—that ignorance and fear were man's greatest enemies, and education and courage were his greatest strengths. She had always believed in her father's teachings. She would be damned before she would falter now!

Those noble thoughts ringing in her mind, Gillian suppressed a gasp as the person ahead of her moved to allow her clear view of the deck for the first time and a familiar squat figure came into view.

That vile man again!

A blustery gust stole John Barrett's words as he conversed with a young seaman standing at the head of the gangplank, but it was plain to see by the purple color that had transfused Barrett's complexion that the two men were arguing. Barrett regarded the other man with a glint in his eye that could be considered no less than savage, and Gillian was reminded of a wild boar she had seen pictured in one of her father's books, an animal written to have killed for the pure pleasure of the act.

Mesmerized by the viciousness displayed in Barrett's countenance, Gillian was unprepared for the lightning-quick movement of his hand as he delivered a powerful, unexpected blow to the seaman's face.

A deep cry of rage resounded from the quarterdeck above as the seaman staggered backward, almost losing his feet. Looking up, Gillian saw a tall, powerful figure clothed in black arched over the rail the split second before he moved down the steps in a stride so smooth and rapid as to appear a great bird of prey swooping down upon the deck.

Gasping, Gillian clutched the gangplank rail, her gaze riveted on the big man's face. Dark brows furrowed over black furious eyes, handsome chiseled features tight, a thin scar stretching the length of one sun-darkened cheek adding silent menace to the overall threat of his expression, he strode to Barrett's side to face the man with barely suppressed rage.

His voice low, deep, and rigidly controlled, traveled with surprising clarity in the sudden silence that had settled over the ship.

"You will apologize to Mr. Cutter, Mr. Barrett."

"I will not!" Barrett's reply was followed by a short laugh that again raised the hackles on Gillian's spine as he continued. "As you have reminded me, Captain Andrews, you are master of this ship. But as I have reminded you, *I* am

Supercargo. As such, I am this man's superior. I will not abide insolence from him!"

"Mr. Cutter was acting under my orders and in my capacity. His authority in this instance is unquestioned. In striking *him,* you were striking *me."*

Pausing, the captain repeated more stiffly than before, "An apology is in order. I insist upon it. Without it, the *Colonial Dawn* will not sail."

"Oh, ho!" Barrett's full face grew livid. "You would have me believe you would jeopardize the voyage and chance losing your ship for the sake of a common seaman?"

The captain's expression hardened. He did not reply.

Silence stretched between the two adversaries . . . growing longer, stiffer, more intense, until . . .

"All right!" His small eyes blazing, his broad form trembling with rage, Barrett turned abruptly to the seaman standing nearby. "You may consider an apology extended!"

The captain addressed his first mate directly. "Is Mr. Barrett's apology acceptable, Mr. Cutter?"

Barely discernible satisfaction flickered across the young man's bruised mouth. "Aye, sir."

The captain paused briefly. "Proceed with the interviewing, Mr. Cutter."

Barrett's florid countenance twitched revealingly as the captain maintained a rigid stance beside the gangplank and the questioning of the transportees resumed.

A slow contempt rose within Gillian as the line inched slowly forward. That captain . . . he did not fool her! For all his posturing, he had no true concern for the men or women being herded onto the ship like so much cattle! If he had, he would not have become involved in this immoral trade! Nor was he concerned for the rights of his seamen, for if he was, he would not have accepted a person as odious as Mr. Barrett as Supercargo!

Shivering as another frigid blast abraded her, Gillian listened as the interviews continued. Her lips twisted with contempt as the same question was asked of each transportee before stepping down onto the deck.

"Have you become part of this group legally, by due process of law? Answer yes or no."

The wind whipped more cruelly than before, increasing Gillian's shivering despite the heat that burned within. Turning to look behind her, she saw Adria's face was blanched of color, her shuddering more pronounced as they neared the head of the gangplank. The knowledge that her sister was shaking as much from fear as from the unrelenting cold flushed Gillian's anger to sudden fury.

They had been robbed of their rights as Englishwomen! They had been treated like criminals because of debts their noble, idealistic father had incurred before his unexpected death! They had been sentenced to be shipped without their consent to a land far from their home to repay his debts with years of servitude. They were to be put on the auction block and *sold* to the highest bidder! They had become little more than *slaves!*

Incensed, her heart pounding, Gillian stepped to the head of the gangplank. A sudden gust of wind whipped once more, dragging her hood from her head to flay her small, perfect features with loosened silver-blond strands of hair, but she did not feel the cruel bite of the cold. Scorching the young seaman with an imperious glance as he repeated his question, she allowed her gaze to touch briefly on John Barrett's tight, ugly expression before meeting the captain's unexpectedly intense gaze for the first time. Infuriated by the boldness of the dark eyes that assessed her openly, Gillian felt her control snap.

"You ask me if I have become a part of this group by legal means? Well, I have a question as well! Is it legal to make a freeborn Englishwoman a slave?"

"So it's you again!" Barrett pinned her with a furious gaze. "Answer the question, bitch!"

Gillian's face flamed. "Were I you, I would look to my own origins for the proper application of that name, sir!"

A muffled sound escaped the captain's throat the moment before he halted Barrett's threatening step forward with the flat of his hand and a soft command.

"Answer the question, madam."

Turning on the captain in burgeoning rage, Gillian hissed, "I will not dignify this farce with a response!"

Black eyes darker, more fearsome than the fires of Hades, caught and held hers. "Answer the question."

"You speak of legalities . . ." Gillian's response dripped with scorn. "What of moralities . . . or of the *immorality* of making a free man a slave? Or is that simple premise above you?"

The heat of the captain's gaze intensified, and Gillian raised her chin defensively. She would not reveal that those eyes as black as ebony seemed to penetrate her soul, affecting her as no others had ever affected her before. Nor would she accede to the trembling somehow unrelated to fear that they evoked as she continued with open contempt. "But I waste my breath, don't I? You are no more than a slaver trading in your own countrymen's blood! And slavers are interested in profits, not moralities, aren't they?"

"Shut the woman up! I've had enough!" Interrupting with unrestrained venom, Barrett attempted another threatening step toward her. "We have no time for a discourse on moralities, most especially from a harlot who sells herself on street corners!"

"Liar! How dare you say—"

"You call me a liar . . . ?" Spittle spraying from his lips with the fury of his reply, Barrett rasped, ". . . you, a whore whose only truth lies in the coin that crosses her palm after she has sold her flesh for the going price of the day?"

"Liar!" Enraged, Gillian spat, "You low, vile beast! You cannot recognize a woman of virtue because you are a stranger to noble emotions! You are contemptible and corrupt, and were I a man I—"

Her furious tirade halted by a soft sound of despair from behind, Gillian turned in time to see the trembling hand Adria reached toward her. Gasping, Gillian was paralyzed by terror as Adria swayed weakly on the narrow plank, tottering—

Swept from her feet and deposited on deck before she had time to react, Gillian stood frozen as the captain moved past her to snatch Adria to safety the second before she slipped into the sea.

Fear, horror, and rage converged in Gillian's mind as the captain stood Adria beside her, continuing to support her with his arm. Her shock erupted in a single, scathing hiss.

"Take your hands off my sister!"

"Your sister?"

Momentary incredulity flashed as the captain glanced between the two delicate faces looking up at him, duplicates of each other in every way except for the venom glowing in the brilliant blue of Gillian's eyes as she ordered with increasing enmity, "Take your hands off her, I said!"

His strong features tightening into anger, the captain remained motionless for long moments before dropping his hands abruptly to his sides. His expression caustic, he dipped his head in mocking courtesy.

"You're *welcome,* madam."

Turning, he addressed his first mate in a clipped tone. "Finish up here and get the cargo below. If anyone interferes, clap him in irons!"

Intent on Adria's shaken state, Gillian did not follow the captain's stiff progress as he strode away. Feeling the weight of someone's gaze as she was shoved roughly into place in line, she cast a glance over her shoulder to see John Barrett staring malevolently. Her brief, cutting glance dismissed him as she turned back to Adria.

Unseen from the quarterdeck, however, the gaze of dark, angry eyes lingered.

Ungrateful witch!

Beautiful ungrateful witch . . .

Inwardly fuming, his broad palms tightening around the quarterdeck rail in a choking grip, Derek watched as the stream of transportees continued. His ears keenly attuned to the question repeated over and again before each individual stepped down on deck, he struggled to keep his gaze from drifting to the slender, haughty woman who was silent at last.

His gaze narrowing, Derek recalled the moment the gusting wind had blown back the young woman's hood, revealing her face for the first time. The azure hue of her eyes, fringed with a sweep of lashes so long and dark as to seem unreal, had momentarily stunned him. She had the small, delicate features of a porcelain doll, hair as fair and glowing as if molten silver and gold had been woven into each strand . . .

And a tongue as sharp as a razor . . .

The haughty witch had drawn blood with each syllable pronounced in her well-spoken tone.

Derek gave a short, caustic laugh. So much pride for a whore . . . *too* much pride for the recreant sister who was her mirror image.

Derek's gaze drifted toward the women once more. The two phenomenal beauties were as dissimilar as they were alike and each was equally flawed. One, faint of heart, was cowed; the other, excessively bold, breathed fire.

Derek suddenly realized that a conscienceless part of his anatomy was responding of its own accord to the bold blond beauty, caring little about her flaws. He was momentarily amused. But he was not a fool. Were he the most desperate of men, and were she the only whore left in the world, he still would have no part of the tart with the rapier tongue.

Suddenly uncomfortable with his thoughts, Derek drew his powerful frame erect and turned his attention to the work in progress below the masts. A quick assessment there and a check of the rising tide revealed they would soon be ready to sail.

Moving on to the urgent press of duty at hand, Derek turned his back on the transportees below, dismissing the beautiful, arrogant whore from his mind.

$\mathcal{T}wo$

Impossible . . . impossible . . .

"Impossible!"

The single word whirling in Gillian's mind burst from her lips as she looked around her at the forbidding hold that was to house the transportees for the duration of their voyage across the ocean.

Adria stood silent and shaken behind her as Gillian observed their surroundings more closely. Dark and dank, deep below main deck where there was little light and the air reeked with the fumes of pitch, bilge water, and other more formidable odors, it was a prison far more intimidating than the debtor's prison Adria and she had inhabited during their weeks of confinement. Shivering, she suddenly realized there appeared to be no provision to alleviate the cold that penetrated to the bone, despite the fact that they would sail through winter seas during the severest months of the year.

Her lips tightening, Gillian scrutinized the narrow cots spotted with stains of former occupants, placed side by side without adequate space for walking between. She noted with dismay the short partition in the rear corner where little privacy prevailed, marking the spot intended for bathing and other matters of personal nature.

Gillian's mind reeled with shock. Could it be that such were the total accommodations provided for over one hun-

dred and twenty of their number? Where had space been
provided for the few moments of privacy necessary to maintain simple human dignity . . . for dining in a civilized manner . . . for doing laundry . . . for exercise beyond a few
shallow steps on the crowded deck around them?

Gasping as she watched the frantic claiming of bunks by
the transportees still filing in, Gillian realized that most appalling of all was the fact that no arrangement had been
made for the separation of the sexes! Men and women would
be lying side by side with no more than a few inches between cots for the duration of a voyage that would last eight
weeks at the minimum!

Was the captain of this ship insane?

"What's yer problem, yer highness?" A familiar voice to
her rear turned Gillian toward the sour-faced guard she had
encountered earlier. His sneer indicating that he had not forgotten the reprimand he had suffered because of their exchange, he continued with barely concealed satisfaction.
"The accommodations not to yer likin'?"

"You odious man . . ." Hot color flushing her cheeks, Gillian stared back into the fellow's rheumy eyes. "You're enjoying yourself, aren't you?" Indicating the transportees
swarming between the narrow cots, she continued tightly.
"You see these pathetic wretches scrambling for a place to
rest their weary bones. In their misery they don't give
thought to the comforts *due* them as human beings and as
Englishmen, even in their dire situation. But neither my sister nor I have forgotten who we are and what we are! We
aren't animals to be herded together without thought to human dignity! I demand—"

"Yer demandin' days are over, yer ladyship!" Shoving her
roughly, the guard watched as she staggered backward, his
sneer widening to a gap-toothed smile as the backs of her

legs struck the edge of the cot behind her and she collapsed to a seated position on its surface.

"That's right, yer ladyship!" The guard's short laughter darkened the color that flooded Gillian's face as he went on, "You did well to claim yer place before all the cots are taken and ye find yerself sleepin' on the deck for the duration of the voyage."

Noting out of the corner of her eye that Adria hastened to claim the cot beside her, Gillian stood up abruptly. "You can't threaten me! You're no more than a servant of the Crown while I am—"

"While you are barter to be sold in payment of debts *due* the Crown!"

Stepping out from where he had stood unseen behind the guard, the ugly toad of a man called by the name of John Barrett walked closer.

"But you are very lovely barter indeed, both you and your sister, despite your disagreeable tongue."

Barrett's leering gaze strayed toward Adria, who maintained her silence beside the cot she had claimed. He laughed aloud at her expression of fixed fascination as she returned his stare much like a frightened bird hypnotized by a snake.

"Your sister seems to find me fascinating." He laughed again and licked his full lips, heightening his toadlike appearance. "I confess to finding you both equally engaging."

"I fear you interpret my sister's observation incorrectly, Mr. Barrett. I know her well, and I know I am not remiss when I say she finds you as totally repugnant as do I."

Shocked gasps followed Gillian's bold declaration. Not turning to ascertain their origins, Gillian held Barrett's gaze unflinchingly as his eyes narrowed into vicious slits.

Gillian's anger heightened. The audacity of the overstuffed buffoon! His bold advances toward her sister and herself had been insufferable and humiliating. She had put him in his place and he now sought to cower her! She would show him! She would stand her ground and prove to him and everyone else who thought to treat her sister and her as less than they were that Adria and she were not common rabble, that they could neither be trifled with nor—

Gillian's valiant thoughts came to an abrupt halt as John Barrett took a sharp step forward. Unwilling to retreat, she stood stiffly silent as he spoke in a tone heavy with threat.

"I fear you speak carelessly and may yet regret your words. Your lives—yours and your sister's—are not your own anymore, you see."

"Sir, my name is Gillian Harcourt Haige. My sister's name is Adria Harcourt Haige. We are Englishwomen! We claim the privileges of Englishwomen and as such are entitled to—"

"Can you truly be the fool as you seem to be!" His words a biting hiss, Barrett took another threatening step toward her. "You have no rights! As official agent of the London Transport Company and Supercargo of this ship, I hold your life in my hands—*my* hands—until we reach Jamaican shores! And it will be *I* who will sell your indenture to your new master when we reach port!"

Pausing to allow his words to take full effect, Barrett continued more lethally than before. "Do not delude yourself that your future will brighten once you are properly sold, for you will be no more than the property of your new master. According to law, you may be hired out, resold, or auctioned—even if it means separating you from your family."

Adria's soft sob punctuated another brief pause, but Gillian refused to respond as Barrett pressed. "As your master's property you may be beaten, whipped, or branded if you

displease him. If you run away, you may be punished by
extension or multiplication of your term of indenture . . . or
worse. Fool! You are no longer an Englishwoman! You are
chattel—a form of currency to be spent or used as your
master sees fit! *You have no rights!"*

Adria's sobbing the only sound in the silence around
them, Gillian maintained a rigid stance as John Barrett's
gaze burned hotly into hers, then dropped to rake her person
with slow, humiliating intimacy. Looking back up into her
eyes, he spoke again.

"You find me repugnant? I promise you, before this voyage is through, you will be begging for my favors. Perhaps
I will consider your petitions . . . if you speak sweetly
enough. Perhaps then I will indulge you—alone, or with
your sister in loving concert."

Gillian's shocked gasp raised an expression of triumph on
Barrett's features and he laughed aloud.

"Oh, yes, my proud, beautiful whore . . . we will see."

John Barrett turned away with characteristic abruptness,
leaving a reverberating silence behind him. Trembling in its
wake despite herself, Gillian raised her chin as she turned
to meet Adria's terrified expression.

Her voice emotionless, she stated, "Dry your eyes, Adria.
The day either you or I will go begging to that man will
never come."

The courage of her words ringing hollowly in her mind,
Gillian did not wait for her sister's response as she turned
to the chores awaiting her.

Standing a short distance away, Christopher Gibson stood
stock-still, stunned by the latest encounter between the arrogant blond transportee and John Barrett.

Was the woman mad?

Christopher ran a calloused, manacled hand through his curly brown hair in an unconscious gesture as he recounted in his mind the beautiful fool's behavior of the past few hours. In her first untenable act, not only had she managed to raise the ire of a dangerous whore with whom she would be spending the next eight weeks of their voyage, but she had also treated him and his well-meaning advice with contempt after he had saved her from the whore's malicious attack. She had proceeded to compound the peril of her situation by responding with similar contempt to a captain whose commanding presence would demand respect from even the most demented—after the captain had done her the service of rescuing her sister from near tragedy! And then, in a moment of supreme audacity, she had offended—no, she had held up to *open ridicule*—the man to whom her welfare had been entrusted, the man who was also the most notorious of all the agents in the employ of the London Transport Company!

John Barrett's words rang again in Christopher's mind.

Can you truly be the fool you seem to be?

Could she?

Watching as the object of his incredulity picked with disdain at the cot she had involuntarily chosen as her own, Christopher was further astounded as she withdrew a spotless linen pillow slip from her hand baggage, and with great delicacy, covered the stained pillow as if the ugly scene between her and the equally ugly and menacing John Barrett had never happened at all!

Christopher's mouth fell slack.

Could the bold beauty truly be the fool she seemed to be?

Oh, yes, she could . . .

His sudden urge to laugh interrupted by a rough jerk on his arm, Chris turned as a harsh, nasal voice sounded in his ear.

"Ye'll do well to stay away from that one." Fumbling with the key as he sought to unlock the shackles on Christopher's wrists, the guard glanced up briefly. "I've been told to release yer irons, since there's no place fer ye to run, but these irons can be snapped back on just as easy as they come off, ye know, so it'll be to yer advantage to heed my warnin'."

Indicating with a jerk of his head the arrogant blonde who still fussed with her pillow slip, the guard continued. "Master Barrett has his eye on that fancy whore and her twin, and I'm thinkin' her sass has only whet his appetite more hotly. She's a proud one and he has a mind to bring her down a peg or two."

Looking up as the wrist irons popped open, the guard hesitated, adding before reaching down to unlock the ankle irons as well, "He's a master of that game, is Master Barrett. Like he says, he'll get her to come beggin'. He has his ways . . ."

"I have no doubt he does."

Relieved to be free of their weight, Christopher rubbed his wrists as the ankle irons were released as well. A familiar bitterness surged. As a child living on the edge of an estate where his father served a titled family as groom, there had been little prospect of chains in his future, despite his family's scanty resources. His parents' situation had changed drastically, however, after the death of the estate patriarch. He had carried the memory of his mother's tears and his father's despair with him when their dire financial situation had forced him out on his own when little more than a boy. Taking to the sea, he had come home often enough in the years following to see the steady deterioration of his parents' circumstances. On his final visit, he had returned to find his mother dead and his father rewarded for a lifetime of service by being turned out into the street when he had become too ill to serve any longer.

Deepening bitterness heated the fair skin beneath Christopher's beard as he recalled the day after he had buried his father, when he had returned to the estate to claim what was left of his father's meager belongings, only to be told by the arrogant, titled master of the house that his father's things had been burned as the trash they were. He did not clearly recall the rapid progress of events that followed, except that the drunken swine had spat on his parents' memory.

Christopher's pale eyes went suddenly cold. He was told afterward that he had attacked the surly bastard. In truth, he did not doubt it, although the hot haze of fury that had suffused his mind did not allow him the satisfaction of total recall.

He remembered very clearly, however, awakening in prison with irons on his hands and feet. Young, healthy, and labeled as dangerous, he had been assessed as ripe for transportation. The legalities performed, his fate had been quickly sealed. He had learned many valuable lessons in the time since. Included among them was the truth about the justice of English law, the futility of rebellion against it, and the unexpected realization that the weight of shackles did not burden the body alone. Those realities firmly established in his mind, he had since vowed that once freed from his shackles, he would risk bearing their weight again for *no* man.

The guard drew himself to his feet as Christopher responded, "Your warning is appreciated, but you may be sure I've no thoughts in that direction. That woman is a fool and too proud for my taste. She's bound for trouble, and I'm not looking for more."

"Smart lad. If I don't miss my guess, there's some females

in this group who are already castin' warm glances yer way. Ye've but to bide yer time and ye'll find yer bed warmed as often as ye like before the voyage ends."

Nodding his thanks as the guard took his leave, Christopher scanned the crowded area briefly. Without undue conceit, he knew the guard's words were true, but he doubted he would take advantage of any willing females who were part of this transportation. Particular in his tastes, he had not seen a one who appealed to him.

Halting his gaze as it drifted back to the beauteous but overly proud blond whore, Christopher unconsciously shook his head. Oh, no! The guard's advice had been sound. He had already lost his freedom. He did not intend to lose his life as well.

Echoes of familiar movement topside raised Chris's gaze toward the deck above. The voyage would soon begin, but his hands would not be among those who would strain at the ropes in the raising of the sails. Nor would he pass this crossing with fresh wind in his face and the taste of salt spray on his lips.

Surveying the dismal surroundings he would inhabit for the next eight weeks, Christopher found his gaze settling again on the blond harlot as she busied herself at her cot a few feet away.

What had she said her name was . . . Gillian Haige? If there were any who did not know that name now, he was certain they would before the voyage was over. Haughty as she was, she was destined to learn her lessons the hard way. He supposed she deserved what she would get.

But, yet . . .

His gaze lingered.

* * *

Adria glanced around her. The bleak, airless quarters, the grunting and cursing of fellow transportees claiming bunks nearby, the suffocating odors growing stronger with each passing moment—all combined suddenly to raise a momentary wave of nausea that was almost overwhelming. Swallowing against it, Adria shuddered.

What were Gillian and she doing in this horrid place?

Her eyes dazed, Adria pushed back a pale strand of hair only a shade darker than her smooth, colorless cheeks. It seemed only yesterday that she had been in her beloved kitchen, near a warm cooking stove with the scent of fresh bread molded by her own capable hands scenting the air. She could almost see Father in the sitting room with one of his many students, and Gillian, Father's most intelligent and eager disciple, in her usual spot at his side. She could almost hear Father calling her as he had so many times, asking her to set another place at the table for the penniless scholar.

The image vanished and Adria's desperation deepened.

She would not hear Father call her . . . ever again. She would not see approval in his gaze as he praised her cooking and housekeeping, or her creative stitchery, all tasks she adored. She would never again hear him whisper with a pride that touched her heart that his daughters were opposite sides of a beautiful, matchless coin, necessary sides that complemented each other with their differences. She would never again hear his reassurance that one day Gillian would depend on her gentleness just as she depended on Gillian's strength. She had known him to be sincere, even while she had railed against the fate that had made her as timid and shy as Gillian was fearless and bold.

But Father was gone. With him had disappeared their modest house and all their possessions, save the few personal belongings Gillian and she had been able to wrest from foreclosure. Those had been black days, filled with despair.

Strangely, however, even during the darkest of those days, she had never . . . *never* . . . considered that in losing all, Gillian and she would lose their freedom as well.

Sounds overhead grew suddenly greater, wrenching Adria from her sober thoughts: stamping feet, loud, angry voices, the creaking protest of the ship, and the hard, metallic sound of iron grating against iron as the anchor was raised.

The moment of departure was upon them! Suddenly panicked, Adria managed a hoarse rasp.

"Gillian . . ."

Gillian turned immediately toward her. Her expression was sober but miraculously unmarked by fear.

"What's the matter, Adria?"

"All that noise . . ."

Surprising her, Gillian smiled. Without conceit, Adria acknowledged that Gillian's smile was beautiful. Despite their similarity of feature, she had never been able to match its stunning intensity.

"It would seem we're about to sail, Adria, so take heart. The sooner we're under way, the sooner we'll arrive at our destination, and the sooner we'll make progress toward regaining our freedom."

"But four years . . ." The period of indenture assigned them in payment of their father's debts stretched out endlessly before Adria's mind. "Four years is such a long time!"

"It will only be long if we allow it to be."

"B-but that horrid man . . ." Adria's voice dropped a notch lower at the thought of John Barrett. "You heard what he said. He frightened me."

Gillian's eyes glowed with familiar fervor as her expression sobered. "He can frighten you only if you allow yourself to be frightened. Don't worry. We shall *will* the time to pass quickly."

Adria was suddenly ashamed. Forcing her chin higher in imitation of her sister's spontaneous gesture, she acknowledged with silent despair that try as she might, she could never imitate Gillian's spontaneous courage.

Her reward was another flash of Gillian's brilliant smile, and for a moment, Adria almost believed.

Striding down the passageway with quick, angry steps, John Barrett pushed his cabin door open with a savage thrust of the hand. He stood in the doorway as it snapped back against the wall and took a deep breath, holding it for an extended period in an attempt to regain control of the rage that boiled within.

He surveyed the cramped quarters with distaste. The room was small—too small for a man of his importance! A table, a chair, a washstand, a small potbellied stove, and a bunk bed, over which hung an oil lamp which he knew at first glance was inadequate to light even this small closet of a room. He recalled the captain's cabin, spacious in comparison, and his expression turned feral.

Noting a moment later that his baggage had been delivered to his quarters as he had ordered, he nodded stiffly. It had better have been!

A tight smile touched Barrett's lips. But then, the guards making this voyage with him worked for the London Transport Company and most of them had served under him before. They knew what to expect if they did not obey his orders exactly as given.

Barrett's smile faded as he glanced back toward the narrow bunk where he would sleep for the next eight weeks.

The angelic features of the beautiful blond whore returned to mind and his agitation returned full measure.

Totally repugnant, was he?

Bitch!

Taking two steps into the cabin, Barrett reached back to slam the door closed behind him. He then snatched up the leather case resting beside the table and withdrew a stained folder. He leafed through the sheets, his fingers clumsy with haste, cursing as the list he sought eluded him. Finding it at last, he held it up to the light.

The bitch had said her name was Gillian Harcourt Haige . . .

Barrett's lips drew back over his yellowed teeth in an angry grimace. He would not forget the way she had pronounced it, as if she were royalty and he was dirt beneath her feet!

Finding the name at last, Barrett read eagerly, his gaze narrowing before he slapped the papers down on the table in disgust. Information about the bitch was inadequate, listing no more than her original date of confinement, the goal in which she had been held pending transportation, and stating her term of indenture as four years in payment of her father's debts.

Barrett's aggravation increased. How had he missed seeing her at the time of pickup?

No . . . how had he missed seeing *them?*

Recalling almost in afterthought that there were not one but two of them, two beautiful wenches who had almost escaped his notice, Barrett paused. No, that wasn't true, either. There was only one. The second sister was a pale shadow of the first, an imitation, a poor copy, without any of the original's fire. He sensed the second sister would be a lifeless, dreary piece in bed who would hardly be worth the effort.

The first sister, however . . .

Barrett suddenly laughed aloud. His imagination taking sudden flight, he saw the haughty bitch on her knees before him, begging to come to his bed. He saw her pleading and crawling, then dancing to his tune.

Oh, yes, he would make her please him. There were so many ways for her to pleasure him, and with her, he would explore every one.

His heavy lids drooping with sensual cravings aroused at the mere thought of the beautiful blond witch, Barrett laughed again. Trickles of perspiration slid from his temples to streak his cheeks as an intense heat pulsed more strongly and the swelling in his britches hardened.

He was already hot, just at the thought of her!

Gripping himself, Barrett twisted his enlarged member, his eyes slowly closing as he manipulated himself with pleasure. Repugnant, was he? Perhaps that was so, but he had never disappointed a woman with the eager tool between his legs. He had been told countless times, by those who were experienced enough to know, that there were few to match it. He had also been told that where he was lacking in height, he had been more than well apportioned in the most important area of all.

And, damn it, it was true! He recalled only too well the cries of the maids he had all but torn asunder with his avaricious cock! But he had shown them no pity. He had needed no one to tell him that despite their cries, he had pleasured those fainthearted wenches far more completely than any man ever had before. In their sobs and cursing of him, even in the blood that he had often drawn in the heat of his passion, he had read the ultimate of satisfaction.

Suddenly impatient with the constraints of clothing, Barrett pushed aside his coat and pulled down his britches, laughing aloud once more as his male part snapped up firm and erect. Saliva drooling from the corner of his lips, he worked the heated flesh more urgently, indulging the pictures slowly taking shape in his mind.

Oh, yes, it would be the proud slut first! He would teach her to beg as only he was capable of teaching. And when she had finished pleasing him to his satisfaction . . . when she had worshiped his proud manhood as many times and in as many ways as he so desired, he would show her what it was to *want* in return. Only then, when she was truly ready, when she cried out for him to bring her to climax, would he show her what a man—a *real* man—could do for a whore like her!

Yes, it would be a satisfying experience which he would repeat over and over again, as many nights as it took to convince himself that she was truly his *slave.* Then . . . *then* . . . he would bring in the sister—the pale shadow who would lie with them both to duplicate her sister's efforts and increase his pleasure twofold. He would teach them some new tricks and he would teach them to perform at will. And when he had them properly trained, he would . . . he would . . .

A sharp cry escaping his lips as his straining member erupted on cue, Barrett leaned back, catching the sticky spray in his hand.

His jowled face wet with perspiration as his heated convulsions finally stilled, Barrett smiled. The britches hanging around his ankles limiting his step, he walked to the washbowl and poured it half full, then washed his hands free of his body secretion. Amused that the haughty bitch had already afforded him a measure of satisfaction without her knowledge, he silently vowed that she would give him much, much more before he was through.

It occurred to him that the arrogant witch was not a practiced whore as he had originally thought. He was determined, however, that by the time he was done with her, she would be.

Grunting as he pulled up his britches, Barrett adjusted his clothing and took a deep breath. He would go back to the work of settling his charges in to his satisfaction.

He paused, considering. What was their exact number? One hundred and twenty? He should have no less than ninety left when they reached port . . . or eighty-five. He shrugged. Either number would be satisfactory and would make for a profitable voyage. The rest be damned.

And if the two sisters did not make it to their destination . . . well, he would have had his fill of them by then, at any rate.

Glancing briefly into the cracked mirror hanging nearby, Barrett wiped the perspiration from his forehead with the back of his sleeve. The haughty bitch had worked him into a sweat! She'd pay for that too . . .

. . . and pay, and pay, and pay.

Snowflakes flurried on the frigid, offshore wind, obstructing Derek's vision as he strained to see the men scampering up the shrouds and out onto the footropes below the topsail yards. His teeth clenched, his gaze intense, he watched their progress across the yards as they clawed at the lines holding the sails furled with one hand while using the other to hang on to the swaying rigging.

Derek's tension mounted. Hands frozen by the cold, no matter how experienced at their work, would have difficulty maintaining their grip. Personal concerns for his seamen aside, he could not afford to lose even one of them. A winter voyage was difficult under any conditions. Somehow, he sensed this one would set a new standard in that direction.

Waiting for the exact moment, Derek raised his speaking trumpet to his lips as the men on deck awaited their cue.

"Man the topsail sheets and halyards!"

Racing to the sheets, the sailors grasped the halyards, moving automatically to Derek's commands as the sails rose amid a bedlam of twittering boatswain's pipes, grunted curses, and the stamping of heavy feet.

The crack of canvas overhead as the sails filled firm and true at last, brought the first flicker of satisfaction to Derek's face. Looking back toward shore through a thickening veil of swirling snowflakes a few moments later, Derek felt his momentary satisfaction fade. If he did not miss his guess, this wind which had cooperated so well by starting their voyage off at a vigorous pace would mount rapidly, so much so that—

Turning at the sound of a step behind him, Derek squinted against the rush of the wind as his first mate stepped up onto the quarterdeck.

"We're satisfactorily under way, Captain." And then with a less formal air, "We're in for a blow, all right." Silently studying the serious, whipcord-thin, bearded fellow returning his stare, Derek was reminded of his first meeting with William Cutter on a Philadelphia dock. They had been years younger then—Cutter, the son of a seafaring family between sailings; and he, who had never known his true parents at all, about to make his first voyage as captain of his own ship. He had been impressed with the quiet young man, noting that Cutter was experienced, intelligent, and not intimidated in the least by his manner. He had signed him on as first mate for a voyage that had proved to be exceedingly difficult, and Cutter had proved his worth.

His trust in Cutter allowing an easy exchange of thoughts he indulged with few others, Derek nodded. "If I were a more superstitious man, I'd say this voyage was cursed. I've never seen an angrier sky or felt a sharper bite in the wind. We're in for a blow, all right, or some foul weather at the very least."

Cutter paused, hesitant. "Aye, but I've a feeling that won't be the worst of it." Derek's gaze tightened as Cutter continued. "There's them below, sir."

The image of haughty silver-blue eyes flashing briefly added a sharpness to Derek's voice as he questioned, "What about them?"

Cutter hesitated, and Derek prompted, "Speak up, William. You know you can speak freely with me."

Cutter frowned. "I've not sailed a transportation before, but it seems to me that Mr. Barrett's provisions fall short of those necessary to provide—"

"I'll thank you to mind your own business, Cutter!"

Stepping up onto the quarterdeck behind Cutter unexpectedly, Barrett glared at the first mate with unconcealed hatred before addressing Derek directly.

"I resent this man's interference and his inference that conditions below are lacking! I am in sole charge of the transportees. My men, and *only* my men, will guard them, feed them, and see to their needs for the duration of the voyage, and *I* will oversee all. I hope that is understood!"

Relinquishing any pretense of courtesy, Derek responded, "We've have had this discussion before, Barrett. I don't intend to have it again!"

"Perhaps you're satisfied, Captain, but I am not! I suggest you instruct your men as to our discussion because I will not tolerate their intrusion into my areas of authority aboard this ship! I do not believe I need remind you that any challenge to my authority in your name will result in revocation of all compensation due you."

"I've already told you—"

Barrett rounded on Cutter with unexpected heat. "I would have your first mate confirm—"

"No!" His expression darker than the sky overhead, Derek took an angry step forward. "As captain of this ship, *I* speak for my men. So, I will repeat one last time that this voyage will be conducted in adherence with the terms of my agreement with the London Transport Company. Having said that, I order you to leave the quarterdeck now, Mr. Barrett, or I'll have you forcibly removed!"

Barrett's eyes bulged. "You wouldn't dare!"

Derek's jaw tightened as he turned toward his first mate. "Mr. Cutter, instruct Morris, Phelps, and Twinning to come up here to remove Mr. Barrett from the quarterdeck."

"Aye, sir."

"That won't be necessary!" Halting Cutter's departure, with a snarl that twisted his heavy features into a grotesque mask, Barrett rasped, "I ask you to remember that this is the second time today that you have expelled me from this deck. Your attitude will not go unreported, Captain."

"Nor will yours, Mr. Barrett."

A furious glare his only response, Barrett turned stiffly toward the steps. Barrett was making angry progress across the main deck when Cutter spoke again.

"He's a bad one, sir. It's going to be a long eight weeks."

The events of the morning flashed unexpectedly before Derek's mind in a fragmented parade that concluded with the vivid image of angry blue eyes in a rigid but hauntingly beautiful face. Cutter's comment echoing in his mind, Derek was struck with an eerie premonition.

Eight weeks that could prove to be a lifetime . . .

Eight weeks ahead of them . . . eight weeks that could prove to be a lifetime . . .

Gillian closed her eyes as the howl of the wind grew louder and the storm that had grown increasingly violent since they had left London earlier in the day tossed her violently on her narrow cot. The excessive wind and high seas had forced the closing of the hatches, eliminating what little air and light the transportees had known before. The sounds and smells of human purging had become overwhelming shortly afterward.

Incredulous that at day's end the pounding of the storm still continued unabated, the rain and sleet battering the hull like a million relentless hammers, Gillian fought her anxiety. The hammering reverberated in her mind, prompting a growing fear that the wooden vessel with its creaking groans of distress could not withstand much more of the ferocious assault.

Another shrieking gust and the ship pitched deeply, throwing nearby occupants from their beds as a low chorus of moans resounded once more. Steeling herself against the sounds of renewed purging sure to follow, Gillian did not have to wait long. The retching, coughing, cursing, and crying of the past few hours resumed, seeming to intensify in volume until the dark deck they inhabited, lit by a few dim, swaying lanterns, appeared a scene straight from the depths of Hades in all its misery.

Uncertain of the exact hour, Gillian knew only that she was somehow grateful that the long day was finally ending as she looked at the cot beside her where Adria lay motionless in sleep. Exhaustion had been her sister's savior. Weakened by hours of the retching from which Gillian had so far been spared, Adria had been reduced to a state where she had been unable to lift her head from the pillow.

Scorning the filthy blankets they had been issued, Gillian had drawn her sister's cape more tightly around her as she had slipped into merciful oblivion, but her sister had trembled from the cold even in her sleep. Despairing, Gillian had finally spread the stained blanket atop her sister's cape, realizing she would soon be forced to do the same for herself, if merely to survive.

Her gaze dwelling on Adria, Gillian felt the rise of another concern. Adria's health had always been fragile. How much more of the mental and physical abuse sure to follow would her dear sister be able to withstand?

Gillian's lips tightened. In truth, she could not say for certain whether it was the battering of the storm or the foul-smelling fare they had been served as their first meal of the day which had truly been responsible for bringing her sister down.

Gillian's stomach turned once more as she recalled the rancid smell of the meat which most of their number had devoured without question, the bread that was already stale and spotted with mold, and water that had the taste of being stored for an inestimable period, despite their recent sailing. She recalled that they had not been offered a warm drink to stave off the cold that had continued to deepen despite the overflowing number squeezed onto their dark quarters. Were she of a weaker disposition, she would admit that she yearned with a desire that was almost debilitating for a hot cup of tea—a staple of which she had never thought to be

deprived and which she had always considered her right as
an Englishwoman.

Gillian's delicate jaw stiffened. But she was *not* an Englishwoman anymore, was she? The loathsome Mr. Barrett
had pronounced Adria and her, and all those who shared
their fate, mere chattel of the Crown!

A short, sardonic laugh escaped Gillian's lips. Were her
circumstances any less dire, she might challenge that statement even now, but she knew she could not. In a dark moment of truth an hour earlier, she had forced herself to admit
that everything the horrid toad of a man had said was true.

Seconds later, however, Gillian had earnestly vowed not
to allow that reality to overwhelm her. She had forced op-
timistic thoughts, reasoning that the present situation was
purely temporary. Adria and she would have their full rights
as Englishwomen restored once their terms of indenture had
been served. Unlike the moaning majority around them, at
the twins' present age of twenty years, Adria and she would
survive their indenture with the better part of their lives still
ahead of them, able to resume productive lives.

Inherent pride surged anew, lending a new light to Gillian's delicate features as her thoughts took wing. After all,
was she not more learned and more well read than most
men? Could she not cipher? Was she not proficient in the
keeping of accounts? Despite her gender, was she not ready
to meet the world on its terms and—

The ship dipped unexpectedly, almost dislodging Gillian
from her cot as if in vehement negative response to her silent
deliberation. The retching around her began anew and Gillian's stomach churned dangerously, wiping prideful argu-
ments from her mind as she struggled against the enervating
sounds.

The wind shrieked, rocking the ship wildly. The creaking

groans of the *Colonial Dawn* grew louder, the lurching more pronounced. Gillian could not see the sea, but she knew their vessel was no more than a toy being pitched and tossed at will by the great, angry swells.

Gasping as the ship plunged more deeply than before, Gillian clutched her bunk tightly.

Another breathtaking drop raised a shriek to her throat!

She heard a crack . . . a scream!

Panic swelling, she scoured the darkness for a rent in the hull . . . for the gush of water that would sweep them away . . . for the icy kiss of death that she—!

Sanity abruptly returned.

There had been no break in the hull. There was no icy stream to carry them into the sea . . . only fear that had been momentarily overwhelming.

Gillian breathed deeply in an attempt to control her trembling. Disgusted with her brief lapse even as the wind howled anew and the vessel continued its mad ride, she drew her cape more tightly around her, then carefully covered herself with the stained blanket as well. In a rare reversal of roles, she realized it was time to take a page from Adria's book—to escape the present by pretending it did not exist at all.

That determination in mind, Gillian struck the raging tempest from her mind. Smoothing her pillow slip with her palm, she placed her cheek against it. The fine linen against her skin, a touch of home, was reassuring even as the howling wind continued its raging abuse and the sounds of distress continued around her.

Closing her eyes, Gillian summoned brighter thoughts. Adria and she would be in a comfortable home surrounded by fine things again. This current unpleasantness was temporary.

The soft line of Gillian's jaw hardened. As for the vile Mr. Barrett, she would someday make him eat his words.

Appearing unbidden from the dark recesses of her mind, black eyes from within a harshly handsome face taunted her, and Gillian felt the rise of a familiar contempt. The captain of the ship—the man with ultimate authority—*he* was responsible for the miserable conditions to which his "cargo" was subjected! For all his pretended concern for legalities, he was no better than that foul toad with whom he was at odds!

Gillian's contempt intensified. There were some who would sell their souls in their greed. No one need tell her that the captain was one of those.

Bastard . . .

That silent profanity echoing in her mind, Gillian closed her eyes.

Riding the frenzied plunging of the ship with the aid of long practice, Christopher Gibson lay silent on his cot amongst the sounds of worsening misery. Having heard similar sounds many times before, he was not affected. Instead, he watched with amazement as Gillian Haige, splendid even in her present state of dishevelment, lay her cheek against her spotless linen pillow slip and closed her eyes.

Incredible. He had watched the bold beauty as she had maintained her poise throughout the day in spite of John Barrett's repeated visits, the horror of an escalating storm that had almost shaken even his composure, a meal fit for swine, the foul odors of sickness all around her, the dependency of a sister who could not seem to raise herself above her fear, and the uncertainty of a tomorrow that might never come.

Catching himself in an involuntary surge of admiration, Christopher summoned the return of caution. He reminded himself of the woman's ungracious arrogance, recalling that his words of caution had been greeted with contempt even though he knew that even now, Maggie the whore watched and awaited her opportunity for revenge.

Those words of prudence fresh in his mind, Chris allowed his gaze to travel a face that was totally angelic in repose despite the fire he had often witnessed there.

She was unbelievable.

Yes.

Without fear.

Yes.

She was not without failings.

No.

Failings overshadowed by her courage.

Yes.

He admired her.

No.

Yes.

Damn! He did.

Sleep eluded Gillian as the wild pitch and toss of the ship continued. Sensing the weight of someone's gaze, Gillian moved uneasily.

Her eyes snapping open, Gillian caught and held an unexpected gaze from the shadows nearby—the young man who had prevented her fall on the dock that morning. She had noticed earlier that the manacles on the fellow's wrists and ankles, signifying his designation as a dangerous prisoner, had been removed. She had been somehow relieved. The young fellow's eyes had not held John Barrett's evil sting or Maggie the whore's viciousness. Nor had his gaze somehow tightened her stomach into knots of an unnamed emotion that continued to haunt her, as had the dark eyes of the heartless captain.

She had been agitated. She had not expressed her gratitude and was sorely remiss.

Managing a small smile, she silently thanked him, hoping the moment had not gone unnoted as she closed her eyes to sleep.

A low hiss escaping her lips, Maggie the whore glared at the exchange of glances between the blond bitch and the young prisoner a few cots away. Jealousy flared anew.

So young . . . so pretty. All the men wanted her . . .

Maggie's coarse skin blanched as the ship's rolling increased and nausea swelled once more. *She* had been pretty once. Men had trailed at her heels and her pockets had been full of money. But that had been long ago. Her pockets had gradually become more difficult to fill when younger whores had come onto the scene.

Whores like the blond witch.

Maggie's envy swelled as she recalled John Barrett's lustful glances at the haughty beauty during his repeated visits below. He wanted her, but the witch was too independent and too *stupid* to know what refusing him would cost her.

A stiff smile twitched at Maggie's lips. She would revenge herself on that one and she would gain John Barrett's favor as well. She would then prove to him that she had more to offer than a haughty witch with a pretty face did. She need only watch and wait. Her chance would come.

A sudden violent roll caused the ship to creak loudly in protest, wrenching Maggie from her thoughts as her stomach rebelled once more. Drawing back from her bucket moments later, she wiped her arm across her mouth, her fury increasing as she observed the blond witch riding the storm without any problem at all.

Damn her!

Her time would come.

His oilskins plastered against his frozen skin, Derek walked down the passageway toward his cabin with a wide practiced stride as the ship rocked and dipped beneath his feet. He pushed the door open and stepped inside, grateful for the warmth that greeted him. Weary to the bone, he hardly reacted to the meal on the table nearby, simple fare due to the fury of the storm.

Stripping down to the skin, he walked naked toward the potbellied stove glowing nearby. He snatched up a drying cloth warming there for his use. It was hot against his skin as he dried his face and wiped the icy crystals from his heavy black hair. Ignoring the chill that pervaded the cabin, he ran the comforting cloth against a lightly furred chest that was heavily muscled from years before the mast and a broad stretch of shoulders stiff from hours of bracing himself against the wind, briefly closing his eyes.

The last few hours had been hell, the fury of the storm a match for any he had ever encountered. Worse, the storm showed no signs of abating.

His thoughts slipping to the events of the day and the men under his command, Derek reviewed their performance in his mind. His seamen had followed his commands with courage and skill. He had come close to losing Dan Phelps on the mast and Dick Twinning in the swing of a loosened spar, but good fortune had prevailed.

Running the cloth against his flat stomach and hips, Derek briefly massaged the length of long, powerful legs aching from the arduous hours of the storm's abuse, then tossed the cloth aside and reached for the fresh change of clothing awaiting him. A fast meal, a hot drink, and he would be back on deck within the hour.

Derek's thoughts slipped to the passengers below as he finished dressing—his "cargo" confined in an airless hold with hatches secured. First to mind was the image of the beautiful blond witch. What had she said her name was? Oh, yes, how could he forget? Gillian Harcourt Haige . . .

His stomach knotted inexplicably as the image grew more vivid. The beauteous whore had doubtless spent a night below that she would not forget. He wondered if she was still haughty or whether the sea and its fury had brought her down a peg or two.

Derek frowned. One hundred and twenty people cramped into the dark misery of that hold . . . He would see them brought up into the sun in rotating shifts at the first break of sun so they might recuperate from—

Bringing his thoughts to an abrupt halt, Derek shook his head. No, he would not. The "cargo" was not his responsibility on this voyage. He had had that called to his attention too explicitly to be ignored.

Staggering at an unexpected lurch of the ship as the wind screeched to new fury, Derek snapped abruptly back to the present. It was just as well. It appeared he would have his hands full on this voyage, in any case. If he were to judge from this first day under way, he would say it would be a challenge to survive.

The glint of amber liquid in a nearby bottle catching his eye, Derek poured himself a healthy portion and downed it in a gulp. Instantly warmed from within, Derek closed his eyes, only to snap them open again at a heavy pounding on his door.

He opened the door to Cutter's concerned report.

"It's the spar, Captain. It's loose again, swinging free toward the rigging."

Out of the cabin and into the passageway in a moment, Derek slipped on his coat and oilcloths and stepped out into the fury of the storm awaiting him.

Three

Two weeks at sea . . . she did not believe it could have been such a horror.

Glancing up toward the reopened hatches, Gillian stared at the narrow shafts of golden sunlight beaming down into the squalid darkness around her. The soft groaning and cries of despair had all but ceased the previous day as the most recent storm had gradually blown itself to a halt. Instead, soft, incoherent mumbling had begun in all quarters, sounds of pure, human misery that grew more unnerving by the hour.

Gillian raised her hand to her hair, briefly touching the tangled mass. Uncombed, unwashed, her clothing unchanged since she had boarded the ship, she despised the unkempt condition that had been forced upon her. "Restrictions." That was the word the guards had used to refuse their desperate number the simple necessities that might afford them a remnant of human dignity.

Had anyone asked, she would have denied that any vessel could have withstood the battering theirs had sustained. Days of ferocious wind, freezing rain, and angry seas had produced unalleviated sickness that had left Adria and countless others too weak to lift their heads, air that grew increasingly foul, and endless, bone-chilling cold.

Then, miraculously, the sun had broken through and the hatches had been reopened.

The small patch of blue visible overhead had been their only exposure to the sun, however, with even those transportees physically capable denied an outing on deck. Incredulously, also denied had been fresh water and soap so that those so inclined might rinse the stains of sickness from their bodies and feel human once more.

Gillian frowned. For the life of her, she could not understand how she had come to survive without succumbing to the torturous stomach ailments that had struck the majority. Father had always joked that she had a will of iron and a stomach to match, but, somehow, recalling those words evoked little of the former pleasure she had received from them.

A few others had weathered the storm as well as she. There was the thin, gray-haired man who occupied the cot in the corner, the husband and wife who had spent their time on their knees in fervent prayer, and the curly-haired fellow with the pale eyes who had helped her that first day. She had not learned their names. She did not expect she ever would.

For the word had been passed . . .

A familiar fury rising, Gillian recalled John Barrett's brief visits below during their ordeal. The despicable cur's gaze had spoken the words he had not needed to utter. No one would come near her or even acknowledge her and Adria's existence for fear of incurring that foul man's wrath.

Cowards, all of them! But that was all right. She would take care of her twin sister and herself. She would—

A soft moan turned Gillian toward Adria's cot as her sister moved with growing discomfort. Except for short trips to relieve herself, which she had not been able to accomplish without aid, Adria had not left that cot for a week. In her extreme physical distress, Adria had not been able to keep down any of the food or water they had been given so sparingly. Frightening her even more was Adria's marked deterioration in the past two days.

Struggling to conceal her concern, Gillian touched her sister's shoulder lightly. "You must try to help yourself, Adria dear. Come, try to sit up for a while."

Surveying Adria's wasted color as she raised her to a seated position, Gillian felt despair surge anew. Her skin gray, the lifeless blue of her eyes deeply ringed, her gown stained from endless purging, Adria was a study in human misery, a faded picture of the young woman who had boarded the ship two weeks earlier.

Supporting Adria with her arm, Gillian reached for the biscuit lying uneaten on Adria's plate. She attempted a smile.

"You must try to eat, dear."

Adria shook her head, her skin blanching further. "No, I think not."

"Adria, please . . ."

Almost beside herself with concern, Gillian stroked her sister's wan cheek. Her heart gave a frightened leap at the heat there.

Fever!

Panicking, Gillian glanced around her. Across the way a gray-haired man moaned in the throes of a fever that had struck him a day earlier. His condition had seen rapid decline since. During the night a woman a few feet farther down had begun mumbling incoherently, stopping only when she had slipped into a sleep from which she had not yet awakened. Behind them another had been similarly stricken . . . and another, and another.

"Guard!" Allowing Adria to lie back against her pillow, Gillian called out sharply once more. "Guard!"

Appearing out of a shadowed corner, the sour-faced guard she had come to know as Willard Swift walked toward her. He halted a few feet away.

"What is it yer wantin', yer ladyship?"

The man's mocking tone sent a hot flush to Gillian's cheeks. "Fool! I've no time for your simpleminded witticisms! I demand to see the doctor!"

"Oh, do ye now?" Swift's expression hardened. "While yer at it, would ye like to see the prime minister, too? Or maybe the queen herself?"

"Damn you for the fool you are!" Gillian's temper flared. "My sister is sick. She needs attention from a competent physician. She needs medicine."

Swift glanced toward Adria's cot. "Aye, I'd say that's so."

"She needs a doctor *now,* damn you!" Gillian took a sharp step forward, ignoring the attention she stirred as she pressed, "I demand—"

"Save yer breath, yer ladyship. Ye have my permission to see any doctor ye want." A cruel smile played at the corners of Swift's mouth as he continued smugly, "That is, if ye're certain yer sister and ye can walk on water."

"Walk on water?"

"Aye, because the only way she's goin' to see a doctor is to *walk* back to port!" Swift laughed aloud. "And ye call me a fool! There's no doctor on this ship!"

"No doctor . . ."

Gillian glanced at Adria. Adria's eyes were glazed as she attempted a smile. "I don't need a doctor, Gillian. I'll be up on my feet tomorrow. Please don't worry."

Gillian snatched up the cup nearby and started toward the rear.

"Where do ye think yer goin'?"

Gillian darted Swift a deadly look. "My sister needs water."

"She's already had her quota of water this afternoon. She'll not get more until supper."

"Her quota . . ." A slow rage transfusing her, Gillian turned toward the guard. "You're telling me you would limit the drinking water of a woman who is ill?"

"Drinkin' water is limited for every one of ye . . . with no exceptions."

"On whose command?"

"On my command . . . on Master Barrett's command . . . on command of the captain of this ship, and ye be *damned!*"

"Oh, no, not I!" Unwilling to submit to the man's abuse, Gillian responded with mounting heat, "It will not be *I* who will be damned! It will be you and your vile masters who will be damned to hell, to burn for all eternity for your crimes against human decency!"

"Bitch!"

Unprepared for the swift rise of Swift's fist, Gillian saw only the bright burst of color as it smashed against her jaw with a sharp, cracking sound. Staggering backward, she heard her own shocked gasp as it rang hollowly in her mind, reverberating as the world swirled around her.

Falling, the light rapidly fading, she heard someone laugh.

It occurred to Gillian in her last conscious thought before darkness assumed control that she did not see anything funny at all.

She had gone too far, damn her!

Grateful that night had finally fallen, that the sea was calm enough so the hatches might remain open, allowing fresh air despite the frigid temperature it also invited, Christopher strained his eyes into the darkness around him. Most were asleep.

But was *Maggie* asleep?

Christopher cursed under his breath. The vicious whore's gaze had seldom left Gillian or him during their stormy voyage. He suspected the reasons for her interest in them were many.

He knew the first was Maggie's hatred for the beauteous Gillian Harcourt Haige . . . who was everything she wanted to be.

He suspected the second was Maggie's obvious, purely carnal interest in him. Christopher shuddered at the thought. He'd cut off his damned male member before he'd sink to pleasuring himself with that hag!

No doubt the third was her desire to ingratiate herself with John Barrett, which she suspected she would be able to do most easily by reporting his or anyone else's attentions to Gillian Haige. But he had been too smart to give that damned whore the chance she awaited. He had had no intention of going anywhere near the haughty blonde . . .

. . . until now.

Muffled sounds of distress continued in the darkness, accompanied by ragged snores and coarse, grunting sounds that revealed some were content to take their pleasures where they might in the face of an uncertain future.

Christopher's gaze slipped toward the cot a few feet away as he recalled the scene he had witnessed earlier.

Gillian Harcourt Haige . . . Her behavior during the past week had proved to him that she was a woman of unusual courage. The scene he had witnessed between the guard and her a few hours earlier, however, had proved to him that she was also a fool.

Chris grunted with disgust. Her vicious verbal assault on Will Swift had been a mistake. It had accomplished nothing more than to push the fellow past reasonable restraint and have him turn more firmly against her than before, which would no doubt be costly in the weeks to come. Yet, the sound of Swift's hand striking Gillian Haige's jaw had shocked and enraged him. He recalled the stricken expression on her beautiful face as she had staggered backward, collapsing onto her cot. He remembered her sister's panic as that fragile shadow of a woman had dragged herself to her feet and had tended briefly to Gillian before succumbing to her own weakness . . .

. . . while he had done nothing at all.

That had been hours ago. Night had fallen, food and water had been distributed and left for the two sisters, both of whom had barely stirred. A dark brute in the corner had slipped over to them with a covetous eye on their ration of biscuit. He was uncertain what he would have done if he had not been able to catch the bastard's eye in silent warning, and if the fellow had not turned to run like the rodent he was.

Christopher's amazement at his own depth of concern for a woman who had done no more than speak a few arrogant words to him had not affected his increasing anxiety as time had passed and Gillian Haige had not regained full consciousness.

He had suffered in the time since, waiting for Maggie's watchful eyes to close, watching the shallow rise and fall of Gillian's breast, counting every breath she breathed as one voice in his mind had urged him to help her, and another had demanded that he did not.

The weight of chains, ever fresh in his mind, had prevailed.

Glancing a final time at Maggie's prone figure, silent and unmoving in sleep, Christopher rolled out of his cot and crept toward the sisters. His heartbeat climbing to a booming thunder in his ears, he paused between them at last. He leaned toward the silent Gillian, freezing into motionlessness as he viewed the great, purple swelling on her jaw.

His hands suddenly shaking, he touched her cheek. Her skin was smooth, incredibly soft, and comfortably warm, but she remained unmoving under his touch and his anxiety increased. Reaching for the cup of water left with her biscuit by a tight-faced Swift, Christopher paused, then searched beneath her cot. A quick exploration of the bag he found there produced a lace-trimmed white handkerchief. Somehow he had known he would find one in there somewhere.

Dipping it into the cup, Christopher ran the cool cloth across Gillian's clear, unmarked forehead. She did not stir.

Trepidation mounting, Christopher repeated the process again and again, running the cloth against her cheek, along the curve of her jawbone, carefully avoiding the bruised area as he trailed it across the fine line of her lips. It occurred to him that this woman was more beautiful upon close scrutiny than he could have believed possible, that her skin was—

Catching his breath as a soft whimper escaped her lips, Christopher froze. Waiting, he was still unprepared for the moment the dark fans of her lashes lifted, for the dazed brilliance of her eyes as they met his, for the hoarse catch in her voice as Gillian rasped, "W-what are you doing?"

Sharp, unreasonable anger flaring, Christopher hissed, "Damned fool! Don't you have any sense at all? Look what you've done to yourself!"

Gillian blinked. "W-what are you talking about?"

"You almost got yourself killed!"

Pausing to search the darkness around them, Christopher leaned closer. "I'll be back in chains again if Barrett discovers I came anywhere near you, so you'd damned well better watch what you do from now on or you'll find yourself on your own again."

"I—I don't need your help. I don't need anybody's help."

Christopher's jaw clenched. "Don't you?"

Gillian stared at him for long, silent moments, seeming to debate that statement in her mind before she responded softly, "I don't know you. You were delivered here in chains. How do I know you're not a dangerous criminal?"

Christopher paused. "Do you think I am?"

Gillian's gaze flickered. "No."

Uncertain why her response pleased him and angry that it should, Christopher questioned flatly in return, "I don't know you, either. You're said to be a whore. Are you?"

"How dare you ask—"

"Are you?"

"No!"

Christopher's lips tightened. "Too bad. It might be easier if you were."

"If you're referring to the attentions of that revolting beast, John Barrett—"

An unexpected stirring turned Christopher toward the cot beside them as a voice similar to Gillian's in tone but not in vigor inquired softly, "Is that you, Father?"

"Adria . . ." Gillian sat up unsteadily. A slow panic invaded her expression as she leaned toward her sister. "Father is dea—" She swallowed, then spoke more softly, "Are you all right, dear?"

Adria's small, warm hand slipped unexpectedly into Christopher's as her gaze, a shade lighter, a shade less brilliant than Gillian's, met his. The love he saw reflected there startled him as Adria responded weakly to her sister's question.

"I'm fine, now that Father is here."

Her head still reeling, her jaw throbbing, Gillian stared at Adria. Incredulous at her sister's unexpected response, she reached out a shaking hand to touch Adria's cheek. The intense heat there sent waves of shock pulsing through her.

Silent, trembling, she looked at the curly-haired stranger kneeling between them. He was a felon she had first viewed in chains. His first words to her had been sharp, despite the spontaneous aid he had afforded her. Her friendly overture that same night, prompted by remorse for her ungracious behavior toward him, had been ignored. Yet now, two weeks later, he was suddenly at her side, reprimanding her again.

Sharp words prompted by concern . . .

. . . And she did not even know his name.

Despising the tremor in her voice, Gillian whispered, "Adria's fever is mounting. She needs a doctor."

The young, bearded face so close to hers did not change in expression. "You heard what Swift said. There is no doctor."

"Medicine . . . Surely the ship hasn't sailed without medicinal supplies of some sort!"

"If there's medicine aboard, you may be sure it isn't for the likes of us."

"The likes of us!"

"Bond slaves . . . chattel . . . currency to be spent as—"

"I'll not listen to such rot! We're human beings!" Gillian felt a new desperation rising. "Adria is sick! Surely there's something . . . someone aboard who can help her!"

"There's John Barrett . . ."

"That evil scum!"

"There's only one man who has more authority than he does."

Gillian's heart skipped a beat. "The captain . . ."

"But I doubt that you'll see him down here. He's set John Barrett in charge."

"He made a mistake in doing that."

The pale eyes holding hers appeared momentarily amused. "Captains don't make mistakes."

"This one did! And I'm going to tell him so!"

"Don't be a fool!"

Gillian blinked at the sudden anger flashing in the young fellow's eyes. Concern again . . .

Gillian whispered abruptly, "Are you my friend?"

Hesitation . . . caution . . . "I have no friends."

Gillian glanced again at Adria. Her sister's hand rested trustfully in his.

"You're holding my sister's hand."

"She's holding mine."

Gillian's throat was suddenly tight. "Yes, she is." Gillian paused. "I don't even know your name."

Again hesitation. "Christopher Gibson."

"My name is Gillian Haige. My sister's name is Adria."

"I know."

"You know my name?"

"There's not a person down here who doesn't by now."

Gillian looked back at her sister. Her eyes closed, still clutching Christopher Gibson's hand, Adria moaned. The soft, pathetic sound sent a flush of anger to Gillian's face.

Animals. They had been treated like animals, yet she had been maligned and physically abused when she had protested! But she was *not* an animal and she would not remain idly by as her sister's condition was callously allowed to worsen, as if she was of no significance at all!

"I'm going to speak to the captain!"

"You'll never get that far."

"The guards are asleep. I'll be able to slip past them."

"Barrett will put you in irons if you're caught—as a lesson to the others."

"I have to try."

"You're making a mistake."

Gillian's expression did not change.

Christopher Gibson's pale eyes flickered. "Do what you want. I'll have no part of it."

Making the only decision her conscience allowed, Gillian silently slipped off her cot and into the shadows. She glanced back one last time before reaching the staircase to see that Christopher Gibson still held Adria's hand.

"Damn it, Cutter! That isn't fast enough! I'll need that mast repaired and the sails patched by tomorrow afternoon, at the latest."

"The men are working on the rudder, sir. It's not been an easy job and they're weary."

"No more weary than I!"

Derek's heavily muscled chest heaved with increasing agitation as frustration soared. The smaller man did not respond, allowing Derek the necessary moments needed to draw his anger under control and continue steadily, "I know the men are exhausted. Not many of them have ever experienced the likes of the weather we've survived these past weeks. To be honest, neither have I."

Visions of mountainous waves sweeping the deck, coating the surface with a glaze of ice that complicated the vicious swing of loosened spars and a cracked mast, returned vividly to Derek's mind. He had slept and eaten little during that time and had remained on deck until he had been almost frozen clear through, with one emergency after another claiming his attention. The emergencies finally in check, he had waged a desperate battle simply to keep the ship afloat.

"The damage to the ship isn't our only problem." Derek frowned, the thin scar that marked his cheek deepening the unintended menace of his expression. "We've already lost more time than we can spare, and we're not yet under full sail. There will be more storms ahead, and more delays to tax our supplies. As for our 'cargo' . . ." Derek hesitated. "I don't trust Barrett. The sooner we reach port, the better."

"We're three men short, sir, with Haskell, Linden, and Walters on the injured list."

"Can they sew?"

"Sew?"

"The sails, man, the sails!"

"As good as any, I suppose."

"Then put them to work helping Sawyer."

"Aye, sir."

Derek paused. He needed no one to tell him that his men were doing their best to get the ship under full sail again. He also needed no one to tell him that it was up to him to make sure they gave their all to this damned, cursed voyage.

"That'll be all, Cutter."

"Aye, sir."

"Cutter . . ." Halting the smaller man as he turned toward the door, Derek added, "Issue an extra ration of rum tonight. Tell the men they're going to need it."

Cutter's rare smile flashed. "Aye, sir."

Staring at the door long after it had closed behind his first mate, Derek turned abruptly. His shoulder, struck earlier that week by a swinging spar, screamed in painful protest at the sudden movement. Raising his fist slowly upward,

Derek rotated the muscle as he glanced toward the potbellied stove in the center of the room. He frowned at the inadequate heat it generated, the fire visible through the grate unexpectedly summoning a vivid, flame-haired image to mind.

You can't forget me, Derek. I won't let you. My obeah is all around you. You're tied to me, darling. Your voyage will be difficult, and in the howl of the wind and the rage of the sea you will see me . . . calling you back.

The darkness within Derek stirred.

No, damn it! He wouldn't *see* her! Nor would he believe in obeah, gris-gris, or any of the nonsense Emmaline employed in her attempt to win him back!

Thrusting the persistent image from his mind, as well as the throaty, melodious voice that accompanied it, Derek walked stiffly toward the desk nearby. Lying open on its surface was the ship's log and beside it, various lists supplied to him at the beginning of the voyage.

His log reflected long days of hell on the sea. The lists reflected a growing threat. A damaged ship and dwindling supplies—a deadly combination.

Sitting, Derek raked his hand wearily through his hair, then picked up his pen and pulled the log in front of him. Suddenly more fatigued than he had realized, Derek looked longingly at his bunk before applying his pen to the page in front of him. Meticulously, he recorded it all: the result of the painstaking inspection of damages and repairs he had done that morning, his realization that more time would be lost than they could afford, the specter of more storms to come on the winter sea . . .

Emmaline . . .

Derek tensed as the red-haired image appeared before his mind once more, only to be unexpectedly supplanted by a haughty, fair-haired image with eyes sparking fire.

Derek expelled his breath in a low growl. One specter was as unwelcome as the other . . . and, each, he feared, was equally dangerous.

Reaching for the nearby bottle, Derek poured a liberal amount of the amber liquid into his glass. He took a deep swallow, then again picked up his pen.

Gillian paused to take a breath. She had made it this far. She had slipped past the sleeping guards and up the staircase to the main deck. Her first breath of fresh air in two weeks had been an icy blast that had set her to violent shivering.

Uncertain of her direction, she had made her way across the deck and opened the door there, finally ending up in a narrow passageway where she was presented with several more doors.

Realizing that the success of her furtive mission, perhaps even Adria's life, depended on the right choice of doors, Gillian hesitated.

Drawing back into a shadowed crevice at the sound of a step, Gillian held her breath. A slender fellow stepped into sight from a staircase at the opposite end of the passageway. She recognized him as the man who had been struck by John Barrett that first day, the one called Cutter. He turned toward a door nearby and knocked. Entering at a muffled reply, he did not bother to close the door behind him as he spoke briefly.

"The men asked me to thank you for the rum, Captain. They said to tell you they'll drink to your health."

Another muffled reply and Cutter stepped back out into the passageway and disappeared in the direction from which he had come.

Captain . . .

Gillian paused at the same doorway a moment later, suddenly uncertain. How could she reach a hard, soulless man who would traffic in the bondage of his own countrymen? Would she find a spark of decency she might fan into flame—or would she soon be wearing chains as Christopher had warned?

The only battle truly lost is the one never waged at all . . .

Gillian's spine slowly stiffened as her father's words rang in her mind. Her hand was steady as she reached for the knob and turned it slowly.

Stumbling forward into the cabin as the door was jerked suddenly inward, Gillian was saved from falling by the powerful arm that clamped around her waist from behind. Pulled back against a hard, male form, Gillian gasped, unable to move as a deep, heartstoppingly familiar voice rasped in her ear.

"All right, madam! Whatever your game is, it is over!"

His arm clamped around her waist, her silver-gold hair beneath his chin, Derek felt the woman's shock as he jerked her backward, confining her tight against the length of him. He was unprepared, however, for her clear, furious voice as it echoed sharply in the cabin.

"Release me! I demand you release me this moment!"

"You demand . . . ?" The voice and words suddenly familiar, Derek slackened his hold and turned the woman roughly toward him. Even standing in the shadows of the overhead lamp, she was immediately recognizable. His arms dropped to his sides.

"So, it's you!"

Glorious blue eyes turned to frigid ice. "Am I to believe you recall our first meeting, Captain?" Gillian Harcourt

Haige laughed shrilly. "That's strange, I would have thought you had paid as little mind to it as you paid to your 'cargo' below."

Derek was momentarily silent. Two weeks in the lower region of the ship had left its mark on the woman before him. Her clothes were wrinkled and stained, her hair was in disarray, and her face was pale and marked by a weariness and strain that was not concealed by the angry glint in her eye as she glared at him imperiously.

But she was still a glorious witch.

"What are you doing here, madam?"

The blue eyes glinted more dangerously than before. "I prefer to be addressed by my name, Captain. It is *Mistress* Gillian Harcourt Haige."

"Of course. How could I have forgotten?" His expression tightened. "I repeat. What are you doing here?"

"That's simple. I have come to speak to Lucifer himself."

Derek paused, a slow anger growing at the woman's sheer audacity. "Explain yourself, *madam.*"

Gillian's face flushed angrily. "Need I explain? Surely, *Lucifer* must be your name, for only the devil could have consigned our party to the hell we have suffered below!"

"I asked you to explain your presence here, madam!"

"Mistress Haige."

"Explain yourself now, *madam,* or you won't get another chance."

"Have you not been listening? I've come to protest conditions below that have induced a suffering and despair among your 'cargo' that is beyond endurance. Sickness rages unchecked without—"

"You overestimate the power of my control, madam. The weather, good or bad and the sickness it induces, are beyond those limits."

"Are filthy, lice-ridden cots and threadbare blankets that are little protection against the cold beyond your control, too, Captain? Is moldy biscuit, rancid meat, and water hardly fit to drink someone else's province? What of soap and water? A breath of fresh air? Have you made the decision that we below are not worthy of seeing the sun until we reach Jamaican shores? If you have, you have made a mistake, sir. Because, you see, if conditions continue, we may not *reach* Jamaican shores!"

"Are you threatening me with rebellion, madam?"

"Oh, you would like to think that, wouldn't you, so you might go below and crush whatever spirit is left! No, sir! I won't give you that opportunity. I've come here with a warning of another kind—to tell you that there is fever below!"

"Fever . . ."

"My sister is one of the many so afflicted and her health is rapidly deteriorating! I spoke to your lackey and asked that she might see a doctor. His response was that there was no doctor. I asked that she might have some medicine to relieve her distress. His response was that there was no medicine for *her.* I asked for a cup of water—*a cup of water*—to wet her parched throat. His response was that there was no water to spare, even for those who were sick. When I demanded who had put such inhuman restrictions upon us, he replied that he, Mr. Barrett, and the *captain* had set them! And when I told him that he and those responsible would rot in hell for their inhumanity—"

Gillian Haige's voice broke unexpectedly and Derek took a spontaneous step forward, only to halt at the sight of a huge purple bruise on her chin previously hidden by the shadows.

A cold rage rose within Derek. "How did you come by that bruise, madam?"

In control once more, the haughty blonde, still beautiful despite the grossly swollen mark, did not flinch under his intense scrutiny.

"By speaking the truth."

His chest beginning a slow heaving, his eyes black, angry daggers, Derek turned abruptly toward the door. Pulling it open, he shouted into the passageway.

"Mr. Cutter!"

At the door in a moment, the first mate blinked with surprise at Gillian's presence as Derek spoke in a voice soft with controlled menace.

"Take Mistress Haige back below. Inform the guard that he will answer to me directly if Mistress Haige suffers in any way for her short stroll on deck."

"Aye, Captain."

Jerking her arm free of Cutter's grip as he attempted to lead her from the cabin, Gillian turned to Derek with a glance of pure rage.

"Is that all? What of conditions below—the filth—the suffering . . . the medicine needed? For God's sake, an extra ration of *water!*"

"Take her below!"

Silent, rigid as Cutter took her arm, Gillian Harcourt Haige did not look back.

Four

Hours had passed since Gillian had been returned to the hold and morning had dawned with calm seas, but Will Swift still glared. Her rage unabating since her brief, volatile interview with the devilish captain, Gillian ignored the threat in the angry guard's eyes as she looked again at her sister's shivering form. Swift was a swine, no better than the man from whom he took his orders! She would not deign to give him any notice at all.

In a brief breach of caution, Gillian glanced toward the cot a short distance away where Christopher Gibson lay. Her newfound friend had been absent from Adria's bedside when she had been forcibly returned below the previous night. He had been lying on his cot, ostensibly asleep when she had been ushered down the steps to Swift's startled gasp, but she had sensed Christopher's scrutiny. She had felt his covert gaze through the night and she had longed with a fervor she had not believed possible to share with him her outrage at the response the captain had given her protests.

Gillian's fury increased. Captain Derek Andrews had proved himself to be everything she had thought him to be, a cold, unfeeling bastard of a man with a heart as black as the clothes he wore. He—

A soft whimper beside her interrupting her raging thoughts, Gillian glanced toward Adria's cot. Adria's fair hair was darkened with perspiration despite the unabating cold, her gaunt face unnaturally flushed, and her gaze disoriented as she mumbled softly, incoherently.

Concern a tight knot inside her, Gillian picked up the nearby cup and held it to her twin sister's lips as she whispered encouragingly, "Come, dear, try to drink."

Her eyes flickering open, Adria managed a brief smile that left Gillian aching. Sensitive and loving with never a harsh thought in mind, dear, sweet Adria had always been everything she was not. Despite her timidity, Adria had given generously of herself in times of need. Gillian recalled the many occasions Adria had tended the motherless Potter children who had lived nearby. Poor, sickly creatures, they had always been suffering from one ailment or another. The children had loved Adria, seeing beyond her shy exterior to her gentle heart.

A cruel fate had rewarded Adria poorly for the consideration she had showed others, however. Now in need herself, Adria was suffering without relief, with all comfort denied her.

Adria's lips parted and Gillian tilted the cup. She watched as Adria swallowed laboriously, her own lips dry. Unsuccessful in obtaining another ration of water, she had sacrificed her own so Adria might have some relief from her fever, but she knew that sacrifice was not enough.

The cold . . . the unrelenting cold . . . She feared it would be Adria's ultimate undoing.

A shiver ran down Gillian's spine as she adjusted her own blanket atop Adria. She had surrendered that sorry piece of cloth to her sister days earlier, but it did little to still the shuddering that appeared to be shaking Adria apart. Growing more vivid in her mind with each passing hour was memory of the lung fever that had taken their mother when

Adria and she were young. She could barely remember their mother's beautiful face, but she remembered with frightening clarity the sound of her mother's breathing, heavy and labored, worsening until—

A rattle sounded softly in Adria's throat and Gillian caught her breath. She saw Christopher sit up abruptly. He was almost on his feet when Adria's breathing returned abruptly to its former labored rhythm. Relief brought a surge of tears to Gillian's eyes, as did confirmation of her new friend's watchful concern.

A sound on the staircase to the upper deck drawing her attention, Gillian saw Will Swift race up the steps. Meeting the tall, familiar figure dressed in black halfway as he descended with the first mate behind him, Swift spoke in a panicked tone that carried easily in the sudden silence.

"Master Barrett gave me orders, Captain. Yer not to set foot down here amongst this rabble."

Even at a distance Gillian could see the stiffening of the captain's broad frame. His harsh reply was succinct.

"Get out of my way."

Stumbling backward, Swift watched with open anxiety as the captain descended. Her position beside Adria's bed allowing her to observe the captain unseen as he walked slowly between the narrow rows of cots, Gillian felt a familiar contempt rise.

Bastard . . . There was not a trace of compassion in the dark eyes that appeared to skim the filth, the congestion, the absolute misery, as if it were an everyday occurrence.

Her breathing growing more agitated by the second as the captain drew closer, Gillian met his gaze with eyes blazing as he stopped momentarily beside her. Not bothering to speak, he looked briefly at Adria, then continued on.

Within a few minutes he had turned back in the direction

from which he had come. Broad shoulders erect, his expression unaffected, he started back up the staircase without a word.

Bastard . . . bastard . . . bastard!

Gillian turned toward Adria, struggling against tears. He had done it purposely . . . flaunting himself, the captain of the ship, the ultimate authority who refused to help them!

Agitation almost overwhelming, Gillian leaned forward to stroke Adria's fevered cheek. Her shaken whisper held the determination of a vow.

"I'll find a way . . ."

Watching as Gillian whispered into her sister's unhearing ear, Christopher glanced toward the staircase in time to see the captain pause midway. The momentary intensity in the captain's gaze as he looked back at Gillian jolted Christopher with surprise.

So, that was the way it was . . .

Noting that Gillian had not seen the captain's glance, Christopher saw Gillian's expression grow increasingly desperate as her sister's shuddering increased.

Adria was worse. If he did not miss his guess, she would not last the week.

"What is the meaning of this, Captain!"

John Barrett was incensed! Being ordered to appear in the captain's cabin before he had even had an opportunity to finish his breakfast—it was an outrage! Unwilling to submit to being summoned in such a manner, he had angrily dismissed the two louts who had delivered the message, only to find himself being forcibly removed to the captain's cabin as if he were common trash!

And here he stood, still in the grips of the two burly seamen as the surly captain sat at his desk, not even deigning to look up!

Barrett's short, squat figure plumped with suppressed rage. His beefy chest heaving, his eyes bulging as he licked his lips in a characteristic display of agitation, he became increasingly toadlike in appearance as he struggled to shake off the sailors unrelenting hold.

"Tell your men to unhand me this moment, or I swear I will make you regret—"

"I suggest you mind your words, Barrett." Derek Andrews's expression was cold as he looked up from the ledger in front of him, then drew himself slowly to his feet. "You're on thin ice at this moment . . . very thin."

"Oh, am I!" Saliva trickled from the corners of Barrett's thick lips as he rasped, "Tell your men to release me, I say!"

"My men will release you when *I* order your release, and not before. For the moment, I'm satisfied with the status quo."

"You are . . ." Twitching as he attempted to rein his fury under control, Barrett paused. "All right, Captain. Have it your way. What do you want of me?"

"I want an explanation for the conditions below in the hold."

"Conditions in the hold?" Barrett attempted a step forward. His lips jerked into a barely controlled snarl as the hands on his arms tightened to the point of pain. "What business is that of yours? I have sole responsibility for the cargo!"

"You have sick people below! What provisions have you made for their care?"

Barrett exploded. "How dare you question me!"

"Answer me! What provisions have you made?"

"None! None are necessary! The strong will survive!"

The captain went momentarily still. "And the rest?"

"The rest are a poor investment! We're better off without them!"

"We are . . ." The black of the captain's eyes turned to brittle onyx as he continued in a tone deepening with menace, "I will not ask you if you've conducted other transportations in this manner, because it's of little consequence at this point in time. The fact is that this is *my* ship, and you'll not be allowed to conduct *this* transportation under these conditions. This vessel will not function as a prison ship, with all its horrors."

"Let me remind you that the contract you signed with the London Transport Company states—"

"The contract be damned!" The captain took another step closer. His heated breath fanned Barrett's face as he rasped, "You will see to it that the mess below is cleaned up! You will issue adequate rations with special provision for the sick. You will provide water and soap for those who would use it. *You will do your best to correct the situation before it is out of control, or you have my word that I will take that responsibility out of your hands! Is that understood, Mr. Barrett!*"

"You have no right to—"

"Do you understand?"

"Bastard . . ."

The captain's mien grew rigid as his voice dropped to a grating softness. "Do . . . you . . . understand?"

Barrett shuddered with fury. "I understand!"

Allowing the weight of his words to linger a moment

longer, the captain looked up abruptly at the seamen still holding the furious supercargo under restraint.

"Deliver Mr. Barrett back to his cabin."

A sound resembling a growl escaped John Barrett's throat as he attempted to free himself once more.

"Tell these damned fools to release me, Andrews, or you may mark my words that you will regret it!"

Silence Barrett's only response, the captain turned away as Barrett was all but lifted from his feet by the seamen who, less than gently, ushered him out the door.

The cabin door clicked closed as a protesting John Barrett was dragged from his cabin, but Derek experienced little satisfaction at the result of the heated encounter between them.

Oh, yes, he had known men like John Barrett before . . .

Walking to the nearby porthole, his broad frame trembling with rage, Derek stared at the play of sunlight on the choppy water beyond as memories returned in bitter torment. He was intimately familiar with conditions like those below. A Jamaican prison offered the same questionable charm—a dank, reeking cell where the shadows were filled with the sounds of tiny, scampering feet; poor food; little water; and the weight of shackles that rubbed a man's flesh raw.

Lacking in the intense cold below, however, a Jamaican prison offered intense and unrelenting heat instead. Deficient in the torment of the storm, it provided the endless, backbreaking labor of the sugarcane fields. But the suffering was the same, as was sickness without relief, and jailors who enjoyed their power over such misery.

He had given five years of his life to such a prison . . .

A familiar, fiery-haired image again appeared before

Derek's mind, and the darkness within him deepened. He had been barely twenty when he had arrived in Jamaica as a seaman aboard the *Royal Wind*. On his own most of his life, the sea had been his only home and his only stability, and the women who had touched him had been casual encounters along the way. He had thought he was content to have it remain that way until he had met Emmaline.

With hair as bright as flame and eyes as green as the sea, the daughter of a drunken and penniless sugar estate overseer, Emmaline had been the most beautiful woman he had ever seen. He recalled with startling clarity the impact of his first face-to-face meeting with her on a Kingston street. He had been knocked breathless. There was not a man alive who could have convinced him that the innocence in those wide, green eyes had been feigned. Nor could any man have made him doubt the love he had seen reflected there as she had lain in his arms during the long weeks following.

Strangely, after all that had passed between them, he was still certain Emmaline had loved him—in her way.

Derek paused on that thought, the darkness within stirring more painfully than before. Unfortunately, he was now just as certain that the youthful British seaman in whose arms he had found Emmaline lying had believed just as strongly that Emmaline had loved him.

Raising hands that had unconsciously tightened into powerful fists, Derek stared at them coldly. Emmaline's smile had been openly taunting when he had found the seaman and her together. He did not recall how the savage fight between that fellow and him truly began. One thing had remained torturously clear, however. Beaten and bleeding, the British seaman lying dead on the ground at his feet, he had turned to look back at Emmaline . . . and she had still been *smiling*.

A taste bitter as gall rose in Derek's throat.

He had seen that smile over and again in his mind during his years in prison. It had haunted him through the long days he had labored under a broiling sun. It had bedeviled him through the endless nights he had lain sleepless in his cell. It had tormented him with each step he had taken that had clanked with the sound of chains.

A part of his soul had withered and died under the glow of that smile.

Contrarily, Emmaline had blossomed. She had married a wealthy planter more than twice her age shortly after he had been sentenced to prison, a man able to give her everything she had ever wanted.

Almost everything . . .

The red-haired image returned to taunt him. It beckoned with sultry, silent promise, turning Derek's jaw to stone.

No, never again, Emmaline.

The vision before his mind's eye changed unexpectedly, supplanted by the fair-haired image of the only woman he had ever met to match Emmaline in beauty, and Derek's frown deepened. Sisters under the skin, each was dangerous and vicious in her own way. He wanted no part of either.

A spontaneous tightening in his groin took that moment to belie Derek's denial as the vision of blazing azure eyes persisted and the heady scent of the woman he had held briefly in his arms returned.

No! Damn her! Damn them both! Never again!

With the slam of his cabin door, Derek left the haunting wraiths behind him.

"It wasn't my fault, I tell ye!"

Swift's nasal twang slipped into a pleading whine as rage

darkened the already rabid coloring of John Barrett's heavy features. Summoned to Barrett's cabin a few minutes previous, he had entered to be struck with terror at the man's obvious fury.

His newly stained britches damp expression of that terror, Swift persisted, "It was the blond witch! It was her fault! She slipped past me and the other guards in the dark and went straight to the captain! I didn't even know she was gone until Cutter brought her back. There was no stoppin' the captain when he came down into the hold the next mornin'."

"So, she went to Andrews . . ." Hot jealousy scorched Barrett's mind. "The fancy bitch must have paid him well for his interference in my affairs. Nothing else could have convinced that hard-nosed bastard to risk breaching the terms of his contract!"

"She didn't have a penny to pay him, sir! I can vouch for that."

Barrett's glance grew contemptuous. "Stupid fool! A woman such as Gillian Haige has another form of currency far more valuable to a man than money!"

"But she wouldn't . . . I mean, *he* wouldn't . . ." Swift shook his unkempt head. "Everybody on the ship knows ye want that woman for yerself and—"

Swift halted abruptly at the sharp twitch of Barrett's livid countenance.

"They do, do they?"

Swift took an involuntary step backward. "But nobody's said nothin' about ye, sir! I mean . . . everybody knows ye'll get what ye want in the end. That blond bitch ain't no match for ye, and neither is that captain, for all his black looks and demandin' ways. He ain't—"

"I'm not interested in your assessment of Captain An-

drews!" Cutting the stammering fellow short, Barrett gave
a short laugh that sent a chill down Swift's cowering spine.
Swift's shaking became more pronounced as Barrett took a
step closer. "As head guard, you are responsible for this
entire debacle!"

Swift swallowed. He nodded with an odd, jerking motion.
"I suppose I am in a way, but I promise ye that I'll not—"

"It's too late for promises! The damage has been done!
The captain has had the gall to *order* me to remedy everything below—to improve the food and allow a greater ration
of water . . . to make special arrangements for those who
are sick . . . to treat those worthless dregs of society as if
they were royalty! It's a joke, that's what it is! I won't do
it! I won't let that blond bitch manipulate me through the
hands of her bastard lover!"

Barrett's gaze became more intense, pinning Swift with
menace. "And neither will I allow you to escape unscathed
for the damage you have done!"

"It wasn't my fault, I tell ye!" Swift clasped his hands in
a shaken plea. "Ye know I've been loyal to ye—more than
loyal—in the many times I've sailed with ye. Nothin' like
this has ever happened before. It's that blond witch, I tell
ye! She had it in for me and for ye, too. If I had it to do
over, I'd knock her harder than I did, so hard that she
wouldn't never get up!"

"You struck her?" Barrett's bulging eyes narrowed. "Did
you mark the bitch?"

"Not much . . . not so's she's marked for good, that is.
She was gettin' out of hand and she—"

"Where did you hit her?"

"On the chin is all . . . to stop her from talkin'."

"Fool! You gave the bitch the proof she needed to plead
her cause to that bastard!"

"I didn't mean it, sir! I didn't know what she would do!" Panic invaded Swift's mind. He had seen those who had been made to suffer John Barrett's punishment before. He'd do anything to escape it.

Swift's terrified expression clearly reflected his thoughts as he rasped, "I'll make it up to ye, Master Barrett! Ye've but to ask and it'll be done. Please, tell me what ye wish me to do!"

Harsh laughter sounded in John Barrett's mind as he observed Swift's burgeoning panic. Stupid, ignorant coward! It was a wonder that the witless cur had been with him this long without fouling up his affairs. But there was a usefulness in the terror he saw in this man's eyes . . . and he, John Barrett, was a man who knew the true value of fear.

Allowing long moments for the obtuse fool's trepidation to deepen, Barrett began softly, "You would make this embarrassment up to me then . . . would you, Swift?"

"Aye, sir. I would." Swift's voice trembled. "Y-ye've but to ask."

"You may redeem yourself in only one way, you know . . . if you're man enough."

"I'm man enough, ye'll see."

Pausing a moment longer, Barrett turned toward the case behind him and reached inside. His hand closed around the cold handle of a pistol and he smiled. His smile became a leer as he withdrew his hand and held the deadly instrument up to Swift's view. "One shot during the night—a quick push overboard—and you will have restored yourself in my eyes."

"A shot, sir?" The stain on Swift's britches widened. "It's the captain yer referrin' to?"

"The captain."

Swift's eyes bulged. "But what if—"

"A shot in the dark and a push overboard is all! If you can't manage that much to prove your loyalty . . ."

Waiting for his unfinished statement to register fully in Swift's mind, Barrett then thrust the pistol toward him. "I want it done quickly . . . when Andrews goes up to check the watch tonight."

Swift stared at the small firearm for long moments, then reached out a shaking hand. His knuckles whitening as he clutched the handle tightly, Swift looked up abruptly. "It'll be done, sir. Tonight."

Swift made his unsteady departure through the cabin doorway moments later and Barrett sneered. Cowardly fool! He'd do what he was told, all right. He was too frightened *not* to!

Suddenly laughing aloud, Barrett wiped his arm across his damp forehead and turned back toward his desk. Catching a glimpse of himself in the cracked mirror nearby, he turned, preening with a growing smile.

Revolting, was he? When the captain disappeared, Cutter would assume the helm but *he* would be the final authority on this ship. The blond bitch would find him appealing enough then! He'd have her at his mercy. He'd have them all at his mercy, every last damned person on this ship!

Barrett abruptly frowned. He'd have to get rid of Swift, of course. He'd have to make sure the cowardly fool never betrayed him. But that would be easily accomplished once in port, and his loss would be of little consequence.

In the meantime, however, he would have to make a pretense of complying with the captain's wishes. Those below would have a cooked meal tonight—perhaps a hot drink, too! The low scum would be incredulous at their change of fortune.

Barrett's expression settled into a sinister smile. They

would all pay a high price for the captain's interference in the days to come. But the strong would survive—he had told Captain Andrews that, hadn't he? It amused him to think that the arrogant fool had probably assumed he would be among them.

But he was wrong.

Gillian stared with disbelief at the unexpected fare that had been delivered for the evening meal. A bowl of soup, a large piece of bread, and a cup of hot, steaming tea . . .

Somehow, it mattered little that grease was already congealing atop the bowl and that the meat lying on the bottom appeared little more than gristle and fat. Nor did it touch her mind to complain that the bread was lightly spotted with mold. As for the tea . . .

Gillian reached for the cup, looking up sharply as it was drawn back unexpectedly from her grasp. Her breath caught in her throat as she met Will Swift's gaze of pure hatred.

"Aye, ye do well to fear me." Will Swift's grating whisper was meant for her ears alone as he continued, "Ye think ye've won the day, don't ye. Well, ye're wrong! Ye don't know how wrong ye are, so enjoy yer meal now, for ye've bitter days ahead." Swift's gaze tightened. "I've made it my mission, ye see, to make the weeks to come as hard as any of those ye'll ever know."

Refusing to acknowledge the shivers crawling down her spine at the menace in Swift's tone, Gillian retorted sharply, "It will do you no good to try to frighten me, for I know what you are." Her brilliant eyes sparked fire, "You are a mean *little* man, hardly worthy of the name."

"Bitch . . ." Swift's shaking became more pronounced. "If it was up to me, I'd dispense with ye and all the trouble

ye've caused the easy way—over the side! But that's not
Master Barrett's way. The truth of it is that I'm thinkin' he
has other plans for ye that'll accomplish my purpose even
better. Of course, when he's through with ye, ye'll be
mine . . ."

Swift laughed, a cruel sound that sent Gillian's flesh
crawling as he continued, "I can see that I've whet yer
imagination for what's to come, and that's fine. Enjoy yer
meal, yer highness. Ye have my word that I've made ye no
promises this night that I will not keep."

Swift walked away, leaving Gillian momentarily frozen
with horror. That ghastly little man . . . He was a malicious,
cowardly beast. The worst of it was that she knew he had
meant every word he had said.

Looking at Adria abruptly, Gillian released a relieved
breath. Thankfully, her dear twin sister had been spared
overhearing Swift's threats. She must also hope she might
spare Adria Swift's wrath as well, but at the moment . . .

Her spirits plummeting unexpectedly, Gillian felt the heat
of tears rise. Their first hot meal in over a week did not
grant her any illusions. She was certain the command had
come directly from the captain—Swift's anger could be explained in no other way—but she did not fool herself that
the captain had responded out of the goodness of his heart.
She had spoken to the man and felt his coldness. She had
seen his face as he had observed the misery his "cargo"
endured. There had not been a trace of compassion in that
harsh, handsome face. Rather, he had realized she had spoken the truth, that their number would be drastically reduced
by the time they reached their destination if some changes
were not made. She had brought Captain Derek Andrews's
attention to the threat against that which he valued most.

Profit. Proving he was the man she believed him to be, he had taken immediate steps to eliminate that threat.

Adria's stirring drew Gillian from her thoughts the moment before her eyes opened. Her smile weak, Adria whispered unexpectedly, "Wh-where did Father go, Gillian? I was so relieved to see him."

Gillian touched Adria's forehead. Barely controlling her shock at the intense heat there, Gillian adjusted the pillow under Adria's head, then reached for the bowl nearby. She scooped up a spoonful of the rapidly cooling contents as she spoke encouragingly.

"Come, dear. We have some nice soup to eat tonight. You'll feel much better after you've had some."

Obediently opening her mouth, Adria swallowed with obvious difficulty before pressing, "I want to see Father, Gillian. Please tell him I'm asking for him." She glanced around her. "I—I don't like this place. I'm going to ask him to take us home."

Gillian's smile was stiff. "Father is out, dear. But he'll be back later tonight. You can talk to him then. In the meantime, you must try to finish this soup, and then some tea."

"Tea?" Gillian's heart broke at the flicker of pleasure in her sister's dulled eyes. "Father brought us tea?"

"Yes, dear. But first the soup."

Adria took a few spoonfuls more, her eyelids heavy as she whispered, "I'm so tired. Tell Father I want to see him . . . please."

"Yes, dear, but—"

"When he comes home, he . . . I . . ."

Adria's voice trailed away as her eyes closed, and a deep sense of hopelessness welled within Gillian. Adria's condition was worsening rapidly.

Feeling the weight of someone's gaze, Gillian turned to see Christopher looking intently at her.

He had heard. He knew.

With a catch in her throat, Gillian wondered if he also feared that Adria would not survive.

Laying down his pen, Derek reread his latest entry into the ship's log. Satisfied, he allowed his gaze to travel to the shimmer of silver moonlight on the brief patch of water visible through the porthole. The sea was smooth, almost peaceful. The velvet darkness of the sky above it was clear and filled with stars.

The ring of the ship's bell on deck drew Derek's dark brows into a frown. He counted, one, two, three, four. Ten o'clock. It was midway through night watch and time for him to make a final check on deck before retiring for the night. It had been a long day.

Forcing himself to his feet, Derek stretched his tall, muscled length stiffly, then reached for his coat. He emerged onto the main deck minutes later, pausing to look around him as the frigid night breeze blew the cobwebs from his mind. The creak of the masts and the soft lapping of waves at the ship's hull the only sounds in the darkness, Derek breathed deeply. They had suffered two weeks of bloody hell on this voyage, during which he had entertained the thought that the *Colonial Dawn* might not survive the battering of the endless storms. Seven weeks of uncertain seas lay ahead of them, as well as the prospect of short supplies and countless problems with their unusual "cargo." Derek breathed deeply once more. At the present moment, however, with sharp ocean air in his nostrils and a glowing path of moonlight on the placid sea appearing to lead straight to heaven itself, Derek felt a familiar passion soar.

The sea was a hard and demanding master who was often cruel. But the sea was also a gentle, bewitching mistress who spoiled a man for all others. This final check on deck during night watch was his private time with that mistress. She did not disappoint him with her beauty and he knew—

A soft rustle of movement in the shadows nearby brought Derek's mind to spontaneous alert. He heard it again, the shuffle of a step, the rasp of an indrawn breath—

"That's right, Captain." The familiar voice was soft and nasal. Derek turned slowly toward it, as it continued, "Aye, ye may turn around and see who is to send ye to yer maker this night."

The glint of metal in the meager light caught Derek's eye as he turned toward the thin fellow shivering in the shadows behind him. Every nerve in his body rigid, he responded in a deceptively casual tone.

"This is a poor joke, Swift. I find it unamusing."

"Yer not meant to find it amusing, sir." Swift's voice was low, barely controlled. The hand pointing the pistol straight at his heart was shaking; the finger that was curled tightly around the trigger was twitching. Derek was intensely aware that any movement on his part at that moment could result in a spasmodic tightening of that finger and a bullet he would not be able to avoid, as Swift continued, "I find it no more amusing than ye."

"Then why do you perpetrate such a joke?"

"Are ye daft?" Swift's voice drew harsh with panic. "Do ye not see there's no joke intended here? I'm to keep my own life only at the expense of yers! I've been sent to kill ye!"

A chill unrelated to the cold night air crawled up Derek's spine. "Need I ask who gave you that command?"

"Could there be any other?" Swift shook his head. "It's Master Barrett, all right. It's him."

Derek attempted a quick step forward that was stopped by Swift's sharp warning. "Step back or ye'll force me to do the dirty deed here and now!"

Derek paused. "So, you're not the fool I thought you to be."

"What's that ye say? Ye believed me to be a fool? Aye, most do, but I'm not. Master Barrett believes me to be a fool, too." Swift shuddered. "He thinks I can't see that I'll soon follow ye from this life if I do what he commands me to do this night." Swift shook his head, momentarily incredulous. "All because of that blond witch below! She's put a curse on this voyage, I tell ye!"

"Mistress Haige?"

"Aye, it's her fault!" Swift became visibly distraught. "What with flauntin' herself in front of Master Barrett, and then lyin' down for ye so ye would take up her cause below . . ."

"Is that what Barrett thinks?"

"Aye, that's right! He's jealous, he is, with her wantin' nothin' to do with him. She's put him all out of sorts . . . made a devil out of him, and made him turn against them who was most loyal of all."

"He turned against you?"

"Aye!" Swift's pistol slumped downward as his tone took on a pleading note. "I've no desire to shoot ye, Captain . . . nay, not especially seein' that Master Barrett won't be able to leave me be afterward for fear of me talkin' about what I done." He nodded. "That's why I'm doin' my talkin' now . . . to ye."

"You're a wise man, Swift. You've made the right move." Derek took a step forward that snapped the pistol back up toward his chest. Wary, Derek continued more softly than before, "You're right. You'd soon follow me on my way if you killed me now. Barrett wouldn't be able to afford to let you live." Derek paused. "How did he expect to get away with such a plan, anyway?"

"I was to shoot ye and push ye overboard. Master Barrett was to take control of the ship then and have his way with everyone."

"Do you want that to happen, Swift?" Derek pinned the smaller man with his gaze. "Do you want Barrett's control to be unopposed?"

"Nay! I told ye, I didn't! He'll have me killed . . . I know it."

"Then why are you still pointing that gun at me?"

Swift paused, then spoke more softly than before. "I'm waitin' for ye to convince me that I shouldn't do it . . . that ye'll reward me for savin' yer life."

"Reward you . . . for pointing a pistol at my chest?"

"Aye. But it would be a humble reward, sir."

"What are you asking?"

"I would have ye protect me from Master Barrett."

"Protect you? You have the pistol. You could turn it on him for your own protection and everything would be done."

"I'm not a murderer, sir."

Derek paused. "Not even at the expense of your own life?"

Swift delayed his response, his gaze filled with fear. "I've no desire to lose my life, sir. I've not been the man I should be, and I've my doubts that the afterworld will be any better than this one has been for me."

"So you're saying . . . ?"

"A guarantee, that's all I ask . . . that ye'll not let that man get me while aboard this ship. That's all I want and I'll hand the pistol over. I've no desire to use it, ye see . . ."

"Because you like me . . ."

"Nay!" Swift frowned. "I don't like ye a bit! But I don't dislike ye enough to see ye dead at my hand!"

Derek felt a strange urge to smile as he stretched his hand cautiously toward the shaken guard. "You have my word, Swift. Give me the gun."

"Ye're sure . . ."

"Give it to me."

The gun in his hand, Derek lost the inclination to smile. Turning on his heel, he ordered sharply, "Follow me."

The sound of footsteps outside his cabin door brought Barrett alert. The abrupt crack of splintering wood and the snap of the door lock jerked him upright in his bunk the moment before several men burst through. Rough hands dragging him to his feet, he protested sharply, "What's the meaning of this? Are you men insane? I demand—"

His voice trailing off in astonishment as Captain Andrews stepped into view in the doorway with a familiar, cowering figure behind him, Barrett swallowed convulsively.

"I—I demand to know—"

"Don't waste your breath, Barrett!" Closing the distance between them in a few quick strides, Andrews stood towering over the smaller man, his voice soft with menace. "If I were another man, I'd do to you what you would have done to me this night. It would be far easier that way."

"I don't know what you're talking about!" His throat tightening, Barrett glanced toward Swift. "If this man has said something against me, it's a lie! I reprimanded him today for the conditions he allowed to get out of hand below. I told him I was going to report him to the company upon arrival in port. He was angry and is obviously attempting to get his revenge."

The captain held Barrett's pistol up to his view in lieu of response, and Barrett swallowed convulsively. "Sw-Swift stole that pistol from my cabin!"

"I didn't, sir!" Swift took a jerking step forward. "He speaks nothin' but lies! I'd not do such a thing. I'm no fool! It'd be the death of me."

"The lies are yours." Barrett's words were a menacing hiss. "And they *will* be the death of you!"

"Nay . . . nay . . . It's ye who wanted the captain dead, who wants him dead, still! And it's ye who'll see the deed done unless he does it to ye first!"

"Enough!" His expression contemptuous, the captain silently signaled his men and their grips on Barrett's arms tightened.

Gasping as he was raised from his feet and dragged toward the doorway, Barrett shouted, "Stop, I say! I demand to know what you intend to do with me!"

Barrett was still shouting . . . still protesting, as the iron bars of the brig slammed closed behind him.

Five

"She's dying, isn't she . . ."

Her shaken question grating on the nighttime silence of the hold as Christopher Gibson crouched beside her, Gillian stared at Adria's still, wasted form.

Conditions had improved below since John Barrett had been removed from authority on the ship two days previously. Had Adria's condition not been so dire, she might have celebrated the obese toad's incarceration in the brig, where his circumstances now matched their own in terms of general discomfort and unrelenting cold. The reason for the man's unexpected imprisonment was not known, but she was certain it had little to do with his handling of the "cargo." Were she not so exhausted and at the point of despair, Gillian realized she might actually be tempted to laugh at the idiocy of entertaining that thought, even for a moment. Rather, she suspected Barrett had done something that had threatened the captain or the ship in some way. She knew nothing else would have made that cold, dark-eyed devil take such a drastic step.

The result had been favorable, however. Protesting loudly and swearing vengeance, Barrett had been suitably confined sometime during the night two days earlier. The following morning, Will Swift and the guards had delivered buckets of water and a brutish kind of soap below so those confined

might use them to wash themselves and clean their surroundings. Some of her fellow transportees had taken advantage of the opportunity. Others had not.

Gillian's jaw tightened as she recalled the captain's brief
visit shortly afterward. He had been openly displeased that
so few had seen fit to improve their living conditions when
granted the opportunity. She had seen contempt in his gaze,
as well as a heated, unidentifiable emotion as he had glanced
her way.

Noticeably absent from the captain's demeanor, however,
had been any trace of compassion for Adria's illness or the
condition of the others similarly afflicted below, and Gillian's fury had soared to new heights. She had been tempted
to shout and rail at him for what he had allowed to happen,
but, distracted by Adria's sudden, violent coughing, she had
allowed the moment to slip away. When she had looked
back, the captain had been gone.

Hot meals had continued to be served once a day, along
with treasured cups of tea. Water and soap had been made
available upon request. The guards had become less vocally
abusive and Will Swift, in particular, had kept his distance
from her.

But it was too little, too late.

One of their number had already died. If she did not miss
her guess, the gray-haired fellow in the corner would soon
follow.

Gillian's heart gave a nervous leap. Adria's fever had
reigned unchecked and she had grown markedly weaker. Her
calls for their father during the night had brought Christopher mercifully to Adria's side, and only the warmth of his
hand in hers was now able to appease her.

Gillian glanced at Christopher's youthful, bearded face as
he crouched between her cot and Adria's. The semidarkness

around them rang with choked snores, the heavy breathing of sleep, and the delirious mumbling of the afflicted as Christopher held Adria's hand. Her question went unanswered as he returned her gaze of silent concern.

Emotion tightened Gillian's throat. Christopher had remained constant throughout three long nights. She had heard him whisper words of encouragement to her rambling sister and had even seen him elicit a brief smile when she had believed Adria was no longer capable of the effort. She had seen sympathy in his pale eyes, and with the silent comfort of his presence, he had touched her heart.

He was her friend.

Belief in the honesty of that friendship, forced Gillian to press him once more.

"Adria's dying, isn't she . . ."

Gillian's gaze was direct and startlingly intense in the limited light. Christopher felt it sear him with its crystalline heat, demanding a response as Adria's hand lay hot and limp in his. He was tempted to release it so he might be free to comfort Gillian, but he hesitated, as much for Adria's sake as for his own.

He had been so determined to distance himself from the sisters' distress. Somewhere in the middle of the previous nights past, however, in the midst of wary admiration, concern, and the nudge of simple human decency he had attempted to suppress, he had broken his own cardinal rule. He had allowed their problems to become his.

Gillian searched his gaze, reading the response he withheld. When she spoke again, her words were more a statement than a question.

"Adria's dying."

Adria's breath rattled in opportune response that left Christopher no choice but the truth.

"Yes."

Gillian's sudden paling was obvious even in the limited light. Christopher moved spontaneously toward her, only to have her draw back as her expression grew dogged.

"I won't let her die."

"You don't have any choice in the matter, damn it!" Christopher glanced around them. Satisfied his outburst had not been overheard, he released Adria's hand and grasped Gillian's shoulders. They were surprisingly fragile under the heavy weight of her cloak as he shook her lightly. "You've done all you can. The rest is out of your hands."

"I can't . . . I *won't* accept that!" The full power of her gaze burned into his, searing him as Gillian continued earnestly, "Adria's a part of me—the best part. She would never abandon me, and I won't abandon her!"

"Why do you torture yourself, Gillian!" Sometime during the longs days past, he had begun using Gillian's given name in the manner of friends, but Christopher was nonetheless harsh in his attempt to free her of misguided self-reproach. "Adria's sick. Fever is burning away her life. You've done everything you possibly can for her. All that's left is to give her whatever comfort you can until—"

"No!" Gillian was suddenly shaking, her eyes filled to brimming. Her beautiful face was a study in anguish as she whispered, "There must be something else I can do. Something . . ."

Christopher swallowed thickly as his father's pain-ravaged face flashed briefly before him. He knew what it was to stand helplessly by as a loved one died slowly. He ached for Gillian's torment.

Resisting the urge to draw her close and comfort her in

his arms, Christopher whispered in return, "There's nothing you can do for Adria, short of getting her out of this damp, freezing hell and into a warm, dry bed where she might stand a chance of surviving. You mustn't blame yourself."

"There must be something I can do . . ." A single tear trickled down Gillian's pale cheek as she looked up at him in agonized appeal. "I must help her, Christopher, some way . . . *any* way . . ."

Christopher stiffened.

"You've thought of something." A hysterical note entered Gillian's voice as she pressed, "Tell me what it is!"

Christopher remained silent.

"Tell me."

Silence.

"Tell me!"

Still no response.

"Tell me, *please* . . ."

The ringing of the ship's bell topside registered in the back of Christopher's mind.

One . . . two . . . three . . . four . . . five . . .

Half past the hour of ten . . .

The sound reverberated, blending with the echo of Gillian's heartshaking plea as he struggled with his conflicting thoughts. Surely Gillian knew there was only one way she might be able to help her sister . . .

Christopher's jaw locked under his beard and the knot in his stomach tightened cruelly. The words he spoke more painful than he had believed possible, he whispered, "There might be a way, but the price would be steep."

Gillian went suddenly still.

* * *

His eyes narrowed into slits, Will Swift leaned back in his chair, pretending to sleep while on guard as Gillian Haige crept up the staircase toward the top deck.

So, the proud whore was attempting to sell her wares again . . .

Swift suppressed a laugh, enjoying himself. The captain had all but ignored the conniving bitch since the night she had last visited him in his cabin. He had dismissed her with a casual glance when he had come down into the hold, and the fury in her eyes had been unmistakable. He had put the arrogant witch solidly in her place and now she had gone begging.

Swift's satisfaction was keen and strong. Gillian Haige had met her match in that cold-hearted devil. She would get nothing from that man but what he *chose* to give her, that was for sure.

Swift nodded and settled more comfortably into his chair. He would give the blond witch enough rope to hang herself. Knowing her sharp tongue and high-handed manner, she surely would.

Then he would enjoy her fall.

And he would be waiting.

Content for the first time in days, Swift closed his eyes.

Her heart pounding, Gillian moved silently down the familiar passageway toward the captain's cabin. Fury, frustration, and deep anxiety increased her shuddering as she paused briefly, staring at the door. Tossing back her hood, she raised a trembling hand to her carelessly upswept hair, suddenly realizing that she had not viewed her reflection since she had boarded ship. She fingered the loosened strands and attempted to tuck them into a semblance of order.

A new anxiety beset Gillian. She knew that the liberal use of the harsh soap and water most recently offered could have done little to contradict weeks of cruel conditions and neglect. It was her guess that she looked little different than the others in her party. Her skin was probably unnaturally pale, her eyes deeply shadowed, and the natural luster of her hair and gaze dulled by poor food and distress. The lack of bathing and laundry facilities had doubtless destroyed any aura of gentility that might have remained.

She had little to offer, yet . . .

Glancing down, Gillian saw a sliver of light coming from underneath the door. The captain was still awake.

Memory of the greeting she had received the previous time she had attempted to enter his cabin uninvited was vividly clear in Gillian's mind. About to knock, Gillian paused, then reconsidered. She could not chance rejection before she had even gained entrance.

Quietly twisting the doorknob, Gillian pushed the door open. Gasping at the sight of a gun pointed straight at her, she stood stock-still.

"So, it's you again!"

Retaining her composure with sheer strength of will, Gillian responded with a boldness she did not feel, "Yes, it's I. You may lower your gun, Captain . . . unless you fear that I may have a weapon hidden in my skirts and intend shooting you when you do!"

The captain's gun remained steady. "It would not be the first time, madam."

Madam . . .

The bastard . . .

"I assure you that is not my intention."

"What *is* your intention?"

Suddenly aware that a door nearby had opened, Gillian glanced back to see the first mate's startled expression. A slow heat rose to her cheeks as she stated flatly, "I would prefer to speak to you in private, Captain . . . if I may."

The captain's mien remained stiff. "Are you asking permission to enter my cabin, madam?"

Gillian gritted her teeth. "Yes."

Silent for long moments, the captain slapped his gun down on the nearby desk and took a few quick steps toward her. Snatching her inside, he slammed the door shut behind her and demanded harshly, "All right, what do you want?"

Her chest heaving, realizing that the captain had again knocked her off stride, Gillian attempted to recoup her senses. But, damn him, he was so close! He towered over her, the muscular breadth of his shoulders broader than she had remembered under his customary black shirt, the masculine scent of him and the power of that dark-eyed stare more intimidating than she had recalled in her most vivid recollections. Strangely breathless, she was momentarily at a loss.

"Speak up, madam! I don't have time to waste!"

"Do you not!"

Suddenly realizing the sharpness of her retort would do little to aid her cause, Gillian continued more softly than before. "My sister is ill."

The captain's gaze flickered briefly the moment before he turned abruptly and walked back toward his desk. He turned to face her again just as abruptly. "I've done all I can for those below."

"It isn't enough! My sister's condition is worsening. If she isn't removed from the cold and damp, she—"

"I've done all I can!"

"No, you haven't! She must be removed to different quarters."

"That's impossible. There are others just as sick as your sister down there."

"I don't care about them! I care about her!"

"I've done all I can!"

"I'll *pay* you for special consideration for my sister!"

"Madam . . ." The intensity of Derek Andrews's gaze deepened. "Do you take me for a fool? If you were in a position to *pay* anyone, you would not be a part of this transportation, would you?"

Ignoring the sudden swell of nausea rising within her, Gillian unclasped her cloak. Allowing it to fall to the floor, she walked slowly toward him, her gaze unwavering as she raised her hands to the buttons on her bodice and began unfastening them. A slow heat rose to her face, the intensity of the captain's stare increasing her trembling as she slid her arms free of the garment.

The bodice fell to Gillian's waist, exposing the chemise beneath. The room was unnaturally silent as she moved her fingers under one strap, and then the other and slipped them from her shoulders. Strangely, she was unaffected by the chill air of the cabin as it met the naked flesh of her breasts. She spoke softly, in a husky, tremulous tone totally unlike her own.

"I will pay you well . . ."

The captain's dark eyes narrowed as his gaze dropped slowly to the softly rounded mounds, then traveled back up to meet hers once more. An unexpected sneer drew back the captain's lips, exposing well-shaped white teeth contrasting vividly with his weather-darkened skin as he responded harshly, "You're unclean, uncombed, and the truth be stated, since I'm master of this ship, you are mine to be taken any

time I should choose. Why should I bother to strike a bargain
with you?"

Gillian forced herself to walk closer to the heinous captain. Near enough to feel the heat radiating from his massive
frame and to sense the emotions he withheld, she whispered
more softly than before, "Because I will make the bargain
worthwhile . . ."

So, she was a whore, after all . . .

Silent, somehow angry to have that fact confirmed, Derek
studied the beautiful woman standing so temptingly close.
His gaze trailed her upswept hair, glorious despite its disarray; her clear, fair brow, noting the translucent quality of
her skin despite her unnatural pallor. He noted the light
shadows beneath her brilliant azure orbs that lent a new air
of fragility to her magnificent beauty.

Derek tensed at the unwanted emotions stirring inside
him. Gillian Harcourt Haige had not flinched under his scrutiny, even as his gaze had caressed the graceful curve of her
neck and shoulders and lingered on the gently rounded perfection of her rose-crested breasts. Her breasts were beautiful. He had but to reach out and—

Silently cursing the responsive hardening in his groin,
Derek felt a new anger rise. Whatever else lay behind the
gaze of those intense blue eyes returning his stare, it was
obvious that the splendid witch meant every word she had
said.

Damn her. She knew the truth about him, all right! She
knew he had been unable to get her out of his mind since
the first moment he had seen her. She knew her soft white
flesh would be difficult to refuse despite the spontaneous
conflict between them. He had no doubt she also knew that

as she stood so exposed before him, it was all he could do not to take her then and there.

Derek's jaw stiffened. Yes, she knew . . .

And *he* knew . . . the danger in accepting what she offered.

He also knew, however, that if he didn't accept her offer, someone else would.

That thought somehow more than he could bear, Derek was incensed to realize that the arrogant Gillian Haige had gained a hold on him, despite himself.

Allowing his gaze to linger, Derek prolonged the silence between them. He did not fool himself that this haughty whore had approached him with her bargain because she found him personally appealing. Hell, no! From the look on her face, she'd as soon have struck a bargain with the devil himself.

It was his damned, untoward luck that the devil wasn't available . . . and he was.

An abrupt decision made, Derek commanded, "Cover yourself, madam!"

Steeling himself against an unidentifiable rise of emotion as Gillian fumbled with her chemise, hot color again tinting her flawless skin, he continued with calculated coldness. "I may give you a try. It's up to you, of course, to prove you're worth my trouble. I'll send for you when and if I decide to accept your offer."

The furious tightening of Gillian's splendid lips providing little satisfaction as the tugging in his groin became more pronounced, Derek scooped her cloak from the floor and slipped it around her shoulders. He wrapped her tightly before shouting, "Cutter!"

The door opened too quickly for his satisfaction. He

thought he saw Cutter's rare smile flash as he instructed, "Take this *lady* back below."

Turning toward the porthole, Derek stared out into the darkness of night as his cabin door closed behind him. He listened to the retreating footsteps, reasoning that the beauteous bitch might yet provide the only compensation he would receive for the damned, miserable voyage still ahead of him.

Derek felt tension heighten within him.

Or was it lust?

Whatever it was, he was determined. It would not become his master.

"Ye're back quickly, yer highness . . ."

Gillian looked into Swift's leering countenance as she stepped back down onto the deck of the hold. His nasal tones grated on nerve endings rubbed raw by her confrontation with the cold and arrogant Captain Derek Andrews a few minutes previous. Cutter's retreating footsteps echoed in the silence behind her, but she did not spare him a glance as she responded, "I thought I would take a stroll on deck for some fresh air, but it was colder than I thought."

"Lyin' bitch!" Swift's expression turned suddenly vicious. "The captain turned ye down, didn't he! Hah! He's smarter than I thought he was!" Swift took a step closer. "Well, well . . . ain't that a shame. I'm thinkin' ye'll be turnin' yer sights toward some of the others, now that the captain's out of yer reach. Ye might even find old Swift appealin' . . . might ye not, *darlin'?*"

The taste of bile rose abruptly in Gillian's throat.

"I'd sooner die!"

"But not before yer sister, poor thing. She needs yer care,

don't she?" Swift smiled, his yellowed teeth glinting in the meager light as he winked suggestively. "Ye may win my favor yet, ye know, if ye try. Of course, I have my preferences. I like to see a woman on her knees, pleasurin' my more manly parts some before I give her her due. Aye, it takes somethin' a little bit more than the average to please me. Ye may give that some thought, yer highness . . . now that the captain is beyond yer reach."

"Filthy swine!"

Swift laughed aloud, then snapped abruptly, "Get back to yer cot, ye haughty bitch! Ye've no one to protect ye now, so ye'd better not turn the sharp side of yer tongue toward me again, or ye'll feel the flat of my hand!"

"You wouldn't dare . . ."

"Oh, wouldn't I?"

Prepared to stand fast under Swift's menace, Gillian turned abruptly at the sound of a hoarse, broken summons.

"Gill—Gillian . . ."

Beside her sister's cot in a moment, Gillian mentally chastised herself for allowing Adria to hear her exchange with Swift as Adria spoke in frightened confusion.

"Wh-what was that terrible man talking about, Gillian? Why did he say those horrid things to you?" Adria turned unsteadily toward Christopher where he sat beside her. "W-why didn't you stop him, Father? He was going to hurt Gillian. He—"

"Don't worry, Adria." Christopher interrupted Adria's fevered anxiety with his steady tone. "I won't let him hurt Gillian. Go back to sleep."

Her anxiety abruptly vanishing, Adria smiled weakly as she returned Christopher's gaze with a tremulous whisper.

"I . . . I love you, Father."

Momentarily silent, Christopher instructed softly, "Go back to sleep, Adria."

Her strength draining as Adria's heavy lids fell obediently closed, Gillian sat on her cot abruptly. The cot sagged with Christopher's weight as he shifted to sit beside her. Turning at his touch, she looked up into his tense expression.

"What happened upstairs?"

Gillian laughed abruptly, recognizing the note of hysteria in the sound as she responded, "The captain said he might give me a try . . . but I'd have to prove I'm worth his trouble."

Christopher's expression tightened.

"He said he'd send for me when and if he decided to accept my offer."

The pale eyes returning Gillian's stare went suddenly hard, but she was unprepared for the choked sound of rage that escaped Christopher's throat the moment before he slid his arms around her and crushed her comfortingly close.

Unable to speak for the emotion that closed *her* throat, Gillian remained silent and motionless in Christopher's embrace. Allowing him to draw her closer, she was unaware until the moment that his fury turned to gentle words of comfort, that she was crying . . . as she had never cried before.

Morning had come with all its torment. Groans and moaning complaints had proliferated, but some confined in the hold had remained ominously quiet. Gillian was uncertain of the exact moment when she had realized that the old fellow in the corner would never awaken again. The guards had removed his body, cursing at the weight of him, and she had steeled herself against the splash she had imagined she had heard just prior to their return.

Afternoon had arrived and with it their hot meal for the day, but Gillian had had little appetite. A hard knot of grief had settled tightly within her as she had stared at her sister's gaunt, colorless face. Adria had been delirious most of the night and morning. With Barrett's threat removed and the need to conceal their friendship gone, Christopher had remained at her side throughout the long ordeal, but even he had been unsuccessful in getting Adria to take more than a sip of water.

Adria's evening meal of hardtack and tea still lay where it had been served. Gillian knew it would remain untouched as had Adria's food throughout the day. She dared not allow herself to think how high Adria's fever had soared . . . nor how much more the delicate balance of her life would be able to sustain.

Seated beside Adria as Christopher, exhausted by the long night behind them, dozed on his cot a few feet away, Gillian looked up at the late-afternoon sky visible through the hatch overhead. It was streaked with glorious shades of pink and blue that were rapidly succumbing to darkness. She dreaded the fall of night, when Adria's fever and delirium would worsen. The sea had been calm throughout the day, doubtless allowing the ship to make up valuable time lost in the storm, but the speed of their progress toward their destination mattered little. Adria would not live to reach Jamaican shores.

Gillian reviewed in her mind the confrontation she had had with Captain Derek Andrews the previous night—as she had countless times since.

She had tried. How very hard she had tried.

Her face flaming anew, Gillian recalled the moment she

had slipped the straps of her chemise from her shoulders. Mortification had expanded within her, flushing her with heat as the captain's coal-black eyes had trailed her face, the length of her neck, the slope of her shoulders, and had paused to caress with an almost palpable touch the virgin flesh of her breasts. Unable to catch her breath, she had been strangely dazed when he had looked back up to capture her gaze once more. She had thought for a moment that he was going to take her there and then—but, abruptly, everything had changed. His eyes had returned to a brittle onyx harder and blacker than the stone itself. Then he had spoken, demeaning and humiliating her, and she had realized for the first time how well his stark black clothing suited him, for it was as black as his heart itself.

Yes, she had tried, but a voice in the back of her mind had allowed her no rest with its badgering. Had she tried hard enough? Had pride gotten in the way of her effort to save Adria's life? Should she have smiled and cajoled . . . petted and pressed the hardhearted beast? Or had Captain Derek Andrews's obvious contempt for her stemmed simply from sensing the truth, that her bold facade was all bravado, that she knew little about the intimacies of pleasing a man and was not certain she truly could.

Most important of all, should she have taken a step further by telling him she would do anything to please him? For she was now certain she would. Having returned to see death hovering ever more closely over Adria's still form, she had realized that given another opportunity, she would sacrifice the last remnants of her pride, or even her life, in order to afford her sister a chance to survive.

A soft sound of despair escaped Gillian's throat. It ended in a silent prayer for one more chance . . . one more chance to save Adria from meeting her end in the darkness of this reeking hold.

Her introspection brought to a sharp halt as a guard stopped to light a swaying lamp a few feet away, Gillian realized the sun had indeed set and night had fallen. She glanced at Adria, unnaturally silent and motionless between intermittent bouts of shuddering. She wondered if her dear sister—

The sound of footsteps on the staircase turned Gillian to the sight of the first mate descending into the hold. Watching as the young fellow stopped to talk to Swift, she saw Swift turn toward her with a look of unconcealed malice. Her breath caught in her throat. Could it be . . . ?

She was frozen, unable to move when Swift reached her side. She blinked as Swift grasped her arm and jerked her to her feet.

"All right, ye bitch! The captain's sent for ye! Ye're to warm his bed for him, but to my mind, I'd rather have a viper on my bosom than ye!"

"I'll take the woman from here."

Turning toward Cutter as he appeared suddenly beside them, Swift growled low in his throat. "The prisoners are my responsibility. I'll take this one up."

"No, you won't." Cutter's soft reply was reinforced by an air of authority totally unaffected by his modest size. Waiting the few moments for his tone to register fully with Swift, Cutter turned to address her directly.

"If you'll follow me, Mistress Haige . . ."

The first mate's simple courtesy almost her undoing, Gillian paused for a steadying breath. Her smile had never been more sincere as she responded simply, "Thank you, Mr. Cutter."

But her smile faded as she followed the sober first mate

toward the staircase to the upper deck. She felt Christopher's gaze, but she dared not look back. She dared not see herself in his eyes, or in the eyes of those silently observing. She dared not glimpse what she had become.

But most of all, she dared not ponder the outcome if she failed.

Her breathing ragged as she watched the light-haired bitch climb the staircase to the upper deck, Maggie the whore silently raged. Swift, the cowardly bastard that he was, was shaking with fury, but he had not the spine to run up behind the doxy and yank her back down where she belonged!

Well, if he wouldn't do it, she would!

Attempting to draw herself to a seated position on her cot, Maggie was struck with a bout of deep, convulsive coughing. Unable to halt the body-wracking spasms, Maggie rolled to her side, struggling for control as the pain in her lungs deepened with each indrawn breath. Weakened from the exhausting attack when it finally ceased, Maggie glanced back at the staircase only to realize it was too late. The slut was gone.

Raising a trembling hand to her forehead, unmindful of the odor of heavy perspiration that rose from her armpits despite the damp cold, Maggie attempted to swallow. Aye, she was sick, all right. She'd never been sicker, with a stubborn fever nagging at her and a cough that would give her no rest, not to mention the soreness in her throat that had left her unable to swallow anything other than the pisslike gruel they had been served.

Maggie gave a low, angry snort. And while she lay suffering, the slut was on her way to lie with that great beast of a man, Captain Derek Andrews . . .

Maggie's frustrated envy soared. It should be she, not that fair-haired harlot who should be lying on her back in the captain's bed! She was more experienced than the bitch. She could do more for a man like the captain than that one could! It wasn't fair! With John Barrett out of the way, the young Gibson fellow was already fawning over her, but the greedy witch wasn't satisfied with him. She—

Her angry thoughts halting briefly for another painful bout of coughing, Maggie wiped her arm across her mouth and attempted a deep breath. John Barrett's short, squat image appeared unexpectedly before her mind, and Maggie paused. Aye, John Barrett was the one to fix it all . . .

Maggie gave a scoffing laugh. There was not a man below who believed for a moment that John Barrett would not best the arrogant captain once Jamaican shores were reached! Nor did a one of them think for a moment that Barrett did not have a special revenge in mind for the captain for tossing him in the brig like a common criminal. Ah, yes . . . but if Barrett knew the captain was now making free and easy with the woman who had spurned him . . . who had laughed in his face . . .

If Barrett knew . . .

Besieged by another bout of coughing, Maggie struggled for breath, each jerking gasp raising her to greater heights of fury. She was sick . . . suffering . . . and the haughty, fair-haired slut was lying in the captain's clean bed, spreading her legs.

She'd put an end to it, she would! She'd see that tip-nosed whore taken care of, if it was the last thing she ever did! She knew the way . . .

That thought driving her, instilling her with a strength she had not realized she still possessed, Maggie slipped off her cot and crawled silently into the shadows.

* * *

Cutter halted at the door of the captain's cabin. He glanced at Gillian briefly as she raised her hand to knock.

"That won't be necessary, Mistress Haige." Cutter's voice was polite but lacking warmth. "The captain's on deck. He told me to tell you to make yourself comfortable and to use the facilities made available to you . . . if you wish, of course."

Cutter turned the knob and pushed the door open. Gillian entered obediently, her heart beginning a slow pounding as she scanned the cabin. She released an anxious breath when she realized she was indeed alone.

A closer look and she saw it, near the potbellied stove glowing warmly in the center of the cabin. A large copper bath tub . . .

Beside it in a moment, Gillian slid her fingers into the water. It was warm . . .

A large drying cloth was draped on a chair beside the stove, absorbing its heat, and on the notched ledge of the tub was a bar of soap. She picked it up and smelled it.

Lavender . . .

Her trembling hand closing around the elegantly shaped bar, Gillian felt a hot flush of rage transfuse her. So, the filth below was to be endured with no more than a bucket of ocean water and some putrid soap occasionally provided to alleviate it! And the unrelenting cold . . . it was to be expected, of course, because those confined there were little more than animals, the entire lot of them, to be sold at auction upon arrival at their destination! They deserved no better!

But in the captain's cabin, filth and cold would not be abided!

Trembling, Gillian closed her eyes. Managing to draw her rage under control, she opened them determinedly. She could not afford to consider the cruel inequities the captain maintained. Neither could she afford to think past the moment before her, the second chance she had prayed for and been granted. She would not let it slip from her grasp.

Unclasping her cloak, Gillian dropped it on the floor and began stripping off her clothes. If the captain would have her clean, she would be clean. If he would have her waiting for him when he returned, she would be waiting. If he would have her smile when he snapped his fingers, she would smile. She would be all and everything he wanted her to be . . . if it would earn her the chance to save Adria's life.

Naked, her clothing on the floor around her feet, Gillian carefully removed the pins from her hair and allowed the heavy strands to fall down onto her shoulders. Ignoring a momentary chill, she slipped first one long leg and then the other into the warm water of the tub.

A slow sense of unreality unfolded within her as Gillian lowered herself into the tub. The water warmed and caressed her skin as she sank beneath the surface. She allowed it to envelop and soothe her as she held her breath, bursting up to the surface with a gasp at the last possible moment. Momentarily exhilarated, she picked up the soap and breathed deeply of its scent. A frown gradually returned as she rubbed the soap against her hair and raised a heavy lather there. Then her face, neck, and arms. . . . The sweet scent grew stronger as she scrubbed her breasts, the flat expanse of her stomach, the dainty crevice between her thighs, the long length of her legs, slender and graceful as she raised them briefly from the water's warmth to continue her determined task.

Totally engrossed, Gillian was jolted abruptly back to the

present by the sound of a step in the passageway outside the door. She went momentarily still . . . but the footsteps continued on.

Her lips tightening, Gillian returned to the chore before her, scrubbing herself more diligently, leaving no patch of skin untouched before standing abruptly and snatching up the warm cloth awaiting her.

The hard knot in the pit of her stomach expanded as Gillian rubbed herself dry, then leaned forward, her hair a pale, shimmering cascade as she used the brush placed conveniently nearby to remove the tangles.

The gleaming strands lying against her slender back minutes later, Gillian reached for her clothes, then halted. They reeked of the filth below.

Making a decision, Gillian walked to the cabinet nearby. She pulled the door open, her heart beginning a heavy pounding as she withdrew one of the two black shirts hanging there. She slipped it on, her lip twitching as the distinctive male scent of its owner touched her nostrils.

Because I will make the bargain worthwhile . . .

Had she really said those words—she, who had never known a man's intimate touch? Had she raised the devil's anticipation for something she could not deliver?

Silently railing against her inexperience, against the trepidation that grew stronger with every step she took, against the harshly handsome image that allowed her no rest, Gillian walked toward the oversize bunk in the corner of the room. She paused briefly there, staring at its unexpectedly broad surface. Whatever happened this night, however this intimate encounter concluded, she would keep in mind one calming thought—that one day *her* time would come.

Her face an exquisite mask of solemn determination, Gillian drew back the blanket, and slipped underneath.

* * *

John Barrett snarled and gripped the threadbare blanket more tightly around him. He still could not quite believe that he was confined in a narrow, rank room no more than eight feet square with ventilation and natural light only from a barred door—a room that was located no more than a few steps away from the putrification of the hold where the dregs of London society languished! Nor could he believe that he, John Barrett, who was so far above those miserable wretches in worth, was being forced to endure their same circumstances at the hands of a bankrupt ship's captain who, for all his autocratic air of superiority, had not the worth of a single hair on his head!

The urge to shout, to shatter the stench of the night with his demand to be freed from his unjust imprisonment rose sharply within Barrett, but he did not. He would not give the bastard captain that satisfaction!

Twisting and turning in his attempt to find a measure of comfort for his bulk on the narrow cot, Barrett paused at the sounds of scampering feet in the darkness. His rage returned. Rats—how he hated the slimy creatures! He had been visited nightly by them, their small eyes glowing in a darkness alleviated only by the small lamp provided him. Becoming increasingly bold, they came nearer each night until he was certain he would soon awaken to find them gnawing on his hide!

John Barrett snorted, incredulous at what he had been made to endure. Food fit for swine, constant dampness and cold, primitive conditions that allowed him no more than a wooden bucket to relieve himself and another bucket of saltwater to cleanse himself—as if he would dare expose his bare flesh and risk lung fever!

Captain Derek Andrews would like that.

A silent oath rose in Barrett's mind. He would take his revenge for each and every minute he was forced to remain in this putrid hole. But unlike before, a shot in the dark would be too quick. When he exacted his revenge this time, it would be slow, so it might be savored and enjoyed. The formula was easy enough. He would find what the surly captain valued most—his ship, no doubt—and he would take it away. Then he would reduce the man to ashes, step by step, and when he was done, he would grind those ashes into dust under his feet. He would dance a jig upon them! Better yet, he would—

"Master Barrett . . . Master Barrett, sir, are you in there?"

A bout of wicked coughing followed the whispered inquiry and John Barrett went momentarily still. A woman's voice. . . . Could it be . . . ?

"Master Barrett, sir, it's me."

On his feet in a moment, John Barrett rushed toward the door and peered into the darkness beyond, only to stop still at first sight of the woman standing there. His lips twisted with disgust as he identified the malodorous figure to be the crone, Maggie.

Disappointment added a new harshness to his tone.

"Filthy hag! What do you want?"

The woman's bent frame straightened the second before she launched herself at the door with a hiss.

"Filthy hag, am I?" The woman's eyes were wide and slightly unfocused in the semilight as she continued. "Well, maybe I am now . . . bein' sick as I am, but I wasn't always this way. I was—"

"What makes you think I'd be interested in the ramblings of an addled doxy! Get out of here and leave me alone!"

"Nay, not yet!" The woman pressed closer, her voice more harsh. "I've not yet said what I've come to say!"

"What could you possibly have to say that would interest me, you slovenly witch!"

The woman growled low in her throat, then smiled with true evil as she whispered, "I've come to report to you, sir . . . to tell you that while you lie here in your foul cell, the captain is upstairs in his cabin and—"

"Fool!"

Impatient with the woman's ramblings, Barrett reached through the bars to push her away. But the whore was too quick for him. Dodging his thrust, she stepped back and laughed aloud.

"Don't you wish to know how the blond slut has survived your imprisonment, sir? Don't you wonder where she is now while you're lyin' all alone in your cold cell?"

Barrett felt a slow rage rise within him. The hag . . . the filthy hag was taunting him!

"Since you're too much the gentleman to ask, I'll tell you, then. The blond slut is lyin' in the captain's bed right now! She's spreadin' the legs she clamped tight for you. She's lettin' the captain make the most of the comfort between them and she's doin' it gladly!"

Barrett's breathing grew ragged. The captain and the blond bitch . . . together . . .

Turning his fury on the woman before him, Barrett shouted, "Foul crone! Get away from me!"

"What's the matter, sir? Does it bother you to know that the bitch scorned you, swearin' she'd rather die than let you taste her honey, and then went crawlin' up to the captain again, beggin' and whinin' for him to take her."

"You lie! The bitch is too proud to crawl!"

"The captain's a *real* man, sir. He's taught her how!"

"You lie!"

"Nay . . . nay . . . he—" The filthy hag was taken by a harsh bout of coughing that cut short her response as Barrett gripped the bars with growing rage.

"Get away from me, you obscene witch, or I swear I'll make you pay for this."

"Make me pay for tellin' the truth . . . for comin' to report to you when everyone else has turned against you?"

"You speak lies!"

"Nay, I don't!"

"Yes, you do! The captain's too hard-nosed a bastard to get involved with that bitch!"

The woman came a step closer. "And if I can prove to you that I'm tellin' the truth . . . if I promise to keep reportin' to you, lettin' you know the goin's-on so's you'll know who to pay back and who to reward . . . ?"

"Whom to reward . . . like you?"

"Aye, like me."

"I'll see you rot in hell first!"

Her indrawn breath a harsh rasp, the whore spat in return, "And I, you!" She laughed shrilly. "But I've accomplished my purpose, all right. You may lie there through the night and imagine the whore you lust for lyin' with the big, black-hearted captain between her thighs . . . and you may choke your stiff cock, knowin' that while you do, the slut is takin' care of that service for the man you despise . . ."

"Get out of here, bitch, I warn you . . ."

"Gladly!" The woman coughed harshly again, and with a brittle laugh, was gone.

Standing in her evil wake, John Barrett gripped the bars of his cage with a strangling grip. If it was true . . .

Shuddering with frustrated wrath, Barrett turned back to

his cot. Wrapping his blanket around him, he lay down and closed his eyes.

If it was true, he'd break the man more cruelly than he had planned . . . and he'd make the woman crawl more than she had ever crawled before.

The echo of the ship's bell topside echoed in the darkness around him and Barrett unconsciously counted.

One . . . two . . . three . . . four . . . five . . . six . . .

He'd make her crawl.

It was his solemn vow.

The bells sounded, rebounding in the clarity of the night as Derek strained his gaze into the darkness.

One . . . two . . . three . . . four . . . five . . . six . . .

Derek shrugged the broad width of his shoulders against the night chill. It was getting late. It was time to retire.

A familiar uneasiness nagged, the thought of the woman who awaited him in his cabin deepening his scowl. The blond whore had offered herself to him and he had accepted her proposition. It was a business agreement, an exchange of services—pure and simple. There was no reason to believe she would not be ready and willing when he returned . . . and no reason for the feeling slowly growing within him that he would live to rue this night.

But . . .

Suddenly incensed at the ambiguity that set his heart to pounding at each thought of the bold, blond witch, then perversely kept him on deck in the cold when she could already be lying beneath him, Derek slapped the ship's rail with the flat of his hand, turning at the angry crack of sound toward the cabin below.

Walking down the passageway toward his cabin moments

later, his expression tensely drawn, Derek pondered his obsession with Gillian Haige, which had blossomed since he had ordered her from his cabin the previous night. The glint of her hair had haunted his dreams, the glow of her skin had taunted him, the warmth of the rich flesh that awaited him had kept him restless through the long night, twisting and turning as her body scent had lingered in his nostrils.

He could no longer deny that he wanted her. She had become so deeply insinuated into his senses that there was now only one way he could free himself from the hold she had so artfully secured.

Pausing again at his cabin door, Derek cursed under his breath when he realized that the hand he raised to turn the knob was trembling.

Damn! He was shaking with hunger for a woman like an untried youth!

Anger soaring, Derek pushed his cabin door open. The lamp had burned low, leaving the room in shadows as he stood in the doorway. He scanned the confines, his mood darkening when the woman was nowhere to be seen.

The conniving witch was gone.

Entering, he was about to slam the door closed behind him when a circle of clothing lying on the floor beside the copper tub caught his attention. He recognized the cloak and stained dress . . . and the camisole that the sultry enchantress had slipped from her shoulders with long, slender fingers.

A few steps farther revealed the water in the tub had indeed been used. The fragrance of lavender still wafted from it, but where was she?

A flicker of movement from his bunk caught Derek's eye. He walked toward it, only to halt abruptly in stunned incredulity at the sight that met his gaze.

Surely this ethereal, pristine vision in his bed, her exquisite features angelic in sleep, her hair a molten, silver-gold
halo spread across the pillow, could not be the haughty
whore, Gillian Harcourt Haige!

Derek moved closer, entranced. The aura of youth and
innocence radiating from her in repose was unexpected. It
glowed in the translucent perfection of her skin, in the thick
brush of lashes against unlined cheeks, in the delicate planes
of her face, and in the warm, red color of her slightly parted
lips.

Gillian moved, turning her face toward him in sleep. She
frowned and Derek was jolted abruptly from his daze by the
haughtiness flashing briefly as she mumbled a harsh, incoherent word.

The blond witch's seraphic expression returned a moment
later, but it was too late. The illusion had been dispelled.

A short, self-derisive laugh escaped Derek's lips. Fool that
he was, he had almost made the same mistake again! He
had almost forgotten a lesson rigidly taught and painfully
learned. That lesson was simple. There was no innocence in
women. The female of the species was born with danger in
her smile and deception in her heart. The extent to which
she used that deception was simply a matter of degree.

Derek pulled off his coat and dropped it on a nearby chair.
His hands were working at the buttons on his shirt as he
acknowledged that the true danger lay in forgetting that the
welcome of warm, female arms was not always true; that
the kiss of ruby-red lips often lied; that the sweet, moist
flesh sheathing his would sheathe others in turn, and even
the passion of the moment was often feigned.

Roughly stripping away his shirt, Derek felt the bite of
the chill air against his heaving chest, but it did little to cool
his rising passions. Quickly divesting himself of the rest of

his garments, he stood naked looking down at the beautiful woman in his bed.

His brief smile was cold.

Gillian Harcourt Haige . . . now you are mine.

His passion soaring hard and true, Derek drew back the blanket only to halt abruptly once more as he noted the black sleeping garment she wore. The bold little witch . . .

Sliding into the bed beside her, Derek caught his breath at the rush of pleasure singing through him as he drew Gillian into his arms. Warm . . . and so very sweet, she melded to the curve of his body without resistance as he breathed in the fragrance of lavender laced with a scent he recognized as distinctively her own. It set his pulses racing as he trailed his lips along her temple, the line of her cheek . . . as he swallowed her brief, whispered word with his kiss.

The first taste of her stoked the fire within him to a roaring blaze. She tasted good . . . so damned good . . . as his kiss surged deeper.

A comforting warmth enclosed her, and Gillian sighed. It soothed a tormented dream of a great black raptor soaring above her. It tempered the menacing shadow, mellowed the shrill calls, gradually dulling the threatening dives and transforming them into graceful, fluttering flight.

She felt gentle wings touch her temple, her cheek. She felt them brush her lips. She tasted the honey.

So sweet . . .

The warmth surged, deeper, hotter . . .

Gillian awakened slowly from her sleep. The room had been comfortably warm, the bed soft and clean. The dark fabric of her impromptu sleeping garment against her skin had been unexpectedly soothing as she had pulled the blanket over her and settled into the captain's broad bed. She had waited, listening intently for approaching footsteps in the corridor outside the cabin door, tension high. But as the minutes had slipped away, exhaustion had gradually assumed control. She was uncertain of the moment when the shadows of the room had begun to pale and the comfort to numb her senses.

But that comfort was rapidly changing to an aching sweetness that devoured her with its heat. She separated her lips, welcoming it, her eyes flickering slowly open . . .

Gillian jumped with a start! She was lying in the captain's arms! His dark, familiar visage was only inches above hers. His breath was sweet against her lips. He was stretched out full against her beneath the blanket.

And . . .

Gillian gasped.

He was *naked*.

The captain's coal-black eyes searched hers in direct challenge that could not be ignored, and Gillian swallowed convulsively. She had made this man a promise that he expected her to keep.

Her heart pounding, Gillian felt the heat of Derek Andrews's gaze burn into hers. She saw a new light in their dark depths that mesmerized her, holding her fast. It numbed her anxiety, strangely dispelling her fear as her gaze traveled the taut planes of his face. He *was* handsome . . . more so than she had realized. His hair was so dark, as black as a raven's wing. She reached up tentatively to smooth a heavy lock from his forehead. It was cool and thick to the touch. Her hand lingered, exploring the curve of his brow and the short, dark brush of his lashes. She followed the line of his cheek, defining with her fingertips the path of the fine scar that stretched its full length. She frowned, her gaze flicking back up to meet his.

The captain responded softly to her unspoken question.

"A souvenir . . . from a woman."

Startled by her own reply, she whispered, "I'll not scar you."

His mouth covered hers then, hungrily, almost angrily, and Gillian indulged its tumultuous assault. She gasped as he crushed her against the hard, muscular length of him. Her breath caught in her throat as her breasts met the furred surface of his chest. A thrill unlike any she had ever known shot through her as he held her inexorably fast, the hard rod of his passion stiff against her softness.

His strong hands both rough and sweet, the captain stripped away her makeshift sleeping garment, his mouth clinging and his body heat searing. Naked against his nakedness, Gillian gasped aloud as a maelstrom of unfamiliar emotions soared higher, brighter, within her. Hardly conscious of the moment when he threw back the blanket covering them, baring her flesh, she lay strangely immobile as he consumed her with his gaze. Her eyes flickered briefly closed as he touched her tentatively, stroking her cheek, the curve of her neck, the slope of her shoulder. She caught her breath as his hand closed around her breast. She waited with heart-stopping expectancy as he lowered his mouth to the pink crest and covered it with his lips.

Hot, liquid fire raced through Gillian's veins as the captain kissed and fondled the aching bud, then raised his head to whisper soft, incoherent words against her lips. Overwhelmed by a hunger too new to comprehend, Gillian parted her lips under his, accepting the probing warmth of his tongue, gasping anew as his hand slid down her body to nudge the warm nest between her thighs with an intimate caress. She curled around his touch and he groaned softly. The sound of his pleasure struck a vibrant chord within her, as did his husky whisper, a tone unlike any she had heard him use before.

"You respond to me like a flower to the sun, Gillian."

Gillian . . .

Her name on his lips set Gillian to quivering anew as he stroked the tender bud, rasping, "Let the flower bloom . . . let me feel its dew."

Gillian's eyes fluttered closed as his touch grew more bold. She had not known it could be like this! She had not known that the heights could be so high . . . that the glow could be so bright . . . that this man could raise her above the world around her with his touch and that the pulsating heat within her could grow so strong, so—

"Open your eyes, Gillian."

The unexpected harshness of the captain's tone snapped Gillian's eyes open to see a torrid emotion that mirrored her own reflected in his eyes as he rasped, "I want you to look at me. I want you to be sure who's making you feel what you feel. I want there to be no mistaking who's holding you . . . now . . . in the palm of his hand."

Helpless under his sensual caress, Gillian shuddered more violently than before. She was tottering precariously on the edge of the vibrancy he had brought to life within her as Derek demanded urgently, "Look at me, Gillian."

Gillian's eyes met his in silent response, and his voice dropped a husky notch lower.

"Give to me. Let your body melt and spew its heat, Gillian. Let it give to me and I'll give to you. I'll give and give and—"

Rapture burst white and hot within Gillian, blotting out all sound. She cried out aloud against the unexpected glory, winging . . . soaring . . . her body pulsing with convulsive ecstasy as the captain consumed her cry with his kiss, drinking in her rapture, absorbing it within him—making it his.

The rhythm stilled. The room went silent as Gillian twitched in final, ecstatic throes, as the captain relinquished her mouth at last to rasp, "If I hadn't felt the wetness of you, if I didn't know for sure, I wouldn't have believed—"

Halting abruptly as an urgent light midway between pleasure and pain flashed in the darkness of his eyes, Derek slid himself unexpectedly atop her. Gillian was unprepared as he lifted himself slightly, then drove himself hard and true within her.

Shock . . . pain . . . a startled sense of uncertainty!

Derek went suddenly still. He looked down at her for long moments, his expression blank, before beginning a slow, gentle rhythm within her.

Gillian caught her breath at the new realm of emotions assailing her. The rhythm was balm to her pain, soothing to her senses. It raised her to a new plane of sensation that eliminated conscious thought and response. Uncertain of the moment when her arms slipped around the captain's neck to enclose him, when her body first moved to join his sensuous dance, Gillian clutched him closer, the cadence consuming her until she was meeting him thrust for thrust, until she—

The sudden eruption of the captain's passion was unexpected. Gasping aloud, Gillian shared in the burst of splendor as his body throbbed hard and true within her, as the beauty expanded, raising her with him on high, wide, glorious wings . . .

And it was done.

Stillness reigned once more in a silence punctuated by gasping, labored breaths.

Cold reality abruptly returned.

Abruptly conscious of the captain's weight lying intimately upon her, Gillian felt her throat choke closed.

It was over. She had done what she must.

But . . .

Had it been enough?

Anxiety returning, Gillian saw the captain's eyes harden as he raised himself above her . . .

A virgin . . .

Gillian Harcourt Haige was a virgin!

Suddenly furious, Derek cast the word from his mind.

No, Gillian Harcourt Haige *had been* a virgin.

Now she was not.

And a whore was a whore, after all . . .

Six

The morning stench of the hold seemed somehow more vile since Gillian had returned below. It assailed her strongly, raising a wave of nausea as she looked at Adria with growing despair. Her sister was motionless except for the shuddering that now wracked her awake or sleeping. She was slipping farther away with each passing moment.

The hiss of virulent whispers continued, but Gillian determinedly ignored it. It had started the moment she had been brought back down into the hold the previous night. She had heard the names called out at her as she had passed, the snickers, and the obscene offers in grating male voices that had not been dared before. The humiliation of it had been almost more than she was able to bear.

But Adria had heard none of it.

Her throat choking with unshed tears, Gillian stared at Adria's colorless face. She might be tempted to think that Adria's oblivion was a blessing, but she knew it was not, for she knew what it foreshadowed. Adria, dear, gentle Adria, could not last much longer.

"Gillian . . ."

Gillian turned at the sound of Christopher's voice, her expression blank. He had been at Adria's bedside when she had returned. Her degradation complete, she had not been able to meet the question in his gaze. She had not spoken a word to him in the hours since.

Christopher's hand closed on her arm, tightening when she attempted to pull it away. She heard the anger in his voice as he rasped, "I want you to tell me . . . I have to know. Is everything all right?"

"All right?" Gillian stiffened.

Christopher's hand tightened almost to the point of pain. "What is it, Gillian? Did he abuse you in some way?"

"Abuse me?"

Gillian looked up abruptly. She was strangely immune to the concern she saw in the strained lines of Christopher's face as he waited for her to continue. A hard knot of mortification, rage, and another soul-wrenching emotion to which she could not put a name squeezed tight within her as she held his gaze for long, silent moments.

Her response came abruptly, in a pained rush.

"It was all for naught . . . all of it!" Pausing to swallow a hot surge of tears, Gillian glanced around her, making certain they could not be overheard. "Captain Derek Andrews sampled what I had to offer and found it lacking."

"Lacking!"

"He left the cabin almost immediately afterward, without a word. He dressed as if I wasn't there and walked out the door. I waited there, uncertain what to do, until . . ." Hot color flooded Gillian's cheeks. ". . . until Cutter came to the door and said the captain had given him orders to bring me back here. It was all for naught, Christopher, and now Adria will . . . she'll—"

Gillian's voice broke, despite herself. Unable to continue, she felt Christopher's hand slide comfortingly up her arm. She leaned spontaneously toward that comfort, only to have a whispered epithet from a nearby cot jerk her rigidly erect once more.

"No, Christopher, please!" Gillian halted Christopher's furious lurch toward the voice with a soft plea. "What he said is true, after all."

"No, it isn't!"

Gillian shrugged. "What anyone calls me isn't important. What really matters is that you would give Swift the opportunity he's seeking to vent his spite on you if you acted rashly. I don't want that to happen, Christopher. I don't want to be responsible for your suffering, too."

Christopher's jaw tightened. "You're not responsible for Adria's illness."

"I should have been able to help her."

"No."

"I wasn't *good* enough. I—"

"Gi-Gillian . . ."

Adria's weak summons turned Gillian abruptly toward her sister's cot. Her tears welled as Adria looked at her, studying her strangely. "Yo-you look different. You—"

A harsh bout of coughing interrupted Adria, violently wracking her emaciated frame as Gillian glanced fearfully at Christopher.

In control once more, Adria persisted with sudden, feverish intensity, "You do, Gillian. You look . . . beautiful."

Rage simmering, Christopher watched Gillian's anxious ministrations to her sister—the gentle stroking of Adria's brow, the cup she raised to Adria's lips, the soft sound of her voice as she coaxed Adria to drink.

You look beautiful, Gillian.

Adria's whispered words rebounded in his mind.

No, Gillian did not *look* beautiful. She *was* beautiful.

Christopher's jaw hardened with frustration. Gillian's beauty came from within. It had little to do with the color of her hair or the perfect symmetry of the features she and Adria shared. Nor was it affected by the change in her appearance after returning from the captain's cabin—the fresh, clean glow of her heavy tresses and perfect skin, or the scent of lavender that clung persistently.

Christopher's frustration heightened. The bastard . . . he had made certain Gillian had *bathed* before he touched her, as if the filth to which *he* had subjected her and everyone else below had made her unfit for his attentions.

Christopher fought to curb the intensity of his emotions. Gillian's humiliation had been written in the flush of her face as she had descended back into the hold, in the defensive rise of her chin as she had suffered insults from the darkness, and in her pained voice when she had said those words he still found too incredible to be true.

He found me lacking.

Lacking . . .

His stomach twisting into a hard knot, Christopher watched Gillian's graceful movements as she ran a cloth across Adria's perspired face. Only a fool would find Gillian Haige lacking in any way. She—

Heavy footsteps descending the staircase interrupted Christopher's angry thoughts. Turning, he watched as Cutter descended into the hold with two seamen close behind him.

The first mate spoke to Swift in a tone that carried clearly over the misery around them.

"The captain has instructed that Mistress Haige and her sister be removed from the hold and installed in a cabin above."

A heated flush suffused Will Swift at Cutter's words. Momentarily incapable of response, he stared at the slight first mate and the two burly seamen behind him.

The haughty slut had won . . .

Nay, he'd not have it! He had been enjoying the blond witch's comeuppance after Cutter had brought her back below. Despondent as she had been, he had begun to entertain thoughts of the more personal vengeance he had hinted at before, one that would put a proper subservience in the witch's voice as she begged his favor.

Aye . . . but now the black-hearted captain would steal that vengeance from him. He'd not stand for it!

Taking an aggressive step toward Cutter, Swift gave little heed to the tensing of the seamen behind him as he grated in response, "Nay! Ye'll not take either of them harlots from this hold! They're in the charge of the London Transport Company until they reach Jamaican shores! Legally so! With Master Barrett incarcerated, their care is left to me and the other guards! I'll not have ye nor nobody else remove them filthy beggars from their proper place!"

Cutter's eyes grew cold. He turned deliberately to the seamen behind him. "Linden . . . Haskell—take the women and their belongings upstairs."

The big men moved to his command.

"Don't take a step toward them harlots, I tell ye!" Swift's eyes grew dangerously bright. "The one's in a bad way. If anythin' happens to her, I'll report the matter to the London Company! They'll take ye all to the courts, they will!"

"Before you do that, you'll have to get past Captain Andrews." Cutter's eyes turned to ice. "It'll take a better man than you to do that."

His narrow chest heaving, his mouth dry, Swift glanced

at the transport guards cowering in the shadows behind him.
The craven weaklings . . .

Swift's anger soared a notch higher as he nodded with a
spasmodic jerk of his head. "All right then, it'll be as ye
say . . . for now! Ye've gained the day, but I warn ye, ye've
not heard the last of this!"

Livid at Cutter's dismissing glance, Swift trembled with
fury as the three started toward the pale witch who watched
in silence, standing so still that she could have been carved
from stone.

"Careful! Careful with her, please!"

Her expression a mask of concern, Gillian watched as a
big, sandy-haired seaman answering to the name of Haskell
lifted Adria up into his arms. Adria's eyes flickered open at
the sound of her sister's voice, fear registering in the fevered
glow of her eyes the moment before she was struck with a
bout of violent coughing.

Waiting until the vicious spasm had stilled, Gillian spoke
softly in an attempt to assuage her sister's anxiety.

"Father's arranged to have us taken to another room, dear,
just as you wanted. We'll be together. It'll be warm and
comfortable there."

"B-but I wanted to go home . . ." Her breathing labored,
Adria looked weakly around her. Her gaze halted on Christopher where he stood a few feet away. "Father, please . . ."

Cutter glanced between Adria and Christopher. His frown
prompted Gillian's whispered response.

"It's the fever. Christopher's hair and beard resembles our
father's. She's confused."

"Father, please." Adria's shuddering worsened. "I'm
afraid . . ."

Cutter's soft command was firmly issued. "Talk to her, Gibson."

Gillian saw Christopher's resentment at the first mate's tone, but his voice was reassuring as he took Adria's hand. "It'll be all right, Adria. You'll soon be home, I promise you."

Her lips stiff and pale, Adria attempted a smile. "You promise? You've never broken a promise to me, Father."

Christopher's voice was husky as he urged, "Close your eyes, Adria. Everything will be all right."

Adria obediently closed her eyes and Gillian fought an almost debilitating sweep of emotion as the small entourage started toward the staircase. Ignoring Swift's low curse as she passed, she kept her gaze trained on the deck above, realization gradually dawning.

She had done it. She had gotten Adria out of the filthy death trap that had been consuming her.

The cold wind whipped cruelly, negating the brilliance of the morning sun as Gillian stepped up onto the main deck of the ship. Glancing toward the quarterdeck, she saw the captain's broad, black-clad form silhouetted against the blue of the sky as he stared through his spyglass at a point in the distance. Her face flushed with a sudden rush of heat as the moments spent in his arms the previous night returned vividly to mind.

Gillian swallowed convulsively. She did not know the woman she had been last night. That woman who had lain in the captain's arms without a trace of shame had been a stranger, a wanton who had responded to him with a spontaneity beyond her control. That woman had savored his kisses and his intimate caresses and had longed for more.

The fine line of Gillian's jaw tightened. But that woman had faded at the onslaught of harsh reality moments later, when the captain had separated himself from their intimate joining without a word and, leaving, had sent Cutter back to remove her from below.

Her humiliation had been complete. She had thought she had not pleased him. Indeed, perhaps she had not. She was still uncertain.

Her anxieties rising as the wind whipped more strongly and Adria's shuddering grew more pronounced, Gillian assessed her sister's wasted face. As it was, it might yet be too late.

That thought almost more than she could bear, Gillian entered the familiar passageway and followed the brawny seaman as he carried Adria toward a door a few feet from the captain's cabin.

So conveniently close . . .

Cutter pushed open the door and Gillian followed him inside. The big seaman carried Adria in behind her and placed her with surprising gentleness on the bunk nearby as Gillian glanced around her. The cabin was modest in size, provided with a smaller version of the potbellied stove in the captain's cabin. It was pleasantly warm. There would be no bone-chilling dampness here. The bunk would only accommodate one comfortably, but even the hard floor was preferable to the filth of her cot below.

Gillian moved aside as the other seaman placed their bags on the floor nearby, her gaze jerking to an abrupt halt at the small black case resting beside the nearby desk. The initials "J. B." jumped out at her and Gillian went abruptly cold.

Cutter replied to her unvoiced question as she looked up.

"Aye, this was Mr. Barrett's room, but he won't be needing it for the remainder of the voyage."

Momentarily unable to respond, Gillian turned at the sound of Adria's voice.

"Gill-Gillian . . . ?" Gillian walked toward her sister and took her hand. The heat emanating from her twin sister's frail form sent a chill of panic racing down her spine as Adria's gaze grew disoriented.

"I-I want to go home, Gillian."

"We will."

"I want to go home now."

"Soon, dear."

"Mistress Haige . . ." Gillian turned toward Cutter as he addressed her. "Is there anything else you'll need right now?"

Dare she? Gillian took a steadying breath.

"Yes, there is. I'd like a kettle . . . or a pot—something I can put atop the stove to boil water freely. I'll need soap, and water for both drinking and bathing. And I'll need a supply of tea . . . so I may brew it at my convenience." Gillian glanced toward the box beside the stove where the fuel was in short supply. "And I'll need that box refilled so I may make sure the fire does not go out."

She thought she saw a smile twitch at Cutter's lips. "Will you need anything else?"

Gillian paused, then added boldly, "The copper tub . . . I would have it delivered here."

"A bath tub?"

Cutter turned at Haskell's unexpected comment, directing his response as much to the surprised sailor as to Gillian. "I'll have it brought up as soon as possible. Anything else?"

"No, nothing else right now." Suddenly realizing one thing had gone forgotten, she added two words she had never spoken with more sincerity. "Thank you, Mr. Cutter."

Her thoughts flying to the work ahead of her, Gillian hardly heard the heavy footsteps of the three men as they moved toward the door, or the resounding click as it closed behind them.

Each grating rasp of breath increasing her pain, Maggie struggled to draw herself to a seated position on her cot. Still staring at the top of the staircase where the blond witch and her sister had disappeared from sight, she supported herself on one arm, coughing raggedly as she glanced toward Swift, then toward the bunk where Christopher Gibson lay with his arm across his eyes.

Her coughing stilled, Maggie breathed deeply in an attempt to clear the cobwebs from her mind. So, the blond whore's visit to the captain's bed had won him over. She'd not thought the haughty bitch had it in her.

Maggie's lips twisted into a sneer. Aye, the witch would have it soft, now, "installed in a cabin above," as the first mate had declared so loudly that no one could miss the words.

She had no doubt whose cabin that would be . . .

That thought striking her with unexpected amusement, Maggie laughed aloud. The sound deteriorated into another bout of coughing that turned her perverse amusement cold as she struggled to draw an even breath once more.

Her chest heaving, Maggie looked around her. Her expression darkened. No one had as much as raised an eyebrow at her distress. There was not a one in their filthy party who gave a bloody damn what happened to her. But there were some who cared about the blond bitch, all right! There was Swift, who had been openly salivating over the slut and who was still shuddering with rage that she had been removed from his grasp . . . and Gibson, who mourned the loss of his lover in silence.

Maggie's malevolence swelled. Gillian Haige, who had pretended to be so much better than she, but who had paid for her new quarters with her lily-white flesh—there was only one other person who hated the arrogant trollop as much as she did.

Only one . . .

Maggie's blue lips spread in a leering smile. She would feed that one's hatred as hers had been fed. She did not fear his threats . . . for she had no doubt that she would soon be beyond them.

Sliding to the edge of her cot, Maggie struggled to draw herself to a standing position. That feat finally accomplished, she walked unsteadily toward the shadows with a fixed smile.

Derek lowered the spyglass in his hand, acutely aware that he had stared blindly through the instrument for long moments, pretending involvement with a nonexistent point in the distance as Gillian Haige had crossed the deck below him. It was done. The beauteous witch and her sister had been removed from the hold and would soon be installed in Barrett's room. The intimate agreement between Gillian Haige and him had been sealed.

Derek shook his head, incredulous.

He must be out of his mind . . .

Diverting his gaze toward the clear sky above him, Derek scowled. Favorable weather persisted. The ship's repairs were progressing well, and they would soon be making full time once more. It was his intention that as soon as the ship was fit, he would squeeze as much possible distance into the day as the ship could sustain.

Derek's scowl deepened. The reasons for that decision

were many, but the strongest lay pulsing insistently in the area of his groin as the woman now being installed in the cabin beside his plagued his mind.

It had been a long night. He had realized soon after leaving his bed and the beautiful woman in it, that the only salvation he could manage from his dilemma was to distance himself from her so he might think more clearly.

Awakening his surprised first mate, he had ordered the woman to be delivered immediately back below. Cutter's surprised reaction had somehow darkened his mood.

The deed done, he had returned to his empty cabin to find that it was not *his* cabin any longer. For the scent of Gillian Haige had lingered. It had lingered in his bed, on the shirt he had slipped from her smooth skin, on the air, and in his *mind*. He had not been able to free himself from it, or from thoughts of the moments she had spent in his arms.

Oh, yes, he remembered. As flower to the sun, she had bloomed for him. He was certain her reactions were not feigned. He had been fooled too many times by the acting of accomplished whores to have allowed himself to be deceived again. But, somehow, that certainty had only increased his confusion.

She had been a virgin. She was now a whore . . . and so very willing . . .

Somewhere in the middle of the night as the scent of Gillian Harcourt Haige had closed around him and the memory of her sweet, intimate flesh had grown ever more vivid in his mind, he had told himself that only a fool or a eunuch would turn down what she offered. The agreement was fair and mutually advantageous . . . and there were at the least, six long, lonely weeks at sea ahead of him.

A stunning red-haired image appeared suddenly before

his mind and Derek's scowl deepened. If anything, the blond whore would keep Emmaline and her "obeah" at bay . . . for if there was one thing that had been proven, it was that when Gillian Harcourt Haige was in close proximity, all other women faded from mind.

Derek gave a low, caustic snort. Perhaps Gillian Haige was the medicine he needed . . .

If the patient could survive the cure.

The direction of his own thoughts suddenly infuriating, Derek muttered a low curse. He would give her some time to settle in and then he would face Gillian Haige and set the rules for their liaison—strict rules that would bear no deviation.

And then he would see . . .

"She's gone, you know . . ."

John Barrett's head snapped up from the bowl of foul gruel that constituted his morning meal. He gritted his teeth tightly shut.

That filthy witch again . . .

The hag approached his barred door, the sight of her almost as sickening as the odor that clung about her as she came to a awkward halt a few feet beyond. Barrett turned his back to her with a growl.

"Get away from me, bitch!"

"Nay . . . nay, you should not talk to me so, sir . . ." The woman leered, her rotted teeth glinting strangely in the light as he glanced over his shoulder. "Did you not hear what I had to say? The bitch is gone."

Gone? Impossible.

"Your mind is addled! Leave me alone or I'll see that you're made to pay for this harassment."

"Oh, sir, did you forget?" The woman's leer broadened. "I'm the one who's walkin' free on this ship, not you."

"I warn you . . ."

"She's gone . . . her and her sister. The captain's installed them in a cabin above to serve as his doxies."

Barrett's head came up with a jerk.

"Aye, both of 'em. They'll have some fun, won't they?"

Barrett turned slowly back toward the lewd crone. "I tell you now to leave me be."

"I couldn't do that, sir." The woman took a step closer. "Since it's *your* cabin the bitch has taken over, I thought—"

"My cabin?"

"Oh, did I not tell you? The blond slut's lyin' in your bed right now. It's a pity that it's not with you, but she'll keep your bed well filled, of that I'm sure. That randy fellow, Chris Gibson, is mournin' even now because he was left behind. He's waitin' his turn. And then there's Swift who's been crawlin' after her in the dark ever since the captain threw you in here."

"Swift?" A low trembling began inside Barrett. "He wouldn't dare! He said—"

"He turned you in to the captain, didn't he, sir? He was pantin' after the bitch as she crawled up them steps. I'm thinkin' her hot flesh had more to do with him turnin' against you than anythin' else. Seems she preferred *him* to *you* . . ."

Enraged, Barrett charged the door, stretching his arms out between the bars as he strained to reach the woman standing just beyond him. His unexpected rush sent the woman a step backward that set her to coughing anew as Barrett shook with frustrated fury.

"Bitch . . . bitch . . . bitch . . ." Watching her shattering spasms with soaring malevolence, Barrett waited only until her breathing was in partial control once more before he rasped, "You come here to torment me because it gives you pleasure, don't you? Filthy hag . . . you will pay for each and every word you have uttered here this day. I will have my satisfaction wreaked on you so that you will regret each letter . . . each syllable . . . each fraction of the words you have spewed."

"Sir . . ." The hag wheezed, her tormenting smile weak. "Am I to understand that you don't appreciate my service?"

"Repulsive shrew . . ."

"Well, since you do, you must make me another promise as well." The hag's eyes grew strangely bright. "You must promise me that when we meet in hell, you'll say hello, so I might have the pleasure of knowing you are burning with me there for all eternity."

Barrett's flailing arms strained toward her and the hag laughed again. "Nay . . . nay . . . you must cool your hunger for me. It's not my time yet. I'll be leavin' you now, but before I do, I would have you know that all I've reported about the blond whore is true . . . and I would have you remember me as your faithful servant—" Maggie's leer faded, "although, behind them bars as you are, you're even less than dirt under my low feet."

Swaying as Barrett choked on his rage, Maggie turned away. As she moved out of sight, Barrett heard her mumble, "Aye, I did what I came to do. The blond bitch will get her due."

Hatred a white, scalding heat inside him, his jealous rage overwhelming, Barrett knew instinctively that the hag had not lied. The blond slut was lying in his cabin . . . in his bed . . . with the bastard captain between her thighs.

Maggie, evil witch that she was, had been right. He would see that Gillian Haige got her due.

* * *

Derek's mien grew increasing darker as the morning grew late and the steady stream of traffic across the deck continued. Agitation growing, he had watched the unexpected progress of events that had begun with Haskell dragging the copper tub recently removed from his cabin across the deck for the second time that week. He had seen the raised brows of his men, but he had not flinched under their speculative glances.

The parade had continued. He had maintained his silence as Haskell and Linden had drawn buckets from the sea, one after the other, and had delivered them below. Other buckets of water that he could only assume came from their drinking supply had gone the same route. Then, empty pots and pans . . . and a kettle.

Derek inwardly groaned. He had made a mistake, all right. He had forgotten—no, he had *chosen* to forget Gillian Harcourt Haige's supreme arrogance at their first meeting. Now certain of her position, she obviously intended making the most of it by reverting to her old, demanding ways that would keep his men running to her commands if he allowed it.

But he would not!

Haskell appeared on deck again, interrupting Derek's agitated thoughts as he hastened in the direction of the galley, and a discordant note rang inside Derek's mind.

Something was missing from the picture . . . something intangible.

Of course! Resentment! That's what was missing! There had been no sign of resentment in Haskell's expression as he had hurried back and forth across the deck like a harried housemaid. Nor had he seen as much as a flash of resentment on Linden's weathered features as he had followed the same beaten course.

Haskell emerged from the direction of the galley, and Derek's thoughts stopped dead.

What in hell—?

Balancing the tray he carried as if it were made of pure gold, his large, beefy hands awkward at the task, Haskell turned again toward the cabins below. The tray itself was covered with a white cloth . . . *a white, spotless cloth* . . . as if it were being taken to the queen's royal chambers! Most incredible of all, testing believability as ocean swells rose and fell as far as the eye could see, was the single flower standing fresh and proud in a glass of water on the tray!

A flower for a whore in the middle of the ocean . . .

A flower? Hell, no, it wasn't a flower! It was the last straw!

Derek started down from the quarterdeck with a growl. He glowered as he turned onto the trail worn hot and deep into the ship's deck by the big, anxious feet of Haskell and Linden.

Gillian turned at the sound of Haskell's familiar heavy step in the doorway of the cabin. She glanced at the tray in his hands, her gaze halting briefly on a small red flower there. She looked up at the seaman's broad, ruddy face. He flushed unexpectedly.

"It's from the cook, ma'am . . . since your sister's so sick and all."

Gillian's throat was momentarily tight. "Please thank him for me." Turning back to Adria, she pleaded softly, "Try to help me, dear."

Adria responded weakly to her urging, struggling to raise

herself from the bed with Gillian's help, but it was to no avail. Frustration soared as Gillian glanced back at the copper tub partially filled with water from which the chill had only been slightly removed. She needed to get Adria out of her clothing and into that tub. It was her only hope of lowering the fever that was rapidly consuming her sister. The treatment was unorthodox, but she recalled that Adria herself had used it in helping one of the Potter children when the child had been severely convulsed by fever. The child's temperature had dropped almost immediately, and while the child had not ultimately survived, she—

Gillian swallowed purposefully. But Adria *would* survive. She would *make* her survive.

"Mistress Haige . . ." Gillian turned toward Haskell as the seaman continued hesitantly. "Would you like me to help you lift her?"

Looking up, Gillian saw the fellow's concern. The two rough seamen who had been running to her bidding for the last hour were not at all the callous individuals she had originally believed them to be. She had misjudged them, and she was suddenly sorely ashamed.

Her tone reflecting that realization, Gillian responded softly, "If you could help me to raise Adria to a seated position, Mr. Haskell, so I might undress her." She blushed. "I mean, if you could just—"

"Yes, ma'am."

The big fellow approached and Gillian relaxed, momentarily relieved. In a few minutes she would be able to—

Adria's sudden, blood-curdling shriek as Haskell leaned over her was unexpected. The sharp, shattering sound reverberated shrilly against the walls of the cabin as the startled seaman bolted upright and looked at Gillian. Another scream sent him stumbling backward.

"Father . . . ?" Adria's voice was a shaken plea as she glanced around the cabin, her fevered gaze frenzied. "Father? Where are you? Y-you said you'd take us home!"

"Adria dear, don't get upset. This man is trying to help us. His name is Mr. Haskell. He—"

Halting as Adria was seized by a violent bout of coughing, Gillian stood helplessly by until the spasm ceased and her sister continued weakly, "I-I don't want him to help us! Call Father! He'll come!"

"Ma'am . . ."

Haskell's tentative step forward set Adria to shrieking anew. Retreating in a rush, as she continued screaming, Haskell bumping heavily into the man entering the cabin behind him. Gillian heard the captain's muttered curse as the two broad figures collided, then the anger in the captain's voice as he demanded, "What in hell's going on in here!"

Her eyes widening at the captain's intimidating figure, Adria went suddenly silent. Taking Adria's hand as she began a soft whimpering, attempting to quell her sister's fears, Gillian turned briefly toward the captain's towering figure.

"She's delirious. She's afraid of Mr. Haskell."

The captain spoke in sharp command to the seaman behind him. "Get out of here, Haskell!"

The man backed out the door and the captain turned back to Gillian. Her first direct contact with this man since the intimacy they had shared the previous night left Gillian strangely shaken. Silent, she saw the tightening of his lips as his gaze raked her face, as he looked at Adria assessingly. She saw a flicker of something else in his gaze as he turned back to her abruptly.

"She wasn't this agitated downstairs with all that filth around her. What's upsetting her here?"

"She's afraid. She's asking for our father."

"Your father . . ."

"He's dead."

The captain's black, piercing gaze held Gillian's. It kept her immobile, sending little tremors down her spine as it dropped briefly to her lips, then snapped back up to meet hers. She was unprepared for the captain's emotionless tone as he stated flatly, "Then there's no help for it."

In a moment he was gone as quickly as he had appeared, leaving an unexpected void in his wake.

Silent, Gillian stared at the doorway through which Captain Derek Andrews had disappeared. She recalled that he had looked at her like that the previous night before he had left her.

In her mind she was already on her way back below.

Seven

The morning wind had freshened since Derek's encounter with Gillian Haige and her fevered sister in their newly assigned cabin below. Standing at the quarterdeck rail, keenly attuned to the movement of his ship as it began heeling over, he squinted up at the masts where the jibs and topsails cracked loudly, then looked down at the deck and called out abruptly.

"Set the sails, Mr. Cutter!"

Silent as his first mate barked orders that sent the men scampering up the shrouds anew, Derek observed as the topgallant and royals were set, the courses dropped into position, and the spankers were hauled to the top of the gaff to flap freely on the mizzenmast. He studied the direction of the wind once more, satisfied that it was astern, knowing that progress would be fast and true that day if the favorable conditions continued.

Conditions in the sisters' cabin, however, were another matter.

Derek's mind returned to the scene below as it had countless times since he had left the two women an hour earlier. Chaos, that's what it was . . .

Derek's jaw tightened. He had seen the panic in Gillian Haige's eyes as she had looked at him from her sister's bedside. Her sister's condition had worsened immeasurably since he had last seen her. It had not been any wonder that Haskell, an experienced seaman and a formidable man in every way, had been struck impotent by the sick woman's screams. Had it not been so tragic, he supposed the sight of that big man impaled by the woman's terrified gaze might have been almost comical . . . but it was not. The young woman had been so wan and colorless as to seem almost devoid of life. Her eyes had been frantic, searching, and blackly ringed. He had seen death hovering above her in that moment. Having seen death many times, he was no stranger to its specter. He had faced it without flinching—until he had viewed it through Gillian Haige's eyes.

The pain he had experienced in that moment had been unexpected. It had grown in intensity, becoming his own. When a few words had revealed that he was helpless against that pain, a familiar door had closed in his mind. Reacting instinctively, he had turned his back and walked away.

But the dull ache within him remained.

"Captain . . ."

Derek snapped toward the sound of Cutter's voice as his first mate stepped up onto the quarterdeck beside him. He met Cutter's gaze as his first mate reported, "The sails are set and the course is holding true. Are there any further orders, sir?"

Derek frowned. "And the situation below?"

Cutter hesitated. "With the Mistresses Haige?"

Derek nodded.

Cutter hesitated again. "It isn't going well."

"Meaning?"

"Mistress Adria Haige's agitation is increasing. She wants to see her father."

Derek's scowl deepened. "There's no help for that. Since her father is dead, there's only one way she'll see him again."

"No, sir, that's not exactly true."

Derek was momentarily disconcerted. "What are you saying?"

"There is a man below who—"

"A *man* below?" Derek drew back. He should have known. With Gillian Harcourt Haige there would always be *a man* . . .

"Yes, but this man, sir, is—"

"I think there is little you might say in that vein that will be of interest to me, Cutter."

"Sir, Mistress Adria Haige thinks the fellow is her father."

"Her father?"

"Mistress Gillian said his hair and beard are similar to their father's and her sister has confused the two men in her mind. I've seen the fellow's affect on her. The young woman is very docile when he's near."

"This man . . ." Derek paused. "Describe him to me."

"He's young, well built, with curly hair and a dark beard—the fellow who was brought aboard in chains—one of the few below who looks to have earned a living with the strength of his back."

Derek's small smile was hard. No more need be said. He had seen the fellow looking at Gillian when he had been below. He had recognized that look.

"Sir . . ."

Derek recognized that tone as well.

"What is it?"

"I've taken the time to look into the situation during the past hour. I think this fellow will be able to help ease the sick woman's anxiety."

"You do . . ."

"Yes, sir."

Long silent moments passed. The wind gusted and the

sails flapped noisily overhead as the ship sliced cleanly through the sea of whitecaps stretching out as far as the eye could see. Derek stood rigidly erect against the battering gusts as an emotion as hot and piercing as a blade slashed mercilessly at his innards.

Again, it came down to a matter of *another man* . . .

The flames licked out at her as Adria struggled fiercely to escape them.

They seared her skin.

They ignited her mind.

She cried out . . . but no one heard her!

Where was he? Father . . . Father?

Adria strained her eyes, but she could not see clearly through the haze surrounding her. Father had been with her earlier. She had felt his hand soothe her brow. She had heard his voice speaking calmly. She had seen his face, his features indistinct as he had consoled her.

He had promised her . . .

"Father!"

"Adria dear, please calm yourself . . ."

It was Gillian . . .

"Father!"

He had promised her he would take her home, where it was warm and safe, where she could work in the kitchen she loved and could take care of those she loved.

But the fire burned hotter.

The flames surged higher.

The pain in her chest stole her breath.

She was helpless here, where it was hot and dark and foul.

"Father!"

She wanted to go home.

But she was tired of running.

She was losing her strength.

The flames were consuming her.

"Father! Help me!"

Wait . . . she saw him!

"Father . . . ?"

He was close . . . so very close.

"Father . . . ?"

She felt his breath on her cheek.

She felt his hand on her hair.

His voice was sweet to her ears.

"I'm here, Adria. Everything will be all right now."

Father.

Joy leaped inside her.

She loved him so.

Shaken, Gillian saw the terror leave Adria's eyes. She saw peace overtake her sister's gaunt face as the mask of fear that had distorted her features for the long hour past faded.

Adria's eyes closed. She went suddenly still and Gillian gasped. "Oh, no, please . . . She's not—"

"She's asleep, Gillian."

Looking at Christopher where he knelt beside Adria, Gillian struggled to respond.

"She's all right, Gillian. She's sleeping."

But the concern in Christopher's eyes reflected her own. "She's so ill, Christopher. What if she—?"

"I'm here now. Everything will be all right."

Christopher's light eyes consoled her and Gillian almost . . . *almost* believed him.

* * *

Adria shuddered.

The fire had turned to ice.

It enveloped her.

It chilled her blood.

Suddenly angry, Adria opened her eyes to the haziness of an unfamiliar cabin. She was floating.

Water . . . it was so cold . . .

She looked around her. She saw him.

"I'm cold, Father."

Father smiled. "You'll be better soon, Adria. The water will make you feel better."

"No, it's cold."

"Rest, Adria. Close your eyes."

Dear Father. She could see that he loved her. She knew he would take care of her as he always had. She tried to close her eyes . . .

"I'm cold, Father."

"Adria dear . . ."

She heard Gillian's voice.

"Just a little longer and you'll feel better. I promise."

Adria shook her head. "Father promised me. I want to go home."

Silence.

"Father!"

"Yes, Adria. Just a little longer and you can go home."

A little longer . . .

Adria closed her eyes.

"She's cooler. Her fever is going down."

Gillian looked up at Christopher, her relief intense when

she saw confirmation of her assessment in his sober expression. Somehow, there was no embarrassment in the realization that Adria lay in the copper tub between them, her nakedness dimly outlined beneath the water covering her.

Together, she and Christopher had removed Adria's clothing. Together, they had raised Adria to her feet and slid her into the copper tub. Together, they had waited as the cool water had slowly taken effect, Christopher talking, reassuring Adria as Gillian had bathed her twin sister's emaciated form.

Gillian frowned, anxiety returning. "Is it warm enough in here? I don't want Adria to get chilled when we take her from the tub."

"It's warm enough."

Adria coughed.

"Let's take her out now."

Christopher nodded and Gillian spoke softly to Adria. "Try to stand up, dear. Come, we'll help you."

"I'm tired." Adria's voice was weak. "I can't."

"Yes, you can."

"No . . ."

Gillian's anxiety mounted.

"Adria . . ." Adria's eyes struggled to open at the sound of Christopher's voice. "That's right, look at me, Adria. We want you to help us get you back to bed now."

"I'm tired, Father."

"It won't take long."

Gillian swallowed against the knot in her throat as Adria managed a nod. The knot tightened as Adria strained to lift herself and Christopher encouraged, "That's right, Adria. I'll help you."

Miraculously, Adria remained standing with Christopher's support as Gillian rubbed her dry. Back in the bunk minutes later, Adria was silent as Gillian touched her forehead. Encouraged, Gillian looked at Christopher.

"She *is* cooler."

Adria coughed again and Gillian's frown returned. Filling a pan from the bucket nearby, she placed it atop the stove before turning back to Christopher. "The steam will help Adria breathe more easily. She'll be better soon. I know she will."

When Christopher did not reply, Gillian repeated, "She will."

"Gillian . . ."

"She *will.*"

During the silent moments that followed, Gillian scrutinized Christopher soberly. Yes . . . his sandy-brown hair was curly, like Father's. Like Father's, his beard was shot with threads of red, but the resemblance ended there. Christopher's eyes were gray and paler than Father's had been. And his skin was fair, lightly freckled across the ridge of his cheeks. His sturdy, muscular frame was totally unlike father's, but she saw that intangible quality surpassing mere physical resemblance that Adria had recognized. It was a quality that her slender, intellectual father and this husky, broad-shouldered young man had in common. Unable to put a specific name to it, Gillian knew only that it had touched both Adria and her deeply.

Adria had trusted Christopher instinctively.

Gillian abruptly realized that she had, too.

Christopher turned away and Gillian was struck with sudden panic. "You aren't leaving . . ."

"No, I'm not."

"But . . ."

"Cutter told Swift before we left the hold that the captain had ordered me to stay here as long as I'm needed."

Gillian's mind jerked to a jarring halt for the fraction of a moment it took for the significance of Christopher's statement to register in her mind.

"The captain did that?"

Christopher nodded, frowning at the inopportune interruption as a knock sounded unexpectedly at the door.

Responding, Gillian saw Haskell standing hesitantly in the passageway. "I brought you a tray, ma'am."

Startled, Gillian glanced out the nearby porthole to see that the sun was already making a rapid descent toward the horizon. Somehow the day had slipped away.

"Come in, Mr. Haskell." When he still hesitated, Gillian almost smiled. "Adria's sleeping. She's feeling a little better."

The big seaman nodded. "I'm glad, ma'am. The captain will be glad to hear it, too. He was disturbed. He's been glowerin' all day."

Her gaze flickering, Gillian did not immediately respond. "Where is the captain now?"

"He's on the quarterdeck, ma'am."

"Thank you for bringing the tray."

Waiting until the door had closed behind the burly seaman, Gillian ignored the tray he had left behind and walked toward the washbowl in the corner of the room. Filling it, she washed her hands and face fastidiously. She then withdrew a brush from the bag Linden had carried in earlier and smoothed back the silver-blond strands that had worked loose from her tight bun. She took a steadying breath before she picked up her cloak, slipped it around her shoulders, and turned toward Christopher abruptly. Her heart began a slow pounding as she spoke.

"I'm going to talk to the captain."

Not waiting for his reply, Gillian slipped into the passage-way and pulled the cabin door closed behind her.

His broad shoulders hunched against the chill wind, Derek raised his spyglass to the horizon. A brilliant sky streaked with pink and gold glittered against the lens as he stared a few moments longer, then gave a low snort of disgust.

What exactly had he been expecting to see? The *Colonial Dawn* followed familiar shipping lanes, but there was little possibility of encountering another vessel at this time of year when captains with more choice than he would have waited the few months needed to offer safer passage for his ship.

Derek lowered his glass, his gaze remaining intent on the horizon. He had sailed many difficult voyages, but this one surpassed by far even the worst he had experienced. Were he a different man, he might now be in a state of panic at the shambles that had become of it with the influential agent John Barrett confined in the brig below, vowing vengeance; with the violation of his contract with the London Transport Company threatening his financial ruin; and with the fever and ague sweeping those below growing worse with each passing hour until it was possible that even his crew was at risk.

And that was not the worst of it!

Damn that Barrett! Determined to have a more precise picture of the supply situation, he had gone below a few hours earlier to personally check the stores Barrett had brought aboard for his charges. He had discovered them to be inadequate, with much that was remaining unfit for human consumption.

Barrett, bastard that he was, had assessed the situation

well. Indeed, only the strong *would* survive the hardships to come.

With little he could do about the situation as it stood, he had made provisions that would grant those below the greatest degree of comfort affordable. Cutter was at that moment implementing his orders.

As if those concerns were not enough to burden him beyond endurance, then there was the woman . . .

The setting sun allowing greater bite to the gusting wind, Derek scowled up at the sails flapping wildly overhead. Hoping to get as much time out of the day as he could, he had decided to wait a little longer before sending the men aloft again to—

"Captain . . ."

Derek stiffened at the sound of a soft, female voice behind him. He had avoided the memory of that voice during the long day, as well as the pictures that had accompanied it, recollections so graphic in detail that he—

"May I speak to you, Captain?"

Derek turned abruptly. His teeth clamped tightly shut as his body reacted spontaneously to the incredible beauty of Gillian Haige as she stood behind him.

Angry at his susceptibility to her appeal, Derek snapped, "It is customary to request permission before stepping onto the quarterdeck, madam."

He saw the woman's gaze flicker the moment before she replied with the barest trace of her former hauteur, "I'm afraid I'm ignorant of maritime etiquette, Captain."

The wind gusted savagely, blowing back Gillian Haige's hood, loosening strands of silver-gold to fly about her face as she struggled to secure it once more. Stunned to see that her hands were shaking, Derek stepped automatically toward her. Catching her hood, he drew it back up to cover her head, then wrapped the flapping folds of her cloak more tightly around her.

His hands somehow refusing to relinquish her, Derek questioned gruffly, "What do you want, madam? It's cold . . . too cold for you to be up here this time of day."

"I wanted to talk to you."

Gillian Haige's lips were so close. They parted slightly, reviving the memory of the sweet taste of her mouth, a memory so vivid that he was swept with an almost irrepressible longing to taste it once more.

Desire pulsed hotly, darkening Derek's scowl. "I have no time for small talk, madam."

"I've come to thank you for—"

"Neither do I have time for gratitude."

"You will have it anyway."

"No, you are wrong!" Determined not to allow this beauteous female to control him with the wealth of warm, white flesh awaiting him beneath the folds of her cloak, Derek forced himself to surrender his hold and take a step backward. A sudden blast of wind again rocked the ship roughly, almost knocking Gillian Haige from her feet. His patience snapped as his arms snaked out to steady her once more.

"Return to your cabin, madam! The weather is worsening. It will soon be dangerous on deck."

"I'll leave after I've said what I came to say, and that is . . . " Gillian paused, continuing a moment later in a voice barely discernible above the howl of the wind, "that Adria is resting. Christopher Gibson is with her now."

"Gibson . . ." The name emerged from Derek's lips in a growl as a familiar agitation soared.

"Thank you for granting Adria the peace of mind of having him near."

"I told you, I don't want your gratitude."

"I know what you want from me, Captain." Gillian Haige's brilliant gaze held his. "You've fulfilled your part of the bargain we struck, and I'll fulfill mine, but you've gone farther than you need have to accommodate Adria and me. I couldn't let that go unacknowledged. I've come here now to tell you that neither will I allow it to go uncompensated. *Favor for favor,* Captain."

Derek searched the beautiful face so close to his, his breathing growing ragged. "I wouldn't make any promises you don't intend to keep, madam."

"I always keep my promises, sir."

Restraint slipping briefly from his grasp, Derek cupped the back of Gillian's head with his palm, holding her fast as he covered her mouth with a hot, lingering kiss. His heart drummed loudly over the whistle of the wind as he drew back abruptly with a harsh, shaken rasp.

"Tonight, madam. Tonight . . ."

"What's that ye say?" Swift's chin dropped in astonishment at the words Cutter had just uttered. He sputtered, finally managing, "Ye cannot do that! It's contrary to legalities!"

"Captain Andrews is the law on this ship, Mr. Swift." Those words allotting him a satisfaction he had desired from the first moment he had laid eyes on Swift's weasellike countenance, Cutter continued. "The decision stands. You are to be relieved of your authority here. You'll function as one of the guards, nothing more. I will oversee the condition of the passengers and—"

"Passengers! Are ye daft! They be *prisoners* and *felons* to be transported because of their crimes!"

"They are human beings, and many of them sick! New

directions are to be followed in their care, which will begin tomorrow, at dawn. They will be brought onto the deck in alternating shifts for air and exercise."

"Nay, nay, ye're askin' for trouble!"

"All those capable of working will apply the mops, soap and water that have been provided until the stench of this place has been relieved."

"Impossible! They're animals, satisfied to lie in their filth. They'll not do it!"

"They will, Mr. Swift."

"Nay . . . nay . . ."

"If *they* won't, you and your fellow guards will."

"Nay!"

"Those who are capable of work and refuse to work, will not *eat*."

"Hah!"

"Including the guards . . ."

Swift's lips snapped tight.

"Those who are well will help those who are sick."

"It will not work, I tell ye!"

"Each well person will be assigned one who is sick to care for."

"Ye're crazed!"

Cutter's gaze became intent. "Crazed I may be, but through Captain Andrews, my word is *law*. You have your orders, Mr. Swift. I'll be back tomorrow to check your progress."

Turning abruptly toward the staircase, Cutter climbed toward the deck above, a rare and satisfied smile on his lips.

Tonight, madam, tonight . . .

Those words rang over and again in Gillian's mind, setting

her hand to shaking as she raised another spoon of gruel to Adria's lips.

"No, please, no more . . ."

Adria turned her head and rolled to her side as a deep bout of coughing shook her. Weakened, she fell back against the pillow, her eyes fluttering closed.

"Gillian . . ." Adria's lips hardly moved with her words. Her eyes remained closed. "Do you think—" Harsh coughing interrupted her whispered question for long moments more before she continued in a fading voice. "— think we'll ever get back home?"

Gillian swallowed against the aching lump in her throat. What could she say in response to her sister whose skin was now a faded gray, whose listless blue orbs were deeply sunken, whose lips had surrendered their former rosy hue for a lifeless shade of blue?

"Gillian . . . ?"

"Adria dear, you and I . . . we must both believe we'll be home soon. If we believe—"

"Father!"

Adria's eyes snapped open wide with her cry and Gillian jumped with a start. Her heart plummeted to her toes at the fever she saw glittering brightly in eyes that had been listless moments earlier.

Adria's agitation expanded. "Call Father for me, Gillian! He's somewhere near. I know he is."

"I'm here, Adria."

Looking up, Gillian realized Christopher had entered without her realization. She saw the bucket in his hand— cool water to bathe Adria's fevered brow. He moved to Adria's bedside.

"Father . . ." Adria struggled to smile. "Gillian said—"

"I heard her, Adria. You'll be home soon. Try to rest, now. I'll take care of you."

"But . . ."

"Close your eyes, Adria."

Adria's eyes dropped obediently closed.

Gillian turned away from her sister's bedside and walked toward the washbowl, pausing briefly to stare at her reflection in the cracked glass above it. The sight brought tears to her eyes, so greatly did Adria's and her formerly identical images now differ.

Breathing deeply, Gillian cast the thought aside as she bathed her face, then reached up to loosen the pins in her hair. The heavy mass fell about her shoulders as she reached for the brush nearby.

"You're going to him now?" The sharpness in Christopher's voice turned Gillian abruptly toward him. Her face flushed as she glanced at Adria, and Chris responded curtly, "Don't worry, she didn't hear me."

Gathering her hair into her hands, Gillian twisted it expertly into a confining knot at the nape of her neck. Agitation twitched at her lips as she reached for her cloak.

"I'm sorry." Christopher stood up and took a tentative step toward her. "I'm angry because I feel responsible, because I'm the one who suggested—"

"No, don't be sorry. I'm not." Gillian turned to face him. "If there is one thing I've learned since Father's death, it's that the hard realities of life will not be ignored. Father . . . dear Father . . . was a teacher. He ignored realities in the pursuit of a noble dream. In so doing, he taught a hard lesson he never intended. I've made myself a promise that I won't do the same." Gillian attempted a smile. "I'm dealing with reality. I've told myself there is no true shame in that. I—I hope you don't think—"

Christopher took her hand. His manner was sincere, but his smile was forced. "Don't worry about what I think, and don't worry about Adria. I'll take care of her."

His words soft consolation, Gillian stepped into the passageway.

Bloody hell . . . she was feeling worse!

Maggie attempted a deep breath that resulted in another round of coughing that left her limp. She glanced around her, assessing the ragged chorus of coughs in the darkness. Aye, she had lots of company in her distress, but that thought gave her little consolation. She rubbed a shaky hand across her perspired brow. There was only one thought that would give her any relief now.

Glancing toward the handsome young Christopher Gibson's empty cot a short distance away, Maggie managed a smile. Aye, in her younger days, she would have had that one many times, she would. There had been few to top her on the London docks then, and there were few who ever would, that was for sure.

Maggie's yellowed smile broadened. She'd been no more than a lass of eleven when she'd entered the occupation at the urging of her ma, and she had enjoyed it from the first, like her ma before her. There had not been a cocky young sailor on the dock who had turned her down when she'd given him the eye, and she had given every one of them their money's worth and more.

Maggie sniffed. She'd had more men than she could count since then. There had been Charlies, Timothys, Williams, Johns, and Patricks, and so many more with no names at all. Hah! She'd liked them the most—those fellas who got right to it without the small talk that stole her precious time.

She had liked the feel of their hands on her and in her, and she had liked the taste of them in her mouth.

Christopher Gibson—aye—she could've done much with him and for him.

Maggie paused in her reverie for another bout of violent coughing. At the sound of a familiar step approaching, she looked up to see the sour-faced Will Swift. Taking her opportunity, she barked hoarsely, "Where is he?"

Swift halted abruptly, turning toward her with a snarl.

"He?" Swift's tone was deprecating. "Ye're wastin' yer time askin' about any man, old whore that ye are! There's not a one, even down here, who'd be desperate enough to have anythin' to do with ye!"

Maggie's lips stiffened. "The young fella, Christopher Gibson, where did he go?"

"What business is that of yers, ye old hag?"

Maggie smiled, deciding on caution. "Old hag I may be, but I have my fantasies left. You above all must understand, seein' the way you were starin' after that young Haige slut when she went upstairs."

"That bitch . . . I'll get my dibs on her."

"Like I'll get mine on young Gibson."

"Hah! Ye're dreamin', all right!" Swift swept her with another disparaging glance. "He's upstairs with the Haige harlot now."

"He went to the slut?"

"Aye, he did. At a direct order from the captain—bastard that he is."

"But he's been gone all day!"

Swift laughed sharply. "Ah, so ye noticed! Well, ye may cease yer waitin'. Gibson won't be comin' back."

"What's that you're sayin'?"

"The wench has him for as long as she wants him . . .

for as long as she can keep the captain convinced that she wants him there for the sake of her sick sister."

"Her sick sister be damned! The bitch wants him for herself!"

Swift's smile became a leer. "Aye, that's the truth of it, I know, and it's sad, ain't it? Ye're down here with so little while that doxy is upstairs gettin' so much."

A hot flush of anger started Maggie coughing anew. The pain in her chest deepened, stealing her breath as Swift observed with a growing smile. "Sick, are ye? Maybe ye should talk to the captain and he'll put ye upstairs in a room of yer own, just like he did for 'her ladyship'." Swift laughed aloud. "Ye have about as much chance of that as Master Barrett has of seein' the light of day before he reaches the other side of the sea!"

Eluding Maggie's grasp as she reached for him, Swift snarled, "Get away, ye filthy witch! I've no more time for ye!"

The heat of her hatred matching the fever consuming her, Maggie struggled for breath as Swift strode away. A single thought finally emerged from the wild disorder of her mind as her rage soared. It was the blond witch's fault! The slut had displaced her in a realm where she had once reigned supreme and now she was floundering!

Aware that she was powerless to affect revenge, Maggie thought again of the one who was not, only a short distance away. She hoped . . . she prayed to the demon who would doubtless soon have her soul that he would grant her the strength to visit her reluctant ally one last time.

That thought driving her, each labored breath she breathed marked by pain, Maggie struggled to draw herself to her feet.

* * *

The sound of Derek's steps echoed in the silence of his cabin as he walked toward the porthole and stared out at the sea beyond. Whitecaps glittered under a clear, moonlit night sky. The expected storm had not materialized beyond a choppy sea and a relentless wind. He had scrutinized the weather diligently, satisfying himself that the remainder of the night would go uninterrupted before allowing more intimate thoughts into his mind.

But that had been an hour ago, and anticipation of the night to come had been building ever since.

More agitated than he cared to admit, Derek paced a familiar path toward the potbellied stove, halting to run his hand through his hair in a anxious gesture.

Damn it! Where was she!

A knock on the door and Derek turned abruptly. His expression stiff, he steeled himself against the sudden pounding of his heart and the flush of hunger for the woman who doubtless stood on the other side as he ordered sharply, "Come in."

Gillian Haige entered and closed the door behind her. Her image was almost celestial in its flawless beauty despite the stains on the dove-gray gown visible beneath her cloak.

Derek struggled for control. She was a witch. The incredible blue of her eyes stole his will, drawing him to her. It changed caution to a desire so strong that he could retain no other thought but of the warmth of her lips under his, the taste of her in his mouth, and the sweet yielding of her flesh.

Suddenly disgusted with his weakness, Derek frowned. No, he would not allow her to control him. He was too old and too wise to fall into that familiar trap.

Realizing as a slow shuddering began inside him that in

another moment it would be too late, Derek forced a grating harshness to his tone.

"We have some things to discuss, *madam.*" Extending the mental distance between them, he continued. "I would have certain issues clearly understood before we proceed to the business of the night."

The business of the night . . .

The captain's emotionless words echoed on the silence of the cabin as Gillian stared back at him. She was suddenly incredulous at her own stupidity. Whatever had made her believe, even for a moment, that this great, intimidating devil looking at her with eyes as unfathomable as the sea had even briefly shared her distress at her sister's illness?

The truth, however, was now clearly reflected in those cold black eyes. The captain had brought Christopher upstairs to care for Adria for one reason alone—so Adria would not interrupt their . . .

. . . business of the night.

"Madam?"

Madam . . .

Spontaneous anger flared, quickly draining as a note in the captain's tone sounded a warning bell in the back of Gillian's mind. He was angry, not the same man who had taken her briefly into his arms on the quarterdeck hours earlier, the man whose mouth had claimed hers with startling passion, whose eyes had radiated a sensual heat that had set her to trembling.

Gillian took a shaken breath, intensely aware how much depended on the course this night would take as she responded, "I heard you, Captain, but I thought matters between us had been settled this afternoon."

The chill in the captain's voice deepened. "You were wrong."

The captain closed the distance between them. He was so close . . . close enough for her to feel the heat of his breath on her cheek, to experience again a thrill she could not deny as his gaze dropped briefly to her lips. Growing increasingly confused as the captain's gaze traveled her face with expanding heat, Gillian questioned, "I don't understand. Why are you angry?"

"Don't try to charm me, madam. I'm immune to your wiles."

"Charm you? Are you determined to read motives that don't exist into everything I say?"

"You waste your breath with denials."

"I've already told you that I—"

"I'm not concerned with what you told me! I'm concerned with what I am about to tell you."

Gillian's heart skipped a beat as the captain continued.

"There are certain details that I will not allow to be compromised." His expression hardened. "The first is that while our agreement prevails, you will have no contact with my men without my permission."

Gillian did not respond.

"Nor contact with anyone below."

She maintained her silence.

"I would also have it clear from the first that our association will be of no specified duration, that it will continue only as long as it pleases me to have it continue, and that it will entitle you to no special privileges once we reach Jamaican shores, when you will revert to your former status."

Gillian's jaw slowly stiffened. "Is that all, Captain?"

"No." The dark eyes above hers grew frigid. "I fear you'll

find the final condition to our arrangement the most difficult."

"And that is . . . ?"

"Fidelity, madam." The captain's gaze grew hard as stone. "I will not suffer your entertaining any other men in your bed during our association. Should I discover that you have . . ."

Gillian's face flamed. The captain paused, his voice hardening as he continued. "Or should I discover you've violated any of the conditions I've just listed, you and your sister will be returned below immediately."

Humiliation a tight knot in her chest, Gillian remained momentarily silent. Aware that the captain had offered the ultimate challenge to her resolve, a challenge she must meet, she began cautiously. "I know I did not endear myself to you when I first boarded this ship, Captain. In defense of my actions, I can only say that I felt they were justified."

The captain's lips tightened. She halted his attempted withdrawal with the touch of her hand on his arm, a contact that set her to trembling as she continued more softly than before. "But we have made a bargain. Whatever has happened since this afternoon to make you believe I would not keep to its terms, I give you my word now, that as long as you will deal fairly with Adria and me, I will deal fairly with you."

Her heart beginning a heavy pounding, Gillian proceeded more softly than before. *"Favor for favor*—I will give you all I have to give, and I will give it willingly. I will do my best to extend to you the comfort you have extended to Adria and me, and I will do it without restraint. As for another man . . ." Gillian's voice dropped to an unsteady whisper. "I am *yours* and *yours alone,* Captain, for as long as our agreement endures."

Gillian remained unmoving under the captain's tense perusal in the long, silent moments that followed. She was breathless under its intensity as he whispered, "You have the face of an angel, did you know that, madam? But I've known too many 'angels' with hearts as black as pitch."

Lowering his head, he pressed his mouth to hers. He drew back slowly to whisper, "Your mouth is sweet as honey . . . but I've also known too many women whose honey turned as bitter as gall." He paused once more before continuing. "Yet your eyes are so clear that I could almost make myself believe I can see into your soul. Do I see the truth there, madam?"

Gillian did not respond.

"I want to believe you. It would be so much easier if I could."

Hardly aware of the words she spoke, Gillian whispered, "Tell me what I might do to help you believe me, Captain."

The captain searched her face even more closely. Then he kissed her again, more slowly, more deeply, his mouth searching and lingering . . .

Gillian was shuddering when the captain drew back from her. She heard the deep ring of passion in his voice as he whispered, "You've made me many promises, so I'll make you one in return. I promise that I will give to you as much as you give to me . . . and that I will make the nights sweet when we lie together . . . sweeter than you ever dreamed."

Curving his arm around her, the captain drew her toward the familiar bunk at the side of the cabin as a swell of emotion unlike any Gillian had ever known rose within her. She was shuddering so intensely that she could barely stand as they stopped beside its broad surface, as she spoke in a shaken whisper.

"There is only one thing more I would ask of you."

The black velvet eyes looking into hers turned slowly cold. "I should warn you, madam. You are not master of this situation as you might surmise from what I have said. You tread on uncertain ground." He paused. "But ask. Because the truth is that you will never have a better chance than now of having your favor granted."

Gillian took a quaking breath. "My request is simple. I ask that you call me by my name."

The captain's gaze slowly consumed her. "Mistress Haige . . . ?"

"No . . . Gillian."

Another moment's silence passed between them before Gillian was suddenly in his arms.

She heard him say it the moment before his lips covered hers. It had a loving sound, the way he rasped . . .

"Gillian . . ."

Maggie the whore's familiar voice hissed from the darkness, raising John Barrett's head from his pillow. Cursing softly, he ignored the furtive summons, only to hear the call once more.

"Come to the door, Master Barrett. You must hurry, 'cause my time is short, and I've much to tell you."

Hatred as bitter as bile rose in Barrett's throat as he remained stubbornly unmoving.

The old whore's voice grew louder.

"You may pretend to be asleep, Master Barrett, sir, but I know better. I know there's little sleep behind bars, 'cause I've spent some time there in my day." The old hag paused to cough violently, then rasp more hoarsely than before, "Of course, I was not like you . . . accustomed to the best in life and then thrown down so low that you must listen to the ravings of an old crone like me without any protection at all."

The old witch laughed loudly then, the shrill sound turning him to see that the effort had caused another bout of coughing that had reduced her to her knees.

Barrett smiled, refusing to acknowledge her. The filthy hag would soon tire and go away.

"The blond bitch has *two* men now, Mr. Barrett, sir." Another piercing laugh. "Two strong, strapping fellows, and she services them well."

Liar.

"Christopher Gibson went up to her this morning. Your friend, Swift, said he'll not come back until the slut has no further use for him—by order of the captain himself."

"Liar."

"Two in her bed now, each petting her white flesh . . . and neither of them is you. Poor Master Barrett . . ."

"Liar!" On his feet despite himself, Barrett stared with true loathing at the old witch. "You will live to regret your lies!"

"Oh, but you're wrong, Master Barrett, sir!" The old whore strained for breath. "I'll not regret what I tell you this night. It's my legacy, you see." The old hag's eyes were feverishly bright. "It's all I have to give and I leave it to you, so it may eat at your innards as it did mine." Again the brittle laughter, then the coughing. The old witch swayed as she clutched the bars, and Barrett sneered.

"Go back to your sty, you old sow. I don't believe a word you say!"

"You do."

"No! Go away!"

"You do believe me, I can see it in your eyes! It's your final gift to me, so I thank you. I know you will guard my legacy well because you will remember that the bitch spit on you as she did on me." The penetrating laughter sounded more weakly. "Imagine, putting the two of us on the same level. Will you ever forgive her, *Master* Barrett?"

The witch cackled again, then turned away and slipped into the darkness as Barrett cursed aloud. He turned sharply at the sound of scratching feet in the darkness surrounding him. Picking up a metal cup nearby, he threw it in the direction of the sound, a unholy cry of fury rising in his throat. But it went unuttered because he knew—the old whore had not lied!

Barrett's fists clenched tightly closed. So, two men now fondled the blond bitch's flesh. Two men now sank themselves deep inside her.

Barrett nodded, his jowled jaw twitching. His time would come, and when it did . . . when he was done with her white flesh . . .

. . . when he was *finally* done . . .

Rasping, Maggie fell again to her knees, but she did not feel the pain. Instead, a picture of John Barrett's rage rose bright and clear within her disoriented mind.

John Barrett, the pig that he was, would make the blond slut pay.

Too weak to stand, Maggie crawled slowly toward her cot. The floor was sticky with dried and rotting waste and her cot was so far away. The rank darkness around her was filled with the sound of snoring, coughing, and rattling breaths, but she heard none of it as she indulged her fantasy. The bitch lay in a clean bed now, but her day would come. John Barrett would take his due and would take it well. If she could, she would be there, watching every sadistic turn, every perverted twist the bastard's revenge would take, and she would—

Suddenly seized by a new bout of coughing, Maggie fell weakly to her side. The spasm passed, leaving her gasping as she looked up to see her cot only a few feet away. Managing to draw herself to her knees, she was pulling herself back up onto its surface when she tasted it.

Blood . . . her mouth was filled with it! Warm and bitter, it gagged her, flooding her throat, her lungs—stealing her breath! She was drowning in it!

A sharp, fervent plea rose within Maggie. No, not yet! She wasn't ready to have the devil take her!

Choking . . . gasping, her plea went unuttered, only to have another sound emerge from her throat in its stead.

A death rattle . . .

Oh, the terror of the harsh, grating sound . . .

A horror that was all the greater because . . .

. . . the death rattle was her own.

Perspiration dripped from Christopher's forehead as the air in the small cabin grew heavy with steam. Glancing back at the pot of water boiling on the stove nearby, he shook his head unconsciously. Gillian had seemed so sure the mist would relieve her sister and help her breathe more easily, but he was uncertain. He had heard too many times that a damp mist killed for him to feel secure.

Yet, Adria did seem to be breathing easier.

Frowning, Christopher touched the gray skin of Adria's forehead, silently acknowledging that the resemblance between the sisters waned more each day. In his eyes, the woman lying on the bunk beside him had always been a pale shadow of her twin sister. But in her wasted state with the physical likeness deteriorating, even the shadow was fading.

Christopher stroked back a damp wisp of hair from Adria's cheek. Her hair was still beautiful, however, if only for its resemblance to Gillian's. The clear skin stretched tautly over classic cheekbones was still without blemish. The fine features, more clearly defined by her emaciated condition, were still perfection itself. She was Gillian—without being Gillian.

He knew, however, that the dissimilarity between the two sisters went deeper than present appearance. There was fire inside Gillian, an indomitable spirit that would not allow her to suffer the adversities of life without protest. She was an incredible light to which he had been drawn like a moth to the flame from the first, despite her apparent arrogance. She was quick and courageous, and when she loved, she was also self-sacrificing.

That last thought twisted the knife of pain within Christopher that had plunged deeply hours earlier, when Gillian had pulled the cabin door closed behind her.

Damn the bastard who now held her in his arms!

Damn the inequities of life that forced Gillian to trade her body for her sister's life!

Damn the cruel twist of fate that had brought Derek Andrews to this ship as captain and had delivered him there in chains!

For if the situation had been reversed . . .

Pain slashed deeply once more and Christopher was suddenly perversely amused at his own depth of agitation. Where was the man who had boarded the *Colonial Dawn* determined he would not risk the weight of chains again for any man? Where was the man who—

Christopher drew his raging thoughts to an abrupt halt.

Senseless questions! That man was gone. He had gotten lost in the brilliant blue of Gillian Haige's eyes. He knew he would never find his way free of their spell again.

Adria twitched suddenly, drawing Christopher abruptly from his thoughts. He frowned as her breathing grew more rapid, more labored. Watching her intently, he saw the new sheen of perspiration that covered her brow the moment before her eyes snapped suddenly open and she rasped unexpectedly, with startling clarity, "Who are you?"

The sound of her own hoarse voice foreign to her ears, Adria looked at the bearded young man crouched beside her. Disoriented, she glanced around her. She was lying on a bunk in a small cabin that was vaguely familiar, but—

Adria turned back to the frowning young man, her gaze blurring. He was vaguely familiar, too. His curly hair, the reddish beard—he reminded her of Father. But there was something else.

"Don't you remember me, Adria?"

That voice . . .

Fear accosted Adria abruptly as memory failed.

"Wh-where's Gillian? Who are you and what are you doing here?"

The young man frowned. "My name is Christopher. Gillian asked me to watch over you while she's gone."

The young man's words whirled confusedly in Adria's mind. She was tired. Her head and throat ached. It was difficult for her to breathe, and she was thirsty.

"I'm thirsty."

The young man smiled briefly and she saw it again, a glimmer that was strangely familiar, something to which she could not quite put a name. It struck a chord of warmth inside her and she attempted a smile in return as he raised her slightly and held a cup to her lips. His touch was as gentle as his voice.

"No, don't drink too much at once. I'll give you more in a few minutes."

Adria was too weak to object. Her head began a slow pounding.

"I want to see Gillian."

The young man's pale eyes flickered strangely. "She'll be back soon."

"Where is she?"

"Go back to sleep, Adria."

Her eyelids were so heavy.

"I want Gillian . . . please."

The young man held the cup to her lips again. Waiting until she had drunk more, he whispered, "Gillian will be back soon. Go to sleep."

Adria looked into the soft gray eyes so close to hers. She sighed at the comfort they afforded.

Suddenly secure, accepting the solace of the strong arms that still held her, Adria allowed the hovering darkness full rein.

"All right, lift!"

Cursing aloud when their effort failed to budge Maggie the whore's lifeless bulk from the floor, Swift glared at the guard who stood at her feet. "Come on, Dobbs, try again!"

Grimacing when another attempt failed, Swift cursed more loudly. Filthy whore—filthy to the end . . . leavin' all her blood behind her.

"Niles!" Disregarding muttered epithets from cots nearby, Swift shouted again as the dozing guard raised his head,

"Get your arse over here! We've another to be rid of to-night!"

"Leave her there till tomorrow!"

"Leave her where she lies!"

"Be quiet, all of ye!" Turning with a growl toward the voices from the darkness surrounding them, Swift hissed, "It would serve all of ye right if I did let this one lie. By tomorrow, ye'd change yer tune with the smell that would be comin' off of her!"

Struggling up onto the main deck with the weight of the old whore minutes later, Dobbs and Niles protesting every step of the way, Swift breathed deeply of the night air in an effort to clear her stench from his nostrils. He grunted as they moved laboriously toward the rail.

A smile touching his lips for the first time since he had heard the old hag's death rattle and gone to confirm her death, Swift turned toward the two men awaiting his command.

"Are ye ready?"

Swift's smile turned to a sadistic leer. They had done this often enough to have the practiced feel of it, they had. Strangely, he almost enjoyed it as he shouted, "All right, one . . . two . . ." Swinging the whore's limp form, they gained the proper momentum as Swift shouted, "Three!"

Releasing their hold with a flourish, the three men watched as the body sailed over the rail and disappeared into the darkness of the sea.

"And good riddance to her!"

A cold gust of night wind raised the hackles on Swift's spine and he shivered before turning to the men beside him. He saw Niles's dour expression and Dobbs's unexpected smile. He laughed aloud as Dobbs said unexpectedly, "That's one less we have to worry about."

"Aye, ye're right!" Swift laughed again. "I'll check her name off the list tomorrow." He paused. "Come to think of it, what *was* her name?"

Dobbs shrugged. "Maggie, wasn't it?"

"Aye, Maggie . . . but Maggie what?"

"Maggie the whore. What else?"

Swift paused to consider. The description was apt. It would do.

He could not quite believe it.

Incredulous, Christopher pressed his palm against Adria's brow. Her skin was comfortably warm and her breathing was easier than it had been for the past week. He glanced back at the water boiling low on the blackened stove nearby, making a mental note to refill the pot within the hour. He touched her moist brow once more. She truly might survive . . .

Adria's gaunt face twitched in sleep and her breathing grew suddenly ragged. Stiffening, Christopher held his breath. In a moment she was sleeping peacefully once more.

His relief intense, Christopher realized he could no longer deny that his depth of concern for the sick young woman beside him was stronger than he had acknowledged. He supposed he couldn't have expected any less. Had he not spent endless hours beside her bed, assuaging her fears and comforting her as he would a child? With Gillian's aid, had he not undressed her emaciated body and helped lower her into a bath as he would a child? Had he not consoled her in her uncertainty and breathed confidence into her with the sound of his voice during her fevered delusions? Had he not fed her, bathed her brow?

Had he not held her *life* in his hands?

A whimper escaped Adria's lips and Christopher responded with an instinctive word. The whimper ceased and Christopher's frown tightened. Yes, in her need, Adria had touched him.

But there was only *one* Gillian.

Gillian, who was now lying in another mans arms . . .

His thoughts suddenly too painful to bear, Christopher adjusted Adria's blanket, then lay back against the pallet prepared for him on the floor and closed his eyes.

But the image remained.

The rustle of bed linens, soft, gasping sounds, the glimmer of lamplight against pale flesh—

The loving continued.

Lying between the warm thighs of the woman in his arms, Derek laved the honeyed hollows of her mouth with his kiss. Drawing back, he traced the outline of her lips with his tongue, tasting her skin, trailing his hunger for her along her jaw to the fragile shell of her ear. She shuddered, drawing soft, incoherent words from a font of tenderness within him as the joy of her swelled firm and true.

Would he never get enough of Gillian?

Gasping culmination had rung in his cabin only minutes earlier as the passion that had soared between them had burst into flame. He had been left breathless, consumed by the blaze, Gillian's ragged breaths matching his own in the aftermath of the splendor they had shared. He had seen the reflection of that glory shining in Gillian's eyes as he had raised himself above her, still sheathed by her intimate softness.

He had allowed his gaze to linger, and rapture had soared anew.

Drawing back abruptly, Derek stared down at Gillian in wonder. What was it about this woman that drove him to such depths of passion? Beauty was not new to him, nor was youth, or eagerness . . . or lust. Uncertain, he only knew that an indefinable quality unique to her lit a spark within him that had not been struck before. He was aflame with it. It heated his flesh. It boiled his blood. It made him *need* as he had never needed before.

Slipping to his back beside Gillian, Derek drew her atop him. He saw her eyes widen as he lifted her easily and fitted her intimately to him. A silent groan echoed in his mind as he slid within her once more.

Gillian gasped at the rejoining of their bodies. The sound reverberated in his mind, striking a new level of intensity within him.

In his need, Gillian possessed him, but he would possess her as well. In his hunger, she obsessed him, but she would be obsessed as well. If she would leave her mark on him, he would leave his mark on her, indelibly, never to be forgotten.

Sliding his hands up her rib cage in a sweeping caress, Derek held Gillian erect as he began a slow, intimate rhythm within her. A wave of elation too sweet to contain swept over him as her beautiful face twitched with mounting passion, as her lips separated, as a soft sound of pleasure, incredibly sweet to his ears, escaped her lips.

His heart pounding, his breathing rapid, Derek studied Gillian's enraptured countenance. No, her passion was not feigned. Her moistness bathed him. Her trembling echoed his. She was tinder to his match, spark to his flame.

Drawing Gillian down upon him, Derek felt the perfect, rounded globes of her breasts brush his lips. He tasted their swells, bathed their burgeoning crests with his kiss. He drew from her tender flesh until she cried out aloud with bliss.

A familiar throbbing began within him and Derek growled a soft curse. No, not yet! He had not had enough of her!

Shifting until he was again atop her, Derek fought to suppress the force building within him as he scrutinized Gillian's flushed face. Her eyes were closed, her lips parted. He sensed the emotions she struggled to subdue, felt the throbbing need building within her.

But doubt lingered.

"Open your eyes, Gillian."

The edge to his tone raised Gillian's heavy lids with uncertainty as he rasped, "Tell me what you see."

Gillian's response was a shaken whisper. "I see you."

"Say my name."

"Captain."

"No . . ."

"Derek . . ."

Derek thrust within her. "Say it again."

"Derek."

He thrust deeper. "Again."

"Derek . . ."

"Again . . . again."

Her rasping whisper becoming a driving rhythm that thrust him warm and deep within her, Derek was uncertain of the exact moment when impetus became cataclysm, when cataclysm propelled him beyond control, when he was projected high into a realm of shuddering joy, clutching Gillian close in a moment of matchless, shattering ecstasy.

Breathless and spent, the moistness of mutual passion slick between them despite the cabin's chill, Derek raised himself above Gillian so he might look down at her once more. The molten gold of her hair splayed across the pillow, her exquisite features motionless and serene, Gillian was a portrait of sensual beauty almost too perfect to be real.

Myriad riotous emotions assaulting him, Derek spoke in a grating whisper.

"Open your eyes for me, Gillian."

Gillian's eyes opened slowly. He saw the lingering shadows of passion there . . . but there were other shadows as well. He tensed. "What's wrong?"

Gillian avoided his gaze. "Nothing."

"Tell me."

"Nothing is wrong . . . nothing."

Gillian looked away, but not before he saw the revealing brightness in her eyes.

Cupping Gillian's face with his palms, Derek turned her back to face him. He found her gaze free of the emotion he had glimpsed briefly there and a knot akin to pain twisted tight inside him.

A deep sadness welling, Derek stroked her cheek, then kissed her lips. He heard himself whisper, "Gillian . . ."

He heard himself repeat her name over and again, in soft, loving litany as Gillian's arms slipped around his neck, as she drew his mouth down to hers, as the wonder began anew.

The lamp had burned low.

Stirring on his pallet, Christopher glanced at Adria, then at the flickering flame.

Gillian had not returned although it was almost morning. Struck with the pain of it, Christopher closed his eyes.

The lamp had burned low.

Gillian opened her eyes to the shadowed cabin, her gaze

snapping to the big man sleeping beside her. Derek breathed slowly, heavily. He lay on his side, his arm wrapped around her, his lips against her hair. She felt his nakedness warm against her, and she remembered . . .

A flush of heat transfusing her, Gillian perused the face so close to hers, searching. Nothing about him had changed. His face was still handsome, his features severe even in sleep. The enigmatic darkness of his eyes were shielded from her gaze by lids fringed with thick, short lashes that lay motionless against his weathered cheeks. His still lips were full and warm.

She remembered those lips . . . the warmth of them . . . the taste of them. She had lost all coherent thought once they had touched hers.

But sanity returned.

She had stayed too long. Adria needed her.

Shifting subtly, Gillian attempt to lift Derek's arm from around her. She felt him stiffen the moment before his eyes opened, his gaze meeting hers.

Touched by panic as a familiar magic assumed control, Gillian whispered, "I—I must go. Adria needs me."

Derek's arm tightened. "Gibson is with her."

"Yes, but—"

"Do you trust him?"

"Yes."

He inched closer. His lips touched hers. They spoke no more.

Eight

Gillian opened her eyes with a start. She glanced around her. Narrow shafts of morning sunlight shone through the porthole of the captain's cabin, relieving the former darkness of night.

The rumpled bunk beside her was empty.

Harsh reality returned.

A plethora of emotions rocking her, Gillian briefly closed her eyes. She was uncertain of the hour, but it was obvious that Derek had cast aside the previous night's vigorous love-making, the *business of the night*, the moment the new day had begun.

Unlike her.

Heat rising to her cheeks despite the chill of the cabin, Gillian threw back the blanket and stepped down onto the floor. Her flush deepened at her nakedness. But there had been little use in donning a sleeping garment of any kind. Derek's attentions had been constant through the night, as had been the power of his passion. Even now, in retrospect, her heart pounded at the memory of the long hours she had spent clasped tight against the hard wall of his body, at the way he had—

Uttering a low groan, Gillian reached for her clothes. The night was past and matters of far greater urgency prevailed.

Her hands trembling, Gillian dressed quickly, a slowly

encroaching fear expanding. Derek had asked if she trusted Christopher to care for Adria. She had responded that she did. To her chagrin, she was intensely aware that had her feeling been to the contrary, it would have made little difference while she had lain in Derek's arms. For the touch of his lips had left her powerless to resist him.

Clothed, Gillian smoothed her hair with a few strokes of her hand before twisting it into a knot and securing it at the nape of her neck. She swallowed against the sudden lump that had formed in her throat. Somehow, in the midst of all her rationalizations and determinations, it had never occurred to her that she would find bliss in the warmth of Derek's arms . . . that she would be transported beyond herself to a realm where all else faded into obscurity in her mind.

Guilt, mortification, fear, all flooding over her in successive waves, lent an urgency to Gillian's steps as she walked rapidly toward the cabin door. Once outside, she paused, turning toward the cabin next door.

What would she find within?

Adria had been so ill.

Adria had been so weak.

Oh, God . . . what if . . . ?

Her heart pounding so loudly in her ears that all sound momentarily dimmed, Gillian thrust the door open with a shaken breath to see—

"Gillian?"

Adria's feeble voice the first she heard, Gillian stood transfixed. Adria's gaze was clear despite her pallor. She spoke with obvious anxiety. "Wh-where were you? I was so worried."

Christopher stood sober and silent nearby as the door swung closed behind her, and Gillian was struck with a sud-

den, choking emotion. Adria, sweet Adria, so ill, so close
to death, had been worried about *her,* while she had been—

Humiliation, embarrassment, *shame*—unable to escape
their debilitating rush, Gillian closed her eyes. She did not
realize she was swaying until Christopher's arms closed supportively around her and she heard his voice in her ear.

"Are you all right, Gillian?"

Gillian's humiliation deepened. "Yes, I-I'm fine."

Christopher leaned closer, his gaze concerned.

"We lost another one of the transportees during the night,
sir. That makes eight so far."

Cutter's voice was level, betraying little emotion, but
Derek knew it was a facade. The intolerable situation that
had been forced upon them all by the machinations of fate
and greed sat no more easily with Cutter than it did with
him as he responded sharply, "Barrett will have much to
answer for when Jamaican shores are reached."

"I wouldn't depend upon Swift or any of the other guards
to back you up with the truth, sir. They'll take the side that
nets them the most. If Barrett can convince them that it'll
be to their benefit to say you are responsible for the loss of
life below—"

"No, it won't come to that." Derek's hard smile did not
reach his eyes. "You may rest assured."

Cutter nodded. "Aye, sir." He hesitated. Amusement
flashed briefly. "The cleanup below begins this morning.
Swift is in charge."

"With a mop and a pail?"

"Aye, sir."

Derek grunted in lieu of a smile. "Keep me informed of
the progress."

"Aye."

Watching as his first mate exited the quarterdeck, Derek withheld a yawn. He was more tired than he had realized. Morning had come too quickly to suit him. It had been more difficult than he had believed possible to separate himself from Gillian's tender flesh upon awakening.

A familiar spot of heat expanding in his groin, Derek emitted an unconscious growl. Was there no satisfying his hunger for the pale-haired witch?

Turning abruptly, Derek stared unseeingly toward the horizon as he hunched his broad shoulders against the wind. He had just completed an inspection of the ship. The last of the repairs had been completed and the vessel was making good time since setting sail. It appeared the worst was over above deck, and with Cutter in charge of the hold, he had no doubt conditions would soon be secure there. All was approaching stability—except within his own cabin walls.

Gillian . . .

Derek unconsciously mouthed her name. The warmth elicited astounded him. He had never known a woman who stirred him more.

A red-haired image flashed briefly before Derek's mind, accompanied by perverse gratification.

No, not even she.

That consolation brief, Derek frowned darkly. He had been relentless in his hunger for Gillian last night. Somehow, each touch, each taste of her sweet flesh, had whet his appetite for more. Lust? No, it was more. There was something about the witch that set him afire. Nagging him still was the realization that although he had taken her again and again, that fire still burned.

Derek unconsciously set his stance against another chilling gust as the deck rocked beneath him and canvas cracked loudly overhead. Gillian had been sleeping soundly when he had left her that morning. Her lips parted, she had been breathing in a light, delicate snore. His lips twitched in a smile. He must tell her about that snore tonight.

Tonight . . .

The scowl returned. He was tired and becoming more irritable by the moment. He intended to retire early and he had no intention of waiting long past dark for the wench to come scratching at his door at her convenience. He need make that perfectly clear.

His jaw firming, Derek turned abruptly toward the quarterdeck steps. He had been up for hours, but the morning was still young. So deep had been Gillian's slumber when he had left her that there was a chance he might find her still abed.

Halting the obvious progression of that thought, unaware that his pace grew increasingly rapid, Derek crossed the deck in broad strides. He turned down the passageway toward his cabin minutes later. Hesitating momentarily outside, his heart pounding, he pushed the door open.

His cabin was empty.

More disappointed than he dared admit, Derek turned toward the supercargo's cabin with a frown. He raised his hand to knock, reconsidering when he saw the door standing slightly ajar.

He pushed it open.

Still supporting Gillian in his arms, Christopher turned with a snap as the cabin door slapped back against the wall behind them. He felt Gillian jump with a start as the captain stood framed in the doorway.

His tone ominous, Derek spoke in soft command.

"Take your hands off her."

The echo of chains resounded in Christopher's mind as he held the captain's cold stare without moving.

Her face drained of color, Gillian extricated herself from his grip and turned unsteadily. Reaching out toward her once more, Christopher was brushed roughly aside as the captain assumed his place at her side.

His voice dropping in timbre, Derek questioned, "What's wrong, Gillian?"

"Nothing."

Christopher saw the subtle twitch of the captain's scarred cheek the moment before he swept Gillian up into his arms and turned toward the door. Christopher's spontaneous bid to follow turned the bigger man back to face him with obvious menace.

"Stay where you are!"

Frustration soaring, Christopher was still staring at the open doorway through which they had disappeared when he heard a choked sound behind him.

Turning, he met Adria's incredulous stare.

Covering the short distance back to his cabin with rapid strides, Derek entered and kicked the door shut behind him. He carried Gillian toward the bunk they had recently shared and lay her down on its rumpled surface, pausing briefly before sitting beside her. Silent, he scrutinized her sober face. There was no denying her lack of color as she met his gaze.

"I want to get up, Derek."

Derek. The sound of his name on her lips jolted the captain with pleasure so intense that he was momentarily shaken. His reaction was a deepening of his frown as he responded, "What happened?"

"Nothing."

"Tell me."

The fine line of Gillian's lips twitched. "I was worried about Adria. I'm not certain what I was expecting when I opened the door, but she was rational, and I—" She took a steadying breath. "Let me up. I must get back to her."

"Not yet."

"I've spent too much time away from her already!"

"You served her needs well when you were apart from her last night—much better than you could have if you had remained at her side."

Gillian did not respond, and Derek's jaw tensed.

"Or perhaps you've decided to put an end to our arrangement since your sister is so much better this morning."

"No! I—"

"Have you changed your mind, Gillian?"

"No."

"What is it, then?"

"It's nothing . . . nothing."

Derek's eyes narrowed. He stood up abruptly, suddenly certain there was no cause to press her. He had read the truth in Gillian's eyes. It had been a long night for both of them.

Gillian drew herself to her feet. Derek resisted the desire to slip his arms around her, to draw her close, a muscle pulling in his cheek at the realization that Gibson's arms had been as eager as his to enclose her.

No . . .

His jaw tightening, Derek was startled to hear himself say, "When you're done tending to your sister, I want you to move your things in here." Gillian went stock-still as he continued. "I expect you to be installed in my cabin by nightfall."

Using the silence that followed, Derek pressed with a growing ring of menace, "But there is one thing I want to make clear, here and now. Never again, *for any reason,* do I expect to enter a cabin to find you in another man's arms."

He kissed her then, claiming her mouth possessively. Forcing himself to draw back a moment later, Derek muttered a silent curse and turned toward the door.

Battling a draining incredulity, Adria accepted the support of Christopher's arms as he held a cup to her lips. She drank at his urging, unable to meet his gaze as he lay her back against the pillow.

"Adria, look at me."

Adria did not respond to Christopher's soft command. She could not bear to look at him as a tight knot of pain, unrelated to the soreness in her throat or the heaviness in her chest, twisted cruelly within her.

Disbelief surged once more. It could not be true! Gillian was too brave, too strong. She would never submit to any man, much less the black-hearted captain whom she despised.

"Adria . . ."

But there had been no denying the captain's proprietary manner, or the look on his face when he had walked through the doorway and saw Gillian in Christopher's arms. Jealous rage had flashed in his eyes. But it had been the emotion that had followed, emotion she had glimpsed in those deep black orbs only briefly, that had truly shaken her. It had come to life as the captain had swept Gillian up into his arms, and it had flared more hotly when Christopher had taken a step toward them. Its heat had singed her. She felt it still.

"Adria, look at me."

No, she could not.

Stricken by a sudden bout of coughing, Adria strained for breath as the painful spasms shook her. Weak and gasping when they finally ceased, she was unable to speak as Christopher raised her supportively once more. She accepted the cup he held to her lips and drank gratefully.

"Are you all right?"

Adria looked up. This man had been kind to her, but he was a stranger—and a felon. It had come to her in a sudden flash that he was the same man who had been delivered to the ship in chains. Yet, aside from Father, he was kinder than any man she had ever known.

"I . . . I'm all right."

Christopher's voice remained soft, but his gaze grew intent. "You mustn't condemn Gillian."

Adria turned her head. She didn't want to hear any of this.

"Adria, look at me."

Responding to his command despite herself, Adria looked at Christopher as he asked unexpectedly, "Are you comfortable in that bed?"

His unexpected question surprising her, Adria nodded. The bed was warm and free of the dampness Gillian and she had been exposed to in the filthy hold below. Yes, she was comfortable.

"Are you feeling better than you did?"

Adria considered the question. She did not feel well. Her throat burned and was perpetually parched. It was difficult to swallow. The pounding in her head was unrelenting, but the weight in her chest had lessened and she was able to think clearly for the first time in countless days. She nodded again.

Christopher frowned, his eyes searching her face as he spoke again.

"The reason you're feeling better is because you're away from the damp cold and filth of the hold. Gillian did that for you. You're recovering because Gillian didn't spare herself in your care. You're going to get well because . . ." Christopher hesitated. ". . . because Gillian loved you enough to make sacrifices."

Sacrifices?

The word resounded in Adria's mind as gradual realization dawned.

No!

Adria was still unable to respond as Christopher continued. "You can pay her back, you know—by realizing that Gillian had no choice in what she did if she wanted to save your life, and by asking yourself what you would have done if the situation had been reversed."

"But . . ."

"And by getting well."

Her voice a hoarse croak, Adria rasped, "But what will happen to Gillian now?"

Christopher's expression went slowly cold. "The captain will treat her well until we reach our port."

"But she . . . it will never be the same."

"Nothing is ever the same."

"But Gillian will be—"

Turning abruptly at a sound in the doorway, Adria saw Gillian standing silently there. Her heart wrenched in her chest, the pain almost more than she could bear, when she saw Gillian's hesitation.

A soft cry escaping her lips, Adria raised her arms toward

Gillian. She was not certain what she said as Gillian moved silently to her side and slipped her arms around her. She was conscious only of the words that emerged in a ragged whisper, straight from her heart.

"I love you, Gillian."

"All right, ye bloody leeches, take up yer mops and yer buckets and get busy, I say!"

Hands on his scrawny hips, Swift looked at the ragged line of transportees standing in front of him. A lazy, beggarly lot they were, straight from the pits of Hades. And here he stood, their taskmaster! Aye, he'd get even with the bloody captain for this!

Swift's stubbled face flushed. He nodded to the two guards standing behind the recalcitrant line. "Show them the weight of yer clubs if they don't start swinging them mops soon!"

"No, I don't think so, Mr. Swift!"

Cutter's interjection cut into the growing intensity of the scene as the first mate descended the staircase toward them.

Swift's temper snapped. "Who're ye to tell me how to handle these filthy beasts? I'm in charge here and I'm followin' the captain's order to get this place cleaned up!"

"Not with a bloodbath, you're not!"

"A bloodbath, ye say?" Swift gave a short laugh. "Nay, a few broken bones, and a few cracked skulls for them who're too lazy to work is all. Then the sluggish bastards will pick up them mops."

Cutter's thin face tightened. "The captain will have no bloodshed. There'll be no unnecessary clubbing down here." Cutter's voice was cold. "Just as there'll be no food for those who refuse to work."

"Hah! Ye hear that, ye lazy slugs!" Swift turned toward the men who measured each word the first mate spoke. He saw them gauging his authority, and he'd be damned before he'd let them sense a lapse. "Ye hear what this fellow says? I've tried to tell the captain that sows like ye enjoy wallowin' in dirt, but he don't understand. He thinks ye'll be better for havin' cleaned up this place a bit. I told him that I'd agree to coax ye to do yer work with a tickle from our clubs, but he won't have it. He'd have ye *starve,* instead! And that's what ye'll be doin' if ye don't pick up them mops right now!"

Swift watched the play of emotions on the dirty, bearded faces facing him. He saw the shifting glances, the hesitation. He watched as a short fellow in front leaned tentatively toward the bucket in front of him, then picked up the mop. Palmer . . . aye, he was the weakest of the lot.

A hot, perverse anger suffused Swift as a second and a third took their mops in hand. Nay, it wasn't right, reasoning with them beasts, giving them the idea that they had any choice at all once a command had been given. It made for trouble in the future. There was only one way to handle them . . . to teach them respect . . . and that was with the might of his club, and he—

The rattle of chains behind him turned Swift abruptly toward the figure emerging from the shadowed corner of the hold. His breath caught in his throat as Barrett's burning gaze met his.

Swift gasped. Barrett's face was unshaven, his hair hanging in dirty strands, his clothes spotted and stained . . . but the menace remained.

Trembling, Swift turned sharply toward Cutter. "Wh-who gave the word to let this one out of the brig? Put him back, I say!"

"Mr. Barrett's out of the brig at my order."

Swift was enraged. "I'll not have it! The captain gave his word that he'd keep him confined!"

Cutter raised his brow. "The man's in chains, Mr. Swift. He's going nowhere, except to do your bidding."

"Nay . . . nay . . ." Cutter took a backward step, trembling under Barrett's evil stare. "I'll have nothin' to do with him. This man is the captain's prisoner! He's not part of the lot I signed on to guard! I'll not be responsible for him."

Cutter paused in response, then nodded. "There's something in what you say." Surprising him, Cutter addressed John Barrett directly. "If you expect to eat, you'll have to work just like everyone else, Mr. Barrett, *sir.* I suggest you take up a bucket and mop."

Barrett's broad, slovenly figure went still. Stretching his head up from his beefy shoulders slowly, much like a turtle extending himself from his shell, Barrett responded in a voice that echoed queerly inside Swift's thin frame. "I would rather starve."

"So be it." Cutter turned to the quaking guard in the shadows. "You—whatever your name is—take Mr. Barrett back to the brig." The guard remained unmoving. "Now!"

Swift held his breath as Niles poked Barrett with his club and Barrett turned responsively back in the direction from which he had come.

But Swift had seen it. There had been death in Barrett's bulging eyes as the ugly toad had glanced his way.

Aye, death.

Swift turned abruptly toward Cutter. "I'll not have the man out from behind them bars again! There's no trustin' him, even in chains!"

Cutter surprised him with a nod of agreement. "You're right. Mr. Barrett's not to be trusted, but in his present position, he's no different than anyone else. If he doesn't work, he doesn't eat. I'll give the word to allow him only water until he changes his mind."

The slender first mate walked back up the stairs to the top deck as Swift shook with suppressed rage. Aye, him and the captain made a good pair with their eyes as cold as ice and their hearts to match. Damn them both to hell! If he had any luck at all, John Barrett would hold true to his word and would be dead from starvation by the time they reached their destination.

Barrett's rotund image returning sharply to mind, Swift gave a grunt of disgust. But there was little chance of that! Barrett could live off the fat stored under his pampered hide for that short space of time and more!

A shiver crawled down Swift's spine. He had no recourse but to keep his distance from the evil toad.

Aye, he would. It was the best chance he had of surviving.

Morning had passed into afternoon, and afternoon was waning in the small cabin where Christopher and Gillian worked at Adria's beside. Foregoing conversation and striking all thought from her mind, Gillian had allowed herself consolation in Adria's slow but visible improvement.

Gillian assessed Adria's sleeping face. Adria's fever had returned briefly, but it had responded well to sponging with the cool water that Christopher had hauled directly from the sea and she was resting comfortably. Water continued to boil atop the potbellied stove nearby and Adria's breathing was less labored. Her dear sister had even managed to take some gruel and eat a small piece of bread.

Gillian took a deep breath, allowing herself the satisfaction of inroads made into other areas as well. Working by her side, Christopher had also hauled the water she had needed to wash the pitifully few undergarments and the change of clothing that had gone unlaundered since they had arrived on the ship weeks earlier. Through it all, he had not forced a word of conversation beyond that offered, and she had been infinitely grateful for his sensitivity.

Glancing again toward the porthole as the sun dropped slowly toward the horizon, Gillian realized she could not put off the moment any longer. As if sensing her thoughts, Christopher halted abruptly in the task of feeding the ever-hungry, potbellied stove and turned toward her.

Gillian met Christopher's gaze squarely for the first time since she had returned from Derek's cabin that morning.

"Adria's much better, isn't she?" She felt the intensity of his perusal as she continued. "Her fever is down and her breathing is improved. I can't thank you enough for taking care of her as you did last night. If it hadn't been for you . . ."

"You don't have to thank me, Gillian. I'm out of that pesthole below. I'm eating the same food as you and the crew are eating, and I'm sleeping where it's warm."

"That isn't why you've helped us."

"No, it isn't."

Gillian was momentarily silent. "Somehow, when I saw you that first day in chains, the last thing I expected was that you would become . . . a friend."

Christopher's gaze held hers. "What are you trying to say, Gillian?"

Gillian averted her eyes. When she did not respond, Christopher gripped her lightly by the shoulders. Gillian glanced nervously toward the door and Christopher dropped his hands to his sides.

"Is that the problem . . . that he's jealous of me?"

When Gillian still did not respond, Christopher continued softly, "I don't want to make any trouble for you with him. Adria's much better. Maybe it would be better if I went back below."

"No!"

"But—"

"Adria will need you when I'm not here." She paused, her face coloring hotly. "I'll be moving my things into the captain's cabin tonight."

Gillian's color deepened when Christopher did not respond. "Will you stay to care for Adria until she's well?"

Christopher's response was a stiff nod.

"I'll never forget what you've done for us." Gillian paused, raising her chin. "It's getting dark. I have to go."

Christopher's hands snapped out unexpectedly, gripping her shoulders, halting her as she attempted to leave. He turned her back toward him, his expression intense, his tone sharply controlled as he spoke softly. "There's one thing I must know, Gillian." He hesitated, pinning her with his gaze. "Does he treat you . . . gently?"

Somehow incapable of verbal response as emotion welled once more, Gillian gave a short, jerking nod. She closed her eyes briefly as Christopher's hands dropped back to his sides.

Snatching up her bag, Gillian turned toward the door. She did not look back as it closed behind her.

The rumbling of John Barrett's empty stomach echoed in the dank cell as he inwardly seethed. Standing up, he walked toward the barred door, his mind returning unexpectedly to Maggie the whore's visit the previous night.

So, the foul crone had died. If he were to believe what

she had promised him, she was waiting for him in Hades right now.

Barrett laughed harshly. If she was, she would have a long wait. He'd not give her the pleasure of seeing him there . . . not yet.

Barrett's laughter abruptly faded. Actually, he had not been as pleased as he had thought he might be at the news. It had occurred to him during the long night past that a distorted mind such as Maggie's was fertile ground on which to bargain and play. He might have found good use for her, were she still alive. He might even have been able to convince her to steal some food for him with the promise of a reward when they reached Jamaica.

Barrett gave an angry snort. That possibility was now past. During the hungry silence of the past few hours, he had been forced to concede to himself that he had handled the whole situation with Cutter that morning very poorly. His rage at seeing the puny wretch, John Swift, in a position of authority over him had overwhelmed his better sense. He had *reacted* rather than reasoned, and the result had been the situation in which he now found himself.

Barrett rubbed his empty stomach, a slow fury building. No, he would not go without food. He would not subject himself to that hardship. He had already decided that he would take up the bucket and mop, instead. And while he used that mop, he would amuse himself by counting each and every swipe he took across the filthy deck, knowing that the count, however high it grew, would match the lashes he would have applied to Swift's bony back when the time was ripe.

Barrett breathed deeply as his rage swelled. The count would also be in keeping with the humility he would demand from Captain Derek Andrews when that black-hearted wretch stood a broken man before him, and with the homage Gillian Harcourt Haige and her anemic sister would give his waiting body while they writhed under his iron hand.

Bastards! Bitches!

They would all be on their knees before him!

Suddenly shuddering, frothing with frustrated wrath, Barrett fought to bring his riotous emotions under control, knowing that when it came, revenge would be sweet.

Agitated, Derek paced his cabin. He glanced again at the glorious pink path the setting sun had lit across the sea as it sank into the horizon, but his thoughts were too similar to those of the previous night to allow him peace.

Damn her! He had told Gillian Harcourt Haige he wanted her installed in the cabin and waiting when he returned! He had thought he had made his point clearly, but it appeared he had not.

Taking a stabilizing breath, Derek drew his broad, muscular physique rigidly erect, his chest heaving under the black shirt he wore. The flickering flames in the potbellied stove reflected demonically in the dark onyx of his eyes as he looked again toward the door.

Derek's shoulder twitched. She was a conniving witch, all right, obviously employing delay to raise his anticipation of the night to come. Well, if that was her ploy, she had succeeded. He was anxious and angry . . . and, despite himself, more hungry for her with every passing minute.

Clamping his jaw tightly shut, Derek sought to control his increasing distraction. When she arrived, he would tell her in no uncertain terms that he would not—

Freezing at the sound of a soft knock at the door, Derek turned slowly. At a word, the handle moved and the door opened. Gillian paused momentarily in the doorway, tentative, her glorious eyes on his face. He saw her hand twitch on the carpetbag she held, a bag incredibly small to hold the bulk of her worldly possessions.

His heart pounding, Derek watched Gillian take a step inside, then another. He was uncertain when he started toward her or of the exact moment when his arms closed around her. He did not recall anything but the flush of heat that suffused him, erasing all rational thought as he swept her up into his waiting arms at last.

Christopher remained staring at the door through which Gillian had left a few minutes earlier. His throat tight, he turned away, his gaze brushing Adria's sleeping form on the bunk behind him. The pain of the moment intense, Christopher heard Gillian's words run over again in his mind.

    . . . *the last thing I expected was that you would become a friend.*

A friend.

Christopher's thoughts rebelled in silent protest.

He recalled Gillian's stiff nod when he had asked her if the captain had treated her gently. It occurred to him that she had not realized how much had hinged on her reply.

Christopher paused at that thought. He supposed it was best Gillian did not know that had her response been else, the captain would not have survived the night.

Nine

The great house of the Dorsett sugar estate stood silent and grandiose in the brilliant gold of the morning sun. Separated by a rise of land from the endless fields where slaves had been laboring since dawn, graceful verandas and balconies extending from the outer rooms overlooking a matchless tropical panorama of dense green foothills in the distance and turquoise Jamaican sea below, the imposing white frame structure conveyed an aura of indolent luxury which exemplified the way of life of those within.

The curtains of the great house swayed in the gentle breeze as the early-morning tranquility was broken abruptly with a sharp, impatient call.

"I said I want you *now,* Lester, not when you're good and ready to come!"

"Yessa, yessa . . ."

Entering the upstairs bedroom in a step just short of a run, the brawny young Negro stopped short at first sight of the woman standing at the open window amidst the diaphanous folds billowing there. He stood stock-still as she turned toward him, her smooth body naked except for the locket that sat in the hollow of her throat. He remained silent as the woman walked sinuously toward him, green eyes glinting as she ran long, slender fingers through the unbound length of hair the color of flame.

"Do you like what you see, Lester?" Coming to stand a hairsbreadth away from the startled slave, she whispered more softly, "Do you?"

Lester did not respond.

"Come now." The woman took a step closer. "We're alone. You can call me by my name. Emmaline is a beautiful name. I want to hear you say it."

The Negro's broad frame twitched. "Massa be downstairs finishin' his breakfast. Him be comin' up any time now."

Emmaline's voice dropped a husky note lower. "You're perspiring, Lester. I can't imagine why. I find it quite comfortable in here with the sea breeze cooling my skin." Emmaline smiled. "Perhaps that's the reason . . . you're wearing too many clothes." She paused. "Take your clothes off, Lester."

Perspiration snaked uneven paths down the massive Negro's cheeks. His broad, flat features jerked nervously as his muscular chest began a ragged heaving.

Emmaline smiled. "I've heard so many good things about you, Lester." She paused to correct herself. "I should say, I've 'overheard' so many good things. Jubba was especially enthusiastic about your last meeting with her behind the sugar mill. She said your 'man stick' was bigger and harder than any she had ever seen." Emmaline glanced toward the buttons on his britches. "I decided then to see if what she had said was really true."

Lester shook his head, a growing panic in his gaze. "Massa comin'. Him goin' to—"

"Take off your clothes, Lester. You wouldn't want me to tell the master you were disobedient, would you?"

Emmaline's gaze grew intense. It refused to relent until Lester's trembling hands began working at the buttons on his shirt. It flashed with triumph as he stripped his shirt away to bare his muscular chest. It narrowed as Lester's hands moved to the closure on his britches.

Emmaline's lips separated with expectancy as Lester released the buttons and drew off his pants as well. Naked before her, Lester shuddered as her gaze roamed his body in slow assessment, coming to a halt on the tight, black curls between his muscular thighs and the limp organ there.

Emmaline raised her gaze slowly to his. "I'm disappointed. Surely you find me as desirable as Jubba." She took a step closer. "Perhaps you need something more. Would you like to touch me, Lester? Do you think my skin would be as soft as Jubba's?"

The young Negro's throat worked visibly.

"Tell me, Lester."

Lester managed a hoarse reply. "Yessa, i-it be fine."

Emmaline's slid her hand down her smooth body. "Is my body as beautiful as Jubba's?"

Shaking visibly, Lester gave a jerking nod. "Y-yessa."

She cupped her hand over the reddish-brown curls of her female delta, her eyes glowing into his. "And tell me . . . do you think it would taste as good as Jubba's if you could have it now?"

The young Negro swallowed thickly. The bulging vein in his neck throbbed visibly.

"Lester?"

"Yessa . . . yessa . . ."

Emmaline took a quick step backward. Her gaze dropped to Lester's male organ, standing hard and true between them. She hesitated, then gave a denigrating shrug. "I think Jubba exaggerated. I've seen much better than that pathetic member before."

The sound of a familiar step on the staircase snapped Lester's head toward the sound. His eyes bulged.

"It be Massa . . ." True terror in his eyes, he indicated the male organ that maintained its formal stance. "Massa take away dis ragin' piece if him find Lester here like dis."

"Oh, would he?"

"Yessa . . . *please.*"

Emmaline's smile changed abruptly to a sneer at his pleading tone. "In that case, I warn you now that if you value that 'ragin' piece,' you'd best be careful about telling your black tarts that the massa's wife is a skinny white stick who wouldn't make your johnny-boy stand up, no way, no how."

The footsteps grew closer to the door and the slave's breathing grew ragged.

"Get out! If you do any more talking about things you shouldn't, I'll make sure the master *finds* you here next time!"

Stumbling as he picked up his pants and shirt, Lester ran toward the open balcony doors. His broad frame disappeared over the rail as Emmaline reached for the gold silk wrapper lying nearby.

Turning toward the middle-aged, corpulent man who entered the room scant moments later, Emmaline casually tied her wrapper. She smiled into his pleasant, lined face as he came to stand beside her. She pressed a lingering kiss against his mouth, then slid her long fingers into the gray hair at his temples.

"I missed you in bed when I awoke this morning, darling."

Robert Dorsett smiled as his beautiful young wife's eyes glittered into his. She was the love of his life, his most precious jewel. He never tired of looking at her.

"Did you, dear?" He glanced around the room. "I thought I heard you talking to someone when I was on the stairs."

Emmaline laughed, her magnificent red-gold mane moving against her silk-clad shoulders as she shook her head. "No, Robert darling. I was singing." She pressed her lips to his once more. "You made me very happy last night."

Robert cupped her chin with his palm so he might study her exquisite beauty more closely. "As you made me. But you always make me happy, dear. You are my greatest treasure." His smile grew strained. "I could never do without you."

Emmaline's smile faded as she slid her arms around her husband's neck. Her gaze suddenly intensely sober, she looked directly into his eyes. Her ardent tone rang with sincerity as she whispered, "My dear Robert, you will never have to do without me . . . not ever."

That thought ran over again in Emmaline's mind minutes later as her husband walked back down the hallway in the direction from which he had come. She turned toward the nearby mirror and stared at the reflection within.

No, Robert would never have to do without her. He was a dear man. He was also mad about her and indulgent of her whims to a fault. She had known the moment she met him that he was the man she had been looking for all her life . . .

. . . although there was only one man she would ever *truly* love.

Sighing, Emmaline slipped her wrapper from her shoulders and dropped it to the floor to assess her smooth, naked perfection in the nearby mirror. She slid her hands up to cup her well-shaped breasts, smoothing them with her palms before slipping her hands into her hair. Lifting the shimmering strands, she allowed them to fall back onto her shoulders in a glittering red-gold cascade.

Yes, she was beautiful. *He* would still want her.

Emmaline's heart began a slow pounding. Her gaze intensified. He was returning to her now, at this very moment. She could feel it. He was sailing toward her across the turquoise sea.

Reaching for the leather thong on her dresser, Emmaline massaged the roughly carved charm strung there. There was no stronger obeah than bone dug from a witch doctor's grave, and no stronger magic than the spell that had been cast from it. She could feel it calling him to her.

He could not escape.

Emmaline smiled as a sudden, breezy gust swirled the filmy curtains around her, wrapping her in the translucent folds. Sending a message across the sea on the current of wind that engulfed her, she spoke in an impassioned whisper.

"Do you hear me, Derek? You cannot escape me. You *will* not escape me. Derek . . . my darling . . . come back to me."

A soft, incoherent voice intruded into Derek's dreams as a sharp gust of night wind rocked the ship. He stirred. He heard the sounds again . . . labored grunts and the scuffling of feet, the crack of heavy fists against bone, a cry of pain and the thud of a body hitting the ground. He saw the red wash of blood and he saw . . .

. . . *Emmaline's smile* . . .

Derek awakened with a start. He glanced toward the porthole to see the dark canopy of night still covering the sky beyond. His hands tightened into fists as he hissed a soft curse.

Damn the green-eyed witch! Would she never let go?

Shuddering from violent emotions relived once more,

Derek threw back the blanket and drew himself to his feet. The chill cabin air touched his naked skin, raising the hackles on his spine and clearing the cobwebs of sleep from his mind. He turned back toward Gillian as she stirred restlessly. She frowned in her sleep, curling into a tight ball as she clutched the blanket more closely around her.

Perverse satisfaction struck him. She had come to depend on his body warmth through the night. He could not count the times he had awakened during the weeks since they had first come together to feel Gillian's breath against his throat as she pressed against him, to feel her palm against his chest, her fingers moving in the dark hairs there even as she slept. During those nights . . . those sweet, sweet nights . . . he had come to know Gillian's body as well as she knew her own. It was a beautiful body, a giving body.

Derek slowly stiffened. There was no doubt in his mind that while Gillian lay in his arms, she was his and his alone. As the light of day dawned each morning, however, as Gillian withdrew subtly from him, the truth renewed itself with glaring clarity.

Favor for favor had again been well served—nothing more.

A familiar agitation thrusting sleep beyond his grasp, Derek reached for his clothes. Dressed moments later, he walked silently to the cabin door. Turning, he glanced back at Gillian, halting as the exquisite warmth of her beckoned with a familiar siren song. The wind howled eerily once more and Derek's gaze slowly hardened. A little longer and he would be far removed from that call and able to put this voyage and everything connected with it behind him.

Derek stepped out into the passageway and drew the cabin door closed behind him. He reached the open deck and breathed deeply of the chill night air as the ship's bell sounded.

One . . . two . . . three . . . four . . . five . . . six . . . seven.

He walked to the rail.

A strange uneasiness stirred Gillian awake. Finding the bunk beside her empty, she sought to clear her mind as she searched the shadows with her gaze. Derek was not in the cabin.

The ship's bell sounded. Counting, Gillian glanced toward the silver shaft of light gleaming through the porthole. Seven bells . . . halfpast the hour of three.

Gillian tensed. Derek should not be up at this hour. Something was wrong.

Sudden anxiety crawled up Gillian's spine as she threw back the blanket and drew herself to her feet. Surely it could not be Adria . . . Derek would have awakened her if something was amiss there. Or would he? He had kept close track of the progress of affairs in Adria's cabin. He had visited briefly each morning, questioning Christopher carefully, and she knew that despite Derek's cold formality toward her sister, had matters not met Derek's approval, he would have taken immediate steps to correct them.

As for Derek's feelings for her, Gillian was at a loss. She dared not dwell on the sensual beauty of the nights she had spent in his arms. Ardent, exquisitely tender, he had grown increasingly passionate, his scope of loving ministrations appearing to know no bounds.

Contrarily, during the daylight hours Derek withheld any spoken word of even casual affection. His proprietary manner retained just below the surface of their relationship a constant, unspoken reminder of the bargain that had brought them together.

Puzzled at the countless times she had turned to find Derek's gaze intent upon her in the intimacy of the cabin they shared, only to have his eyes turn cold at the moment of contact with hers, she had begun to feel he resented the passion that flared when he took her into his arms, and the soul-wrenchingly tender side of himself that emerged.

Often autocratic and terse, he still managed to infuriate her, leaving her vacillating between raging anger and a softer, consuming emotion that she—

Unwilling to face the conclusion of that thought, Gillian thrust it abruptly aside.

As for Christopher, it was obvious Derek neither liked nor trusted him—and that Christopher felt the same.

But Adria's health had been gradually improving. She had been free of fever for the past week, and she had been able to walk about the cabin. Christopher and she had even discussed taking Adria up on deck for a brief period to clear the sickness from her lungs since they had entered warmer waters and they—

A strange uneasiness suddenly swelled, bringing Gillian's thoughts to an abrupt halt.

But Adria had been more pale than usual when she had left her the previous evening. She had begun coughing again. If she had had a relapse . . . if the lung fever had returned despite all their precautions . . . if Adria was now struggling for every breath she took—

Suddenly unable to think past wildly burgeoning fear, Gillian reached for her dress. Pulling it down over her head, she slipped into her shoes.

In the passageway moments later, Gillian paused outside

Adria's cabin, her heart pounding. A faint light flickered beneath the door as she pushed it open abruptly.

"Gillian?" Instantly awake, Christopher threw back the blanket on his pallet. He was on his feet in a moment. "What's wrong?"

A shudder slipped down Gillian's spine the second before Adria raised herself from her pillow to stare uncertainly toward them.

"Is that you, Gillian?"

Moving quickly to her side, Gillian took Adria's hand. It was cool to the touch and Adria's gaze was clear.

Her relief intense, Gillian shook her head. "No, nothing's wrong. I thought . . ." She was suddenly embarrassed at her irrational behavior. "I-I don't know what I thought. I must've been dreaming." She leaned down to kiss Adria's cheek. "Go back to sleep. I'm sorry I woke you."

Back in the passageway, Gillian turned at the sound of Christopher's step behind her. The flickering light of the passageway lamp illuminated his young, bearded face as he hesitated, then spoke with obvious concern.

"Gillian . . . you're sure there's nothing wrong . . ."

Gillian attempted a smile. "I'm sure."

"You would tell me if there was . . ."

"There's nothing wrong."

"That isn't what I asked."

"I said—"

"I know what you said." Christopher's pale-eyed gaze held hers. It touched her heart, as did the sincerity in his voice as he whispered, "You know I'm your friend, don't you?"

Gillian's throat grew tight. "Yes."

"Do you trust me?"

Gillian nodded.

"Promise me you'll tell me if anything goes wrong."

Gillian hesitated. She had already burdened him with so much.

"Promise me, Gillian."

"I promise."

Reentering the cabin as the sound of Christopher's door clicking closed reverberated behind her, Gillian stared at the empty bunk she had abandoned minutes earlier. The strange uneasiness remained.

Succumbing to impulse, Gillian snatched up her cloak and slipped it over her shoulders, then stepped out into the passageway once more.

The wind whistled briefly in a darkness lit only by a pale crescent moon as Derek walked the shadowed deck. He breathed deeply of the sea air, oblivious to the night chill as he studied the swaying masts with canvas tightly furled, as he skirted with a practiced step the organized litter that awaited the next day's hoisting of the sails.

Derek frowned. It was often said that a captain's worth was measured by his ability to judge the direction and power of the wind, and by his knowledge of the capabilities and shortcomings of his vessel and crew. If that were true, his worth was extremely high, for the intricacies of the wind were no mystery to him. Nor were the limitations and strengths of his vessel. He was intimately familiar with every inch of the *Colonial Dawn* and there was not a man on his crew who was not tried and true under his command. He was intensely conscious, however, of the fact that this voyage, in so many ways, still remained the truest test he had ever had of his skill.

Derek paused in his thoughts, running his hand through

his hair in an unconscious gesture of agitation. His dark brows furrowed over the glittering onyx of his eyes as he unconsciously checked off his list of greatest concerns.

First: the condition of his ship. The necessary repairs had been completed and the patches in ship and sail had held up well.

Second: the condition of his "human cargo." Under Cutter's supervision, the situation below had stabilized. There had been no deaths during the past week, a fact that allowed him limited consolation, considering the number already lost.

Third: food supplies for those below. With careful control, supplies had held out better than anticipated, doubtless aided by the reduction in number.

Fourth: weather conditions. Favorable weather had prevailed after the first difficult weeks aboard. Their rapid progress since that time had brought them into more temperate waters. At their present rate, they would dock in Jamaica within the week.

Jamaica—within a week . . .

An image of clear blue skies, brilliant sunshine, and exotic tropical colors flashed briefly before Derek's mind. To think that he had once believed that island to be paradise . . .

Derek's short laugh was void of mirth. Young fool that he had once been, he had seen no farther than the supreme natural beauty of the island. He had neither known nor cared that it supported a dissolute society that existed solely for cultivation of sugar—a money crop that brought wealth to landowners, quick fortune to overseers, and endless revenue to the Mother Country. Nor had he recognized that the society was, at its core, so base and greedy that it perverted the minds, actions, and lives of all it touched—and that in that matchless paradise, there was no truth or validity beyond the wealth and power that money evoked.

It had not bothered him that the island was ruthlessly exploited, that profit was dependent upon the work of indentured servants and slaves who served the sugar crop year round and were often worked until they dropped. In his ignorance, he had actually been amused when he had discovered that no land on the island was wasted on the planting of anything as mundane as food, and that except for the small plots of ground utilized by slaves for their own use, food was imported from the American colonies and Great Britain.

He had dismissed the religion of the slaves, ruled by obeah men, fetishes, and spells. He had ridiculed the powers supposedly evoked by fowls' feet, feathers, teeth and earth from burial grounds.

And he spent little time thinking about the plight of those working in chains . . .

. . . until he had become one of them.

Derek closed his eyes as the pain of the sugar fields returned vividly once more. He had cursed the chains that had bound him, as well as his own stupidity in having allowed himself to fall victim to their weight.

As he had cursed *Emmaline*.

Emmaline, who had been waiting for him when he had emerged from prison, five years older and wiser.

Emmaline who had casually dismissed her marriage vows as she had offered herself to him again.

Emmaline, who had said she still loved him.

Emmaline, who did not know the *meaning* of the word "love."

Emmaline, who had sworn, her brilliant eyes glinting into his, that she would make him come back to her.

Emmaline, whose face had been worn by every woman he had held in his arms since . . .

. . . with *one* exception.

Dismissing Emmaline abruptly from his mind, Derek forced his thoughts back to the two final concerns still facing him.

The first and most odious was John Barrett.

Strangely, Cutter had had little to report regarding John Barrett since he had been confined in the brig below. After his first angry protest at being put to work, Barrett had performed the chores assigned him daily, his chains securely fixed. Will Swift, his fear of Barrett unabating, had kept his distance during the hours Barrett was allowed out of his cell.

Derek's jaw twitched with agitation. He, himself, had had no direct contact with either Barrett or Swift during that time. He was well aware, however, that the situation was soon to change.

Then there was his last order of concern—and the most difficult.

Gillian.

A flush of heat he did not care to identify flashed hotly through Derek's veins. Suddenly angry with the woman who had freed him of thoughts of Emmaline only to obsess his thoughts even more completely, Derek cursed again. They would dock in Jamaica within the week and their association would come to an end. He would then be freed of his—

A soft, rustling sound from the shadows turned Derek sharply. He took an angry step forward as Gillian stepped into view.

"What are you doing on deck at this hour?"

Her face in the shadows, Derek saw only the stiffening of Gillian's shoulders as she responded, "I-I wanted some air."

A sudden gust of wind rocked the ship, throwing Gillian off balance. Reaching out automatically to steady her, Derek felt her shudder as his arms closed around her.

"Some air?" Derek frowned. "You're cold."

"I'm not."

The warmth of Gillian in his arms began working a familiar magic as Derek drew her closer. He fought to retain rational thought as he pressed, "It's dangerous for you to be up here alone at night."

"I'm not alone."

Derek's jaw tightened. "Why were you looking for me, Gillian?"

A silver shaft of moonlight momentarily raised the shadows from Gillian's face. He saw an undefined uneasiness reflected there that matched his own as she responded, "I wasn't looking for you. I mean, I just . . ."

Gillian's voice trailed to a halt, but there was no need for her to continue. He knew.

Gillian remained unmoving as Derek's lips met hers. Her lips separated under his. He tasted her mouth. He fondled her tongue with his, loving the taste of her. He tangled his hands in her unbound hair, drinking deeply of that taste. She was melting in his arms in the moment before he drew back abruptly.

His jaw tightening, Derek grasped her arm, turning her to pull her along with him through the shadows. Struggling to match his long strides across the deck, down the stairs to the berth deck, and along the passageway, Gillian glanced up at him as they reached the cabin door at last.

"Are you angry, Derek?"

Angry.

Inside, Derek swept Gillian's cloak from her shoulders. He unfastened the buttons on her dress and drew it up over her head. He scooped her up into his arms and lay her down on the rumpled bunk, his hands trembling as he stripped away his own clothes as well. In a moment she was again in his arms, her flesh warm against his.

His hoarse reply was succinct the moment before his lips touched hers.

"No, I'm not angry."

Swift footsteps in the passageway . . . the sound of the captain's door snapping closed . . . the murmur of soft voices . . .

Silence.

Adria felt a hot rush of tears.

"Christopher . . . are you still awake?"

Christopher's voice emerged softly from the shadows. "Yes, I'm awake."

Adria's throat was tight. Christopher had been so kind to her. She did not recall a time in the past weeks of her illness when she had awakened from a fevered dream and had not found him there to comfort her. He had bathed her, fed her, soothed her pain. His gentleness had never lapsed. In a way, he was closer to her than any person she had ever known. And if he had never looked at her with the same depth of feeling as he had looked at Gillian, well . . . she understood. There was only *one* Gillian.

"Christopher . . ." Adria's whispered words were hoarse. "Do you think the captain truly *cares* for Gillian . . . at least a bit?"

Christopher's response was stiff. "Try not to think about it, Adria. We'll be in Jamaica soon."

The pain inside Adria squeezed more tightly. "But what

about tonight, and *all* the nights until then? I can't sleep for thinking about Gillian."

"Don't think." Christopher's voice grew gruff. "Put it from your mind. Gillian will be all right."

Adria's voice caught on a sob. "How can you be sure? Even now the captain might be—"

"Go to sleep Adria!"

Christopher's harshness froze Adria into momentary stillness. She heard the regret in his voice, as well as the pain when he spoke again.

"Go to sleep . . . please."

But Adria could not, for in that moment of stark revelation, the burden of Christopher's pain had been added to her own.

The pale light of morning filtered through the rank reaches of the hold, illuminating John Barrett's cell as he drew himself slowly to his feet. A familiar hatred expanded within him as he took the few steps to the corner bucket to relieve himself, then buttoned his britches and jerked them up around his waist.

His clothes were loose. They hung on a body that had formerly been well padded from the rewards of the good life enjoyed to the maximum. But his body was well padded no longer.

Straightening up, Barrett pushed back the limp, greasy strands of hair that had escaped his unkempt queue. No one need tell him that his appearance had deteriorated. He had lost weight. His clothes were filthy and his body unclean. The permanent stench of the hold, remaining despite all effort to erase it, had settled over him like an unwanted shroud. It had seeped into his pores, becoming a part of him until he appeared as wretched as the human filth who inhabited the stinking cesspool beyond his cell.

But he would *never* be one of them!

And he would soon have back his own . . .

Squinting at the sound of an approaching step, Barrett walked toward the barred door of his cell. He stared at the guard who held out a metal plate and cup containing his morning meal. Exercising the moment of control he had practiced daily over the fellow who stood shaking under his glare, he did not move to accept it.

"Take it, Master Barrett, sir." Charles Dobbs's voice held a pleading note. "It ain't so bad as it looks. You'll see."

Barrett did not respond. He knew Dobbs well. The scrawny weasel of a man had worked under him as guard in almost as many transportations as had Will Swift. Dobbs had served him well because he knew that in serving Barrett, he served himself. Barrett almost smiled. He liked that kind of man. That kind of man suited his purposes.

"Come on, sir. Take it. If you don't, I'll have to take it back and you'll go hungry till the next meal."

Barrett remained silent as Dobbs's shoulder jerked nervously. "We're to dock in Jamaica soon, sir. Aye, the ship's made up the lost time because of a brisk wind. We'll soon be free of this vessel and all that happened aboard it." Dobbs's voice dropped a note softer. "You know I had nothin' to do with what happened to you, don't you, sir? I mean, I followed orders, is all. You can't fault a man for that, can you? Master Barrett . . . sir?"

Barrett maintained his silence.

"I don't blame you for bein' angry, with all they've done to you down here . . . with makin' you work like you're one and the same as them others. But I know better, sir." Dobbs took a step closer. "I know you're too smart to let that captain get the better of you, and I know that once we're in port, you'll get your own back on him." Dobbs gave a nervous laugh. "A-and I just wanted to tell you now, that Will Swift ain't no friend of mine. I won't back him up on nothin' he says about you . . . and when it's all over, I-I'd be proud to work for you again . . . if you'd have me, of course."

A slow sense of triumph swelled within John Barrett. So, the rats were already scurrying. That pleased him.

"Master Barrett . . . sir?"

Barrett snatched the plate from Dobbs's hand. He took the cup as well. He turned back to his cot.

"You'll remember what I said, sir?"

Yes, he'd remember.

Dobbs hesitated a moment longer, then turned away.

Barrett sat on his cot and picked up his spoon. His stomach growled in eager anticipation as the stench of the foul mass reached his nostrils. Cursing his faithless stomach for disowning his pallet in its greed, he rapidly devoured the contents of his plate. He gulped the weak, tepid tea, then slapped the empty cup down on the stool beside him with a crack.

No better than piss it was! Yes, he'd get even for this. He'd—

Barrett's head jerked up toward the door at the sound of footsteps again approaching. His protruding eyes focused on Cutter and the two burly seamen behind him as they approached. His jowled jaw clenched tight as Cutter halted at the door.

"All right, up on your feet, Mr. Barrett. The captain wants to speak to you."

Barrett remained seated.

Cutter's bearded face stiffened. "Either you get up or Haskell and Linden will get you up. It means nothing to them if they need drag you across the hold and up the stairs, but it was my thought that you might not like putting on such a show for those you'll be passing."

Barrett did not respond.

Cutter turned toward the smaller figure hidden behind the two silent seamen. "Open the door, Dobbs."

Dobbs hastened to obey.

Barrett rose slowly to his feet as the door jerked open and the two seamen stepped forward. Dragging his chains noisily, he crossed to the door and fell in behind Cutter without a word as the first mate turned toward the staircase to the deck above.

So . . . the time had come . . .

The time had come.

Seated at his desk, Derek attempted to check the document in front of him once again. He scowled, annoyed at his distraction as Gillian moved through his line of vision. He had been intensely aware of the flash of Gillian's white flesh as she had risen hastily from the bunk and slipped into her clothes a short time earlier. He knew she had been surprised to find him still in the cabin when she had awakened, instead of on deck as was his common practice at that hour, but he had not felt compelled to make explanations.

In the time since, he had struggled to maintain his concentration as she had fumbled with the buttons on her dress, as she had washed her face and hands, brushed her hair and twisted it into a quick knot at the back of her neck, and had then turned to chores which included the neat arrangement of the blankets and pillows on the bunk and the return of her few personal articles to her carpetbag after they had served her needs.

Annoyance had swelled his distraction as he had noted out of the corner of his eye her careful repacking of that damned carpetbag, a silent, subtle reminder she issued daily that she would resume residence in the cabin next door without protest . . .

. . . despite the look in her eyes when she had followed him up onto the deck in the middle of the previous night . . .

. . . despite the long, loving hours afterward that she had spent in his arms.

He remembered clearly, however, even if she chose to forget, the soft whimpers of pleasure that had escaped her lips as he had bathed her with his kisses; the shuddering that had overwhelmed her as he had worshiped her body with his; and his name on her lips, rasped with quaking passion, as he had driven full and deep inside her.

And he remembered the joy of her slender arms clutching him close.

He was unable to forget it.

Derek's silent agitation increased. No! He would not allow himself to be manipulated by the warmth of Gillian's arms, by the taste of her lips, by the glory of all that followed as the lamp burned low . . . *or* with the subtle unpacking and repacking of that small bag!

Damn her! He was tempted to tell Gillian to take her bag and leave if that was her true desire!

A familiar tug in his loin silent testimony to the sham of that thought, Derek felt exasperation swell. He had no time for these distractions this morning.

Turning abruptly, Derek snapped, "What are you doing, Gillian?"

Gillian looked up at him. An arrogance he remembered only too well flashed in her reply.

"Tidying up—as I do *every* morning."

Irritation soaring, Derek drew himself slowly to his feet. The spontaneous rise of Gillian's chin and the challenge it implied forced a harshness he had not intended as he spoke in a voice just above a whisper.

"I will have you remember something, Gillian, for your own benefit. This is not *your* cabin. It is *mine*. You are distracting me. Please leave."

Gillian went momentarily still. The fine line of her lips twitched spasmodically the moment before she turned without response and reached for her bag.

Anger exploded within Derek. Snatching the carpetbag from her hand, he tossed it roughly into the corner.

"No, damn it! You'll not get away that easily!"

Their exchange interrupted by an unexpected knock on the door, Derek responded gruffly, "Come in."

The door swung open to reveal Cutter standing there. Derek felt Gillian's shock as John Barrett stepped into view beside him. Cursing his stupidity, intensely aware as Gillian stiffened under Barrett's malevolent stare that had it not been for the personal demons he had been struggling against all morning long, he could have spared her the unpleasant confrontation, Derek addressed Gillian in a softer tone tinged with regret.

"We can continue our conversation later. I believe your sister is waiting for you."

The sound of Barrett's chains grated harshly on the silence as Cutter ushered Barrett inside.

Rigid, Gillian acknowledged neither Barrett nor Cutter as she pulled the door closed behind her.

Her slender frame rigid as she entered Adria's cabin moments later, Gillian remained silent despite Christopher and

Adria's concerned glances. She struggled for composure, all memory of the angry confrontation between Derek and her erased by John Barrett's virulent gaze, still vividly clear before her mind.

She had read a shocking truth there in that one, silent moment.

In response to anxious questions that seemed to echo hollowly from a distance, Gillian heard a hoarse voice hardly recognizable as her own whisper, "It was John Barrett. He's in Derek's cabin. H-he wants to kill me."

Christopher stepped out into the passageway leaving Gillian, still shaken, behind him. Enraged at the captain for having exposed Gillian to such a frightening encounter, he turned hotly toward the captain's cabin. Realizing the error in that course a moment later, he halted abruptly. Turning in the opposite direction, he walked rapidly toward the staircase.

His feeling of impotence never more complete, Christopher took the stairs to the main deck two at a time.

Too incensed to speak, John Barrett maintained his silence. He felt Derek Andrews's scrutiny as he inwardly raged.

Andrews had done it deliberately! The bastard captain had staged the scene specifically for his benefit—specifically to humiliate him! There could be no other reason for having had the beauteous Gillian Harcourt Haige present when he had entered the cabin in chains. Nor could there have been any other reason for the captain to have allowed her to remain just long enough for him to see the revulsion in her gaze when she had looked at him.

Barrett's jaw ticked with fury. But Gillian Harcourt Haige had also read *his* gaze, and he had seen her fear.

Remaining silent as Cutter ushered him further into the cabin, Barrett unconsciously nodded. Gillian Haige's fear was well founded. He would see her suffer for having refused him, only to go willingly into the arms of the diabolic bastard he was now facing. And when he was done with her he would—

"We have some things to discuss, Barrett."

Looking at the bastard captain as he spoke, Barrett snapped his jaw tightly shut.

So, it had begun.

Derek awaited Barrett's response, assessing him silently. Cutter had kept him informed as to Barrett's condition below, but, somehow, he had been unprepared for the drastic change in the man's appearance since he had seen him last. Shocking was the weight loss that left Barrett's clothes hanging loosely on his frame, as was the absolute filth of him. Barrett had been adequately fed, and water and a crude soap had been provided. There could be no reason for the man's physical condition except that the hatred now glowing in his eyes was devouring him.

Cautious of that hatred and the devious mind behind it, Derek spoke again.

"Am I to understand that you have no desire to discuss your situation, *Mr.* Barrett?"

Barrett's lips curled in a sneer. "You didn't call me here to discuss my situation, Captain. You called me here to discuss yours."

Derek paused. "It appears you are confused. *You* are the one wearing chains, not I."

"A temporary state."

"So you would choose to believe."

"It's not a matter of what I choose to believe, Captain! It's a matter of what I know as well as you!" Barrett took an aggressive step forward, snarling as his chains clanked with his step. "You sought to destroy me with these chains, but you failed. Do you think I haven't known from the first that this moment was coming? Do you think I didn't realize that your authority, while absolute on the high seas, will be diluted to impotence the moment you step down on the shore of Jamaica? Do you think I don't know that you are cognizant of the power my name carries and that you realize whatever evidence you present to defend your actions against me will be outweighed by the value placed on that power?" Barrett laughed loudly. "Fool! I knew you would call me to your cabin sooner or later. It was just a matter of time!"

Momentarily incredulous at the audacity of a man who would attempt to take command of a situation while in chains, Derek stared into Barrett's flushed face. His slow smile was cold. "No, *you* are the fool, Barrett." He paused, adding with menacing softness, "My response to all the points you've just made is simple. Did it not occur to you that if it wasn't to my advantage, you would never *reach* Jamaica?"

Barrett went abruptly still. "You wouldn't dare . . ."

"Don't underestimate me."

"You don't have the stomach for it!"

Derek's voice dropped a notch lower. "You forget. I've worn chains. I won't risk wearing them again—*at any price.*"

Barrett's protruding eyes narrowed. His thick lips moved into a harsh semblance of a smile. "So . . . you would have me believe that you would employ no more principle than the situation demands . . . that you are no better than I."

Derek held his gaze. "I simply urge you to *believe* what I say."

Barrett's sneer returned. "I'll tell you what I believe. You called me here because it was to your advantage to call me here, and for no other reason. You've come to realize that bringing me into Jamaica in chains would be a mistake, that according to the terms of the agreement you signed, my authority over the transportees, no matter how vile you deemed it, was unequivocal. To negate those terms was to sacrifice the compensation you were to receive. Without that compensation, your ship would immediately fall into the hands of the receivers awaiting you."

Derek smiled. "And if I report you as having died of the fever that has killed so many below?"

"Don't insult my intelligence! The documents for the transportees need my signature, witnessed ashore, in order for your compensation to be paid. In any other event, you would have to await months of legalities. Your ship would pass into the hands of receivers long before you stood any chance of collecting. You are between the devil and the deep blue sea, Captain!"

Derek's cold eyes turned to ice. "You're right, but there's one point you've overlooked."

"Really?"

"Yes. You have overlooked a simple determination—a promise I have made to myself. Do you want to know what that promise is?"

Barrett did not respond.

"The promise is elementary. If I lose my ship, you will lose your life."

Barrett's jowled cheek twitched. He looked at Cutter who

had remained silent during the exchange, and Derek almost smiled. Cutter did not even blink.

Barrett drew himself slowly erect. "It seems we are at stalemate."

"No, we are not." Derek's cold eyes hardened. "We are at the point where you will ask what terms I have to offer you."

"No!"

"Yes."

"No!"

Derek paused, replying softly, "Your life depends on it."

Aware that the slow shuddering that beset Barrett reflected fury rather than fear, Derek maintained his caution.

"All right!" Barrett snapped erect as his response exploded into the silence of the cabin. "What terms are you offering?"

"The *only* terms I will give." Derek turned toward the desk nearby. He picked up the document there. "This is a confession of your plot to kill me and to assume control of the *Colonial Dawn*. Cutter will witness it, and Swift will attest to it."

Barrett's sneer returned. "You are more of a fool than I thought! Biased witnesses—the man who attempted to perpetrate the crime, then named me as its instigator, and your own first mate. It's a joke! The confession won't hold up."

"Two of your other men will witness your signature as well."

"Liar! None of them will turn against me."

"You're wrong. Dobbs and Niles have already agreed."

"You're bluffing! Dobbs came to me this morning and he—"

"And he told you he wouldn't back Swift up on anything

Swift said. I spoke to him afterward and . . ." Derek paused for effect. ". . . he changed his mind."

Barrett seethed.

Derek felt the heat of the man's hatred as he pressed, "So, *fool* that I am, I have the upper hand, after all."

His chest heaving with the violent emotions he suppressed, Barrett responded, "And if I sign the confession?"

"You will regain your authority over those below once they are ashore in Jamaica. I will return your confession to you when I receive the compensation due me."

"Since you claim that I've already attempted to have you killed and failed, what makes you think I won't try again when ashore?"

"I don't think you're that much a fool, considering what's come to pass during this voyage. But consider this." Derek's dark eyes narrowed. "What makes you think I would hesitate to do the same if I felt seriously threatened by you?"

Barrett's jaw worked convulsively as his complexion darkened to an apoplectic hue. Hesitating for long moments, he finally spat, "All right! Give me the damned confession and get your witnesses in here!"

Derek paused, allowing his victory over the rabid negotiations to settle firmly between them before turning to his silent first mate.

"Bring the witnesses in, Mr. Cutter."

Livid, Barrett turned toward the door as Cutter pulled it open and ordered the three men waiting there inside.

Quick scrapes of the pen, the document signed and witnessed minutes later, Derek watched as Barrett glared at Swift, Niles, and Dobbs in lethal promise. Interrupting Barrett's mute intimidation, Derek ordered, "You may remove Mr. Barrett below, Mr. Cutter."

"Bastard!" Barrett raised his shaking fists, enraged. "You have what you wanted! Remove these chains!"

"They will be removed when we reach Jamaica, not before."

"Bastard . . . bastard . . ."

Frothing with fury as Haskell and Linden entered from the passageway, Barrett shrugged off their grip and turned toward the door.

The cabin was silent in Barrett's wake as his unspoken threat lingered.

Christopher breathed deeply of the salt air in an attempt at control. Frustrated emotions held barely under restraint, his jaw locked beneath the reddish-brown beard glinting in the morning sun, he stared out at the sea. Aided by a brisk wind, the ship sliced through the crystal swells beyond the rail, traveling smoothly under the bastard captain's command. Were the captain any other man, he might have admired him for the skill which had enabled him to turn a potentially disastrous voyage around, against all odds.

But the captain was not another man, and Christopher knew the truth about him. Captain Derek Andrews was an emotionless, unfeeling bastard who did not have the sense to realize that in holding Gillian, he held the world in his arms as well.

The fear reflected in Gillian's brilliant eyes returned to haunt him, and Christopher's torment swelled, even as he recognized the irony of his despair. The uncertainty of his own future—the eight years of indenture facing him—had somehow faded into insignificance in his mind in the face of Gillian's tribulation. Had the situation been different, had he met Gillian before he had been relegated to the ranks of felon, had he—

Christopher closed his eyes, abandoning his torturous line of thought. The past could not be changed. As for the future—

A wildly cracking sound overhead jerked Christopher's gaze upward abruptly to see a freed sail flapping in the wind. He frowned as the sail continued its awkward, threatening dance, a broken line whipping beside it. He saw one seaman, then a second, start spontaneously up the shrouds. He knew the danger there—that a loosened canvas could easily whip a man free of his precarious hold aloft to fall to his death on the deck below. He watched, riveted as the men reached the rigging and attempted to negotiate the foot ropes. He noted their caution and their skill as they inched across . . .

Gasping as the foot rope snapped unexpectedly, Christopher watched, frozen with shock as the first seaman scrambled to retain his hold on the spar, as his hand gradually slipped, as he—

The cabin door closed behind Barrett. The echo of his chains lingered in an unnatural silence broken abruptly as Swift addressed Derek in a quaking voice.

"He-he'll get ye for that, ye know." Emerging from the corner where he had withdrawn, Swift glanced toward Dobbs and Niles a few feet away. "And he'll get us, too, if ye go back on yer word to us. Ye won't do that, will ye, Captain?" Swift's voice became anxious. "Ye'll see to it that we have a place on the next ship back to England as ye promised, won't ye?"

Derek assessed the three cowering guards with contempt. He had no doubt that had they believed they would've fared better taking Barrett's side rather than his, the situation would have turned out quite differently. Ultimately, Barrett had lost for a simple reason. His men had known him too well to trust him.

Holding Swift's terrified gaze, Derek demanded softly, "Listen to me . . . all of you . . . because I don't intend to repeat myself again. You've kept your part of our bargain and I'll keep mine. I will only say one thing more. Take fair warning: Should you decide to change loyalties midstream, you will forever hear my footsteps behind you."

Pausing, Derek allowed the portent of his words to register clearly in the expressions of the three men before he instructed tightly, "Get back to your work."

Alone in his cabin moments later, Derek picked up the signed confession, his expression grim. He had no illusions. The confession offered only limited and temporary protection. This thing with Barrett would not come to a good end and he—

A heavy thud on the deck overhead halted all conscious thought, jerking Derek's gaze abruptly upward. A sound like no other, it curdled his blood the split second before he turned toward the cabin door at a run.

The wind gusted roughly, rocking the ship as Derek emerged breathlessly on the main deck. Pushing his way through the circle surrounding the seaman lying motionless on the deck, Derek knelt beside him. It was Jeremy Stiles, one of the youngest of his crew. He was unconscious, his face raw and bleeding, his brown curly hair matted with blood.

Steeling himself against the sinking feeling in his stomach, Derek examined Stiles more closely. The young seaman's breathing was shallow but regular and, incredibly, there appeared to be no broken bones. It occurred to him with a sudden flash of insight that the same shrouds that had rubbed Stiles's face raw of skin might possibly have saved his life by breaking his fall.

Looking up, Derek saw the blank expressions of the men surrounding him. A fall from the rigging . . . a hazard with which all were familiar . . . a nightmare that never quite died.

Raising his head at a sudden shout from above, Derek cursed low in his throat at the sight of a second man suddenly dangling from the rigging. His hand caught in a snapped line, the seaman swung helplessly with the dip and sway of the ship, much like a helpless fish on a line.

Hardly conscious of the flash of movement from the rail behind him, Derek jumped to his feet, snatching a knife from the sheath of a seaman standing nearby as he raced toward the shrouds. The knife jammed into his belt, he was climbing rapidly, his gaze fixed on the trapped man above him, the heavy, slick ropes swaying with his weight, when he noticed the man climbing beside him.

Meeting Christopher Gibson's gaze briefly, he continued his frantic race upward.

Hardly conscious of the captain's presence nearby on the shrouds as he arrived a short distance from the seaman still swinging wildly from the broken line, Christopher heard a shout that was momentarily lost in the whistle of the wind. Turning toward the captain, Christopher saw him glare as he shouted again.

"Grab him when he swings toward you and hold tight until I can get above him and cut him loose!"

Christopher was momentarily aghast. Was the man insane? The only way he would be able to work his way above them would be by negotiating the rigging—an impossibility without foot ropes in the present battering of the wind.

"Gibson, damn it! Did you hear me?"

Christopher gritted his teeth. "I heard you!"

The ship dipped and the seaman swung wildly toward them again. Christopher strained to catch him. He missed once . . . twice . . .

. . . as the captain slipped up to straddle the rigging and begin inching his way across.

The ominous thud on the deck above . . . the slam of Derek's door and his running footsteps toward the stairs . . . excited shouts echoing . . .

"What was that!"

Gillian's heart began a furious pounding as Adria's gaze met hers.

Adria's eyes widened. "I heard Christopher go up on deck. He was so angry." Her breath shuddered in her throat. "Oh, Gillian, you don't suppose he tried to do something foolish!"

Gillian shook her head, Adria's panic slowly infecting her mind. No, Christopher wasn't a fool. He knew they would soon be in Jamaica, and he knew that once they were—

The shouts from above grew louder, more frantic, and Gillian was suddenly on her feet. Running toward the door, she did not hear Adria calling out behind her.

A few steps onto the main deck and Gillian halted abruptly at first glimpse of the still figure lying motionless on the deck. Her view blocked by the circle of men around the fallen man, she could not see his face, but she saw . . .

The circle shifted and Gillian gasped. The fallen man's curly brown hair was sodden and red with the blood still oozing from it.

His *curly brown* hair . . .

Her breathing suddenly ragged, Gillian attempted a step toward him, but her stiff legs would not obey.

She reached toward him, but her hands remained frozen at her sides.

The blood pooled deeper.

The ship rocked crazily beneath her feet.

The light expired.

Gillian knew no more.

Straddling the rigging, his fingers whitening with his straining grip, Derek inched his way across. He cursed as the loosened sail continued its cracking assault, as Davey Wright continued swinging to and fro at the end of the broken line, as Gibson stretched out again from his position on the shrouds, attempting to catch hold of Wright as he swung his way.

Unaware of the gasps from below as Gibson caught Wright and held him fast, Derek clutched the rigging tightly, his progress painfully slow toward the rope that still held the seaman bound. His hold precarious in the unrelenting wind, Derek struggled to maintain his grip as he stretched an arm out toward the taut rope, the blade of his knife glinting in the sun.

Gasping as the blade made first contact with the rough fiber, Derek gritted his teeth with determination, leaning into the chore with his full weight.

The fibers snapped slowly under the sawing motion of his blade, the first . . . the second . . . the third . . .

Abruptly breaking, the heavy line recoiled, whipping back to strike Derek a stunning blow. Consciousness briefly wavered as Derek breathed deeply in an effort to clear his head. Clarity returning, he glanced down to see Wright and Gibson making their way back down the shrouds. Taking another steadying breath, Derek inched back in the direction from which he had come.

Davey Wright was shaken but unhurt when Derek stepped down on deck to the concerned words of his men. He glanced toward Jeremy Stiles as the young seaman was carried gingerly toward the staircase below. He frowned at the unexpected sight of a second circle of men clustered a few feet farther away, confused to see Gibson on his knees beside a prone figure lying in the center. Gibson raised the figure to a seated position and Derek snapped erect.

Gillian . . .

Derek's spontaneous step toward them halted as he glimpsed Gillian's expression when she looked up at Gibson. Her whispered words escaped him, but the joy in her eyes as she slipped her arms around Gibson's neck and clutched him close struck him an almost mortal blow.

So, he knew the truth at last.

The sun had slipped past the midpoint of the sky when Derek finally returned to his cabin and slammed the door closed behind him. He walked to the porthole and stood stiffly there, staring blindly out at the choppy water beyond.

Jeremy Stiles was dead. The young seaman had never regained consciousness.

Turning, Derek took a few stiff steps toward his desk. He frowned at Barrett's signed confession lying there, then picked it up, folded it carefully, and placed it in his log. He would record Jeremy Stiles's death and the execution of Barrett's confession in his log later that night. What he would not record was a hard truth he could no longer deny, one that had left a ragged welt on his heart deeper than the one that marked his cheek.

His severe features tightly drawn, his bruised cheek adding new menace to his already intimidating appearance, Derek took a tight, controlled breath. Gillian had struck a bargain with him—an intimate bargain. She had been true to that bargain. She had slept every night in his arms and she had given herself to him completely, without holding back.

Derek paused, his frown darkening. Arrogant fool that he was, he had convinced himself that it had meant more.

But he was a fool no longer.

Derek raised his head at a knock on the door. Cutter entered at his response, his expression strained.

"Sawyer will have Stiles's body ready for the sea within the hour, Captain."

Derek nodded. "Tell the men to be ready to assemble."

"Aye, sir."

"There's another matter. Christopher Gibson . . . where is he now?"

Cutter's gaze flickered. "He's next door, with Mistress Adria."

"And Gillian?"

"Aye, Captain."

"Tell him I want to see him—now."

Cutter did not immediately respond.

"Now, Mr. Cutter."

Cutter turned on his heel.

Responding with a gruff bid to enter when another knock sounded on the door minutes later, Derek observed Gibson's wary expression as he stepped into the cabin. He read the silent challenge there. The desire to wipe that challenge from Gibson's face with the power of his fists never stronger, Derek spoke abruptly.

"It's apparent from your efforts in Wright's behalf that you're an experienced seaman . . . is that right?"

Gibson's gaze narrowed. "Yes, it is."

"A seaman would respond with the word 'aye.' "

"I'm not a member of your crew, *Captain.*"

"You have a choice, Gibson." Derek's stance stiffened. "You may become a member of my crew for the remainder of the voyage—replacing Stiles—or you may return to your quarters below. The choice is yours. What will it be?"

Gibson frowned. "Mistress Adria hasn't totally recovered."

"You will vacate the cabin next door immediately, in any case. Make up your mind. I have no time to waste."

"You bast—"

Derek took a short step toward Gibson. His mien darkened as his voice softened with menace. "I warn you not to respond hastily with words you will regret."

Christopher Gibson's broad hands tightened into fists and Derek felt a slow anticipation rise. He hoped . . . he *prayed* . . . that Gibson would be fool enough to swing those fists.

Gibson's jaw hardened, as did the look in his pale eyes the moment before he nodded stiffly. "I'll join the crew."

"Captain."

"Captain."

Derek paused, his chest heaving. "Move your things in with the other seamen. And while you're at it, tell Gill— *Mistress Haige* to come in here."

Gibson did not move.

"That was an order, Gibson"

A long, silent moment passed.

"Aye, *Captain.*"

Alone in his cabin moments later, Derek waited.

Trembling, Gillian strained for control as she paused in the passageway outside Derek's cabin. It had been a difficult day. The series of unexpected events since awakening had shaken her badly. Christopher's announcement moments earlier that he had been asked to join the crew had been unanticipated. She could not help but feel Derek had more surprises in store when he had demanded her immediate appearance in his cabin.

Gillian raised her hand to knock. She was startled as the door opened abruptly to Derek's stiff expression. She stepped inside, gasping as he turned fully toward her and she saw the red welt that marked his cheek. She raised her hand automatically toward it only to have him jerk back from her touch.

The harsh sound of her own voice startled Gillian as she broke the strained silence between them.

"Your face is badly bruised."

Derek's eyes were cold. "The mark of a rude awakening."

Confused by his response, Gillian maintained her silence as Derek continued. "We'll be arriving in Jamaica within the week. I've already made arrangements for Gibson to replace Stiles as part of my crew, which will leave your sister unattended." His eyes turned to stone. "Since your sister's health has always been your foremost concern, I'm releasing you from the terms of our bargain so you may care for her."

Picking up the small bag he had thrown into the corner

earlier that day, Derek held it out to her. "It's over. You may remain in the cabin next door until we dock in Jamaica. You'll rejoin the others below then."

Derek paused. His hand closing firmly over hers as she accepted the bag, he added coldly, "There is only one condition to your occupation of the cabin next door—one I will not allow to be compromised. You will have no visitors in the cabin. Should I discover that any man . . . *any man* . . . has stepped over that threshold, you will return below immediately. Is that understood?"

Gillian nodded.

Derek released the bag into her hand.

"You may leave."

Gillian could not move.

Derek turned his back, leaving her no choice.

As if she ever had one.

Ten

The solemn, steady beating of drums echoed on the still, tropical air, throbbing Pucku's call. Sizzling and cracking, long tongues of fire licked up at the starless night sky from the blaze in the center of the clearing where bared black bodies stood poised, gleaming in the flickering light. The low humming that had begun the moment the flame was struck gradually gained in volume as the dancers encircled the flames. Moving to the sensuous beat, they pumped and twisted, inhaling and exhaling in short barks of sound, the rhythmic stamping of their feet and the harsh barking coughs becoming a gasping chorus of sound that rebounded against the shadowed foliage surrounding them.

The hypnotic rhythm accelerated, growing more savage. The dancers whirled with increasing fury seeking to hold and conquer the throbbing beat that heated their blood and inflamed their minds. The drums beat faster. The momentum grew wilder. The barking coughs rose to a barbarous crescendo as the entranced dancers quaked in the delirium of possession, writhing and thrashing, spinning in ecstatic frenzy, dropping to the ground in increasing numbers to lie benumbed, twitching, speaking in tongues, their minds wandering in the gray, semiconscious vale where their possession had transported them.

Standing in the flickering shadows, excitement pounding

through her veins, Emmaline watched the dizzying scene. Enthralled, she followed the gyrations of the gleaming, scantily clad bodies as the throbbing of the drums continued, as new dancers replaced those who had fallen, as—

Her breath catching in her throat, Emmaline went stock-still as a new dancer emerged from the rough hut in the rear of the clearing. Her eyes grew bright with anticipation as the tall, massive Negro leaped into the midst of those still whirling to the frantic rhythm of the drums, as his wide shoulders and powerful chest shook spasmodically to the pounding beat, as his broad, flat features twisted with the sensations pulsing through his veins, as his eyes rolled and his body quaked, as he sustained a prolonged, violent rhythm more intense, more consuming than those who fell back in the wake of his power. The cadence consumed him, convulsed him, pushed him to greater frenzy, as he gave his all with a barking shout—

The drums fell abruptly silent as he dropped to the ground. Wild with the frenzy of the moment, Emmaline emerged from the shadows in a run. Pushing all others aside, she scrambled to the side of the fallen dancer and grasped his hand, claiming his heed. His eyes were still closed, his breathing ragged, his glistening, perspiration-drenched body heaving as the power of his possession surged through her and she rasped in a trembling voice.

"Speak to me, William Gnu! Tell me what you see." She thrust the leather thong she carried into his hand and squeezed his long, trembling fingers closed around the roughly carved charm strung there. "You gave me this charm for my lover. You told me it would bring him back to me. You gave me the power to touch his mind with it although he is far away . . . but he is close now. I can feel it. I can feel *him*. Tell me . . . tell me what you see."

Her gaze intent on the big Negro's face as his eyes opened into narrow slits, Emmaline waited. She saw his hand jerk tightly closed around the amulet she had placed in his palm and her excitement soared as she asked again, "Tell me, William Gnu."

"Dis man . . . him be de devil's man."

Emmaline shook her head. "No . . . no, you're wrong."

"Him eyes be black as night, him clothes be de same. And him heart . . ."

Emmaline went still. "His heart is mine . . ."

William Gnu's lips jerked spasmodically. "Him heart be cold to woman with hair de color of fire."

A slow rage transfusing her, Emmaline squeezed William Gnu's hand more tightly around the amulet. "You've made a mistake! Look harder!"

"I see him black eyes growin' warm when him see hair shinin' pale, like moon in de sky. I see dat big man snatchin' at dat ragin' woman—"

"What woman?"

"With hair like moon in de sky . . ."

Emmaline began a slow shuddering. "The woman is a streggah! He's had many streggahs, but they mean nothing!"

"Nay . . . nay . . . she not be streggah."

"What is she, then?"

"She be . . . she be . . ." William shook his head. He sat up slowly, then drew himself to his feet, hardly looking at Emmaline or the others who were beginning to stir around him. Emmaline stood up beside him as he turned abruptly toward her, his voice a deep rumble on the silence between them.

"You want dis man?"

Emmaline's beautiful face grew tight. "I *will* have him."

William turned again toward the fire. His intense dark

eyes reflected the fiery glow that danced against the moist sheen of his coal-black skin as he stared long and hard into the flames. He spoke slowly as he raised the amulet high before him.

"What you give Pucku fe dis man?"

Emmaline's response was quick. "What does Pucku want?"

William closed his eyes.

"Pucku want a place dat be safe fe him. Him wants backra man stay away when him people dancin'. Him wants a night fe Pucku alone."

Emmaline nodded. "Give me the obeah I need and Pucku will have his place here."

Nodding, William dropped to his knees beside the fire. Snatching a partially charred branch from the blaze, he drew back and scratched at the ground, his eyes falling half-lidded as he mumbled, "Branch taken from Pucku's fire tell de story. Pucku see. Pucku bring dat man across the sea. Pucku bring him back fe you."

Reaching for the pouch suspended from a string at his waist, William opened it and sprinkled the symbols he had drawn with a pale-gold dust. He then scooped up the dirt on which he had made his marks and, turning with a short command toward a woman nearby, awaited the roughly fashioned pouch she brought back to him before pouring the dirt inside. From his own pouch he withdrew a flat blue stone. He held it up to her, his gaze intense.

"Dis be Pucku's *eye.*" He dropped the stone into the pouch and then the roughly carved amulet. He held the pouch out to Emmaline. "Pucku watch dat ragin' fella. Him bring dat ragin' man back fe you soon."

Emmaline smiled. "He's mine, then . . ."

William turned away abruptly, stepping around those still

lying on the ground as he made his way back toward the hut from which he had emerged.

Watching William Gnu's proud, massive form, the muscles rippling smoothly under his taut black skin as he disappeared back into the hut from which he had emerged, Emmaline nodded. A handsome, randy piece was William Gnu—truly worthy of Pucku's favor. He had had many women. He would have many more.

Emmaline breathed deeply, the force of the moment surging through her. Unlike William Gnu, there was only one man she had ever truly wanted. Her desire for him had been returned with a fervor that had granted her her first experience with true power. She had been excited beyond measure to know she had held that beautiful, dangerous man in the palm of her hand. Her exaltation had been supreme in the moment when that control had reached its height, the moment when Derek—handsome Derek, powerful Derek, passionate Derek—had stood silent and bloodied over the man he had *killed* for the love of her.

The brilliant green of Emmaline's eyes glowed as she looked back at Pucku's fire. She had waited for Derek. She had lived for the day when he would be released from prison. She had met him, promising him all they had had before and more, when they were together again.

But Derek had refused her. He had sent her back to Robert—aging, indulgent Robert, a puppet to her strings—her husband who was no impediment at all to the love they could share.

Emmaline's blazing eyes grew slowly cold. She had promised Derek then that she would allow no woman to replace her in his heart or mind. She had evoked Pucku's powers to sustain that promise, and she had read the truth in Derek's eyes in each encounter since.

He could not forget her. It was a matter of time until he came back to her.

But she was tired of waiting . . .

The drums resumed their pounding and Emmaline's smile slowly grew. She raised the pouch she had received from William Gnu to the fire, speaking into the shower of sparks that burst unexpectedly into the air.

"Do you hear the drums, Derek? They call you to me. You will come back to me now—back into my arms. And there you will stay. You cannot escape, my darling."

Bewitched by the fiery display, Emmaline closed her eyes as the drums throbbed anew and Pucku's power swelled around her. Her graceful silhouette flickered against the shadows of the surrounding foliage, expanding with the rise of the flames, growing ever larger . . .

. . . dancing against the darkness where a concealed figure lay, silently watching.

Derek raised his hand to his pounding head. The throbbing was steady and consistent, like relentless drums as he stared at the empty page of the captain's log in front of him. Powerful and unexpected, the discomfort had started minutes previous when he had returned to his cabin for the night.

His *empty* cabin.

The pounding increased, raising a familiar voice in the rebounding rhythm. Scowling, he determinedly shook off the sound as a refreshing gust blew through the open porthole behind him. The air was almost balmy, despite the lateness of the hour. They would dock in Jamaica before sunset the following day.

Scratching a few words on the page in front of him, Derek

rose abruptly to his feet. Barrett, still in his cell, impatiently awaited their arrival in port when he would be released. He had no doubt the devious bastard would attempt some kind of retribution for the indignities he had been made to suffer, but he also knew the man would not renege on the compromise they had struck. The complications would be too extensive and would cut too heavily into a profit that depended upon quick disposition of their "cargo."

As for Christopher Gibson, he was forced to admit that the fellow had proved his worth since becoming part of his crew the previous week. He did not like the man. He never would, yet he was beholden to Gibson for his heroic efforts on Davey Wright's behalf, and the sentiment of his crew was in his favor.

Derek pulled himself abruptly erect in an effort to dispel the image of Gillian in Gibson's arms. He had put deliberate distance between Gillian and Gibson in the time since. Not willing to explore his reasoning, he only knew that having freed Gillian from the intimacy of their agreement, he would rather have been damned to hell than have allowed Gillian and Gibson to spend the remainder of the voyage in each other's arms.

Agitated anew by his wandering thoughts, Derek unbuttoned his shirt and stripped it away. His shoes and britches followed. Lying naked in his bunk, Derek moved restlessly. He could no longer deny that he missed Gillian's warmth beside him. He missed the even cadence of her breathing, the womanly fragrance of her skin, and the moment of breathtaking wonder each time she opened her eyes and raised her incredibly brilliant gaze to his. He had read so much in those clear eyes as she had lain in his arms. He had read honesty, an unexpected innocence, and a passion that had matched his own.

And once again he had been wrong.

Derek's jaw turned to stone. An empty bed inspired bitter thoughts, but the situation was temporary. He would make good use of the warm and willing arms readily available once ashore. He had driven one woman from his mind with that treatment, and he would drive the other who had insinuated herself there as well.

The pounding in Derek's head ceased. They would reach Jamaica tomorrow, and that would be the beginning of the end of it.

Determined, Derek closed his eyes.

Adria's restless movement in her bunk broke the silence of night in the cabin Gillian and she shared. As sleepless as she, Gillian moved uncomfortably on the narrow pallet Christopher had formerly occupied. Since vacating Derek's cabin, night had become her enemy as it never had before.

Gillian pulled the coverlet up higher around her shoulders. No, she did not miss the strong, possessive arms that had held her close during those long nights. Nor did she miss the security of Derek's muscular body curved against her back, the sound of his even breathing in her ear, or the brush of his breath against her cheek.

Nor did the frigid indifference of Derek's gaze each time they now passed in the passageway stab mercilessly at her heart.

It's over.

Yes, it was over.

Despite his cold dismissal of her, Derek had kept all the promises he had made. The only fault she could find with him was in denying Adria and her contact with Christopher after he had assumed the duties of seaman. Adria had not missed a day in mentioning Christopher's name. Adria, who had already borne so much, had suffered at Christopher's absence, and for that unnecessary cruelty, Gillian knew she would forever hold Derek culpable.

Thankfully, however, Adria was almost well. She had regained her color, and if she had not quite returned to her former strength, Gillian was now certain she soon would.

But another fear had loomed ever more brightly each night as Gillian had lain sleepless. The uncertainty of Adria's and her future was suddenly upon them, and her fear had grown until—

Gillian's thoughts halted abruptly. Her *fear*?

The word echoed strangely in Gillian's mind. *Fear* had not held a place in the vocabulary of the Gillian Harcourt Haige who had walked onto this ship with head held high those long weeks ago! That Gillian Harcourt Haige had rejected fear while still at her father's knee! That woman had been strong, and determined that life would not become her master!

What had happened to that woman?

The pain of abrupt realization was intense. In her inexperience, that woman had made a glaring, rudimentary mistake. Sometime during the long nights at sea, that woman had surrendered a critical part of herself to the power of Derek's embrace, to the deep throbbing of his whispered passion, and to the explosive glory of the lovemaking they had shared. That woman had allowed that part of herself to become dependent on Derek's strengths, rather than her own.

And somewhere during those long, tender nights, that woman had made the crucial mistake of beginning to believe that the ardor in Derek's intimate whispers had meant more.

Anguish swelling, Gillian briefly closed her eyes.

So naive . . .

Such a damned fool . . .

But even fools could learn.

The lesson expertly taught and painfully learned had been simple—the reality that passion was a transient emotion, no matter the depth and power evoked, and that while easy to indulge, it was just as easily betrayed.

She would never suffer the need to have that lesson taught again.

Gillian's eyes grew cold. To say she was the same Gillian Harcourt Haige who had boarded this ship weeks earlier would be a lie. That woman had been intelligent, well educated, and determined, but woefully lacking in experience with certain intimate realities of life. The *new* Gillian Harcourt Haige was not.

Gillian's delicate jaw hardened. Now, so equipped, the new Gillian Harcourt Haige was a match for *any* man.

Adria moved restlessly once more. Her worries overwhelming, she could not sleep. Gillian had been so distant during the past week, and she missed Christopher. She missed the smiling warmth of his light eyes, the sound of his voice, and the support of his touch. But most of all, she missed talking to him and knowing he was near.

Adria raised her hand to the sudden heat in her cheeks. But she was not foolish enough to think there was any hope for the tender feelings she cherished inside her. She had seen the truth each time Christopher had looked at Gillian.

Dear Gillian, always smarter, brighter, more courageous than she. But Gillian had changed in a subtle, indefinable way, and somehow the future had begun to loom even more threatening than before.

Adria's heart skipped a beat. The term "indentured servitude" was so vague. It bespoke only one sure tenet. It was slavery.

The rustle of movement on Gillian's pallet caught Adria's notice. She ventured softly, "Gillian . . . are you awake?"

Long moments passed. "Yes, I'm awake."

Speaking in a rush the thoughts she had not dared to utter in the light of day, Adria whispered, "We'll be docking in Jamaica tomorrow. A-are you afraid, Gillian?"

Another pause. "Afraid?"

Adria's voice dropped a notch softer. "Of what's going to happen to us when we do."

Gillian's response was devoid of emotion. "We'll be all right."

"How can you be sure? What if we're separated? I-I couldn't bear that, Gillian."

"That won't happen."

"How can you be sure?"

"I'm sure."

"But how—"

"I won't *let* it happen."

"But, Gillian—"

"I promise you, Adria. I won't let it happen."

"But—"

"Go to sleep, Adria. It'll soon be morning."

A slow, stunning sweep of realization robbed Adria of response. Somehow, sometime, during the period since the lamp had been extinguished for the night and the moment that had just passed, the old Gillian had returned!

Adria unconsciously revised that thought in her mind. No, that wasn't exactly true. The Gillian who had just spoken to her was different. Her voice had been harder . . . more callous.

Sadness squeezed tight inside Adria. She supposed she knew the reason why.

Oh, Gillian . . .

Eleven

The clear turquoise waters of Kingston Harbor lapped softly against the hull of the *Colonial Dawn* as a golden morning sun shone brightly. Gentle currents of air warmed by its radiance enveloped the crowded dock with a deceiving aura of lethargy that belied the humming activity of the past hour.

John Barrett, restored to his former appearance less considerable poundage that did little to diminish his repulsive demeanor, cracked the gavel loudly on a podium sufficiently elevated by the platform on which it stood to allow clear view of the auction under way. The sound reverberated against the line of waterfront buildings behind him, ringing in the ears of the diverse crowd assembled as he scrutinized it with a practiced eye. He was not pleased.

Notices of the auction had been posted in all the usual places, but the response had been poorer than Barrett had anticipated. Overseers, small estate owners, local merchants, all with dirty hands and critical eyes, all so typical of this damned, steamy island where the dregs of humanity abounded—he was sick of the lot of them! Enthusiasm had been limited since the inception of the auction, and it was rapidly dwindling.

Barrett looked back at the transportees grouped behind the platform, awaiting their individual call. Granted, they were an unappealing group. A chance to bathe, a change of clothes, and a cursory delousing had done little to enhance their appeal. At the present rate, he would end up surrendering the greater part of the lot to soul drivers who would herd them inland to sell to individual sugar estates along the way, causing a costly dip in profits he was not prepared to take.

The crowd shuffled impatiently, and hatred swelled as Barrett saw Captain Derek Andrews standing on the fringe of those assembled. The captain had kept to his part of the bargain, bastard that he was, and he had been forced to keep to his. He had signed the first of the papers that morning, releasing partial payment for the transportation. He knew the captain would not let him out of his sight until the remainder was paid.

Turning back to the business at hand, Barrett motioned the next transportee forward, a surly lout who had been convicted of vicious assault. Although lacking in height, the fellow was particularly broad in the chest and had powerful arms, a perfect field animal if he had ever seen one. He turned back to the crowd with new determination.

"All right, how much am I bid for this fine male specimen?"

The silence that followed heightened Barrett's ire as he pressed, "Note the strength of this fellow . . . the strong arms and chest! You'll get your money's worth and more from him in the fields!"

The crowd barely stirred and Barrett's anger soared. Turning to the guard beside him, he hissed, "Turn the filthy beggar around! These people want to see what they're buying!"

The guard obliged roughly, and Barrett addressed the crowd again.

"Come now, surely you see the value here! What am I

bid for this robust specimen who will serve at your command for eight years or more?"

One bid, then another. The price offered was an insult and Barrett's resentment climbed. Furious when his efforts to boost the highest bid proved a miserable failure, he raised his gavel and pounded it down with a deafening crack.

"Done!"

Silently cursing, Barrett cracked the gavel against the block once more, shouting to the tall, balding fellow in the rear of the crowd, "This one is yours! Come and get him!"

Seething, Barrett signaled the next felon forward.

A resounding slap . . . a pained gasp . . .

Then a raging shout.

"Shut up! Don't you dare cry, you lazy wretch!" Emmaline's brilliant eyes widened as her fury echoed in the vaulted hallway of the great house. "I told you . . . I *told* you I wanted to know the moment the *Colonial Dawn* docked! But you were too lazy to bring the information back to me as you were told! The ship has been here two days . . . *Two* . . ."

Emmaline's wrath knew no bounds. "Where were you when you were supposed to be tending to your mistress's business? Were you with Lester . . . is that it? Were you fornicating behind the barn when you should have been checking the arriving ships as you were told?"

"No, Jubba not be with Lester!" The slender Negresss's voice shook with fear. "Jack be sick. Him can't climb into de wagon fe de achin' in him bones dis week." Indicating the aging house servant standing silent in the foyer, the Negress continued. "Jack go Kingston town today and him see dat ship. Him come right back here."

"You've made me lose time . . . valuable time . . ." Emmaline quaked with frustrated rage. "And you will pay. Both of you!"

"Amassi, mistress!" The shaking Negress's eyes grew wide.

"Have mercy?" Emmaline struggled to overcome her rage. "Yes, I will have mercy . . . if the mercy is due." She raised a trembling arm and pointed toward her bedroom door. "Go! Get my green silk ready!" Emmaline's furious gaze narrowed. "But if your neglect of duties has cost me dearly, it will cost you dearly as well. Your dear Lester . . . he will not be quite the man he was without his 'man stick,' will he?"

Jubba's eyes bulged with horror. "No . . . no!"

"Nor will you be quite the woman you were if you must wear that 'ragin' piece' hanging from a string around your neck until the end of your days . . ."

The Negress gasped.

"Go, damn you!"

Watching as the Negress scrambled to her bidding, Emmaline cursed again and followed stiffly behind.

Derek tensed as the next transportee approached the auction platform. He heard the buzz of interest that stirred the crowd as Christopher Gibson stepped into sight. The reason was apparent as Gibson stood stiff-jawed and erect in front of the prospective buyers. Young, well built, his curly hair and reddish beard neatly trimmed and his light eyes clear, he was also the first of the lot to appear civilized.

Cutter moved subtly at his side as the bidding began and Derek glanced toward him. Purposly maintaining his silence as the bidding progressed, he waited patiently until it had dwindled down to one before raising his hand unexpectedly. Barrett's surprise was apparent as he accepted the bid and worked feverishly to raise it.

Cautiously bettering each bid offered, Derek waited, feeling the heat of Barrett's stare as the bidding finally ceased. Derek gave a low snort. His momentary satisfaction as Barrett turned venomously in his direction was almost worth the price alone as Barrett cracked the gavel against the board with a vicious swing.

"Done!"

Maintaining his position at the perimeter of the crowd as Cutter walked forward to count out the required price, Derek waited. He scowled as Cutter started back toward him minutes later, Gibson walking behind. It was obvious from Gibson's expression that he had not a whit of appreciation for having been saved from the endless, backbreaking labor of the sugar fields. The fool doubtless could not think past the realization that he was bound in servitude for the next eight years to the man who had held his lover intimately close while he had been denied her.

Derek's jaw twitched at the irony of the approaching moment: Two men would soon face each other, neither able to think past the memory of Gillian in the other man's arms.

Suddenly disgusted with his indulgence of the same, senseless torment, Derek watched intently as Gibson strode to a halt beside him. His expression tight, he spoke coldly into the silent animosity of Gibson's gaze.

"I can see you're no more enthusiastic about this turn in your circumstances than I." Derek paused, a harder edge entering his tone as he continued. "I owe you no explanations as to the reason I bought your indenture, Gibson, but I will make one thing clear from the outset so there will be no misunderstandings. I bought your indenture for two reasons. The first is that I am in need of a seaman to replace Stiles on a permanent basis and you have proved your ability to fill that position. The second is that your effort on Davey Wright's behalf has turned the sympathies of my crew in your favor, and I value the concerns of my men. I wish to impress upon you, however, that in buying your indenture, I have spent money I can ill afford to spend—and with that comes a word of advice."

Derek's voice dropped a menacing octave lower. "You had better be worth the price."

Movement at the head of the gangplank a distance beyond suddenly catching his attention, Derek did not see the flash of pure hatred that was Gibson's response to his warning. Unable to draw his gaze from the two, identical female figures who stepped suddenly into view, Derek felt his heart begin a ragged pounding as Gillian and Adria started down the gangplank, the unbound lengths of silver-gold hair streaming past their respective shoulders glittering in the sun.

Derek turned abruptly to Cutter. "Get Gibson back on the ship."

A hot flush of fury coloring his vision as Gibson turned to follow the descent of the two women, Derek snapped viciously, "You're wasting time looking in that direction, Gibson. In the event you don't recall, your time isn't your own to waste anymore. It's mine. In case you have any ideas to the contrary, let me remind you that there's no place you can escape on this island, and there are no ships that will take you on without the necessary papers, should you think to evade your indenture. So, get moving!"

Turning with hard-jawed resentment at Cutter's urging, Gibson walked back toward the ship. Watching intently as

Gibson came abreast of the two women, Derek saw their quick exchange of glances in passing.

Struggling to suppress the surge within him as the guard pushed the two women to a faster pace, Derek noted that the subtle difference in appearance between the sisters that illness had wrought was undetectable at a distance. But he had no difficulty in telling them apart. There was something about Gillian's step, the tilt of her head . . .

. . . as they approached the platform and started up the stairs.

"Are you going out, dear?"

Emmaline snapped stiffly upright at the sound of her husband's voice in the doorway behind her. She turned abruptly to face him, halting her frantic activity as he entered the bedroom and walked slowly toward her. Smiling, Robert noted that the hand Emmaline raised to the upward sweep of her hair was shaking. He also noted that she was clad in incredibly lovely, black lace undergarments in which her creamy flesh was liberally exposed, undergarments which he had never seen her wear before.

Emmaline swallowed, her beautiful face twitching as she attempted a smile in return. "Robert . . . darling . . . I wasn't expecting you home so early. I thought you said you would be in the fields until late afternoon." When he did not reply, she continued in a rush. "I . . . I'm going shopping. Madame Louise has received a new shipment of gowns directly from England, and mine are all so shabby. I want to get there before the selection is gone."

Robert maintained his silence as he continued his slow approach. Emmaline was trembling. He had seen her tremble like that before. He knew what it meant.

Jubba entered in a rush, halting abruptly at the sight of him as she clutched a freshly ironed silk gown in her hand. He saw the welt on her cheek and the redness of her eyes as she glanced at her mistress with obvious uncertainty.

He addressed the shaken slave softly. "Your face is bruised, Jubba. What happened?"

"Jubba . . ." Jubba glanced at her mistress. "Jubba fall and hurt him cheek, massa."

"Hurt your cheek? That's unfortunate. You look unwell. Perhaps you should go down into the kitchen and rest for a while."

Emmaline gasped. "What are you saying, Robert! Jubba's fine! She doesn't need a rest! She's as strong as a horse! I need her now . . . t-to fix my hair and help me dress!"

Robert's slow advance halted at Emmaline's side. Intensely aware of his wife's awesome, youthful beauty, he was just as intensely aware of his own failings in that regard. He had never been considered a handsome man, even in his prime, and he was now old, past the age of fifty. He was short, overweight, and totally lacking in muscle tone. His hair was gray and thinning, and the passage of years had deeply lined his face. He had few illusions about Emmaline or the reason she had married him. Her manipulative personality, her occasional violent outbursts, her addiction to black magic, and her supplication to Pucku—he knew her well. He also knew that despite her claims to the contrary, she had never felt for him the supreme passion that had turned his life around the moment he had first glimpsed her beautiful face.

But all that meant nothing.

Turning back to the uncertain Negress, he ordered softly, "You may leave, Jubba. Go to the kitchen and rest. Mistress Emmaline will call you when she needs you."

"Robert . . ."

"Go, Jubba."

Placing the gown carefully on the lounge beside her, Jubba hurried from the room without looking back. Waiting until her footsteps had faded, Robert turned back to Emmaline's flushed face.

"You look upset, dear."

"Of course I'm upset!" Emmaline's trembling had increased. "I-I had plans and you're ruining them!"

"What were your plans, dear?"

Emmaline blinked. "I told you what my plans were . . ."

"Yes, you did—something about new gowns . . ."

Emmaline took an unexpected step forward, her expression growing suddenly coy. "Yes . . . new gowns, Robert dear." She stroked his cheek with her fingertips in a way with which Robert was familiar. "Don't you want to see me in something new . . . with a deep bodice, perhaps—something colorful that will display my charms to best advantage?"

"You *are* wearing something new, aren't you, dear?" Robert smiled again. "These beautiful undergarments . . ." He slipped the lacy strap of her chemise from her shoulder. He watched it fall before slipping the other from her shoulder as well. He saw her twitch of annoyance and a knot inside him tightened. Gently, firmly, he pushed the chemise to her waist.

"Robert, really . . ." Emmaline shook her head. "I don't have time for this! I have things to do."

Grasping her arms gently, Robert held Emmaline fast as he lowered his head and covered the dark crest of her breast with his lips.

"Robert . . ." Emmaline gasped. He saw her eyelids flicker as he suckled her sweet flesh. "Robert, please . . ."

Drawing back, Robert replied softly, "Please what, dear?"

Slowly, deliberately, he lowered his mouth to the other white mound. He heard her gasp again as he drew deeply from it.

"Robert . . ."

The sound of Emmaline's protest was waning as he pressed her soft flesh passionately, as he wound his hand in the delicate lace shielding her female delta from his touch and rent it in two. He heard her excited rasp as he slid his fingers deep inside her. He felt a warm, sticky surge bathe his hand. He saw her eyelids finally flutter closed as she leaned into his touch, and his smile tightened.

He stroked her with increasing fervor. "I came home early so we might spend some time together this morning. I had some thoughts how I might entertain you." He paused. "Do you like the way this feels, Emmaline?"

Emmaline took a short, uneven breath.

"Emmaline . . . ?"

Emmaline nodded.

"I can't hear you."

"Yes . . . I . . . I do."

He walked her slowly backward, his intimate stroking increasing. "Would you like me to continue?"

Emmaline shuddered.

"Speak up, dear."

"Yes."

The bed struck the back of Emmaline's knees and he pressed her down against it. He crouched in front of her and separated her legs as his voice throbbed, "Do you want me to do this?" He pressed his lips against the reddish-brown nest between her thighs. He found the moist slit there and tasted it with his tongue.

Emmaline shook convulsively.

"Tell me . . ."

"Robert . . ."

Robert licked her moistness lightly and she shuddered again. "I had hoped you would ask me to stay."

"Robert, I—"

Robert's kindly eyes hardened. He slid his tongue slowly along the moist slit, intensely aware of the severity of the tremor that wracked her. "Do you want me to stay?"

Emmaline was shaking uncontrollably. He saw a passion in her narrowed gaze that was not feigned. He had developed that passion slowly, over a passage of years as he had memorized every warm, sensuous inch of her flesh with his lips. He knew he had the power to raise that passion almost at will, that he was the only man who held that power over her—save one. He pressed that power once more.

"Do you, Emmaline?" Ignoring his own growing need, Robert whispered, "I'll leave, if you want me to."

"No! I mean . . ." The brilliant green of Emmaline's eyes caught and held his. He saw surrender there and he reveled in its glow as she gasped, "Please . . . stay."

His heart pounding, Robert remained unmoving as Emmaline cupped his cheeks with her long, slender fingers, as she drew him slowly toward the waiting nest between her thighs. His heartbeat attained the volume of thunder in his ears as his mouth met the wetness there, as he heard her gasp, as she clasped him tight against her.

Cupping her firm buttocks in his palms, opening her up fully to him, Robert indulged the intimate feast Emmaline offered. *His* Emmaline . . . a feast he would not share.

His intense ministrations surged deeper, stronger, and Emmaline cried out aloud at the ecstasy induced.

Robert's heart pounded. He loved her. He would keep her . . . his alone . . . at any price.

* * *

Barrett's gaze glowed demonically as the assembled crowd moved restlessly during the auction's brief lull. The Haige sisters could not be seen by them as they approached, but *he* could see. He had watched out of the corner of his eye as they walked down the gangplank and he had seen them exchange glances with Gibson in passing. He had silently cursed the bastard captain again for having saved that brawny pup from the fields—that one who had spent the voyage in the Haige sisters' cabin, enjoying their charms, while he had suffered the filth and deprivations of the brig.

He had also noted that the bastard captain's expression had remained hard and cold when the two sisters came into his view.

So, the captain had had his fill of them . . . Barrett's bulgy eyes narrowed. Well, *he* had not. There was much he intended to teach them both about the intimate press of the flesh. Oh, yes.

The restless rumble of the crowd grew louder as the pause lengthened, but Barrett was confident their dwindling interest was temporary. Searching out a familiar face within those gathered there, his scanning gaze halted abruptly on the broad, perspiration-marked face of a man in the rear. Charles Higgins, his obese form bulging at the buttons of his frock coat, nodded with his characteristic smile. He had taken special pains to inform Higgins of the Haige sisters' arrival. He had whet the fellow's considerable appetite and he was certain that once the overweight proprietor of Kingston's most popular bordello caught sight of the two women, the matter would be closed. He had also taken pains to elicit an agreement from the fellow, which gave him first dibbs on the sisters, individually as well as working in concert.

Ah, yes, they would make such beautiful music *together* . . .

The two women reached the platform staircase and Barrett scrutinized their appearances more closely. His instructions had been followed to the letter. The women were wearing their hair unbound, the pale, shimmering color particularly eye-catching on an island where dark hair and skin was predominant. They were also dressed in the pale blue cotton gowns he had bought for them upon arrival in Kingston. The color exactly matched the brilliant shade of their eyes, and the delicate batiste, purposely lacking in the proper undergarments, allowed the clear outline of their slender limbs to show through the skirt, while the bodice bared their shoulders to a daring degree, exposing a generous curve of firm white breasts.

Ah, yes . . . that firm white flesh. The crowd would soon be salivating.

The women climbed the staircase. He saw Gillian Haige—unmistakable for the tilt to her haughty chin—turn toward her sister and take her hand as they reached the top. He heard the hush that fell over the crowd as the women stepped into view, the breathless lack of sound that was silent tribute to the phenomenon of two women, so identically beautiful.

Identical . . . except that in the eyes of one was hatred, and in the other, fear, as they looked directly at him.

Barrett sneered. He would choose the former over the latter every time . . . for the sheer excitement of it.

The silence of the crowd slowly changed to an enthusiastic mumbling that grew louder as Barrett left his podium and approached the two. Halting beside them, he grasped a handful of Gillian's silken, silver-gold locks, reveling in the flush of fury that colored her magnificent face as he called out aloud, "All right. What am I bid!"

* * *

Concealed in a doorway nearby, Swift laughed softly at the spectacle progressing on the platform a short distance away. He turned at the nervous pulling of his elbow.

"Leave go of me, I say!" He shook off Dobbs's clutching grip. "I will not miss seein' the bitch get her comeuppance, I tell ye!"

"Aye, so you say . . ." Dobbs face was white with fear. "But is it worth the chance you take?"

"Ye worry for naught!" Dismissing Dobbs's anxiety with a shake of his head, Swift continued. "We've been hidin' since we docked as the captain advised, ain't we? He fixed it so's we have our papers and berths readied on the ship sailin' back to England on the morrow—you, me, and Niles—ain't that true?"

"Aye . . ."

"Barrett, fiend that he is, is too busy gettin' his vengeance on the blond slut to bother with us now. By the time he realizes what happened to us, we'll be gone."

"I suppose . . ."

"So leave me be and let me enjoy meself!" Swift's expression grew harsh. "I've earned it after sufferin' the cut of that one's tongue, and I will not be denied!"

Dobbs took a step back. "You're a fool, puttin' us all in danger for the likes of her!"

"Fool I may be . . ." His gaze intently focused on the platform a short distance away, Swift did not notice that Dobbs had slipped away as he rasped, "but I'll watch the witch pay . . . and that's the last of it."

The excited mumbling of the crowd grew louder as Gillian clutched Adria's hand tighter. She raised her chin stiffly against the intimate scrutiny of the men below, as intensely aware of the transparent quality of the gowns Adria and she wore as she was of Derek's dark, silent presence at the edge of the crowd.

Barrett grasped her hair more tightly and Gillian winced as he shouted encouragingly to the crowd, "Who will make the first bid?"

A first bid sounded, then a second and a third in dizzying succession as Gillian scrutinized the faces in the crowd. The bids continued, rising ever higher, and a growing sense of horror expanded within Gillian. Search as she might, she could not see an honest, concerned face among those staring back at her—nor a decent, civilized thought reflected in the eyes gazing hotly in her direction.

Glancing at Adria, Gillian saw her sister stiffen with fear, and a shudder ran down her spine.

"Come now, my friends . . ." Barrett's voice rose again over the growing rumble below, "We have a marvelous treasure here! Twin beauties at your disposal! Have you ever seen hair of this sheen and color?" Barrett tugged Gillian's hair harder, then released the heavy strands to run his hand along her bared shoulder, "Or skin as clear and smooth as this?"

Gillian shrugged off his touch and Barrett laughed aloud. "Sensitive young ladies, they are! And so full of spirit! Which of you will teach them their place?"

His laughter dropping away as he turned to face Gillian, Barrett hissed, "Turn around, bitch! Give them a show . . . or I give you my word that your sister will pay the price of your reluctance!"

Gillian remained motionless, only to hear Barrett persist, *"Now,* Mistress Gillian Haige. Yes, I know which one you are! Are you contemptuous of me now, Mistress Haige—

now that your protector, the black-hearted Captain Andrews, has turned his back on you?"

Refusing to follow Barrett's direction, hatred surging hot and swift within her, Gillian jumped with a start as Barrett grated, *"Now,* Mistress Haige, or I will turn my attentions to your sister!"

Realizing that the malice in Barrett's tone was not feigned, Gillian released Adria's hand and took a step forward. Her flesh crawled as she turned slowly to Barrett's low encouragement and a new murmur moved over the crowd.

Barrett addressed the crowd anew.

"That's right, gentlemen. We have a fine pair here, a bold sister who would like to entertain you, and a shy sister who needs encouragement. An interesting thought, is it not? *Let me hear your bids!"*

His emotions held tightly in check, Derek tensely observed the growing spectacle. Barrett's hand on Gillian's hair raised a flush of heat within him. Barrett's thick fingers slipping across the bared flesh of Gillian's shoulders sent him a step forward that he halted with tenuous control.

Gillian responded to a whispered word from Barrett by releasing her sister's hand and turning to allow the crowd a better view of herself, but not before Derek saw the flash of fury in her gaze.

The responsive comments of the crowd flushed Gillian's face with hot color and Derek swallowed, his torment intense.

Gillian glanced up unexpectedly, catching his gaze. Derek saw a humiliation in his brief contact with the glorious blue of her eyes that slashed so deeply at his innards as to draw blood. And he saw despair.

Instinct, and a surging anguish that tore at his heart, thrust Derek another step forward before he halted abruptly.

No. He had bled before from the type of wound that Gillian sought to inflict on him. He had barely survived.

Rigid in his attempt to retain control, the effort more difficult than any he had ever sustained, Derek held Gillian's gaze for a silent, timeless moment.

Slowly, with great determination, he looked away.

The shouts of the crowd faded from Gillian's hearing as Derek dismissed her gaze. Somehow incredulous, she watched as he slowly turned and walked away. She jumped with a start as Barrett claimed her attention with his rough grip on her arm.

"Another turn, Mistress Haige . . ."

Gillian remained unmoving.

"I said, *another turn* . . ."

Gillian could not make herself budge as the sounds of the crowd faded, as the brilliant glow of the sun grew more dim, as she swayed—

Adria's slender hand slipped into hers and Gillian felt a hot flush of shame. Damn the malady that had sought to weaken her! She would not submit to it!

Squeezing Adria's hand, Gillian gathered her strength, then rotated slowly to Barrett's command.

She was standing rigidly still as the bids slowed to a halt. She was hardly conscious of the victorious smile that flashed across Barrett's sweaty face before the crack of the gavel shattered the late-morning silence once more. She felt the rough hand of the guard as he urged Adria and her from the platform.

And then she saw *him,* waiting at the bottom.

The man was outrageously obese. His clothing was ringed with sweat, his broad face beaded with it. His rank odor became increasingly offensive as she descended the stairs toward him.

The man smiled, exposing yellowed teeth spotted with decay as he said, "My name is Charles Higgins, ladies. If you will come with me, there is much we have to discuss."

Following as Charles Higgins led them proudly through the crowd, Gillian saw the revealing sneers and heard the lewd comments of some in passing. Gripping Adria's hand more tightly, she continued steadily forward.

Twelve

Gillian sat silently, unable to speak past the thick lump that had formed in her throat. She glanced at Adria, seated beside her on the small cot in the narrow, slovenly room where Charles Higgins had delivered them earlier. She was uncertain how long Adria and she had been waiting for his return. Food and water had been brought to them since, which lay untouched as morning had passed into afternoon and afternoon had begun to wane . . . as her apprehension mounted.

There was no doubt in her mind what kind of place this was. She had known the moment they had approached the wood frame building adjacent to the docks where women sat at the open upper windows, revealingly clad, exchanging ribald conversations with men who passed by.

The cloying smell of the place had struck her with the force of a blow as Higgins had pushed open the door and ushered them inside. The heavy mixture of fragrances meant to cover a pervading odor of perspiration and the intimate mingling of flesh had been enough to make her wretch. It was the sights that had met her gaze as they had crossed the foyer toward the staircase to the upper rooms, however, that had had the greatest impact. Women, in various stages of dress and undress, crowded the parlor room. She had seen their smiles as they had openly encouraged the interest of the men milling there, moving sensuously under their intimate touch.

Unwilling to glance toward Adria for fear of what she might see reflected on her sister's face, she had followed solemnly behind Mr. Higgins as he had climbed the staircase. Low, grunting sounds emanating from the rooms they had passed had been difficult to ignore, and the glimpse she had inadvertently obtained through a slitted doorway of the activity progressing within had set her stomach to churning.

They had been ushered into the narrow room they now occupied. In the time they had spent waiting there since, it had occurred to her that the room they now inhabited was a crib, such as those she had read about and had never truly believed existed.

As Adria and she waited, she had begun to wonder if this crib would be *their* crib . . . and the thought had been almost too terrible to bear.

Adria suddenly shuddered, and Gillian turned quickly toward her to see Adria's face was blanched of color, her eyes wide. Her own nausea intense, Gillian grasped her twin's hand, her whispered words attaining the power of a shout in the silence of the room.

"Adria dear, everything will be all right."

Adria's eyes snapped toward her with startling anger. "I'm not a child, Gillian! I know what kind of place this is."

Gillian's attempt at a smile failed. "There can be no doubt, can there."

"Is this the way we are to end our days, Gillian?" Adria's voice trembled. "Surely someone can help us. Perhaps Christopher can—"

"No. It will do no good to entertain false hopes in that direction. Christopher's life is not his own. We can't depend on him. We can't depend on anyone but ourselves."

"Ourselves? But we're helpless!"

"You can't be sure of that! We must wait and see. Perhaps when Mr. Higgins returns, he—"

"Yes, perhaps when Mr. Higgins returns, he'll bring us back a *customer* to entertain!" Adria's eyes filled. "I would rather die, Gillian! I would rather die!"

The rattle of the door turned the two women abruptly toward it as Charles Higgins thrust it open and stepped inside. It occurred to Gillian that the man had suffered even more in appearance in the few hours since they had last seen him. Greasy hair formerly concealed by his hat lay in limp, uncombed strands against his scalp. His face was flushed from the heat, his clothing more darkly ringed. And his bodily odor had become overwhelming.

The urge to wretch so intense that it left her weak, Gillian struggled for control. Higgins addressed them in a polite tone contrasting so sharply with his appalling demeanor that an aura of unreality began to prevail.

"I'm sorry to keep you waiting so long, ladies, but there was some business to which I needed to attend." Higgins smiled, his yellowed, spotted teeth flashing nauseatingly once more. "I'm not quite certain if it's superfluous at this point in time to recite the terms of your indenture, but I suppose it cannot hurt for you to be totally clear on your situation."

Higgins paused, his manner more that of a concerned solicitor than that of a purveyor of flesh, and Gillian's sense of unreality grew staggering.

"Ladies, the terms of indenture are clear and concise. They are as follows: You have each been sentenced by law to a term of indentured servitude of four years. During that time you are the possession of your master. The work you do, the clothes on your back belong entirely to him. You may be hired out to his terms . . . with all sums earned reverting back to him." Higgins paused for effect, then continued. "You may be resold at his whim. There are no limits imposed on punishment he may inflict if he is displeased with your services, with the exception of purposely inflicting death. Attempts to escape may be punished by extension or multiplication of your time. In that regard, I feel compelled to comment that escape is virtually impossible, especially on this island, that when an attempt is made, wanted posters are circulated throughout the island—throughout the colonies for that matter—describing escapees in detail. Since indentured servitude is an essential and accepted part of the immigration and penal system established by the Crown, cooperation on the part of the population is excellent. I also feel compelled to mention, although it is probably insensitive for me to do so, that it is a common practice to brand habitual escapees so they may be easily recognized."

Despite herself, Gillian's breathing grew ragged. The heat of the room, the airlessness, the overpowering stench . . . the sheer incredibility of the entire sequence of events since Adria and she had stepped up onto that platform and had their lives auctioned away, was dizzying.

Seemingly unaware of her distraction, Higgins continued, "Dear ladies, I don't think I need explain to you the type of establishment this is." He smiled. "But I assure you, my ladies are very happy here. They are adequately clothed, fed, and *entertained*—and, of course, they never lay claim to being terribly tired at the end of their working period since they spend so great a part of it abed."

Charles Higgins laughed loudly at his own joke. The sound rang in the small room, rebounding wildly in Gillian's mind. His laughter fading when Adria and she did not join in, Higgins shook his head sadly. "You are such serious ladies. I would so much have appreciated the opportunity to teach you to enjoy yourselves. But, alas, I will not have that opportunity. You see, I have spent the greater part of the day in very difficult negotiations concerning the sale of your indenture to a third party. Those negotiations were concluded a short time previous. I am now awaiting the purchaser's return with the sum agreed upon. Since the transaction was so profitable, I thought I would extend the favor of saving your new master the need for clarification of your indenture."

Mr. Higgins paused, sincere sadness flickering across his full, flat features. "I fear you will not be as happy with your new master as you would have been with me. He is an intense sort, not known for affability; but, alas, his determination overwhelmed me and I was obliged to consummate the transaction."

Incredibly, Higgins winked. *"Consummate* the transaction—I'm such a clever fellow . . ."

Gillian was speechless.

Higgins turned toward the door at the sound of a heavy step outside. He frowned for the first time. "I think I hear the unpleasant fellow now. You should be quite well acquainted with him."

Gillian became suddenly breathless. The room grew abruptly bright.

The doorknob turned as Higgins continued. "Mr. John Barrett—"

At the sound of that infamous name, the brightness exploded within Gillian's mind, leaving only darkness behind.

"Get out of my way!"

Thrusting Higgins aside as Gillian slipped to the floor,

Derek rushed to Gillian's side. He heard Adria's frightened gasp. He saw her reach shakily toward her sister, but he spent no time on her concern. It was Gillian, her exquisite features lax, her faultless skin drained of color as she lay in a crumpled heap that sent tremors of fear along his spine.

"Gillian . . ." Derek scooped her up into his arms and lay her on the cot, not questioning his instinctive ability to differentiate between the two, seemingly identical sisters. "Gillian . . ."

"Really . . ." Higgins's mumbling tone sent Derek's anger soaring. "How can you tell which is which? But then, of course, I suppose it doesn't really matter."

Derek looked up at the man sharply, gritting his teeth as the fellow looked back blankly and Adria fluttered uselessly beside him. He growled, "Get me water, damn it!"

Adria rushed to the table nearby and poured some water into a glass. She was sobbing softly. Somehow the sound annoyed him almost as much as Higgins's tone when the fellow spoke again. "I hope you don't hold me responsible for this. You may ask this young lady if I didn't do my best to console them . . . to explain their situation in the most generous terms. I was just about to tell them that Mr. John Barrett was probably going to be incensed that I had sold their articles of indenture . . . and at such a profit, especially since he had such a personal interest in them, but I hardly had the chance to—"

"Shut up, will you!"

His patience expiring with a flash of ire, Derek grabbed the glass of water from Adria's hand. "Get out of here! Both of you!"

"But my sister—"

"*Out!*"

"Sir, this is my establishment and I—"

"Out, damn it! Out!"

The door clicked closed behind them as Derek looked down into Gillian's pale face, his heart pounding. Her skin was devoid of color and small beads of perspiration marked her brow and upper lip. Her lips were slightly parted. He could feel the brush of her breath as he leaned closer, as he stroked a wisp of hair back from her cheek. Her eyelids flickered and he spoke for the first time, startled at the rasp of his own voice as he slid his arm under Gillian's head and raised her gently.

"Drink, Gillian . . . just a small sip. That fool should've realized it was too hot in this room to keep you waiting here so long."

Gillian's eyes flickered open. She looked at him strangely, but she did not speak as he urged again, "Drink . . . just a sip."

Gillian's lips parted further. She sipped obediently, her eyes returning to his the moment she had swallowed.

"Are you feeling better?"

Gillian nodded. Derek leaned closer. He saw the responsive widening of her eyes and his heart began a furious hammering as she whispered, "Mr. Higgins said—"

"I don't care what that damned whoremaster said."

"He said that he had sold our indenture . . ."

Derek stiffened. "He did."

"John Barrett—"

Derek seethed. "I don't want to hear you speak that filthy bastard's name . . ."

"He said that John Barrett—"

"John Barrett be damned! Look at me, Gillian . . . and hear what I say." Derek looked into the crystal blue of Gillian's eyes. He saw the confusion there . . . the pain. When he spoke again, his words were harsh, torn from the tight knot of anguish within that bore Gillian's name.

"You belong to *me*."

He swallowed her soft rasp with his kiss. The sound echoed deep inside him, feeding the anguish, stirring it anew. It awakened a hunger he had sought to deny, then had thought to subdue. But he had failed in both tacks. He had acknowledged that failure when it had almost been too late, and he had known there was no option left to him, save one.

Drawing back from her lips, Derek scrutinized Gillian's returning color a moment longer, then mumbled, "You've been in this filthy hole long enough."

Standing abruptly, Derek saw Gillian's uncertainty as he leaned down and scooped her up into his arms. Ignoring her protest, he started toward the door. Outside in the hallway, he paid little mind to Adria's concern or Higgins's surprise as he snapped into Adria's flustered expression, "Follow me, or I'll leave you behind!"

Moments later, Gillian in his arms, he walked out the door onto the street.

Emmaline slowly opened her eyes, her mind cloudy from her nap. She stretched, enjoying the caress of the soft bed linens against her naked skin. She cupped her breasts with her palms, their aching sensitivity stimulating a fresh surge of heat in her groin. She smiled . . . her smile dropping away as reality abruptly returned.

Growing rapidly furious, Emmaline looked toward the window where the light of afternoon was fading, then toward the clock on the dresser. Sitting up, she cursed aloud.

Damn Robert's persistent male member! Try as she might throughout the long morning and afternoon, she had been unable to put it to rest until she had begun to wonder in the back of her mind if her husband, the aging, overweight, benevolent fellow who worshiped her and granted her every wish, had actually suspected where she had been going.

Emmaline unconsciously shook her head. No, he couldn't possibly. She had been too careful. She had never looked at another man in his presence. That had not been as difficult as she had originally thought it might be when she had married Robert, because of his extremely passionate nature. Except for dreams of Derek that would not die, he had satisfied her sexual appetite with surprising consistency, even exceeding his best efforts at times such as that morning when he had—

Emmaline's lips twitched with annoyance. Damn Robert and his horrid timing!

Derek's dark-eyed visage flashed before Emmaline's mind and her heart began a furious pounding. Her rage at Jubba returned. Derek had been in port for two days without her knowledge, long enough to have broken the celibacy of his voyage with one of the local streggahs. Jealousy loomed hotly at the thought. She had wanted to reach Derek before he had had the opportunity to break that celibacy. It had galled her to admit, even to herself, that she needed that advantage after the long years they had been apart. She had been certain that with that advantage and the aid of Pucku's power, she would have been able to win him back forever.

As for Robert . . . Emmaline frowned. Admittedly, she had formed a true affection of sorts for the man, and Derek would never be able to keep her in the luxury she enjoyed with Robert. But Robert was old. She would still be young when he died. With Derek waiting in the wings, her life would be complete.

Slipping to the side of the bed, Emmaline stood up. She

paused in midstep at the sounds of movement from the connecting room. That sneeze—she recognized it. She also recognized the sound of Robert's steady stream as he relieved himself into one of the hand-painted ceramic chamber pots placed for convenience there. Damn the man! He was supposed to have left to check the progress of the harvesting!

Reaching for the wrapper lying on the side of her bed, Emmaline silently cursed again as Robert appeared in the connecting doorway. He was naked except for the cloth covering his private parts, the exposed white skin lightly peppered with gray hair that stretched over his obese proportions an unappealing sight. She hastily slipped her arm into her wrapper, only to see a familiar glimmer in his eye as he approached.

Oh, no . . .

"Did you have a nice rest, dear?"

Emmaline's heart began a slow pounding as she forced a smile. "Y-yes. I did." She belted her wrapper nervously, both astounded and annoyed at her body's reaction to that persistent glimmer. "As a matter of fact, I feel quite invigorated, despite the hour. I thought I'd dress and see if I might yet make it to Kingston in time to see Madame Louise's new offerings."

Robert smiled in return. "Don't you think it's rather late for that?"

"No, not really!" Emmaline drew herself up stiffly. "Of course, if you object to the expense . . . if you feel I'm being too extravagant . . ."

"Everything you do is extravagant, dear. It's one of the things I love most about you."

"Then you don't care if I—"

Robert loosened the cloth around his broad waist and allowed it to drop to the floor as he continued his approach.

Despite herself, Emmaline felt a surge of moistness in the female core of her, and a familiar quaking beset her. It grew stronger as he pushed her hands away from the belt on her wrapper and slowly loosened it.

"Robert . . ." Emmaline's breathing grew uneven. "I . . . it's been a long day. It's getting dark. I'm getting hungry." She shuddered as Robert slid her wrapper from her shoulders. "I'm going to call Jubba."

"Call her later, dear."

Robert lowered himself to his knees in front of her, and Emmaline silently groaned as a hunger that had no relation to the empty growling of her stomach flared. She felt Robert's hands on her hips, and she closed her eyes. She felt his palms cup her buttocks, as he drew her toward him, and she gasped. She felt the touch of his mouth against her . . .

"Robert, I—"

Robert drew back from her and looked up. "Yes, dear?"

Her heart pounding so loudly in her ears that she could barely speak, Emmaline rasped, "Tomorrow . . . I'll go tomorrow."

Robert did not bother to respond.

Gasping, Adria struggled to match the captain's pace as he strode across the cobbled street toward the docks, leaving the house of ill repute behind them. It occurred to her that Gillian's weight was not the reason for his scowl as he carried her sister easily in his arms. She marveled at his strength, even as she suffered its intimidation.

Heads snapped around at every quarter as they passed. She heard the startled comments, the snickers, the coarse jokes, but as frightened and confused as she was, she paid them little mind.

Gillian's unexpected collapse had numbed her. Gillian, always so strong, so dependable . . .

Startled as she had been by the captain's appearance, Adria had obeyed his orders instinctively. It hadn't been until she had been sent outside that Mr. Higgins had explained it was the captain who had purchased their indentures.

The thought had held little consolation.

The captain had emerged from the room with Gillian in his arms, and Adria had felt her apprehension rise with the realization that Gillian had lit a fire in that great, angry man which he resented and despised but was helpless to extinguish. She feared, however, it would be Gillian who would ultimately be most severely singed by that fire.

The captain stepped up onto the dock and looked back at Adria unexpectedly. His expression was dark and impatient.

"If you expect to reach the ship safely, you'd better keep up!"

Glancing around her, Adria needed no clarification of the captain's statement. An entirely new class of humanity had begun emerging onto the docks with the setting of the sun. She could feel the touch of hot, greedy gazes. Those gazes hurried her step, keeping her in the captain's shadow as he approached the gangplank of the *Colonial Dawn*. In a moment they were climbing.

Adria's breath escaped in a relieved sob as they stepped safely onto the deck a moment later. She heard Gillian whisper to the captain, "Put me down, please. I'm all right. My sister needs me."

The captain's response was flat, accompanied by a deepening of his scowl. "Your sister is a grown woman. It's time she began behaving like one."

Hot color flushed Adria's cheeks. Still close behind him as they walked briskly down the familiar passageway, Adria stopped abruptly as the captain halted outside the room she had formerly occupied. He addressed her flatly.

"This is *your* room."

Adria felt a moment's panic. "But what about Gillian?"

A glare his only response, the captain strode toward his cabin. In a moment, the door slammed closed behind them . . .

. . . and Adria's question was answered.

Poor Gillian.

Adria was still staring at the cabin door through which the captain and Gillian had disappeared when she heard a step on the staircase behind her. Another sob escaped her throat as she turned and Christopher's arms closed around her.

"Put me down, Derek."

Derek looked down at Gillian as he kicked the cabin door closed behind them, but he did not respond. His gaze was hard, his jaw locked. She did not believe she had ever seen him angrier.

But there was something else in his gaze as he walked to the bunk and lowered her to its surface. She attempted to sit up, but he restrained her with the flat of his hand.

"No."

"I want to get up."

"I want to talk to you."

"We can talk while I'm standing up."

Derek's dark eyes held hers. "Are you afraid of me, Gillian?"

"Afraid of you?" Surprising herself, Gillian paused to consider the thought. "No, I'm not afraid of you."

"Lie there, then."

"Why must I—"

"Because you suffered an ordeal today. Because you're still pale. Because I want you to." He sat beside her, silent. She felt the weight of his heady perusal as she returned it in kind. She saw anger in his eyes, tension around his mouth. She remembered the taste of that mouth as it had covered hers minutes earlier . . .

But she didn't want to remember the taste of Derek's mouth! She wanted to remember the words that mouth had spoken so coldly, the words that had sliced at her heart.

It's over.

"I want to get up."

"Gillian . . ."

Gillian's lips tightened. "My sister is alone. She needs me."

"Your sister isn't a child! As long as you keep treating her like one, she'll continue to behave like one. Let her be."

"What do you know about it? She's *my* sister, not yours!"

Derek's jaw tightened. "She may be your sister, but for the next four years, she belongs to me—just as *you* belong to me."

Gillian's chest began an agitated heaving. "Yes, duly purchased and paid for, and at an exorbitant price, if I'm to believe what Mr. Higgins said before you arrived." Gillian paused. "Does that mean that from now on you'll expect me to call you 'master'?"

Derek stiffened. "Perhaps."

"That day will never come!"

"Won't it?"

Gillian held Derek's gaze in silent challenge before continuing. "You paid an exorbitant price for two female bond servants. What do you expect to get for the price you paid?"

Derek's jaw twitched. Gillian saw his anger heighten the moment before he spat, "All right, I've had enough of this! It's time for some plain words."

Grasping her by her shoulders, Derek pinned her against the surface of the bunk. His gaze bit into hers. "I purchased your indenture because I wasn't ready to surrender the intimate relationship between us. Whatever you think of that, you cannot deny you'll be better off bound to me than to Charles Higgins." Derek's expression darkened. "Whether you realize it or not, your potential customers were already lining up in the hallway outside your door."

Gillian's stomach twisted. She swallowed against the bile that rose in her throat. "Really."

"Yes, really, but that's of little consequence now. You belong to *me*. You will belong to me for the next four years. Your duties will be simple. You've already had experience in their execution. You'll live in my quarters and you'll sleep in my bed. Your sister will be hired out to work. I will allow interaction between you and her only as long as it proves to my advantage."

"Bastard . . ."

Derek paused. His voice dropped a menacing note lower. "Perhaps I am, but I tell you now, you will not use that name for me again."

"Oh, yes, I forgot. You prefer that I use the term *'master'*."

A long, uncomfortable silence followed Gillian's response.

"Gillian . . ."

Derek's soft, pained pronunciation of her name was unexpected, as was the light mirroring that pain which entered his eyes as he whispered, "Listen to me, Gillian. Anger will avail us nothing. I'm asking you to put it from your mind so you can remember what I remember. Whatever other circumstances prevailed, it was good between us when we were together, Gillian . . . more than good. You were sweet in my arms, too sweet for me to forget. What I ask of you now is no more than you once willingly offered me."

Derek paused. He kissed her gently. She felt his reluctance as he drew back and continued more softly than before. "I want you, Gillian. I want you enough to have put all other consideration aside. I've paid the price and you are mine. However you feel, I won't let you go—but I *will* make you a promise. I promise to make it good again between us . . . as good as it was before. I promise to make your nights sweet while you lie in my arms. And I also promise you that when that sweetness fades, you will not suffer for the time we have been together."

Gillian swallowed. "When that time comes, will you sell my indenture back to Mr. Higgins?"

Derek drew back sharply. "No, damn it! Haven't you heard anything I've said? When the time comes when we can no longer raise the emotion between us that we formerly shared, I will free you of the intimate exchange between us."

Gillian took a stabilizing breath, holding his gaze. "What if I told you that I wanted to be free of such intimacy now?"

Derek stared intently into her eyes. His deep voice was a passionate rumble that echoed in her heart. "I'd know you lied."

Derek kissed her then. The kiss lingered and Gillian knew . . .

. . . the lie would not prevail.

* * *

"Don't cry, Adria."

Christopher drew Adria into his arms. Standing in the small cabin they had formerly shared, he felt the moistness of her tears as she tucked her face against his neck. He felt her shuddering and he drew her closer. Beautiful Adria, a child, where Gillian was a woman. A needy child . . .

"Adria . . ."

Adria drew back and looked up at him abruptly, and Christopher was struck with sudden realization. Sometime during their past days of separation, the gauntness and shadows of her illness had all but faded. Adria was again Gillian's image—glimmering gold hair, brilliant azure eyes, flawless skin.

Christopher swallowed. It would be so easy to make himself believe it was Gillian he held in his arms . . . that it was Gillian whose lips were so close . . .

Christopher halted the wayward direction of his thoughts. Adria was not Gillian. She was a sweet child who was totally dependent on him. That dependence was a burden he had not anticipated but somehow could not ignore. Nor could he ignore the anguish in her trembling whisper.

"What are we going to do, Christopher?"

A familiar frustration stiffened Christopher's spine. "There's nothing we can do but wait and see what the captain has in mind for us."

"But, Gillian—"

Christopher dropped his arms from around Adria abruptly. Holding her gaze with his, he rasped, "This is my fault, all of it."

Adria shook her head, confused. "What are you saying?"

"Adria . . ." Christopher took a slow breath. "I'm the one who told Gillian to offer herself to the captain." Continuing despite Adria's gasp, he whispered, "I told her there was only one way she could save your life. I told her that because it was true, but I never thought—I never dreamed—"

Adria's eyes brimmed. "Christopher, please . . . don't blame yourself. Don't you think I know how you feel?"

Christopher shook his head. "You couldn't."

"Yes, I do." Adria raised her hand to his cheek, consoling him as he had consoled her so many times. "I understand—surely I do." Adria's voice dropped a note softer. "I love her, too, you know."

So, Adria knew . . .

But Gillian did not—Christopher knew that instinctively, just as he knew that Adria, for all her weaknesses, would not lay the weight of that knowledge on Gillian's already overburdened shoulders.

Meeting the sympathetic blue of Adria's eyes, Christopher slid his arms back around her and drew her against his chest. He was powerless to protect Gillian, but he could and he would protect Adria. He would protect her for Gillian, for Adria . . . and for himself.

Yes . . . for himself. It was his only consolation.

"Let go of my arm, I tell ye!"

Swift turned with a snarl, shaking off Dobbs's clutching grip as the growing din of the dockside tavern grew louder. He was in a nasty mood, as he had been ever since that afternoon when he had seen *"Her Ladyship"* Gillian Harcourt Haige, emerge from Charles Higgins's brothel in Captain Andrews's arms.

The sound of shrill female laughter and loud guffaws erupted into a chorus of a racy ditty as Swift turned back to the bar with a furious snort. Carryin' her like a princess,

the black-clad, black-hearted devil had been, with the bitch's
faint-hearted sister trailing at his heels.

Damn the man!

Swift picked up the glass in front of him. He had emptied
it repeatedly and without caution since he had arrived hours
earlier. That lack of caution was reflected in the unsteadiness
of his hand as he raised the glass to his lips and tossed the
contents down with a cough and a growl.

Aye . . . damn the man! He had almost had the ultimate
satisfaction of walking into the haughty bitch's crib and demanding that she service him. It would've been worth any
wait and any price he would've been asked to pay, for the
memory of it would've lasted through the long weeks of the
return voyage across the sea. But he had been robbed of
that satisfaction and he—

"You're a damned fool, Swift!" Dobbs grasped his arm
once more. Jerking him around so that they were face to
face, he hissed, "You can risk your life in your fury at havin'
missed a chance to taste the pale-haired slut, but I'll be
damned if I'll let you risk mine!"

"Cowardly cur! Get out of here if ye're so afraid that
Barrett's men'll find ye! Save yerself and leave me be!"

"Why? So you may lead Barrett's men back to us and get
Niles's throat and mine slit, as well as your own?"

"There's no chance of that, I tell ye! Master Barrett's forgot all about us for the time bein'. Aye . . . I know the
man . . . He can think of nothin' else right now but that the
tart's escaped him again! Right now he's rantin' and
ravin' . . . but even if he wasn't, he's not a clue as to where
we are. We've been hidin' since we reached port. For all he
knows, we've already sailed. He won't be able to find us
before we sail in the mornin'."

"He will."

"Nay . . ." Swift looked up to see Niles enter and make his way directly toward them across the crowded floor. Niles's face was grimly set and Swift gave a short laugh. "What's this? Reinforcements? Are ye intendin' to drag me back to yer hidyhole so Barrett's men won't get us?"

Dobbs's weasellike face grew tight. "If we must."

Swift did not immediately respond as his expression gradually sobered. "It does not bother ye, does it, that the bitch came up on the sunny side of it all, with the bastard captain takin' her back to his cabin and installin' her there like she was a queen."

Dobbs scanned the tavern nervously, then responded with a hiss, "Nay, and neither does it bother Niles. Neither of us had the taste of that witch's white flesh in our mouth as did you. That was your mistake—foolin' yourself that you'd ever have her!"

"I almost did!" Spittle sprayed from Swift's lips as he raised a shaking fist. "I almost had her!"

"Aye." Dobbs nodded toward Niles, giving the signal as they grasped his arms, lifting him to his feet. They ushered Swift toward the door in a rush so rapid that Swift laughed aloud.

"Ye're afraid of yer own shadows, I tell ye! Barrett won't—"

"Be quiet, damn you!"

Ignoring Niles's short command as they emerged out onto the dark street, Swift laughed loudly again. He was enjoying their agitation almost as much as he was enjoying the luxury of being all but carried through the shadows toward the docks.

Ignoring Dobbs's harsh warning and Niles's grumbling words, Swift raised his voice in a song that echoed into the darkness. He closed his eyes, indulging his pleasure as

Dobbs and Niles turned him down a nearby alley, as they drew him along toward the small room they had shared since arriving in port. He was offering another jeering comment on their fear when they released him so unexpectedly that he fell to his knees.

"Ye filthy knaves!" Swift attempted to lift himself upright. "I'll get ye for this, and I'll—"

The sight of the inert bodies of Dobbs and Niles lying behind him brought Swift's words to an abrupt halt—as did the hardly discernible figures moving toward him in the darkness.

He caught his breath as he heard the words spoken in a harsh hiss.

"Mr. Barrett sends his greetin's . . ."

Then a blade at his throat—a hot rush of blood from the wound—and a curse that went unuttered from lips that would speak no more.

Shadows flickered along the secluded shoreline as a rowboat slowed to a halt a distance from shore. The burly, shadowy figures within rolled first one, then a second and a third sack into the dark water.

The splashes rebounded in the silence.

The ripples spread.

The sacks sank and disappeared from sight . . .

. . . as all was claimed by the night.

Night enveloped the cabin in shadows that moved with the ship's gentle sway. Lying in Derek's arms, Gillian felt the familiar pressure of his naked length against her, and she closed her eyes against the bittersweet joy of it. She felt the touch of his mouth against her lips, her throat, her breasts. She felt him probe. She felt him fill her. She heard his whispered words of passion.

Her arms closed around him. Those words would be enough . . . for now . . . until morning . . . until . . .

Thirteen

Emmaline fidgeted impatiently as her carriage rattled along the cobbled Kingston street. It was early morning—far *too* early. Waking at the break of dawn to the sight of Robert dressing for a day in the fields, she had pretended sleep, waiting only until he had left the house before rising, too, and shouting for Jubba.

But the morning had not gone well. The temperature of the day had been uncomfortably warm, the air unpleasantly moist, and the servants annoyingly slow. She had been hot, fatigued, and irritated before the day had truly begun, so much so that she had finally decided upon wearing her pale-green batiste rather than the silk gown she had intended wearing the previous day. She had not accepted that concession with grace.

Granted, the green batiste was as daringly cut in the bodice as the silk. It displayed enough creamy skin and womanly curves to reveal at a glance that the years Derek and she had been apart had increased her beauty instead of diminishing it. The color was extremely flattering, picking up the variegated shades of green that flickered in her eyes, but it lacked the elegance of the green silk. Also, because of the transparency of the fragile fabric, it did not allow the donning of the black undergarments she had saved specifically for Derek's return.

The graceful curve of Emmaline's lips ticked with annoyance. Of course, Robert had rent a part of her perfectly matched black undergarments beyond repair prior to the sessions of unprecedented passion they had spent together the previous day.

The fragile planes of Emmaline's face colored unexpectedly. Damn! She was still uncertain what had gotten into her! She had not truly realized that Robert had acquired so great a skill in arousing her.

Emmaline's lips twitched once more. Were things different at this particular moment in time, she might have been amused at that thought, but she presently was not. Instead, she was merely *tired*. Robert had worn her to the bone through the long day, and his attentions had not relented throughout the night. She had wanted to go to Derek with her energy at its highest level. Instead, she was fatigued, uncomfortable, irritable, and growing more impatient by the second.

But she would be damned if she'd lose another hour before she saw Derek! She had been waiting too long for this moment! She would please him, at *any* expense, and with the aid of Pucku's power, freshly summoned by William Gnu, he would not be able to resist her.

Emmaline gritted her teeth with determination. Derek had belonged to her once. He would again. She would not relent.

Her heart skipping a beat as the carriage turned onto Port Royal Street and the docks came into full view, Emmaline scanned the tall-masted ships littering the harbor for a sight of the *Colonial Dawn*. Anticipation leaped inside her as she spotted the familiar vessel.

"Drive faster, Quaco!"

The elderly driver nodded and slapped the reins against the team's backs. Annoyed when the effort elicited little improvement in their pace, Emmaline snapped, "Make them move faster, Quaco, or you will be sorry that you did not!"

Another slap of the reins sent the carriage a quick leap forward that almost dislodged Emmaline from her seat. Holding on for dear life as the carriage flew over the cobbled street, Emmaline was cursing aloud when they drew to a clattering halt on the dock in front of the *Colonial Dawn* minutes later.

Struggling to set her appearance back to right, Emmaline whispered at the aged driver in an agitated hiss as he descended to help her alight. "You old fool! I told you to drive faster, not to abandon all caution!" She accepted his hand and stepped down onto the dock, staring hotly up into his dark, wrinkled face. "You will wait here for me, and you will not move from this spot for any reason! Do you understand?"

The old slave nodded, and Emmaline sniffed, her temper mollified. The hot sun baking Quaco's brain while she passed the morning in the comfort of Derek's cabin would teach the old dolt a thing or two about guarding his mistress's safety as well as her comfort.

Turning toward the ship, Emmaline straightened her spine and walked determinedly forward. She ignored the inquisitive glance of the tall, well-built seaman on deck as she climbed the gangplank. She did not smile as she stepped down on deck, offering by way of response to his inquiring glance, "I'm here to see the captain. You needn't announce me. I know the way."

A shaft of golden morning sunlight shone through the porthole of Derek's cabin, accompanied by a warm morning breeze that alleviated the nighttime closeness. Derek breathed deeply, conscious of the fragrance of the island that blended subtly with the scent of salt air and sea, giving it new life.

Lying on his side watching Gillian as she slept, it occurred to Derek that Gillian's entrance into his life had much in common with the fragrant breeze now bathing them. She had blended subtly with his life during those long weeks of the voyage, becoming a part of it as much as the floral fragrance of the island became a part of the sea breeze. She had filled his life with her fragrance and her fragrance had become instilled in his senses. Somehow, he had felt unable to breathe without it.

But Gillian belonged to him now. It occurred to him it was somehow ironic that a man who had always discredited the system of indenture should now hold the indenture of *three*.

Two of those indentures he could definitely do without. But the third—

Derek scowled. It had been hard—damned hard—admitting to himself that Gillian had touched him in a way no other woman had ever touched him before. It had been harder, however, admitting to himself that he wanted her even if she did not feel the same about him in return. He had fired back at the viciously nagging voice in his mind that whatever Gillian felt for Christopher Gibson, her feelings had not interfered with the beauty of the moments she had spent in his arms—that when she lay in his intimate embrace, no one stood between them. He believed that to be true with all his heart.

But even if it were not, he knew it would have made little difference—for one, simple reason. In his heart and mind, however temporarily, Gillian belonged to him. He had had no choice but to make that situation a legality from which she could not escape.

Four years.

Would they prove too long . . .

. . . or too short?

And where would Gillian go from there?

A hot rush of emotion swelled as Derek slid his arms around Gillian and drew her close. But he need not concern himself with the future when Gillian was presently lying in his arms. While Gillian belonged to him, he would not contemplate a time when she would not. Nor would he consider a time when any man's arms other than his would hold her or when—

Gillian's eyelids flickered, drawing the heated progression of Derek's thoughts to a sharp halt. He waited for her eyes to open, holding his breath, anticipating the moment her gaze would first meet his. That was the way it should be— *his* eyes the first Gillian would see each morning, *his* gaze the last hers would meet each night—*his* lips the first and last to touch hers.

Derek brushed Gillian's mouth lightly with his. Her lips moved under his kiss. A familiar hunger stirred. His kiss deepened . . .

The click of the passageway door raised Derek's head abruptly, the moment before it opened to slap back against the cabin wall.

Incredulous, momentarily speechless, Derek stared at the woman standing boldly in the doorway. He felt Gillian stiffen as the woman demanded in a voice cold with rage, "Who is this woman, Derek?"

The loud crack of the captain's cabin door reverberated in the silence of Adria's cabin and she jumped with a start.

A brief silence followed, then the mumble of voices growing louder, and Adria began a slow trembling.

Something was wrong.

Unconsciously fastening the last buttons on her dress, Adria walked closer to her cabin door, straining to hear. She heard a woman's voice—but it wasn't Gillian's. In the sharp exchange that followed, Gillian's voice was strangely absent.

Uncertain, shaking harder each moment, Adria listened and waited.

"Get out of here, Emmaline."

Ignoring his demand, her beautiful face flushed, Emmaline stared at Derek with the fury of a woman betrayed. Incensed at her audacity, Derek released Gillian and slipped out from underneath the coverlet, standing naked for the few moments it took to don his britches and face Emmaline once more.

Advancing into the cabin, Emmaline stood rigidly in place as Derek grasped her by the arm. Refusing to move, she stared malevolently at Gillian.

"Who is this streggah?"

"I wouldn't be so free with name calling if I were you."

Emmaline looked up at Derek, rage changing abruptly to an earnest appeal that would once have touched his heart as she spoke in a throbbing whisper. "I was never a streggah, Derek. *You* are the only man I've ever loved. Tell her to leave. You don't need her anymore. I'll give you all the love you will ever need, my darling."

Derek paused, incredulity soaring. If he did not know better, if he had not learned in the most difficult of ways the kind of woman that lay beneath Emmaline's innocent exterior, he would think—

Derek turned to look at Gillian. Her thoughts were written in the pallor of her skin and in the torment in her eyes. No, she didn't deserve to suffer—not from Emmaline's lies.

Derek grasped Emmaline's arm more firmly. She protested vigorously as he ushered her toward the door. Waiting only until it had closed behind them and they were alone in the passageway, Emmaline tore her arm from his grip. She thrust herself against him, winding her arms around his neck, her slenderness tight against him as she pulled his mouth down to hers. He felt her trembling, sensed her growing passion the moment before he jerked himself back from her.

"You're wasting your time, Emmaline. I've told you that before."

Emmaline's expression grew determined. "You didn't mean it then and you don't mean it now. You love me! You'll always love me!"

"I *never* loved you."

"Liar! You loved me! You said you did!"

"I was a young fool. I didn't know the meaning of the word."

"You *killed* a man for me!"

Emmaline's words rebounded in the silent passageway. Astounded, Derek saw it flash again—the same excitement, the same exhilaration he had seen in her eyes when he had stood beaten and bloodied over the dead seaman's body.

His heart turned to stone.

"Derek . . . you know you can't forget me. You love me."

His gaze frigid, Derek spoke in soft response. "Listen to me, Emmaline, and try to understand what I'm saying. I never loved you. I was obsessed by you."

"It's the same thing!"

"No, it isn't. Love has nothing to do with the mindless-
ness that possessed me those years ago."

"No . . . no . . . you loved me then. You love me now."

Emmaline attempted to throw herself into his arms again,
but Derek held her off. "Call it whatever you will, Emmaline, but whatever feelings I had for you then are now
dead. Nothing can revive them. You have a good life. Go
back to it and enjoy—"

"You're angry because I married Robert, aren't you!" Emmaline's eyes grew wide. "What could I do, Derek? My
father was killed shortly after you went to prison and I was
alone! Robert was wealthy and he wanted to take care of
me. But he's old, Derek! He won't live long. When he dies,
we can have everything!"

"No, we can't."

"Yes we can if you'll just—"

Derek looked up at the sound of a step on the stairs. He
nodded toward the tentative glances of Cutter and Haskell
as they descended, ignoring Emmaline as her voice trailed
on. They were standing beside her when he interrupted her
with his flat admonition.

"Go home, Emmaline. Go back to your husband."

Emmaline's face flamed. "It's that pale-haired streggah in
your bed, isn't it! She's amusing you temporarily and you
think you can forget me!" Emmaline did not wait for his
reply. "You're making a mistake. You and she can never have
what you and *I* can have together! I can fill your life with
passion like none you've ever known. You know I can do it,
Derek! Just think back and remember . . ."

"Go home, Emmaline."

Gasping as the seamen took her by the arms in answer
to Derek's silent command, Emmaline stared at him in disbelief. Her head jerked toward the click of a door opening

nearby. A choked sound escaped her lips as Adria appeared in the slitted opening.

"There are *two* of them?" Emmaline's gaze turned hot with fury. "Bastard!"

Derek did not bother to respond.

Her protests halting as Cutter and Haskell turned her firmly toward the staircase, Emmaline waited until she had mounted the first step before calling back to him in malevolent promise. "You'll come back to me, Derek. You'll come back begging. And then, my darling . . . then, we'll see."

Breathing a sigh of relief as Emmaline slipped from sight, Derek turned back to his cabin. He halted abruptly as he met Adria's accusing gaze.

Irate, he growled, "Get back in there!"

Adria's door snapped shut behind him as Derek paused before his cabin.

Trembling with fury, Emmaline attempted to jerk herself free of the two burly seamen as she reached the gangplank. Unsuccessful, she burned them with a hot, imperious gaze.

"I won't be needing your assistance any farther."

"Sorry, ma'am." The taller of the two seamen, a big, sandy-haired fellow smiled uncomfortably. "The captain wants us to escort you off the ship."

Emmaline's eyes shot green fire. "I *told* you that I—"

Emmaline's words were brought to a gasping halt as the seamen grasped her elbows, lifting her with ease as they ushered her down the gangplank. She was seething as they deposited her on the dock, nodded politely, and turned back toward the ship. Her harsh shout at their retreating backs rang on the early-morning silence of the docks.

"You stupid oafs! Your captain has made a mistake today—a mistake he'll regret, and you have compounded it with your mishandling of me! The day will come when your captain will go down on his knees for my return, and when that day comes, you'll regret your treatment of me as much as he! As for the two streggahs below . . ." Emmaline's jaw hardened. "I'll see to it that you both have your chance at them! You are deserving of each other!"

Turning in a rage as Quaco approached, Emmaline spat, "Fool! Where were you when I needed you! Help me up into the carriage! When I return home you may be certain I will tell the massa that you are too old to be of any real use. What will you do then?"

Expecting no response from her raging tirade, Emmaline cast aside the old slave's helping hand and stepped up into the carriage. She sat stiffly, her furious green eyes blazing as the carriage snapped into motion and the face of the woman who had been lying in Derek's bed returned once more to haunt her.

. . . *Woman wit hair like moon in de sky* . . .

Damn William Gnu! He had not told her there were *two* of them!

Damn them both!

She'd have her way and she'd make them *all* pay!

But until then . . .

"Who is she?"

Unable to tear his gaze from the red-haired woman whose carriage was driving briskly away from the dock a short distance away, John Barrett turned toward the lean, shaggy-haired, ill-kempt fellow beside him. When there was no response, he snarled, "I asked you who that red-haired woman is!"

Barrett's gaze snapped back toward the *Colonial Dawn* as the carriage moved out of sight. His mood was vile. He had not forgotten the amused expression on Charles Higgins's face when he arrived at the fellow's seedy brothel the previous evening, nor would he forget the bastard's off-handed response to his inquiry . . .

"Oh, the sisters, yes, they were a true novelty. Incredible to believe, but my patrons were actually beginning to line up outside their door until Captain Andrews showed up." Higgins had then shrugged. "The captain is a rather unpleasant fellow—so much animosity—but I simply could not refuse his offer. I will, of course, refund the sum you paid in advance to reserve the sisters' services." Higgins had then counted out the money. Looking up, the slovenly ass had added with a wink, "In case you should change your mind, I have two very special ladies you might be interested in—both blondes and similar in appearance, and both very, very good at what they do."

Barrett's rage soared anew. He should've known better than to trust the word of an odious degenerate such as Charles Higgins! He had made a costly error, but Captain Andrews's victory was only temporary. He would yet have his revenge on the bastard captain, and he would yet have the pleasure of sating himself on the pale-haired bitch's sweet flesh . . . of bending her to his whims . . . of indulging his most perverted fantasies.

Barrett's jaw locked tight. He had been allowed only one gratification the previous evening—the confirmation that Will Swift and the other two ingrates who had betrayed him would never open their eyes to another dawn.

But that satisfaction had been brief as nagging fury had risen anew, interrupting his sleep, driving him to the early-morning surveillance of the *Colonial Dawn* in the company

of the fellow at his side. So agitated had he been upon aris-
ing that he had neither bothered to bathe nor eat. As a result
he was now hot, tired, hungry, and heavily steeped in his
own bodily odor. Too obsessed to care, Barrett turned toward
the man beside him, his expression grim.

"I'll not ask you again, Peters . . ."

Peters's shifty-eyed gaze met his, and Barrett's gaze narrowed. He had used the services of Peters and his anonymous henchmen before. He had always been satisfied that
they did their work swiftly, competently, and discreetly. He
was secure in using their services because liberal payment
aside, he knew Peters *enjoyed* his work. It occurred to Barrett as Peters smiled unexpectedly, then started to speak, that
the fellow's smile was almost as lewd as the man himself.

"It took a moment to place 'er, Master Barrett. Aye, she
ain't seen too often on the docks, y'know."

"You're wasting my time."

" 'Er name's Emmaline Dorsett. She's a rare piece, is that
one. 'Er husband's old and rich and she's got full rein to do
just about anythin' she likes because of it."

Barrett nodded. He had heard the red-haired witch's furious tirade. A woman scorned . . .

"What *does* she like?"

"She likes black magic, does that one. She likes the power
of it."

"And men?"

"There's a story about 'er. It happened before I came to
the island . . . about 'er lover killin' a man out of jealousy
of 'er. The bloke went to prison for it, 'e did."

Barrett was instantly alert. "What was the man's name?"

"I don't know 'is name."

Perspiration rolled unheeded down Barrett's cheeks as he

snapped, "Find out! Come back with that information and you'll be handsomely rewarded."

"Aye, Mr. Barrett." Peters nodded. "I'll get you what you want."

Anticipation rose inside Barrett. Emmaline Dorsett . . . somehow he was certain the red-haired witch would be the key . . .

His gaze riveted on the *Colonial Dawn* where she rocked gently at her mooring, Barrett was not conscious of the moment when Peters slipped away as a familiar agitation squeezed tight inside him. Gillian Harcourt Haige, the haughty bitch that she was, would pay heavily for the night just past, spent in the bastard captain's arms.

They would all pay—Andrews, the bitch's sniveling sister, the rutting Gibson—he'd see to it! But most of all, Gillian Harcourt Haige would pay for making him suffer anticipation for yet another day.

"I owe you no explanations, Gillian."

"Nor have I asked for one."

The coverlet clutched tightly around her nakedness as she stood beside the bunk from which she had arisen moments earlier, Gillian stood stiff and silent in response to Derek's cold declaration. He had returned to the cabin from the emotional confrontation in the passageway with his jaw set, his eyes cold. It occurred to her as her gaze briefly lingered that the man in whose arms she had awakened minutes earlier was gone. He had disappeared with the unexpected opening of the cabin door, at first sight of the red-haired woman standing there. In his place was this half-naked, intimidating stranger who eyed her with startling coldness.

Approaching to stand towering over her, Derek looked

down at Gillian for long, silent moments. His eyes were veiled, his strong, handsome features harshly composed as he spoke abruptly. "You heard what was said in the passageway?"

"Most of it."

"Emmaline deludes herself with thoughts of what we may again be to each other. I have no control over her delusions."

"She loves you."

"Emmaline loves only herself."

"She wants you back."

"She will never get that wish."

"She's beautiful."

"Yes . . . she is."

Gillian took a steadying breath. "She said you *killed* a man because of her."

Derek's gaze turned to ice. "I did."

Gillian shuddered despite herself, despising the sudden flash of nausea that stole her breath. She halted Derek's sudden step forward with the harshness in her tone.

"I suppose, then, that I should be glad that you do not 'love' me."

Derek paused. His expression tightened into a formidable mask totally devoid of warmth. "In the event you need be reminded, I will say the words again. You *belong* to me, Gillian. It makes little difference what I feel for you. You are mine to do with as I please."

Anger dispelling her brief weakness, Gillian forced a brittle smile, "Yes . . . you are my *master.*"

"I advise you not to forget it."

A world of meaning behind her reply, Gillian responded slowly, "You need not fear that I will ever, *even for a moment,* forget."

Turning her back on the flash of fury in Derek's gaze, Gillian was conscious of Derek's agitated breathing behind her, then the swish of movement as he snatched up his shirt. She heard him walk toward the door, then the sound of the latch clicking as he grasped the handle.

Gillian closed her eyes briefly. Taking a steadying breath, she raised her chin, then dropped the blanket to the floor.

His hand on the door, Derek halted abruptly. His bared chest heaving with emotions under tenuous control, he turned back toward Gillian. His heart skipped a beat as she reached for her clothing, allowing the blanket that had formerly shielded her nakedness to slip to the floor.

Derek followed the smooth, slender lines of Gillian's body with his gaze, the tension inside him increasing. He had returned to the cabin furious at Emmaline's audacity, only to be faced with a silent accusation in Gillian's eyes. Cutting him more deeply, however, had been the coldness he had seen where softness had formerly glowed, and his fury had swelled. That fury had forced harsh truths from his lips, truths that had extended a distance between Gillian and him that had momentarily appeared unbreachable.

Gillian stiffened briefly before picking up her undergarments, leaving no doubt that she was aware of his perusal. He noted with increasing annoyance that she did not turn back toward him as she drew on her underdrawers, then her chemise. Waiting until they were firmly in place, she finally faced him . . . but the effort was wasted. The outline of her rounded breasts was still visible through the fine batiste cloth, as was the shadow between her thighs. He saw her lips twitch as she followed the line of his gaze, and his annoyance deepened. Full-fledged anger soared once more when she spoke with familiar and infuriating hauteur.

"Is there something you wanted?"

Closing the distance between them in a few, quick strides, his chest heaving with emotions held under tenuous control, Derek slipped his arm abruptly around Gillian. He held her fast as he slid his hand underneath the drawstring waist of her underdrawers and cupped the warm nest between her thighs with his palm. At her gasp, he whispered, "It astounds me that you're still unclear on that point, Mistress Gillian Haige. I've already told you what I want from you. What I haven't told you—what I'm telling you now—is that what I want from you has nothing to do with what happened between me and any other woman."

Derek's heart raced as he found the tender bud of Gillian's femininity and stroked it gently. Easily subduing her brief struggles, he whispered, "Understand that, Gillian, once and for all, and understand this—that this emotion we share, this emotion even now surging through you, is the ultimate truth between us."

His intimate strokes growing more searching, his heart pounding with increasing impetus, Derek saw Gillian's angry eyes grow slowly glazed. Lowering his mouth to hers, he trailed his tongue warmly against her parted lips, the responsive moisture that surged against his hand almost stealing his breath as he rasped, "Gillian, don't you see? When we're together there are no other people in the world—only you and me and what we make each other feel. It's happening again. You feel it . . . I know you do. Tell me . . . whisper the words . . . tell me what you feel."

"Derek—" Gillian's voice faded as Derek's stroking touch deepened. She went gradually lax in his arms, her thighs separating, and his breathing grew more ragged.

"I want you to feel good, Gillian . . . that's what I want from you. I want you to feel as good as I feel when I hold you in my arms. I want you to feel wonder when I touch you like this. I want you to know that right here and now, there's nothing more important than the two of us together . . ."

"Derek . . ."

"You know it's true, Gillian. Don't fight what you feel."

Gillian was trembling. Her eyes were passionately narrowed, her face flushed, her lips parted. She was shuddering more intensely. The time was near . . .

Another tremor shook her. "Please . . ."

"Let the passion flow, Gillian. Let it rise. Let it sweep over you."

"Derek—"

The edge of panic in Gillian's voice was reflected in her eyes as well as they widened briefly.

"Let me feel your heat, Gillian. Gillian—"

Gillian's breath caught in her throat as the spasms started, as her slender body throbbed with passion, quaking . . .

Shifting Gillian subtly in his arms, Derek freed her of her underdrawers. Freed of his own clothing as well, he supported her in his arms, holding her upright against him as he fitted himself intimately to her. With a quick thrust, he impaled her lovingly with his throbbing need.

Gillian met his gaze with startled intensity, her eyes slowly closing as Derek began moving sensuously within her, and passion assumed control. A slow exaltation began inside Derek as Gillian's short, impassioned breaths bathed his lips, as she gradually joined the sweet rhythm of their sensuous dance, as their mutual need grew greater . . . stronger.

The moment of culmination came abruptly, their mutual gasps shattering the silence of the cabin as Derek clasped Gillian close, their bodies locked in the release of vibrant emotions soaring once more.

Supporting Gillian, holding her erect as the convulsive spasms stilled, Derek kissed her parted lips gently, lingeringly. He drew back to whisper as her slitted gaze rose to his, "This is what I want from you, Gillian." He kissed her again, tearing his lips from hers to rasp, "And this is what you can't deny me—because this is what you want as well."

Realization shuddered through Gillian as her gaze held his. It reverberated deep within him as he scooped her up into his arms and carried her to the nearby bunk.

No further words spoken between them, minutes later he was gone.

"Where is she, Jubba?"

Robert Dorsett's small smile did not ring true. The frightened Negress trembled under his intense gaze as they stood on the outer steps of the great house, but he felt little of his usual concern as he pressed her once more.

"I asked you where your mistress has gone. I expect an answer, Jubba."

The slender slave raised a trembling hand to her lightbrown cheek. "Jubba not sure, massa. Quaco take de carriage out dis mornin' and de mistress get in. Dat all Jubba know."

Robert paused, his smile fading. The bright morning sun had barely risen when he had slipped out of bed and dressed for the day's work. He had left the house reluctantly. Had it not been for the necessity of his presence in the fields at this crucial period, he would have remained abed, entertaining his beautiful wife. Nothing would have given him more pleasure, although he knew he had all but worn out his dear Emmaline with his antics the previous day. Emmaline had appeared to be sleeping so soundly that he had honestly believed she would lie abed until noon, despite the presence of the *Colonial Dawn* in port.

A familiar agitation stirred within Robert. Dear, beautiful Emmaline . . . self-absorbed, cunning, sometimes-cruel Emmaline . . .

He should have known better.

He also should have known that Jubba's fear of her mistress's unstable temperament during these periods was such that she would not dare say more. He could not really blame the poor slave. He had heard some of Emmaline's threats. They had chilled his blood.

The sun beat down on Robert's shoulders, raising his discomfort as he pressed more softly than before, "When did your mistress leave, Jubba?"

"Dis mornin'."

"What time?" Robert glanced unconsciously toward the position of the sun, not yet at the midpoint of the sky.

"Early, massa."

"Did she—"

The rattle of an approaching carriage interrupted Robert's question. He turned toward the sound as Jubba pointed toward the road. "Here missus come, massa! Jubba go inside now, massa?"

Robert nodded, the sound of Jubba's rapid retreat registering in the back of his mind as he turned toward the carriage's approach. Stiffening, he prepared himself mentally to face Emmaline, as he had many times before when Captain Andrews's ship was in port. He had not long to wait.

The carriage drew to a halt and Robert was momentarily startled. If he didn't know better, he would've thought Emmaline had been crying!

Approaching the carriage in a brisk step, Robert realized

Emmaline's agitation was genuine as she ignored Quaco's proffered hand and reached instead for his.

"Robert . . ." Emmaline grasped his hand tightly as he helped her down. Her voice was choked. "I've had a terrible morning."

Sliding his arm around her, Robert drew Emmaline against his shoulder. She was trembling. Concerned, he drew her closer.

"Emmaline dear, what happened?"

Emmaline struggled to respond. "Everything went wrong. I arose early—s-so I could look at the new shipment of gowns at Madame's. The ride into town was hot and dusty . . . the air heavy. I was so uncomfortable. Then when I got there . . ." Emmaline's lips tightened. "The gowns were terrible . . . all the wrong color and size. I left immediately."

A tinge of misery entered Emmaline's tone as she continued, "Then Quaco drove like a novice on the way home, hitting every rut and bump in the road. He drove so badly that I actually had to make him stop so I could vomit!"

"Oh, my dear . . ."

Emmaline drew back, her green eyes moist, her skin pale. "I'm so glad you're here. You always make me feel better, Robert dear."

Kissing Emmaline's trembling lips, Robert drew her along with him toward the house as he whispered reassuringly, "You're tired, dear. You need some rest. We'll go upstairs and rest . . . together."

Almost tempted to laugh at Emmaline's short, wary glance toward him, he whispered into her ear, "We'll have Jubba bring us up something to eat and then I'll make love to you as I never did before. We'll spend the afternoon lying in each other's arms."

Watching Emmaline's expression carefully, Robert added as if in afterthought, "Then, tomorrow, we'll go to that goldsmith you favor, and we'll have him make up those earrings you've been wanting . . . the ones with the emeralds that match your eyes."

"Oh, Robert," Emmaline attempted a smile, "you are a dear."

Walking up the staircase beside Emmaline, Robert glanced sympathetically toward his dear wife. He recognized the signs.

Captain Andrews had sent her away again.

Robert silently sighed. He was truly grateful that the captain was a stronger man than he could ever hope to be in that regard. He knew, however, he must maintain his vigilance. Emmaline was such a determined young woman.

Robert's eyes briefly hardened. Emmaline was almost as determined as he.

That thought in mind as they reached the top of the staircase, Robert drew Emmaline toward the bedroom with a smile.

Her fingers working nimbly, Gillian twisted her heavy silver-gold mane into a tidy knot and pinned it atop her head. She frowned at the fine wisps that curled at her hairline, despairing at their stubbornness as she turned toward the door. She was annoyed with herself for having allowed so great a part of the morning to escape before checking on Adria, but somehow . . .

Memory of Derek's impassioned attentions earlier returned, raising a flush to her cheeks. Derek was her master. She belonged to him. He had reminded her of that fact too many times during the night and morning past for her to forget it, but she knew that reality had nothing to do with the emotions he aroused within her.

Angry Derek . . . bitter Derek . . . unyielding Derek . . . possessive Derek . . . *loving* Derek, he was all those things. Strangely, he inspired those same emotions within her as well, and she wondered, when he no longer wanted her, would she ever be the same again?

When he no longer wanted her . . .

Gillian stumbled briefly in her step. Annoyed at her lapse, she drew the door open, guilt flushing once more as she approached Adria's door. Poor Adria, waiting and wondering . . .

The thought abruptly occurring that Adria might have heard the explosive confrontation between Derek and his visitor earlier, that she might have been frightened as well, she knocked lightly on the cabin door and then pushed it open anxiously.

The cabin was empty. Stunned, Gillian glanced around her. Adria's bag was still there, neatly stored, and the bunk had been carefully made up. But where was she?

Emerging onto the main deck moments later, Gillian squinted in the brilliance of the sun. She looked around her anxiously, then ran to the rail to look down onto the dock.

Where was Adria?

Panic was making strong inroads into Gillian's mind when she felt a strong hand on her arm. All trace of earlier passion erased from the cold depths of his eyes, Derek demanded, "What's wrong?"

"I-I can't find Adria."

Derek's hand tightened. "She's gone."

"Gone?"

"She went to work."

Stunned, Gillian was momentarily speechless. "To work? Where?"

"The Royal Arms Tavern."

"A tavern!" Gillian gasped. "Adria?" Gillian could feel herself pale. "Surely you're joking!"

Derek's jaw tightened. "She started work in the tavern kitchen this morning. Gibson will be working there, too, until we ship out again."

Adria working . . . ship out . . . Gillian's mind whirled. Anger halted the whirling abruptly. "What about me?"

Derek's gaze grew wary. "What do you mean?"

"Why didn't you send me with them?"

Derek's jaw tightened. "Because you won't be working there. Your duties are of an entirely different nature."

A hot rush of color flushed Gillian's face. "So, I'm to remain on this ship awaiting your whim while my sister does physical labor in a tavern kitchen, exposed to—"

"Do you think I'm a fool?" Derek's features tightened. "I'm aware that Adria is a beautiful woman. Gibson has his orders not to let her out of his sight. He knows what will happen to him if he fails to follow those orders."

"I don't doubt Christopher's intentions! He would protect Adria without any instructions from you, merely because he cares about her as he cares about both of us!"

"Really? Well, perhaps it might be best if Gibson didn't *care* so much! Caring gets in the way of clear thought."

"Oh, yes, it would be a mistake to be motivated by *caring*, wouldn't it, Derek." Gillian forced a smile. "I suppose I should be grateful that no such emotion will ever taint the relationship between us."

Gillian halted abruptly, forcing away another unexpected swell of nausea with a determined breath. She continued a moment later. "In any case, I prefer to work with my sister."

"You have no choice in the matter."

"Do I not?" Control rapidly slipping away, Gillian attempted to shake her arm free of Derek's grasp. "Let me go! I'll find the Royal Arms by myself!"

"You'll do no such thing!"

"I will!"

"No, damn it, you won't!"

Sweeping her from her feet before she was conscious of his intent, Derek carried her across the deck. She was kicking and squirming, protesting loudly, unconscious of the seamen they were drawing from all quarters of the ship as Derek started down the staircase she had climbed only minutes earlier. She was still protesting when he pushed their cabin door open with his shoulder, then kicked it closed behind them. She saw the tight lock of his jaw the moment before he stood her on her feet. She heard the ominous warning in his voice as he spoke softly.

"Don't *ever* do that again."

Gillian returned his stare. "Do what?"

"Disobey me!"

"Oh, yes . . . *master.*"

"Gillian . . ." Derek grasped her arms, his fingers cutting tightly into the soft flesh. "Do you really think I would allow you to work in the Royal Arms Tavern—exposed to lustful stares and ribald comments?"

"But you sent my sister there, damn you!"

"Your sister is protected."

"As I would be!"

"No. No man will extend that kind of protection over you but *me.*"

Gillian was momentarily speechless. "That's absurd! Christopher is capable of—"

Derek halted her response with a hard shake. His gaze was intense. *"No one* but *me."*

Frustration soared, raising Gillian's anger a dangerous notch higher. "Take your hands off me! I won't remain idly by while my sister is sent off to work in a waterfront tavern!"

"You will do what I say."

"I won't!"

"You will, if I have to lock you in this cabin in order to make you stay here!"

Despising the tears that unexpectedly flooded her eyes, Gillian rasped, "It's demeaning! I'm not a concubine! I will not have you make one out of me!"

"You have no choice in the matter!"

"I do!"

"Gillian, I warn you . . . I will do what I have to do to keep you here. If that means selling off your sister's indenture—"

Gillian caught her breath. "You don't mean that. You wouldn't separate Adria and me."

Derek did not respond.

Releasing her arm after long moments, Derek brushed a wisp of hair back from her cheek. She saw a emotion curiously close to pain in his eyes as he whispered, "Your sister is safe. I won't have this discussion again."

In a moment Derek was gone, leaving only harsh reality behind.

"I'm fine, Christopher. Please don't worry."

The aroma of smoke and roasting meat filled the kitchen of the Royal Arms Tavern. Deep male voices echoed in from the public room, mingling with the clatter of dishes and pans, the sizzle of searing meat, and the ring of clipped orders issued by harried barmaids as Adria turned to walk briskly across the kitchen toward the worktable in the corner.

Adria's reassurance was useless. Christopher did worry. He had been worrying since the captain had given Adria and him orders to report to the tavern after the fiasco with that red-haired termagant in the captain's cabin that morning. The captain had been in a foul mood and Christopher had not liked leaving Gillian alone the entire day with him. Nor had he liked being instructed to guard Adria's welfare in a tavern where her unusual beauty was certain to attract attention—as if he would not have acted instinctively in her behalf without the captain's admonition.

Christopher's jaw ticked with suppressed anger. The captain did not fool him! The bastard hadn't issued him those orders out of concern for Adria. He had done it as a deliberate reminder of his power over them.

His stomach churning, Christopher assessed Adria's expression as she worked with nimble, experienced fingers, slipping the crusts she had mixed and rolled earlier onto the meat pies awaiting them. A few slits of the knife and a quick shifting on the metal trays and they were ready for the oven. Adria's face was pink from the heat of the room, but her expression was confident. That unexpected confidence continued to amaze him.

Christopher glanced toward the tavern owner's wife, seated in the corner of the room, her swollen foot resting on a padded stool. He saw that the old woman followed Adria's progress with an expression that was almost euphoric, in sharp contrast with her reaction when she had first glimpsed Adria's fragile beauty and soft-spoken ways.

Peeling potatoes by rote from the endless sack in front of him, Christopher saw Adria hesitate as the tray of pies was taken from the table by a robust young helper and delivered to an oven outside. He saw her concerned expression as she looked at the tavern owner's wife, then walked to her side and leaned toward her with a solicitous whisper. The woman nodded after a brief exchange. Startled, he saw Adria begin to unwrap the woman's bandages. He stood abruptly as Adria stepped back, her face whitening when the foot was uncovered.

Adria turned toward him as he reached her side. She clutched his hand.

"Oh, Christopher . . . look!"

"Aye, 'tis a nasty wound." The old woman winced as she viewed her grotesquely swollen foot. Her small eyes narrowed. "Spilled a pot of grease, I did, and the flesh won't heal. Mr. Healy told me I'd been standin' on it long enough and 'twas time to get someone in to do my job." Mrs. Healy looked up at Adria with a gap-toothed smile. "When you came through the doors with your pretty face and fine ways, I thought I'd soon be up on my feet again, but I was wrong. You're doin' well, dearie. I could not ask for more."

Adria's fair brow knitted with concern. "Did you have a doctor in to look at this? Surely you realize the wound is festering badly."

Mrs. Healy sniffed. "Aye, Mr. Healy called Dr. Clark. Old quack that he is, he did nothin' more than spread some grease on the wound with his dirty hands." She sniffed again. " 'Tis my feelin' I'd have been better off without him."

Adria's hesitation was brief. "I . . . I've completed the chores you've set me to, Mrs. Healy. The meat pies are finished and John is watching the oven outside. The roast will soon be done, the vegetables have been set to boiling, and when Christopher finishes with the potatoes, it will be a simple matter to set them to roasting." She paused again.

"I've yet to begin mixing the new batch of biscuits, but . . . if you would allow me, I'll try to give the wound some ease."

Christopher's hand closed around her arm in silent warning. "You know nothing about doctoring, Adria."

"But I do, Christopher!" Adria turned the bright blue of her gaze up to his. He was momentarily overwhelmed by its ardency as she insisted, "I do! The Potter children at home suffered similar burns in a household fire. Their mother had died years earlier and I helped them through their ordeal. Dr. Foster's treatment was controversial, but the children healed well." She turned back to the old woman who regarded her warily, "I don't mean to frighten you, Mrs. Healy, but you do know what could happen if your foot doesn't heal."

"Aye . . ." The woman's face sank into deeply etched lines. "The old quack's already told me I may lose it to the rot."

Adria's eyes filled. "I wouldn't like to see that. I hope you'll let me try to help you."

Christopher took a mental step backward as the old woman considered Adria's offer. A new Adria had emerged in the confused disorder of the kitchen they had entered earlier, one entirely different from the timid, uncertain shell of a woman he had formerly known. He suspected he had not seen the last of this new Adria's talents as Mrs. Healy responded with a frown.

"There's much to what you say. The truth is that the heat is spreadin' in my limb, as well as the pain. I don't suppose you can do it any harm."

Startling him further, Adria took the old woman's calloused hand in gentle consolation. "It may be difficult . . . the cleansing, I mean. It may cause you some pain at first."

"I'm not a babe!" The old woman was momentarily irate. "I've stood pain before."

Christopher could not believe the beauty of Adria's small smile as she whispered, "Thank you for your confidence in me. I'll do my best."

Adria turned away, only to be halted abruptly by Mrs. Healy. "What will you be needin'?"

"Warm water . . . and soap and clean cloths so I may wash away the festering."

"Don't stand there!" Mrs. Healy addressed Christopher sharply. "You heard her! Draw the water and put it on the fire. There's much to be done here."

At the well moments later, Christopher turned at a gentle tug on his arm and Adria's concerned gaze.

"You mustn't mind Mrs. Healy's gruff ways in setting you to fetching for me, Christopher. She's worried for her health, you see."

Christopher took Adria's hand, his grip tight with concern. "Are you certain you can manage this? It's a nasty, smelly wound."

"Christopher . . ." Rosy color flooded Adria's already flushed cheeks. "I know it's difficult for you to believe in me in light of my behavior since you've known me."

"No, Adria, I—"

"No, I don't blame you, Christopher. I've depended on Gillian's courage most of my life—but I know well how to care for those in need. I have an ease with it, so you mustn't concern yourself about my worth in that quarter."

Christopher frowned. "Your *worth* was never in question in my mind, Adria."

Her eyes moist, Adria nodded, then walked swiftly back toward the kitchen. Silent, and somehow uncertain, Christopher stared after her.

* * *

The light of afternoon had begun to wane. Reclining in her bath, Emmaline glanced at the darkening sky through the bedroom window. Robert had left an hour earlier to return to the fields. Her smile briefly flickered. He had done so at her suggestion after he had first kept his promise to entertain her during the early-afternoon hours.

Emmaline rubbed the fragrant soap against her firm, round breasts. In truth, Robert was a consolation like no other to her. He knew exactly how to soothe both her body and her mind and he was especially creative in the art of lovemaking. She could not remember the number of times he had brought her to climax that afternoon, but she did know that he had managed to erase the morning's torment from her mind for a few passionate hours. His powers of endurance continued to astound her.

Emmaline slowly smiled. But age would tell. Using that realization to suit her purposes, she had ever so innocently shamed Robert into returning to the fields without an opportunity to rest after the afternoon's vigorous activity. She knew what that would mean. He would fall asleep the moment his head hit the pillow that night and nothing would awaken him.

Emmaline's smile hardened. She was depending on it.

Derek's handsome image flashed abruptly before her mind and Emmaline's ire returned full bore. Bastard! He would choose a colorless witch over her, would he? *Two* colorless witches! Well, she would show him . . .

Glancing toward the window once more, Emmaline frowned and stood up abruptly. Water cascaded from the slender perfection of her form, splashing the polished wood floor as she shouted harshly, "Jubba! Where are you?"

Appearing at her side in a moment, the young Negress held up a drying cloth as Emmaline stepped imperiously from the tub and wrapped it around her. She instructed firmly, "You will tell the servants to keep the house silent tonight after the massa falls asleep. If he should awaken for any reason and ask where I am, you will instruct them to tell him that I've been called away because old Mrs. Lindham is sick. You will then send Quashie for me immediately. Is that understood?"

"Jubba understand."

"If anything goes wrong—if the massa discovers anything that will upset him, *you* will be the one to suffer. Is that also understood?"

The young Negress's eyes widened. "Jubba understand."

"I intend resting a few minutes longer. The massa should be home soon. You may tell him I'm waiting up here for him." Emmaline dropped the damp cloth to the floor, then reached up to free the heavy red locks pinned to the top of her head. They fell onto her shoulders in a fiery shower of color as she continued softly, "I will do my best to make *sure* the massa sleeps well tonight."

When the hesitant Negress lingered, Emmaline ordered, "Get out!"

Enjoying her servant's frantic retreat, Emmaline turned toward her bed. The realization that she was anticipating Robert's return with a certain degree of eagerness surprised her.

Glancing at her naked reflection as she passed the mirror, Emmaline smiled. She snatched up a bottle of fragrance and touched it to her neck, breasts, and inner thighs. She laughed. That particular scent drove Robert wild. He could not get enough of her, the dear old fool.

Reclining on the bed, Emmaline arranged the lace-trimmed linens gracefully around her nakedness before lying back and spreading her glowing tresses against the pillow.

She did not have to wait long.

The snap of the front door echoed from the foyer. Emmaline heard the soft buzz of Jubba's voice, then Robert's low tone in response. Eager footsteps sounded on the stairs. They approached her bedroom door.

Smiling, Emmaline held out her arms in loving welcome.

"It went well, don't you think, Christopher?"

Adria glanced at Christopher as they walked across the cobbled street toward the moored ships at the dock. Their first day's work as bond servants in the employ of the Royal Arms Tavern was over, the sun was setting, and they were returning to the *Colonial Dawn* as they had been instructed that morning. She saw his frown and she ventured, "Mrs. Healy appeared pleased with our work and she seemed to be in less pain with her foot."

"Yes."

Adria swallowed, an agitation she had struggled the long day to subdue returning. "You're worried about Gillian."

Christopher nodded.

"I've been telling myself she's all right . . . that the captain will take good care of her. He does seem to value her, don't you think?"

Christopher's strong jaw hardened. "He values her, all right."

Adria flushed, struggling to match Christopher's rapid pace. "Christopher . . ."

The uncertainty in her tone turned Christopher toward her as he continued steadfastly forward. She saw an agitation that mirrored her own in his pale eyes. She had seen it mount as the day had slipped slowly past. She began hesitantly, "I wish . . ."

Adria halted midsentence, realizing the uselessness of continuing. She could not alleviate Christopher's distress, the ache that she knew grew greater each time he saw the captain and Gillian together. Nor could she be all Christopher wanted in a woman, because no matter the duplication of their features, she was not Gillian. She was simply Adria—with all her weaknesses. Her love, however earnestly given, merely would not suffice.

"What's the matter, Adria?"

Christopher cared for her—she knew that to be true. But he *loved* Gillian. That complicated morass of emotions in mind, the question slipped past her lips before she realized her intent.

"What's going to happen to us all, Christopher?"

Christopher's light eyes met hers as he responded with an honesty that darkened his frown, "I wish I knew."

Climbing the gangplank at a pace just short of a run, Adria halted abruptly as Gillian stepped out of the shadows nearby. She heard the anxiety in her sister's voice as Gillian questioned softly, "Are you all right, Adria?"

"I'm fine."

Gillian's face twitched, and Adria was momentarily taken aback. If she did not know better, she would think Gillian was holding back tears as she responded hoarsely, "I was worried about you in that tavern until Derek . . . until I learned Christopher was with you." Gillian glanced at Christopher with an attempt at a smile. "I knew Christopher would take care of you. Thank you, Christopher."

Christopher did not answer as the twin sisters turned toward the cabins below and Adria realized with sudden incredulity that it was *she* who steadied Gillian as they walked.

Adria's heart wrung with pain.

Oh, Gillian . . .

The throbbing of the drums grew louder, stronger, as Emmaline worked her way feverishly along the darkened, heavily foliated trail. She was late!

Struggling to catch her breath, Emmaline pressed forward. Damn it all, what had come over Robert! If she did not know better, she would believe he was employing obeah to instill him with the stamina of a youth! She had been so certain that their last intimate session would put an end to him for the night, but it appeared to have had the reverse effect!

Emmaline stumbled. Cursing, she righted herself and continued on. In the end, she had been forced to drop a powder into Robert's tea in order to put an end to his attentions, but not before she had been so exhausted that she had hardly had the energy to rise from the bed.

Emmaline paused for a short breath. She had barely waited for Robert's eyes to close before dressing and running from the house. She had been determined that *nothing* would interfere with her plans this night.

Emerging at the edge of the familiar clearing as the drums pounded once more, Emmaline saw the dancers moving around the fire. The rhythmic stamping of their feet was already a dull thunder; the chorus of short, barking coughs was approaching crescendo; possession was almost complete as they whirled in wild frenzy, flames flickering, pulsating shadows flashing.

Breathless, her heart pumping with growing excitement, Emmaline searched the frenzied circle for the figure of William Gnu. He was not there. Watching as the dancers dropped to the ground in increasing numbers, she felt a growing disquiet when William Gnu did not emerge.

Disquiet gradually turned to fury.

How dare he! William Gnu, for all his powers of black magic, was a slave! He was Robert's possession, and through Robert, *her* possession as well—yet he had given her a worthless charm! Pucku's eye! Hah! This time she would settle for nothing more than a *real* charm—*real* magic that would cloud Derek's mind to any woman but her!

Ignoring the frenetic throng filling the clearing, Emmaline walked directly toward the hut in the rear. Her step slowed as she neared, as she heard the grunting sounds emanating from within. Stepping into the doorway, she looked down at the couple tightly entwined on a mat in the shadows of the small fire in the center of the dirt floor.

The big man's attention snapped toward her as her words emerged in a heated rush.

"You filthy, fornicating beggar!" He returned her stare without response, his gaze narrowed as she hissed, "Get up—*now*—or I will make you rue the moment you did not!"

Separating himself from the woman beneath him, the slave drew himself to his full, intimidating height as the woman scrambled for her clothes. Clutching her clothes against her nakedness, the woman ran past her into the shadows, but Emmaline did not spare the frightened slave a glance as she disappeared from sight. Instead, she allowed her gaze to linger on William Gnu—the taut planes of his face, his powerful limbs, the breadth of his shoulders and chest, and the male tool that remained firm and hard as he regarded her unblinkingly.

Reaching into her pocket, Emmaline withdrew the stained pouch he had given her. She threw it at him with disdain.

"William Gnu is a fraud! Pucku has deserted him! He is a *buffuto!* He has no power!"

The great black man's face grew grim. "William Gnu speak fe Pucku! Pucku give him strong obeah."

"Your obeah is weak! Your scratchings in the dirt mean nothing! You cannot see with Pucku's eye! Nor do you speak with his voice!"

William Gnu's dark eyes narrowed. "William Gnu see. Him see what Pucku see . . ."

The great black man dropped to his knees by the fire. He reached behind him for his pouch and sprinkled a pinch of dust on the flames. The flames leaped higher, spitting and crackling, drawing Emmaline forward despite herself as William Gnu watched their mesmerizing dance. His powerful body swaying, he spoke slowly, his throbbing tone intense.

"Devil man turn him face from woman wit hair like fire. Him send him away. Him have *two* women wit hair color of de moon . . . but dere be only *one* in devil man's bed . . ."

Emmaline was enraged. "Fool! Charlatan! *One* of them in his bed is too many! You said he belonged to me! You said Pucku would make him mine!"

William Gnu continued his steady perusal of the flames. His body continued its hypnotic sway as he whispered, "Pucku's eye be shaded. Him not see fe de power fightin' him."

"Power? What power is stronger than Pucku's?" Emmaline halted, then gasped. "The blond streggah is a witch! Is that what you're telling me?"

William Gnu did not respond.

"Tell me!"

"Pucku see . . . Pucku see . . ."

"What does he see?"

"Pucku see other backra want dat ragin' woman. Him come from darkness. Him watchin' dat woman . . ."

Emmaline gasped. "Another boss man? Who is he?"

"Him shadow be strong nigromancy. Him take dat woman . . ."

"Who is he?"

"Him be . . . him be . . ."

The fire popped unexpectedly, showering William Gnu with sparks that seared his skin. Leaping back, his eyes widening, Gnu turned abruptly toward Emmaline. The fear she saw there was too wild to be feigned as he rasped, "Dat ragin' backra lookin' fe woman wit hair like fire. Him say him find dat woman, and when him do—"

"He'll find me?" Emmaline felt a slow trembling overwhelm her. "When? When it's too late? After Derek's gone? Tell me who he is?"

"No more . . ."

"Bastard!"

"No more!"

Rigid with fury, Emmaline stared with disbelief as William Gnu strode past her and disappeared into the shadows. The drums halted abruptly, and then she knew.

The "ragin' backra," the raging white boss man William Gnu had described, was the key. Whoever he was—he was the key.

The darkness of the cabin . . . the glimmer of moonlight through the porthole. . the rustle of restlessness . . .

Gillian was intensely aware that Derek lay as sleepless as she although the hour was late. They had had little to say to each other since their exchange earlier in the morning.

The silence had been heavy between them, a silence she broke at last with her hesitant whisper.

"Derek . . ."

Derek did not respond but she felt his acute attention. The words she was about to speak among the most difficult she had ever spoken, Gillian continued softly, "I would ask a favor of you, Derek."

Silence, then his soft response.

"What is it?"

"I want you to tell me . . . I need to know what tomorrow holds . . . how long you intend remaining in Jamaica . . . where you intend sailing from here."

"Why?"

Gillian swallowed. "It would be easier if I knew."

The former sharp edge to his voice was noticeably absent as Derek responded more softly than before, "It wasn't my intention to make you suffer, Gillian."

Gillian swallowed. "I know."

Silence stretched for long moments more before Derek spoke again. "The repairs done at sea were only temporary. I must make certain the ship is seaworthy beyond doubt before I can go forward. Then I will contract for new cargo and set sail."

"Christopher will rejoin the crew then?"

A moment's silence. "Yes."

"What about Adria and me?"

"The repairs will take a while longer."

"And then?"

"I've told you all I can."

"Derek, I want—"

"Gillian . . ." Derek drew her into his arms. She felt his strength envelop her. She heard the desperation in his tone as well as the hunger as he whispered, "Nothing has changed. Nothing *will* change. Whatever happens, you will still belong to *me*."

"Derek—"

Gillian's words were swallowed by Derek's kiss.

She felt its passion. Her own soared anew.

And words were forgotten, for a little while.

Fourteen

Christopher cursed as the heat in the tavern kitchen continued to soar. He glanced around him, frowning at the activity that had not abated since Adria and he had arrived shortly after sunrise. He looked down at the greasy pans piled nearby, awaiting his attention, and he cursed again. They were but a few of the endless mountain of pots, pans, and dishes he had washed at the Royal Arms Tavern in the two weeks past. He sprinkled a handful of sand on the pans, a trick he had learned to aid the scouring. The calluses he had earned by the sweat of his brow had softened and his fingernails had grown as white and soft as a woman's. It occurred to him with disgust that he would be more suited to the position of cabin boy than that of seaman when the *Colonial Dawn* again sailed.

Christopher uttered a silent groan. Never again would he discount women's work as he had been wont to do in the past. It was hot, grueling, and almost past bearing for the tedium involved. Had it not been for the need to protect Adria from the rabble in the public room beyond, which grew greater each day, he would have faced the captain down and declared that his worth was being squandered at such menial tasks.

Adria walked past, her step brisk, and Christopher's thoughts came to an abrupt halt. Strangely, however, Adria seemed to thrive on the monotony of the tavern kitchen. In the short time of their employment there, her color had improved and the fear always present in her eyes during the long weeks of their voyage had disappeared.

Christopher silently corrected his last thought. He had seen fear in Adria's eyes the previous day, but it had lasted only until he had freed her from the embrace of a drunken lout who had taken advantage of her vulnerability when she had carried a tray into the public room.

The fury of the moment returning, Christopher strove to bring his emotions again under control. Strangely, he could not remember his first reaction when he had heard Adria's frightened shriek. Nor could he recall his thoughts when he had dashed into the public room and had seen her struggling in the fellow's arms. He *did* recall, however, the vibrant, bloodred color that had tinted his vision the moment before he had grasped the fellow's collar with a furious bellow and tossed him across the room.

It had been his arms that had closed around Adria then. Deaf to all else but her frightened words, he had drawn her back into the kitchen and had consoled her until her trembling had ceased. He had realized in that moment that the miraculous change in Adria was due partly to the reassurance of his presence. It had made little difference that Mrs. Healy had been as furious as he at the fool who had frightened Adria and that the obnoxious fellow had been banned from returning to the tavern. Adria needed *him*. He had realized at that moment of revelation that he would respond to her need, even at the cost of his life.

That was the way it was.

That would not change.

And he had not needed the captain's charge to tell him to do it!

The bastard captain—Gillian was suffering because of him! He had not had the opportunity to exchange more than a few words with Gillian in the past two weeks, more of the captain's work, he was sure, but he had heard enough of the snickers and comments upon his return to the ship each night to cause his anxiety to mount. Captain Andrews barely allowed Gillian out of his sight, going so far as to accompany her when she went on her daily walks about town. Talk had been rife in the tavern about those walks, about the black looks he sent the way of any man who glanced more than once in her direction, about his possessive stance, about the fact that he carefully avoided the side street where Charles Higgins's racy establishment held sway.

Christopher sniffed. Not that he begrudged the man his anger at the slovenly degenerate who had thought to establish the sisters in his immoral house. Had he his chance at the man he would—

Adria moved into his line of vision again, and Christopher's thoughts halted as she knelt by the smiling Mrs. Healy and began unwrapping her foot. It was not the affected extremity which he studied as Adria worked, however, but Adria's face. Somehow he could not recall why he had never thought of Adria as beautiful when he had always considered Gillian to be so. Because Adria *was* beautiful. She was also kind, gentle, loving, loyal—all those things that Gillian was, although her application of those virtues was distinctly different.

Adria was almost whole again. She had been healed as she now attempted to heal.

Christopher's throat tightened. Had it not been for Gillian, however, Adria would not have had the chance to heal. Gillian, who was still paying the price of her sister's life.

"Gibson! Are you sleepin'?"

Christopher turned at the familiar sound of Mr. Healy's voice. His frown did not intimidate the burly tavern proprietor as the fellow ordered curtly, "Get yourself movin'! Mistress Adria will be needin' clean pans for her pies in a little bit!"

Mistress Adria?

Christopher noted that the other workers did not bat an eye at Healy's respectful reference to his young employee. He knew he should be amused, but he recognized the danger there. Without conscious effort, Adria was making herself indispensable to the aging proprietor and his ailing wife. He wondered what the future would bring when the *Colonial Dawn* again set sail.

If Gillian were separated from Adria and uncertain of her sister's condition, her suffering would be acute.

Left behind with no one to watch over her, Adria would be bereft.

And he . . . ?

His expression grim, Christopher returned to his work.

" 'E's the one, all right!"

"You're sure?"

"I am." Peters nodded, pausing to scan the dank alley where Barrett and he had met with a shifty glance characteristic of his depraved personality. Satisfied they could not be seen, he continued. "I did a lot of diggin', I did. There wasn't too many who were willin' to talk about that Captain Andrews. It's not that 'e's well liked or nothin' like that. Most think 'e's a foul fellow, but it's the look of 'im that puts people off, with a smile never touchin' his lips and 'im bein' so big and dressin' in black like 'e does . . . not to mention them eyes. There's many who say the black 'e wears goes clear down to 'is soul."

Barrett regarded the small man beside him with open disgust. "What are you trying to tell me, Peters? That Captain Andrews is—"

"I ain't tryin' to tell you nothin'!" Anger flashed on Peters's thin, sweated face. "I'm just tellin' you what them around 'ere think about 'im. Most are afraid of 'im. They say 'e's *tallawah*—a *Guzu* man. That's why it took me so long to find out what you wanted to know."

Barrett laughed aloud, a harsh, bitter sound that echoed briefly in the narrow alleyway before he responded, "They say he has strong witchcraft?" Barrett laughed again. "It would be better if they called him devil man . . . a more apt appellation, for I'll soon see him consigned to the place where that dark figure resides!"

"Nay." Peters restrained a smile. "They can't call him that. Most saves that name for you."

Barrett's face flamed. "Enough of this rubbish! Tell me what you learned!"

"I told you, 'e's the one who done it. 'E killed a man for that red-haired Dorsett witch. Talk is that she 'ad 'er 'ooks into Andrews real good, she did, and when 'e found 'er with another fella, 'e beat the fella to death with 'is bloody 'ands!"

Barrett sneered. "Something you would never do."

Peters's lewd smile flashed. "Nay. I favors a knife, I do."

Barrett stared at the smaller man, not daring to reveal the extent of his contempt as the fellow withdrew his spotless weapon and flashed it with an evil snicker. The corrupt swine thought to impress him, but he did not. Neither had Peters fooled him. He was well aware that Peters and his henchmen had spent the major part of the time it took to obtain the information just imparted in a drunken stupor. He had been furious at being kept waiting, but he had not wanted to reveal himself by making inquiries on his own; and he had known Peters would come through, simply because he had been certain the sinister knave would not miss the opportunity to again ply his trade.

Barrett gritted his teeth. The foul smell of the fellow, doubtless emanating from the rotten core of him, was almost beyond bearing as Barrett grated harshly, "My patience is waning. Get on with it!"

Peters exposed yellowed teeth as he responded. "The red-headed witch is out to get Captain Andrews back, all right. She's been goin' to them Pucku ceremonies to get the spirits after 'im."

"The woman is a fool!"

"No, she ain't. People say the captain 'ears 'er voice wherever 'e goes."

"Not when he's sleeping with the blond bitch, I wager!"

"Some say the blonde one's a witch, that she's so powerful that she split 'erself in two so she could better fight Pucku's magic."

"Nonsense!" Barrett's rage soared. "Is this all you have to report?"

Peters's smile grew progressively obscene. "Nay, there's more. It seems Mistress Dorsett found the captain in 'is bed with the blond 'arlot that mornin' we saw 'er rantin' and ravin' on the dock. Rumor 'as it that she begged 'im to throw the blond 'arlot out but 'e refused, and that's when she swore to get 'im back any way she could."

Barrett nodded. That made sense. He had seen the red-haired witch's exit from the ship that day, and he knew jealous fury when he saw it.

"What about *Master* Dorsett? What does he think about his wife's intentions?"

Peters shook his head. "Don't know. 'Is people don't talk about 'im much, but 'e looks to be a fellow who won't get in 'is wife's way."

"Perfect." Barrett reached into his pocket. He saw the gleam in Peters's eyes as he withdrew a small money pouch. He held it out with a devious smile. "For your effort . . ." Snatching the pouch back just as Peters's fingers were to close around it, Barrett continued, "when you complete just one more task."

Barrett's smile became a leer.

The afternoon sun shone down on the group clustered on the dock, watching the antics of a small brown monkey as he danced to a sailor's piped tune.

"Look, the little fellow is actually smiling!"

Gillian's spontaneous comment was followed by her delighted laughter, and Derek was suddenly struck with the beauty of the sound. Standing beside her, it occurred to him that of all the emotions he had succeeded in raising within this magnificent woman, happiness had been lamentably absent.

Gillian laughed again. The musical sound lingered in Derek's mind as he watched her enjoyment of the simple entertainment. The heavy silver-gold strands wound into a loose knot atop Gillian's head glittered as she turned this way and that, following the animal's chaotic performance. Her eyes flashed with an azure hue emphasized by the new, golden tint to her skin lent by the tropical sun. It occurred to Derek that he had not believed it possible for Gillian to become more beautiful, but he had been wrong.

Derek's sober thoughts wandered with the acknowledgment that he had also been wrong when he had thought the plane of beauty they could attain in each other's arms had reached its apex. Somehow, each night brought new wonder, either in the passion of their joinings or in the simple intimacy of knowing Gillian lay beside him . . . his alone.

But there had been other surprises as well in the most recent weeks past. Strangely, in all their contacts, he had never truly grasped the full extent of Gillian's academic accomplishments. Her work with the accounts of his ship that had suffered his neglect as he had busied himself with the problems of a turbulent voyage and then with dangerous and necessary repairs of his ship had astounded him. Her thoughtful calculations had gone so far as to extend to suggestions on more efficient handling of several elements of the ship's repair. He had been uncertain whether to be amused or annoyed in that regard, but one thing had remained clear. Her deductions had been based on mathematical conjecture and clear logic. Derek almost smiled. Unfortunately, some of those ideas had been tried before and had been found unworkable, a point he had deliberately neglected to explain, thereby raising her ire.

Strangely, he had been almost pleased to see anger again flashing in Gillian's eyes. Her brief period of silent distraction after he had purposely separated her from Adria and Gibson's new responsibilities had worried him. He had deliberately limited her contact with Gibson—for reasons too obvious for him to accept with comfort. He knew Gibson resented it. He suspected Gillian did, too, although she had not voiced her resentment.

Gillian's restlessness, however, was apparent. He had rarely allowed her out of his sight since they arrived in

Kingston. Somehow, as dependable as he knew his men to be, he could not make himself trust her safety to anyone other than himself. He knew she chafed at the restrictions and that her devotion to the ship's accounts still left her with restless energy.

Gillian had expressed her interest in visiting Adria in the Royal Arms Tavern many times. Derek drew back spontaneously at the thought. That would never happen. He would not offer Gillian up to the ogling of the type of man who frequented waterfront establishments.

Derek scrutinized the immediate area once more. His concern for Gillian's *safety,* however, was legitimate. Haskell and Linden had been amused when they had reported Emmaline's daily carriage rides past the ship, but he had not been similarly entertained. He knew the true malevolence of which Emmaline was capable, and it had been apparent during their confrontation in the passageway two weeks earlier that her vicious streak had not waned.

Nor did he like the mumblings of black magic associated with her.

Emmaline was up to something.

Derek's blood ran slowly cold. He remembered with chilling clarity the glow of Emmaline's smile as he had stood over that dead seaman so many years ago. He was determined that he would never give her cause to smile that way again.

Abruptly uncomfortable, Derek grasped Gillian's arm. She looked up, her smile fading as he spoke.

"It's time to move on."

There it was again, the delicate flaring of Gillian's nostrils that indicated were circumstances different, she would not have moved at his command in so docile a manner.

Conflicting feelings soared within Derek. Somehow, he

regretted his power over Gillian even as he indulged it; he despised his depth of desire for her, even as he wanted her more each day.

Despairing, he had found that however flawed, the present solution he employed to the dilemma was the only workable one. He was determined that while he employed that solution, he would enjoy it to the maximum.

Foremost, in any case, remained his concern for Gillian's safety. That worry in mind, Derek slid a protective arm around Gillian's waist, drawing her closer as he urged her forward.

"What's wrong with you, Quaco! Must you drive this carriage into every rut in the road?"

Ignoring the aging driver's mumbled regrets as the carriage continued bumping along the primitive thoroughfare to town, Emmaline struggled for control. She was almost beside herself with discomfort. Ever vigilant in protecting her delicate skin against the sun's unrelenting rays, she held her parasol rigidly over her head, her back determinedly straight, but the effort was of little use. The heavy morning air had never been more moist, the road never bumpier, and the sun never hotter than it had been since they had set out for town a short time earlier.

The familiar taste of bile rose in Emmaline's throat. No, damn it! She would not vomit!

Emmaline swallowed hard, silently cursing again. She was wearing a new gown, an exquisite yellow batiste that bared her shoulders and breasts to the daring degree for which she had become well known on the island. She was aware that she looked lovely in every color, but she also knew that the shade and style of this particular garment was especially complementary. She had worn it with the expectation that today, after endless failure, she would finally meet up with Derek on the street and he would be unable to resist her.

It had been a terrible week. Damn that William Gnu! He had disappeared from sight and no one seemed to know where he was. She knew it was not uncommon for the masters of some estates to lend slaves out on occasion during harvesting, but she had dared not ask Robert if that was the case with William Gnu for fear of arousing suspicion of her motives.

As a result of her lack of guidance from Pucku, she had been floundering! Daily trips to town had not availed her of even one face-to-face confrontation with Derek. Nor had she made contact with the "devil man" to whom William Gnu had referred, the man who was the key to winning Derek back again.

Oh, she had done it all! Out of sheer desperation, she had sought out another obeah woman. In the time since, she had been chanted over, spat upon, and sprinkled with duppy dust until her head was spinning. A gnarled chicken foot with the singed feathers of a seabird lay under her pillow, dirt from a new grave lay in a sack under her bed—both powerful obeah—but her dreams had told her nothing. Were she another woman, were she not determined that she would finally have her desire realized, were she not resolute that she would again have Derek at her beck and call, she might have despaired. But she was not another woman. She was Emmaline Dorsett and she would have her way!

Emmaline attempted to swallow. She had taken great pains with her appearance before leaving. She had all but run Jubba ragged, ironing and curling and beribboning her hair. She had been a confection for the eyes when she had left the great house, but with each jolting mile that had rolled on, with each puff of dusty air she had inhaled, with each humid gust that had slapped her damp skin anew, the confection had deteriorated further until she feared, in truth, she would arrive in Kingston a melted travesty of her former self. What was more, her stomach—

Oh . . .

A revolting surge . . . a gasping breath . . .

No . . .

Her hand pressed tightly against her lips, Emmaline grated, "Stop!"

Her parasol abandoned, Emmaline scrambled toward the carriage door and thrust it open, but the carriage continued moving.

Rage battled nausea as Emmaline managed a shout.

"Damn you, Quaco! Stop, I say!"

It happened abruptly—the revolting spasms, the violent purging that left her weak and breathless, clinging to the side of the halted carriage. Raising watery, bloodshot eyes from her humiliating lapse, Emmaline saw Quaco regarding her from his seat.

"Breakfas' better out den in when stomach ailin'."

Declining response to Quaco's comment beyond a murderous glance, Emmaline drew back. She dabbed at her forehead and upper lip. She was wilting badly, but even at her worst, she was miles above that pale bitch in Derek's bed!

Emmaline took a strengthening breath. "Drive on, Quaco!"

Quaco did not respond.

"You heard me!"

The carriage snapped into motion.

Falling back against the leather seat, Emmaline seethed. She had had two weeks of torment, riding back and forth to Kingston with one excuse or another because of Derek.

She could have been lying in a cool, fragrant bath during the worst hours of the day instead of retching over the side of her carriage like a drunken wench! Right now she could even have been reclining on her lace-trimmed sheets with Robert's hands moving lazily along her scented body.

She paused at that thought. It would've been no problem convincing Robert to stay home for a few hours. Robert was truly a homely old toad, but he had such good hands, and he was so anxious to prove, over and again, their expertise. Why, the previous night he had even—

A familiar surge, and Emmaline gulped.

No . . . not again.

Sliding to the side of the carriage in a rush, Emmaline thrust open the door.

Incredulous at the vulgar sounds she made as she retched anew, Emmaline looked up moments later to meet Quaco's gaze.

"Don't say a word, you clumsy fool! Keep driving!"

Collapsed against the seat minutes later, Emmaline was capable of only a weak, trailing whisper.

"Derek . . . my darling . . . you will pay."

"What time did the mistress leave, Jubba?"

Mounted on his great gray gelding, his rotund figure clothed in white appearing all the more bulbous atop the powerfully muscled animal, Robert Dorsett looked down at the slender slave where he had halted her progress across the yard. His pink, smoothly shaven face was flushed and damp as he raised his hat from his balding head and wiped his arm across his forehead. When Jubba hesitated in reply, he pressed with a touch of agitation, "I asked you a question, Jubba."

"Missus leave early."

"How early?"

"Right after massa leave."

Robert frowned. More "shopping." His darling wife was such a devious sort, leaving just after he departed for the fields each morning and making certain to return, almost without exception, before he came home. The dear little schemer did not realize, however, that he was on to her machinations, and that he could be just as devious as she when given proper incentive.

"Which direction did she take?"

"Jubba not see, massa."

"Jubba . . ."

The slender Negress shuddered. "Carriage head fe town."

Robert's frown deepened. He watched as Jubba continued her way toward the kitchen, telling himself as she disappeared within that there was no need for concern. He reminded himself that Lester's loyalties were unquestioned, especially since he had pardoned the terrified fellow when he had been caught leaping stark naked from Emmaline's bedroom balcony weeks earlier.

Strangely, it had not occurred to him to question Emmaline's fidelity with the handsome Negro slave. He knew Emmaline too well to believe she would cuckold him with Lester. Vanity and a perception of her worth would not allow it, especially when he kept her so well satisfied in the more intimate aspects of their married life.

Robert's sagging jaw slowly tightened. No, if Emmaline were to betray him with anyone, it would only be with Captain Derek Andrews. So certain of Emmaline was he, and so confident of Lester's gratitude and determination to absolve himself completely in his master's eyes, that he had allowed one matter to solve the other by equipping the eager slave with a horse and saddle and setting him to a surveillance of Emmaline's covert activities.

Robert looked unconsciously toward the road to town. While annoying him, Lester's reports had also entertained and saddened him. Dear Emmaline was having no success at all in her pursuit of Captain Andrews. She was becoming terribly frustrated. He knew that was true because he knew his young wife so well, and because she was again taking out her frustrations in the most intimate of ways.

A smile tugged at Robert's lips. Dear Emmaline was becoming insatiable.

He was saddened, however, at the realization that *he* was responsible for a great portion of her frustration. He had never truly objected to Emmaline's addiction to Puckamenna. His wariness had begun with the growing prominence of William Gnu at the nights of fitful worship.

Robert's frown returned. William Gnu was too good a puckoo man. His powers to see and to speak with Pucku's tongue were too strong. Robert knew that because he had felt Pucku's powers through William Gnu. His manly parts had known new life since he had begun taking William Gnu's powders. It was as if he were a young man of twenty-five again. So competent was William Gnu and so determined was Emmaline, that he had had no choice but to spirit William Gnu away to a part of the island where Emmaline would never find him.

Of course, Emmaline had searched out an obeah woman in William Gnu's place, but he had the feeling she had as little faith as he in that damned chicken foot with the burned feathers that had been lying under Emmaline's pillow for days, or the pouch with that odoriferous dirt under their bed.

Sadness slowly overwhelmed Robert. He disliked being

responsible for Emmaline's unhappiness in any way, but knew he need be vigilant only for a short time longer until Captain Andrews was able to repair his ship and contract for cargo. Perhaps when the captain was gone, he would bring William Gnu back to ease Emmaline's frustrations.

In the meantime, Lester would watch over Emmaline as he would his own life, just as he had each time Emmaline had made those furtive treks to the Pucku ceremonies when she had believed herself alone. She was such a child, his Emmaline—a spoiled, sometimes dangerous child, to be sure, but nonetheless a child whom he worshipped with all his heart.

Still staring at the empty road, Robert felt sadness well almost to a debilitating degree with the admission that he, who would do anything to make Emmaline happy, could not give her the thing she wanted most.

Yes, he loved her. It was his curse, his bane . . . and the joy of his life.

Knowing the full extent of the danger of his love, Robert turned his gelding back toward the fields.

Her back rigidly erect, her chin high, Emmaline stared directly forward as the carriage rolled onto Kingston's cobbled streets. The sights, the sounds, the *smells* . . .

Ugh!

Emmaline felt a familiar surge.

"Take me to Madame's, Quaco! Quickly!"

Emmaline forced a smile as admiring glances turned her way.

They *were* admiring . . . she was sure. They could not be else, for surely no one noticed that her perfectly arranged red curls were slightly disheveled . . . that her exquisite yellow batiste was spotted with stains she would rather not identify . . . that instead of her former perfection of color, her skin had a decidedly green tinge.

No, they couldn't possibly notice.

Emmaline's smile stiffened. A short visit with Madame, however, and all would be right again. She would be ready to seek Derek out and—

Madame's small shop came into view at the end of the narrow street and Emmaline released a silent sigh of relief. Her torment was almost over.

Alighting from her carriage minutes later, Emmaline instructed tightly, "Do not budge from his spot, Quaco! I want you waiting here when I come out."

Her step imperious despite her disheveled state, Emmaline approached the small shop's door. She ignored the vile-looking fellow who stood nearby, his shifty eyes regarding her intently. She was about to issue him a sharp reprimand for his impertinent gaze when his narrow face creased in a heinous smile.

"Mr. John Barrett sends his regards . . ."

Emmaline's step came to an abrupt halt. She knew that name!

So, *he* was the one.

The time had finally come.

Unusually tense as he walked along Port Royal Street, uncertain of the exact reason for his agitation, Derek surveyed his surroundings speculatively. Nothing seemed amiss. Modest traffic filled the cobbled streets, business at the warehouses nearby was progressing as usual, and he saw no one loitering suspiciously.

Derek's strong features moved into a scowl. Things had

not gone at all well with Gillian that afternoon. She had been resentful and silent after he had drawn her away from the group surrounding the amusing monkey. He was certain she had irritated him deliberately by talking to that old beggar on the road and by smiling flirtatiously at the young fellow who tipped his hat. She had resisted him when he had said they were to start back, and had opposed him further by telling him she wanted to visit Adria at the Royal Arms Tavern.

The result had been conflict that had ended with his almost physically dragging Gillian back to the ship. Worse luck, he had found a message from a commercial agent waiting for him when they arrived. His difficulty in contracting for cargo since arriving in port had both confused and concerned him. He had almost begun to believe that some sort of conspiracy to keep him in port for an extended period was involved. Had the timing been more opportune, he would have been happy to receive the message from the agent. Instead, he was not.

If he had had the chance, neither would he have agreed to meeting at the Royal Arms Tavern, for obvious reasons.

His scowl darkening as he reached the tavern, Derek pushed the door open and entered, squinting as he strained to acclimate his gaze to the dim interior light. He heard the scrape of a chair and then a voice that rang with unexpected familiarity.

"Derek! Damned if it isn't you!"

Derek strained to see through his temporary sun blindness. Could it be . . . ?

The height of the fellow approaching him, the tawny, sun-streaked hair, left no doubt, even while his features were unclear. Damien Straith! Derek clasped the hand extended toward him and shook it warmly.

A ship's captain at the age of twenty-six, one of the youngest and most respected captains in the colonies, Damien had been no more than a youth when Derek had stood convicted of manslaughter, but Damien had demonstrated his individualism even then. He had spoken out vociferously in Derek's defense when all others had turned their backs on him. Derek had never forgotten it.

Derek's rare smile flashed. His rapidly clearing vision revealed that Damien had filled out even more since he had last seen him. The thinness of youth had been replaced with a broad expanse of shoulder and a firm, muscular physique that matched his own proportions. He also saw that the passage of years had added new maturity to Damien's even features, and that the arresting, unnerving quality of his peculiarly clear, translucent gray eyes, a startling physical feature that had stirred persistent speculation on the superstitious island, had not changed. From what he had heard of Damien since, he doubted that his innovative friend would hesitate to use that speculation to his advantage if the opportunity presented itself.

Settled at a table in the corner of the rapidly filling tavern some time later, Derek frowned as he emptied his glass again. He glanced at the clock on the tavern wall.

Damien laughed aloud. "If I didn't know better, I'd think you weren't enjoying renewing our old acquaintance, Derek."

"Thomas Marshall is almost an hour late for our appointment. Something tells me he won't be coming." Derek's lips twitched revealingly. "If I didn't know better, I'd think there was a plot afoot to keep me from contracting cargo back to the colonies."

Damien's expression abruptly sobered. "I've heard a few stories . . ." He hesitated. "We docked only this morning, but it didn't take more than an hour for talk to filter through."

Derek was instantly alert. "Talk?"

"It seems you've acquired yourself some bond servants . . ."

"What about them?"

Low, appreciative comments from surrounding tables raised both men's eyes at that moment to see Adria the focus of attention as she entered the public room from the kitchen and placed a tray of food on the bar. Damien whistled in soft approval as Adria met his gaze briefly, glanced at Derek, then beat a hasty retreat back to the kitchen.

"She's one of your bond servants, isn't she?"

Derek nodded.

"Her *twin* sister, too, I hear."

Derek's gaze narrowed.

"Don't look at me like that, old friend!" Damien laughed. "I must admit I find it hard to believe there can be two such beauties, but I'm not about to go anywhere near women who belong to you."

Derek held the gaze of those peculiarly light eyes in an attempt at clarification he would employ for very few. "Only one of them is *my* woman."

"And not the one who works here." Damien shook his head. "I didn't think so, not with your proclivity for possessiveness, not to mention your disinterest in that one since you arrived—*and* not with that strapping young fellow in the back watching her like a hawk."

"You're referring to Gibson . . ." Derek gave a low snort. "He had *better* watch her closely."

"So, you hold his bond as well . . ."

"Damned if I know exactly how the whole thing happened." Picking up his refilled glass, Derek drained it and slapped it back on the table. "All I know is that it's a damned mess I've gotten myself into, and I've not seen the last of it yet."

Damien scrutinized Derek's troubled expression. "I hadn't thought to see you so affected by a woman after the last time."

"You're talking about Emmaline . . ." Derek gave an irritated snort. "It's not the same. I'll never be that kind of fool again."

Derek returned Damien's intense scrutiny. Derek had heard much about Damien as well during their years of separation. Rumor had it that Damien was a staunch patriot who stood strongly behind the colonies in their position against the Mother Country's taxation policy, and that he avidly and openly advocated rebellion. He had heard Damien was as feared by his enemies as he was respected by his crew, and that while fair in most dealings, he was not above turning the situation to his advantage by whatever means were available to him.

Derek paused in his scrutiny. Damien was all those things. He was intelligent, perceptive, and he was a friend, yet there was no understanding of the true depth of his predicament in the clear, translucent eyes returning his stare.

"You have no idea what I'm talking about, do you, Damien? One woman is as good as another to you."

Damien's fingers trailed absentmindedly along his shirt-front, unbuttoning it midway in concession to the growing heat of the room as he considered his response to Derek's question. He leaned back in his chair, the fine white lawn separating to expose a light furring of golden-brown hair on his tightly muscled chest as he finally shrugged.

"I wouldn't say that, exactly. I do have a particular affection for a wench named Ruby, here in Kingston. I'm looking forward to renewing my acquaintance with her tonight. Her welcome is always warm."

Derek nodded with a raised brow. "I know Ruby well."

"You do." Damien gave a short laugh. "I should've guessed. Then there's Jasmine in Philadelphia, and Lulu in Charleston." He paused to glance at Derek sideways. "Do you know them, too?"

"If I don't know those particular women, I know plenty like them."

"Meaning *your* woman is different . . ."

Derek did not respond.

Damien shook his head. The planes of his face grew pensive. "I've never met a woman who stayed on my mind past the time it took me to close the bedroom door behind me. On the other hand . . ."

Damien's jaw clenched unexpectedly. His expression turned cold. ". . . there is one female I won't soon forget."

Derek was curious. *"Female?"*

"A nine-year-old."

"A *nine-year-old!*"

"Aye, Amethyst Greet, a raven-haired, lavender-eyed brat—a little witch beyond description whom I delivered to port this morning with a group of actors . . ." Damien needed no encouragement to continue. "The little twit was traveling with her mother, a sweet, sickly woman who's an actress with the troupe. The nasty whelp behaved as if the relationship between the two of them were reversed. She got it into her mind that I was interested in her mother and she didn't hesitate to demonstrate in maddening ways too numerous to count that she disapproved."

"Were you?"

"Interested in her mother? In a way." Damien paused. "The woman was a gentle sort, entirely the opposite of her daughter. It was easy to see that she had had a difficult time, what with her husband being killed and being left with a need to support herself in a profession that doesn't cater to women as plain and soft-spoken as she. Her state of health was extremely poor. It grew increasingly obvious as the voyage progressed that she will not live the year out."

"And the child . . ."

"The damned little termagant thwarted my good intentions every step of the way until I was ready to wrap my hands around her skinny little neck and . . ." Damien paused. The golden color of his skin tinted with angry color as he continued with growing heat. "Do you know what the little witch did when she left? She didn't even acknowledge me as her mother said a genuinely warm farewell. When they were making their way across the dock below with the rest of the troupe, she waited until she was a safe distance away before she looked directly at me with those eyes as bright and hard as an amethyst stone. Then she grimaced, stuck out her tongue, put her nose up in the air, and walked off!"

Derek was unexpectedly amused. "She's a child, Damien."

"No, she isn't." Damien's light eyes glared into his. "She's an arrogant, nasty witch in the body of a nine-year-old, but I'd like to see how arrogant she'll be a year from now when her mother's gone and she's on her own in this damned deceiving paradise . . ."

"You might not like what you'll see."

"Aye." Damien nodded. "But then again I might."

Studying his friend's face a moment longer, Derek could not help but hope that Damien never met up with the woman this girl with the amethyst eyes would grow up to be. Somehow, he had the feeling Damien would not fare any better in the encounter than he.

His former light mood replaced by an irritation that obviously still gnawed, Damien stood up abruptly. "It's time to see to my ship." He paused briefly, studying Derek once more. "I have only one other thought to offer—whether it's welcome or not. That other woman years ago . . . what was her name?"

"Emmaline."

"I'd stay away from her, if I were you. I hear she's still on the island and she's as lethal as she ever was."

Derek stood as abruptly as his friend. He accepted the hand Damien offered with another of his infrequent smiles. "I'll do that—only if you'll put the lavender-eyed brat behind you, too."

Watching his friend's broad back slip through the tavern doorway moments later, Derek glanced again at the wall clock. He cursed, then sat abruptly, emptied his glass, and signaled the plump barmaid nearby.

"Fill it again."

He'd wait only a little longer . . .

She was everything she had been described to be . . .

Emmaline Dorsett turned down into the narrow alleyway where John Barrett waited. She approached him with a decisive step, and Barrett felt a familiar hardening in his groin. He had been waiting in the dank corridor between two retail shops for more than an hour since Peters had set up the meeting. Furious at being kept waiting in the company of the swift-footed, long-tailed residents who darted in and out of the shadows around him, he had been dangerously close to departing. His first close look at the her, however, had proved worth the wait.

The extraordinary Emmaline Dorsett drew closer.

Oh, yes, he could see how a man could kill for a woman such as she.

Emmaline Dorsett came to an abrupt halt a few feet from him and Barrett's momentary intoxication faded. Fanaticism burned in the stunning green of her eyes, singeing him. There was a heat inside this bitch not unlike the heat for Gillian Haige that burned within him. He had no need to ask who had lit that fire as Emmaline Dorsett addressed him boldly.

"You are John Barrett?" Her eyes narrowed. "Your man told me you sent your regards."

Somehow annoyed at the coldness of her tone, Barrett raised his dark thick brows speculatively. He allowed his gaze to linger openly on the firm white flesh exposed in the bodice of her gown. "Am I to assume you are accustomed to meeting strange men in alleyways when they send their regards?"

Emmaline's delicate lips twitched. "You may *assume* whatever you wish, but you are more a fool than you believe me to be if you think I would expose myself to an encounter such as this without protection."

Barrett gave a mocking snort. "You need no protection from me, madam."

"So speaks the 'devil man' . . ."

"Who called me that!" Barrett was suddenly enraged by the young woman's presumption—she, who had little room to talk! "I demand to know!"

"Oh, are you sensitive?" Emmaline raised her narrow brows, mocking his former expression. "Who would have suspected it?" Emmaline's mocking expression vanished with the return of her former heat, "As surprising as it may seem with the reputation some have given me, *I*, too, am sensitive—too much so to be looked at as if I were a prize cow up for auction! So, you will keep your lascivious glances to yourself, Mr. John Barrett, or we will not do the business you have called me here to conduct!"

"Oh, won't we?" Barrett's restraint snapped. "You don't fool me, Madam Uppity Bitch! I know the reason you came to meet me here. It was not in spite of what I am called behind my back, but *because of* it! You aren't beyond employing the work of the devil to get what you want, and neither am I! Whether you like it or not, we are colleagues, both devoted to the same cause and bent on achieving our ends any way we can."

"I think it might be best if we clarify that cause here and now."

"The cause is Captain Derek Andrews."

Emmaline's gaze tightened. "I know what *I* want from Captain Andrews. Suppose you tell me what you want from him?"

"My dear lady . . ." Barrett attempted temporary retreat. The bitch was a fool, but she need be carefully handled. He wondered how Andrews could have been taken in so completely that he would kill a man for the likes of her. Barrett continued a tone more softly. "I think we have started out poorly. Perhaps we should try again in a . . ." He glanced around them, "place that would afford us more privacy."

Emmaline Dorsett's eyes grew mockingly wide. "Where would that be, Mr. Barrett? Your bedroom, perhaps?"

Her deprecating tone again igniting a flash of anger inside him, Barrett stepped threateningly forward. The bitch did not cower, enraging him further as he rasped, "You may relax, my dear lady. I have no designs on your flesh. That is the point of this meeting, you see. I *do* have designs on the flesh of the woman your dear captain now keeps in his bed. It is my hope that we may devise a plan between us that will separate the lovers. Then *you* may have the man you desire, and *I* may have *both* women I desire."

"You want *both* of them? You're a greedy sort, aren't you?"

"No more greedy than your dear Captain Andrews, but if I were to be completely candid, I would have to say my intentions are twofold. You see, I'm not as fond of your lover as you. Without going into detail, I will tell you that he and I interacted badly during the voyage. I would have my revenge on certain steps taken against me—certain steps made possible by the abuse of his position as captain."

"I don't believe you! Derek is an honorable man."

"You must pardon my stupidity, madam. Is there such a thing as an honorable murderer?"

Emmaline's reply was unexpected. "Yes . . . there is."

Thwarted by her response, Barrett continued acidly. "Your 'honorable' man was not so honorable during the voyage, madam. He forced his attentions on Mistress Haige and he—"

"Liar!" Emmaline was suddenly enraged. *"She* seduced *him!* She seduces him still!"

"Whatever you choose to think, madam. In any case, my goal is to separate Mistress Haige from your lover."

Emmaline grew abruptly suspicious. "I thought you said you wanted both sisters."

"My dear lady, *one* will affect my revenge, *two* will affect my pleasure . . ."

"Loathsome man!"

"Exactly the type of fellow you were searching for to accomplish your purpose, am I not, Madam Dorsett?"

Emmaline Dorsett smiled unexpectedly. Flabbergasted as much by the beauty of her smile as by the realization that it so effectively hid a heart and soul as black as pitch, Barrett was struck momentarily dumb. His bemusement grew as Emmaline's eyes widened into innocent saucers and she offered softly, "Mr. Barrett, sir, I'm certain I don't know what you mean." She added slowly, "But I do believe that we will work well together, indeed."

Yes, she would do.

Barrett's thought was confirmed as Emmaline continued deliberately. "Now, tell me, what is your plan?"

Derek turned all heads at the Royal Arms Tavern as he bellowed out the last line of the sailor's ditty with a power that rocked the rafters. He cracked a lopsided smile. He had always known his reluctant baritone was unmatched.

Low, rumbling comments sounded at the bar as Derek cleared his throat and prepared to sing another chorus. He was uncertain how long he had been waiting for Thomas Marshall to appear for their business appointment, but the sharp edge of impatience had dulled more with each glass of the tavern's delicious brew that he had emptied. Agitation had gradually been replaced with enjoyment as a few fellows in the corner began singing a familiar seafaring song. He had joined in impulsively, only to have the others fall silent, one after the other, until he had found himself singing alone.

And how the rafters had rung!

Derek shrugged. It mattered little to him that a few unpleasant fellows had complained about his lack of tone and confused lyrics. Nor had his enthusiasm been dampened when some had clapped their hands over their ears and groaned aloud. He was uncertain how long he had been singing chorus after chorus, even though a few, tight-faced souls had commented it felt like years.

But he was thirsty. It was time for another drink.

Weaving his way toward the bar, Derek smiled abruptly as a group of seamen standing nearby swayed uncertainly. He reached for a tall fellow's arm to steady him, laughing aloud as it escaped his grasp.

Derek grinned. The poor sailor was drunk!

Grasping the edge of the polished mahogany bar to steady himself when he finally arrived, Derek looked back, surprised that he had not previously noticed the dangerous slant to the tavern floor that had caused him such difficulty in crossing the room. He made a mental note to call the problem to the attention of the proprietor when he got a chance, then slapped his glass down and addressed the smiling barmaid.

"Fill 'er up, my lovely!"

"Aye, I'll do that for you, you handsome devil!" The plump barmaid winked as she reached for his glass. "You have a right pleasant voice, ducky! Why don't you give us another song?"

A chorus of groans along the bar turned Derek's head with a snap. He raised his dark brows with disdain before turning back to the pleasant brunette with a slurred question.

"What's yer choice, my lovely?"

"Don't egg him on, Sadie!"

"Have a heart, Sadie!"

"My ears are throbbin', I can't stand much more!"

Ignoring the protests, the buxom woman smiled warmly up at Derek. It occurred to Derek that she had a pleasant face. It was round and full, with small features and bright brown eyes. She had not one chin, but two, and both dimpled when she laughed and pinched his cheek.

"Don't listen to them, ducky. They don't know good music when they hears it."

"Sadie . . . !"

"Oh, shut up, all of you!" Turning back to Derek, Sadie smiled again. "Come on, give us another song."

Derek hesitated, insulted by the comments along the bar. "I think not, Sadie." He raised his glass to his lips and drank deeply. He heard a great belch when he was done and he turned sharply to ascertain the source, only to find himself the focus of attention. He continued with a note of haughty reserve. "I think I'll be going. If Thomas Marshall should show up, you might tell him to—"

Derek paused. "Second thought, I'll tell him myself."

Emptying his glass, Derek slapped a handful of coins on the bar, only to have the barmaid grasp his hand as he attempted to draw it back. "Hey, you ain't leavin' yet, are you, dearie?" She leaned forward, her ample cleavage bulging. "I'm through here for the night and I was thinkin' maybe you'd be wantin' to come back to my place for a while?"

Derek shook his head vigorously. "Oh, no!" His grin flashed again. "I've someone waiting for me, you see."

"Not another woman!" The barmaid looked downcast. "And there I was thinkin' that you loved only me."

"Have mercy on the poor fella, Sadie!"

"Aye, he's not *that* drunk!"

Derek's head snapped toward the unsolicited comments. Drunk? He wasn't drunk!

Derek pulled himself erect and started toward the door. He tripped. Damn that floor! Righting himself, he concentrated, putting down one foot after the other, careful where he placed them . . . so careful that he didn't see the table and chairs in his way . . . the trays of food resting on a corner rack . . . the bottles piled nearby . . .

Derek was careening from one near catastrophe to another when he felt a strong arm slip under his and heard a soft, familiar voice in his ear.

"Just lean on Sadie, dearie. I'll get you home."

Derek smiled. He had never met a more pleasant woman. She smelled good, too. Like flowers. Lots of them.

In a few minutes they were out on the darkened street and Sadie was singing. Smiling, Derek joined in. He stopped singing when they finally reached the door of a small, frame house. Sadie took out a latch key, and he drew back, uncertain.

"Where are we?"

"At my house, dearie. I told you I'd take you home."

Derek was suddenly sad. "Sadie, dear girl . . ." Damn if his tongue wasn't so thick that he had trouble getting out the words. "I'll be going home—back to my ship."

Sadie's small eyes filled. "There's too much of me to make you happy, ain't there, Captain." She shrugged. "That's all right. I know some men don't like big women." It was a moment before Sadie's infectious smile flashed once more. "But that don't mean big women can't like them."

Throwing her arms around his neck, drawing him tight against her ample softness, Sadie kissed him full on the lips. The kiss was pleasant and Derek allowed it full duration without response. Sadie winked as she drew back. "That was somethin' to remember me by."

Derek nodded and tipped his hat. Suddenly recalling that he wasn't wearing one, he dropped his hand back awkwardly to his side. His voice was soft with apology. "If someone wasn't expecting me . . ."

"Yeah, I know." Slipping her key into the lock, Sadie pushed the door open with a look of regret. "You're sure you don't want to come in just for a little while?"

"I regret I cannot."

Turning, Derek started back down the street as Sadie's door clicked closed behind him. It occurred to him that he had turned down a generous offer from a truly decent woman. He sighed. But there was only one woman he wanted . . .

Derek glanced up at the night sky, at the moon that was a bright crescent against the backdrop of black velvet overhead. It also occurred to him that it was later than he had thought and, he realized as he glanced around, that he wasn't really sure which of these small winding streets he should turn down to arrive back on the docks.

Derek touched his suddenly reeling head. He was tired. He needed a rest. He took a few steps more, then lowered himself to a seated position in the shadows of a tree and propped his back against the trunk. He'd rest just for a few minutes before going on.

Gillian twisted uncomfortably, then turned to look at the clock on the cabin wall. Catching herself in the act, she frowned and closed her eyes. There was no need to look at the clock. The silver light of dawn creasing the small patch of night sky visible through the porthole was ample indication of the hour.

The knot in her stomach tightened as Gillian turned her face into the pillow. What was wrong with her? So Derek had stayed out all night. This was the first time, but it most assuredly would not be the last. She knew he was all right— more than all right. Adria and Christopher had returned from the tavern hours earlier to say that Derek had started out celebrating with an old friend, and that his celebration had continued long after his friend had left.

Singing . . . Derek had actually been singing . . .

. . . and smiling.

Gillian swallowed against the thick lump in her throat. It was somehow painful to realize she had never seen Derek smile, that the only reaction she had ever stimulated in him had been anger and other, less admirable emotions. It was even more disturbing to acknowledge that Derek had felt the need to go elsewhere for relaxation and enjoyment—for the opportunity to spend a few carefree hours.

Gillian opened her eyes and glanced again at the lightening sky. It was long past the hour for the taverns closing. She wondered who was helping Derek pass those carefree hours now.

A sudden crash sounded on the deck above, and Gillian jumped with a start. She heard voices mumbling. She heard a door slam, then a stumbling thunder on the steps, and a loud thud. She sat up in the bunk as uneven footsteps started down the passageway. She lay back down and closed her eyes the moment before the cabin door was thrust abruptly open.

More stumbling steps and the pervading odor of alcohol . . . Derek stood swaying uncertainly by the bed. She heard his slurred curse and sensed his perusal. Through slitted lids she saw him frown.

The bunk shook as Derek flopped down unceremoniously beside her. He turned toward her and she heard him mumble as he flopped his arm across her breast.

Gillian's eyes slowly opened. She smelled flowers. She inched closer to Derek. He reeked of cheap perfume.

Derek mumbled again, and Gillian listened more closely.

"Sadie . . . only woman I want . . ."

Gillian caught her breath, fighting to withhold a sob at final confirmation of her thoughts.

Sadie, who smelled like flowers.

Sadie, to whom Derek had so easily turned.

Sadie, who was the first in a long line of many to come.

Sadie, who had brought her back to harsh reality when she had almost started to believe—

Her last thought too painful to conclude, Gillian paused a long moment before lifting Derek's arm carefully from across her body. She placed it by his side, her gaze lingering on his shadowed face as a solitary tear fell.

Fifteen

Morning dawned as Adria leaned over the washbowl in the corner of her cabin and splashed cold water on her face. She patted it dry, looking up at the cracked mirror almost in afterthought. She frowned at the image there. Her improved health was as clearly reflected in the blush of her cheeks as it was in the clarity of her gaze and the sheen of her pale hair. The illness that had almost stolen her life was in the past. Gillian had made her recovery possible . . . dear Gillian.

Turning away from the reflection of tears suddenly welling, Adria forced herself to continue dressing, her mind running in the same circles they had since she and Christopher had returned from the tavern the previous evening.

The sight of Captain Andrews behaving so uncharacteristically in the tavern had truly unsettled her. Also unsettling had been the inordinate amount of attention Sadie had showered on the captain as he fell deeper and deeper into his cups. Adria unconsciously shook her head. Sadie was a pleasant woman, but a promiscuous one. She could not count the times the buxom barmaid had taken a fancy to a customer and brought him home with her to continue entertaining him after the tavern had closed for the evening. She knew each and every time it had occurred, simply because Sadie was outspoken about her intimate affairs—almost as if she were proud of her sexual encounters.

Sadly puzzled, Adria frowned. She supposed she could understand that reasoning no more than she could understand a man who would waste time with Sadie while he could be lying in his own bed with—

Suddenly aghast at her own thoughts, Adria halted their progression abruptly. When had her thinking changed to such a degree that she now totally accepted the situation between Gillian and Derek Andrews? Adria searched her mind cautiously. Could it have been when she had first noticed the concern the captain evidenced for her sister? Could it have been when she had first noticed admiration in the captain's eyes—not for Gillian's physical beauty but for her beauty of spirit? Could it have been when she had first begun to suspect that the captain concealed feelings for her sister that far transcended the physical relationship between them?

Adria's throat tightened. Or had it been when she had first seen the warmth in *Gillian's* eyes when she looked at *him?*

Adria steadied herself against her growing distress. Was that why the thought of Sadie and the captain had cut so deeply?

Recalling the anguish reflected in Christopher's eyes the previous night as Gillian had maintained her brave facade in the face of the captain's delinquent return, Adria knew he had suffered for Gillian just as she did—for the same reason—because he loved her.

Adria's torment deepened. Christopher loved Gillian. Adria loved Christopher. And Gillian loved—

Adria impatiently brushed away a tear. She could not recall how long she had lain awake the previous night, waiting for the sound of the captain's step on the staircase. As it had turned out, she had not been able to mistake the hour of his return, and her heart had broken for Gillian's suffering.

Adria turned nervously toward the clock on the cabin wall. She had wanted an opportunity to speak to Gillian before she left for the tavern that morning so she might console her sister however she could, but it appeared there would not be time.

Staring at the cabin door, Adria paused indecisively. Dare she knock on the captain's door?

Paralyzed by uncertainty, Adria waited.

Gillian opened her eyes slowly, carefully, noting that the silver shafts of dawn that had accompanied Derek's return had expanded to full illumination of the morning sky as a familiar wave of nausea swept over her. She turned toward Derek, lying so close beside her. Had it been any other day, Derek would already have awakened and would have been on deck with his men when she arose, but she knew that would not be the case today.

The sickening surge progressed to a familiar churning, and Gillian silently groaned. She raised herself slowly to a seated position in the bunk, battling the rapid deterioration of her control as she crawled over Derek's inert form. Careful not to awaken him, she stepped down onto the floor of the cabin.

Panicking as nausea rose in a jolting rush, Gillian pressed a shaking hand tightly against her lips.

No, please no . . .

Abandoning conscious thought, Gillian rushed toward the cabin door. Outside in the passageway moments later, she ran the few steps to Adria's cabin and burst in. On her knees beside the wastebucket in a moment, she retched in deep,

heaving spasms. She looked up briefly as the ghastly convulsions abated to see Adria staring at her from beside the
closed cabin door before the retching began anew.

Weak and shaken moments later, Gillian leaned back on
her haunches, supporting herself against the bunk as her
eyelids drooped closed. She felt a hand on her shoulder and
opened her eyes to see Adria crouched beside her. Her sister's gaze brimmed as she questioned hoarsely,. "Does this
mean what I think it means, Gillian?"

Gillian could not make herself respond.

"Why didn't you tell me?"

The slow sobbing that began inside Gillian did not reach
her lips as she replied softly, "At first I wasn't sure, then I
didn't want to believe it. But there's no doubt anymore,
Adria. No doubt at all."

Adria slid her arms around Gillian, and Gillian could feel
her sister's trembling, even as Adria spoke in an attempt at
consolation.

"It'll be all right. I know it will."

Gillian drew back, her emotions strictly controlled as she
whispered, "I won't lie to you, Adria. I thought for a little
while . . ." She hesitated and began again. "I tried to make
myself believe that Derek cared for me beyond the pleasures
of the flesh, but I now know that even if that were true, it
means little. Derek is a free man and I'm his servant . . .
his slave. He's made no commitment to me. His actions last
night prove he values his freedom above all, whatever else
he feels."

"What are we going to do, Gillian?"

Gillian shook her head. The nausea was returning, and
with it the accompanying weakness. "I don't know, Adria.
Please, dear, leave me be for a little while."

"Are you sick again?"

"Yes . . . yes."

"H-how long do you think you'll be able to hide your condition from the captain?"

"I don't know. Please, dear . . ."

Gillian leaned back weakly against the bunk, her eyes closed. So intense was her discomfort moments later as she leaned again over the bucket that she did not hear the knock on the door, or Adria's frantic step, or the sound of the door opening.

Gasping, Gillian drew back at the touch of strong male hands on her shoulders.

"Gillian, what's wrong?"

Gillian swayed weakly under Christopher's touch. She looked up at him, her glorious eyes dulled, her magnificent skin colorless, her breathing short, and Christopher's concern deepened. Scooping her up into his arms, he carried her to the nearby bunk and lay her on its surface. Sitting beside her, he brushed her hair back from her cold, perspired cheeks and turned gruffly toward Adria.

"Get a damp cloth. Hurry."

Taking Gillian's icy hands in his, he chafed them nervously. He quizzed Adria sharply as she returned with the cloth.

"What happened to her?"

Adria blinked. She shook her head. "I . . . she . . . Gillian's sick."

"I know she's sick! I can see that! When did she get sick? How—"

"Christopher, please . . ."

Gillian's thin voice turned Christopher back toward her. Her color was returning, but she still looked unwell, and his heart pounded nervously. Gillian couldn't get sick, not now, when the damned captain was already straying. It had been difficult enough knowing that Gillian lay in the captain's bed each night. He had borne the situation with mixed emotions, knowing it afforded him his only opportunity to watch over her and remain a part of her life, ready to console her when the captain started to wander. He had not thought it would be so soon, or that he would suffer so badly at Gillian's anguish . . . or that she might grow ill.

"Christopher . . ." Gillian attempted a smile. It was a poor effort that failed miserably as she took his hand. "I'm sorry I frightened you."

Christopher turned back to Adria. "Get her some water."

"No . . . no." Gillian swallowed convulsively, and briefly closed her eyes. "I'm all right." She took a deep breath, then looked at him again. "I want to sit up."

"No."

"Yes."

Gillian was determined despite her lack of color, and Christopher knew he dared not refuse her. She met and held his gaze as he helped her to a seated position.

"I want you to promise me you won't tell anyone about this, Christopher."

Christopher shook his head, confused.

"I'm not sick."

Christopher did not speak.

"I'm going to have a child."

Her words hitting him with the force of a blow, Christopher could not reply as Gillian continued, "Strange isn't it, that the inevitable should come as such a shock to us all?"

Struggling to control the rising heat of anger, Christopher questioned stiffly, "Does he know?"

The planes of Gillian's face grew rigid. "No."

"He has no idea?"

Gillian avoided his eyes. "I've been able to hide my morning distress from him so far." She looked back up at him abruptly. "I need time, Christopher." The sudden, uncharacteristic welling of tears in Gillian's eyes tore at his heart as she rasped, "I have to have time to think."

"Gillian, I wish—" Christopher halted abruptly. He knew what he wished. He wished he could take her in his arms and tell her he loved her. He wished he could honestly say that he would take care of everything and make it better. But most of all, with all his heart, he wished that the child Gillian carried was his own.

"I know what you wish." Gillian's response interrupted Christopher's thoughts unexpectedly. "You wish you could have saved Adria and me from everything that's happened, but we both know that was beyond your power as well as ours. But I want you to know, Christopher . . ." Gillian's voice grew unsteady, ". . . that whatever happens now, I'll be forever beholden to you for what you've done for us."

"You don't owe me anything, Gillian."

"I do." Gillian glanced at Adria. "We both do."

"I don't want your thanks. I just want to know you'll be all right."

Gillian took another strengthening breath. "I'll be all right. I'm just . . . I just need some time to think things through."

Gillian's uncertainty almost more than he could bear, Christopher slid his arms around her and drew her against his chest. He felt her trembling as he whispered, "If I could only have spared you this."

"Christopher, please, I know you would have—"

Gillian's words halted abruptly at the sound of a step in the cabin next door. Her eyes snapping wide, she slipped

free of Christopher's arms and was on her feet before he
had time to rise. She had thrust the bucket out of sight and
was standing beside Adria when a knock sounded at the
door.

Christopher stood up at the sound of the captain's voice.

"Are you in there, Gillian?"

Gillian's expression hardened. "Yes, I am."

The door opened with a sharp thrust. Christopher's fists
knotted despite himself as the captain, much the worse for
wear, glanced between the three of them. The captain's gaze
lingered briefly on Gillian's nightrail and bare feet before
he demanded, "What in hell's going on in here?"

Gillian regarded him coldly. "You were sleeping. Considering your late return last night, I thought it might be best
if I came in here rather than chance awakening you."

The captain's eyes narrowed. "You were concerned for
my comfort?"

"I was concerned for my own. I thought your disposition
would be foul when you awakened, and I was right."

Not bothering to reply, Derek turned toward Christopher
abruptly. "What are you doing here?"

Christopher barely held himself in check. "I came to take
Adria to the tavern."

"Get going, then!"

Christopher glanced briefly at Gillian, only to hear the
captain growl, "You heard me . . ."

Christopher was ushering Adria down the passageway
when he heard Derek speak again to Gillian.

"From now on you will not leave my cabin unless you're
suitably clothed. Is that understood?"

Gillian's soft reply was indistinct, but the captain's angry
reaction was not.

"Gillian . . ."

The sound of Gillian's light step sounded in the hall, then the captain's following behind, and Christopher's heart sank once more.

"I'm warning you, Gillian . . ."

Following Gillian as she turned imperiously into his cabin, Derek slammed the door behind them. His heavy head began pounding anew and he silently cursed.

Gillian turned toward him, her brilliant eyes flashing. " 'Suitably clothed'—even to visit my sister next door?"

"That's right!"

"That's absurd! The sight of my nightrail is no novelty to Adria."

"Am I to assume it's no novelty to Gibson as well?"

"You may *assume* what you like!"

"I choose to assume that you will obey my orders!"

"And if I will not?"

"Witch!" Derek took a furious step forward. The painful drumming in his head had intensified, his stomach was churning, and his tongue felt as if it had been rolled in down. And still the witch taunted him.

Derek's fists tightened. Were he another man . . .

But he was *not* another man. Derek's fists loosened as he regarded Gillian more intently. "It appears to me that I'm not the only one whose mood is foul this morning."

"Oh, truly?" Gillian's magnificent brows rose with disdain. "I'm surprised you noticed. Your interests seem to be in other quarters of late."

Derek went abruptly still. The conniving witch . . . she sought to agitate him into telling her where he had been until the early hours . . . as if he owed her explanation. Well, he did not!

"You don't fool me, *madam* . . ." Gillian stiffened as he addressed her with the term she despised, and Derek felt satisfaction surge as he continued. "You've somehow gotten it into your mind that I owe you an explanation of my nightly whereabouts when I'm not lying in your bed." Derek grimaced in lieu of a smile. "Well, I do *not!*"

The furious drumming in his head increased to thunder, forcing Derek to speak more softly. "In the event you've forgotten, *I* am the master here. *I* am the one who demands the answers, and *I* am the one in control. *Your* freedom has been curtailed, not mine. My days and my nights are free to do with as I choose, with no restrictions or responsibilities that I do not choose to accept. I will spend my time where I like, and with whom I like, with no explanations due."

Derek paused, deliberately ignoring Gillian's paling. "And when I return from my excursions, I expect to find you *waiting.*"

Gillian's chin trembled. His brief regrets were overwhelmed by a new surge of anger at her soft reply.

"And you called John Barrett vile . . ."

Grasping Gillian's shoulders before he realized his intent, unconsciously amazed that the simple contact had the power to raise the heat of another kind inside him even as he inwardly raged, Derek managed past his growing physical distress, "Don't speak my name in the same breath with John Barrett's."

"The sharp edge of truth cuts deeply."

Releasing Gillian so abruptly that she took a few staggering steps backward, Derek growled, "Get out of here . . . now, before I do something I'll be sorry for."

Gillian's pale face remained defiant. "No. I will not."

"I'm warning you—"

"I will not because my *master* ordered that I shouldn't leave this cabin unless 'suitably clothed' . . ."

"Witch!" His physical distress swelling beyond control, Derek snatched up Gillian's clothing from a nearby chair. He threw it at her with a furious hiss. "Go to your sister's room and don't let me see your face in here again until I summon you!" Derek paused, his bloodshot eyes cold. *"If I summon you."*

Gillian's sober face twitched as she clutched the garments he had thrust at her. Derek had only a moment to consider that brief display of weakness before Gillian picked up her shoes and turned toward the door.

The door latch clicked loudly in the silence of Gillian's wake and Derek closed his eyes. The room spun, and he sat down abruptly. The spinning continued and he lay back on the bunk with a groan of misery.

It occurred to him that he had never dreamed, those long months ago on that frigid London dock when he had first glimpsed Gillian's face, that this complicated, aggravatingly painful morass would result.

Nor would he have believed it.

He still didn't.

And his regrets loomed.

"An obscene child!"

Adria gasped, then looked around her. The early-morning kitchen of the Royal Arms Tavern was at a momentary lull. She and Christopher had arrived a few hours earlier. As luck would have had it, Davey Wright had chosen that morning to walk with them as far as the tavern, eliminating the opportunity to discuss Gillian's shocking revelation. Finally finding a moment when Christopher and she could talk,

Adria had seized her opportunity, only to have her worst fears confirmed.

"Surely you must be wrong, Christopher." Adria's azure gaze pleaded. "No decent person could blame a child for an accident of birth."

"The law is the law, Adria. The illegitimate child of a bond servant is considered an obscene child. The woman is allowed to bear her child, but she must return to her former position as soon as possible afterward to continue serving out her bond. I've seen it happen in Philadelphia. The child is usually sent away to be raised by someone else and—"

"No! Gillian would never allow that!"

"You don't understand, Adria. There's no choice involved." Christopher's expression tightened. "By law, time is also added to the servant's term of indenture to compensate for the master's expenses in the birth of the child. If this were happening in Philadelphia now, Gillian would be required to pay a fine, which would also extend her term of indenture."

"But if the child has been sired by her master, she—"

"That makes no difference. The master isn't held responsible."

"That's unfair! It's indecent! It's—"

"It's the law."

"Christopher . . ." Adria glanced nervously around the secluded alcove where Christopher and she had hidden to talk. "Surely Captain Andrews wouldn't do that to Gillian. He cares for her."

Christopher's jaw twitched.

"He must care for her . . . a little, even if he did stray. You saw him this morning. I can't believe he could turn his back on his own child."

"Adria! Damn it, think what you're saying! Is that what

you want for Gillian . . . to be satisfied to have the child of a man who would keep her waiting in his bed while he makes the rounds of the local doxies?"

"No, but—"

"Gillian has a difficult choice to make."

"A choice?" Adria shook her head, confused. "Didn't you just say Gillian has no choice?"

"She has no choice if she wishes to *bear* the child . . ."

Adria's hand snapped up to cover her involuntary gasp. Her shocked eyes widened. "You're saying—"

"I'm saying the choice is Gillian's."

Adria grasped Christopher's arm. It was rigid under her touch as she rasped, "Gillian wouldn't do that!"

"It's *her* decision."

The sound of a step from the public room beyond snapped both their heads toward Sadie's well-padded form as she appeared in the doorway. Adria's stiffened. The barmaid had been full of cheer since the moment she arrived. She had responded with knowing winks to the coarse comments of a few people about the previous night's activity, and Adria's humiliation had welled for her dear, helpless sister.

Christopher's mouth tightened the moment before he shook off Adria's hand and stepped back into sight, and Adria's anguish soared. Christopher was right in one respect. The present situation could not continue—not without volatile results. It was obvious that despite his straying, the captain still jealously guarded Gillian. It was also abundantly clear that Christopher would not be able to bear Gillian's continued degradation. Dear Gillian had a difficult choice, indeed.

That heavy burden in mind, Adria stepped out of the alcove at the same moment Mrs. Healy limped in from tending the outdoor ovens. Mrs. Healy was recovering well, but that realization meant little to Adria in her present despair. Walking swiftly toward the worktable, her head down to conceal the glitter of tears, Adria took up the floured mass awaiting her and continued her work.

Her preoccupation intense, Adria did not notice the short, lean, foul-smelling fellow who peered in through the open window as she resumed her work—the fellow who had taken to loitering at the rear of the tavern in recent days. She did not see the intensity of his shifty-eyed gaze, or the evil smile that flickered across his face as he considered the conversation he had overheard. She did not see him nod as he silently agreed that the captain's whore had a choice to make, adding mentally that Master Barrett did as well.

Nor did Adria see enjoyment flash as the fellow indulged thoughts of Master Barrett's face when he would say . . .

"She's carryin' the captain's whelp, she is . . ."

"You lie!" John Barrett's eyes bulged under his heavy black brows. "Captain Andrews isn't that much a fool!"

"Aye, I'd say 'e is . . ." Peters shrugged his bony shoulders offhandedly. " 'E barely escaped the clutches of that fat sow, Sadie, only a night ago. It was my thought she'd get 'im, so deep in 'is cups was 'e."

John Barrett was instantly alert. "You're telling me the captain turned the barmaid's offer down?"

"Aye, 'e did. 'E told her 'e 'ad somebody waitin' for 'im. Two sheets to the wind 'e was, too, so much so that 'e spent the next few hours sleepin' under a tree a few feet from the eager bitch's door." Peters frowned. "I could've slit 'is throat as easy as looked at 'im and none would've been the wiser."

"I won't have that, I told you!" Barrett's expression tightened. "Not yet, at any rate. I won't have a quick, easy revenge on that man. I want Captain Derek Andrews to suffer as *I* suffered!" Barrett paused. "No, that's not exactly right. I want him to suffer *more* than I suffered. I want him to know tenfold the anguish I endured in that filthy ship's brig while he was amusing himself with Gillian Harcourt Haige's white flesh." Barrett gave a short laugh. "The rutting fool! Without his realization, he has provided me the perfect vehicle to do just that!"

Not waiting for Peters's reply, Barrett continued tightly. "You're sure the captain doesn't know about the child yet?"

"Aye, I'm sure. It looks like the bitch may decide to do away with it so 'e'll never know."

"No, she'll not dispose of it. I'll make sure of that."

Peters's gaze narrowed. " 'Ow can you be sure the bitch won't just slip away and get it done?"

"The captain will take care of that detail. He doesn't let her out of his sight. No . . . Mistress Haige will have to come up with a plan to escape his watchful eye before she finds someone to accommodate her purpose. That will take a few days, at least."

Peters shrugged again. "What do you want with the whelp, anyways?"

"Are you really that dense, Peters?" Barrett's impatience surged. "Surely you realize that if Captain Andrews would suffer in losing his women to me, he would suffer even more to know that I have his *child.*"

"If 'e cares at all . . ."

"He will. I'll *make* him care."

" 'Ow are you plannin' on accomplishin' all that in a few days?"

"A change of plans and quick action, that's all."

"What about that red-haired one?"

"We don't need her anymore."

"It's my thinkin' it won't be so easy to drop 'er. She's that 'ot for the captain that she'll not leave you be unless you keep 'er informed."

"A few words will put her off long enough to do the trick. Once I tell her what I have planned for the Haige bitch, she'll be satisfied. That witch is so vain that she truly believes once Gillian Haige is off the scene, Andrews will fall into her arms."

"Per'aps he will." Peters appeared amused. "What'll you do with your fine revenge if 'e's satisfied to take the red-'aired wench instead of sorrowin' after the other?"

"You'd like that, wouldn't you?" Barrett's voice dropped to a low hiss as he regarded Peters with open disdain. "You'd like to be able to say I told you so, that I should've allowed you to take the opportunity to slit the captain's throat when it was available to you. Well, I'll answer you with this, my bloodthirsty friend. Should the captain surprise me . . . should he decide to take advantage of the red-haired witch's offer rather than spend his time squirming about the woman who is to bear his child, he will be yours."

Peters smiled. "What'll you do with those 'Aige women then?"

" 'Use them and lose them' . . . I've always found that an efficient motto in my dealings with women. As a matter of fact, I know of a particularly popular house in London where a woman who is large with child demands a greater price from customers with specialized tastes." Barrett paused to consider that thought, continuing a moment later. "But the thought of the child intrigues me. There are so many 'uses' for children these days . . . especially if the child is broken in well . . ."

"Aye." Peters nodded. The thought intrigued him as well.

It raised a responsive swell in his groin as he rasped with growing enjoyment, "Tell me what you wants me to do."

"You're mistaken. It can't be!"

The four walls of Dr. Samuel Phelps's small office rang with Emmaline's shocked exclamation. She had arisen that morning frustrated, and determined that she would not let another day elapse before facing John Barrett with the failure of his plan to separate Derek from the pale-haired Haige women. He had said it was going to be so easy. All he needed was time.

Well, she had done her part. She had made up a story about Derek's being accused of dishonest dealings and had suggested Robert tell local estate owners and overseers they should refuse to ship their cargo with Derek. Robert, the dear, trusting husband that he was, had followed through immediately. Barrett had obviously been similarly successful with local commercial agents, but nothing had progressed past that point, despite the potential of Derek being detained indefinitely in port.

Nor had Barrett contacted her, and she was tired of waiting.

That irritation foremost in her mind, she had been seated in the carriage bumping along the road to town a half hour after Robert had left for the fields.

And then it had begun again . . . the nausea . . . the misery . . . the unfailing motion sickness that had left her no respite of late. Furious as she had hung over the side of the carriage, overwhelmed by the same revolting spasms for the fourth time that morning, she had decided that she would not tolerate the misery any longer. Her unscheduled visit to

Dr. Phelps upon arriving in town and his subsequent examination, however, had left her incredulous.

The lines of Dr. Phelps's aging face creased into a smile. "I assure you, my dear, I am not mistaken."

Emmaline's lips parted in an attempt at a reply. When no sound emerged, she swallowed, finally responding, "Robert is too *old* to have sired a child!"

Dr. Phelps laughed aloud. "Emmaline dear, I should have thought you would've realized by now that your husband is an extraordinary man."

Emmaline shook her head in silent refutation. No, this could not be! The palm of her hand moved unconsciously to her stomach. She was still as flat and firm as a board. There was not even the merest indication of a bulge.

Dr. Phelps continued softly. "Surely you've noticed an interruption in your monthly flow."

Emmaline shook her head. "I'm not particularly regular in that regard. Delays mean nothing."

"Have you felt a sensitivity in your breasts?"

Emmaline considered the question. Her breasts *had* been tender of late. For that reason Robert had been especially gentle the previous evening in his lovemaking. She recalled the ease he had given her as he had laved the erect crests with his tongue. It had felt so very, very good . . . as had his touch as he had massaged the aching swells with his hands, as he had drawn the delicate flesh into his mouth and suckled with gentle persistence. His sensitivity to her reactions had been unrelenting, his ardor intense, and his skill consummate, so much so that in the end she had flung her arms above her head to allow him fuller access, groaning and calling out her pleasure aloud, begging him not to stop.

Hmmmm. . . .

Emmaline shrugged in response to Dr. Phelps's inquiry. "A bit."

"Have you felt a surge in your . . ." The doctor hesitated. "In your carnal desires?"

Emmaline paused in reply. She recalled the particularly heated inner stimulation that had caused her to follow Robert into his dressing room that morning. She had come up behind him and whispered a subtle word into his ear that had stopped him in his tracks and held him immobile as she had gotten down on her knees to pay passionate homage to the swollen, unfailing instrument that had pleasured her so thoroughly the night before.

Robert had *howled* for more.

Emmaline raised a haughty brow in answer to the doctor's question. "Some."

"This nausea and retching that brought you here this morning, it's happened frequently?"

"Oh, yes . . . the motion sickness." Emmaline elaborated, "Any kind of rocking motion seems to start it off all over again."

Those words just out of her mouth, Emmaline silently considered the fact that motion sickness hadn't bothered her in the least the countless times of late that she had been inspired to mount Robert, to sit astride his swollen member, and to ride him until they were both wild with the ecstasy of it.

Emmaline continued in afterthought. "Perhaps it's the smell of the horses . . ."

"So, odors bother you?"

"Yes, at almost any kind of strong scent my stomach begins those revolting spasms."

"This has never happened before?"

"No, but I thought—"

Elaine Barbieri

"Yes, my dear. What did you think?"

Emmaline's lips tightened. "I'm *sure* it is the heat."

Dr. Phelps took her hand, his smile broadening. "My dear, you may believe me when I say it is not the heat. Robert will be overjoyed."

Overjoyed!

Emmaline snatched back her hand. Suddenly furious, she jumped to her feet. "No, he will not! Robert is too old to be a father. For that reason, I will expect you to take care of the matter so Robert will not be forced into this discomfiting situation in his old age."

The doctor's expression grew wary. "Robert isn't as old as you consider him to be, but in any case, if you mean what I think you do, I will have no part of it."

"Oh, will you not!" Emmaline's green eyes iced. "It is my body to do with as I like, is it not?"

"I'm sorry."

"Have it your way, then. You aren't the only person on this island able to perform the service for me!"

"My dear . . ." Dr. Phelps offered more gently, "You must give yourself some time to become accustomed to—"

"I will not!" Emmaline's eyes narrowed unexpectedly with threat. "Neither do I expect to discover that you have taken it upon yourself to inform Robert of your *mistaken* findings."

The old gentleman drew an offended step back. "Madam, confidentiality with regard to my patient's condition is always my first concern."

"It had better be!" Emmaline snatched up her bag and turned angrily toward the door. "Because you are wrong!"

Walking stiffly toward her carriage moments later, Emmaline glared at the stooped Negro driver awaiting her.

"What are you staring at, you old fool?" Cursing as

Quaco opened the door, she stepped up into the carriage and instructed tightly, "Port Royal Street. Hurry!"

"Where be dat?"

"The office of Mr. John Barrett, you idiot!"

"Yessa, missus."

Emmaline sat, her jaw locking as the carriage jerked forward. Her hand moved to her flat waist as the queasiness began once more. Damn it all! She would not suffer the grotesque swelling of form other women appeared to flaunt in their duties as brood mare. She would not chance the ugly puffing of her delicate features that often took place, and she would not subject herself to being seen waddling with the graceless, hideous gait of those women in the last throes of their nine months of humiliation!

Emmaline took a deep breath. Nor would she sacrifice her youth to the desires of a squalling infant when her own personal desires had not yet been met. She would get what she wanted—what she had *always* wanted—if it meant meeting in a thousand alleys or a thousand putrid offices, with a thousand loathsome creatures such as John Barrett. And when she *got* what she wanted . . .

Derek, you darling bastard . . .

Emmaline's eyes grew hot as she shouted at her driver once more.

"Faster, Quaco! I have no time to waste!"

"That will never happen, Christopher."

Silence reigned in Adria's small cabin as Gillian returned Christopher's sober stare. It had been a long, difficult day since Derek had ordered her out of his cabin that morning. Clothed and waiting in Adria's quarters, laboring to escape her whirling thoughts, she had stiffened when she had heard sounds of movement within his room sometime later, when she had heard Derek's door open and close, and the distinctive sound of his step approaching her door. But Derek's footsteps had continued past. She had not heard them again since.

Gillian frowned in recollection. She had gone up on deck a short time later, only to have Cutter approach her as she neared the gangplank, his face characteristically solemn as he stated softly, "The captain left the usual orders, Mistress Haige. You're not to leave the ship." He had seemed disturbed to have been forced to restate the captain's policy, and she had attempted a smile to assuage his discomfort, but she knew it had been a miserable failure. She had returned below shortly afterward to await Derek's return.

She had still been waiting when Adria and Christopher had returned from their day's work at the tavern.

Screeching sea birds skimmed the surface of the sea, their calls echoing eerily through the ship's wooden hull as Gillian continued, holding Christopher's gaze with soft determination. "I will never allow a child of mine to be considered an obscene child."

"Gillian . . ." The pain in Christopher's voice added to Gillian's own. "You must realize you won't be able to hide your condition from the captain indefinitely. Before that happens, you must make some difficult decisions."

Gillian did not respond.

"You realize you have few options . . ."

Gillian maintained her silence.

"Gillian . . ."

Gillian took a short breath. "Options?"

Christopher's expression remained sober. "The first option is obvious. You can tell the captain about your condition and let him decide what he wants to do." He paused, his gaze searching hers. "You would know better than I what his reaction would probably be—if he's likely to accept the responsibility of fatherhood and the accompanying demands."

. . . I am the master here . . . your freedom has been curtailed, not mine . . . my days and my nights are mine to spend as I choose, with no restrictions or responsibilities that I do not choose to accept . . . I will spend them where I like and with whom I like, with no explanations due . . .

Nothing could have been clearer.

"And if he does not choose to accept it?"

"He could send the child somewhere to be raised after it's born so that you and he—"

"No!" Gillian's throat tightened. "What's the second option?"

Christopher paused. "The second option would be not to have the child at all."

"You mean—" Gillian struggled against the great sadness welling within her. Adria whispered a soft word of comfort as she responded, "No, Christopher . . . I couldn't."

Christopher's eyes hardened. "There's only one other option."

Gillian waited.

"Escape."

"Escape . . ."

"We can do it, Gillian." Christopher grasped her shoulders as she turned away. "Look at me, Gillian. We can."

"We?" Gillian shook her head. "Do you realize what you're saying—what you would be risking?" She stared into his earnest light eyes. "This is an island, with no way to escape and no place to hide."

"That's not true."

"If you were caught—"

"We won't be caught."

"How can you be sure?"

"What's your alternative, Gillian?"

"I have no alternative, but *you* do."

Christopher's strong hands tightened almost to the point of pain. "That's where you're wrong."

Silence.

The sincerity of Christopher's husky response almost more than she could bear, Gillian stepped forward into his comforting embrace. Uncertain of the moment tears began falling, Gillian knew only that his soft, incoherent whispers against her hair soothed the deadening ache within her, and that his warmth was balm beyond measure for her wounded spirit. Drawing back minutes later, she did know, however, that she would allow tears to fall no more.

Brushing the dampness from her cheeks, Gillian felt Adria's hand slide into hers as she whispered, "Tell me your plan."

"No, it isn't true!"

Emmaline battled incredulity. She had arrived at John Barrett's office minutes earlier, only to have Barrett steal the wind from her sails with a few, short words.

To hear the same pronouncement twice in one day . . .

Incredulity turned to rage. "She did it on purpose! The witch hopes to trap Derek with the babe she carries!"

"Not so! She's hidden her condition from the captain so far and is considering doing away with the child. I won't allow that, of course."

"Why not?" Emmaline was taken aback. "Surely you realize Derek will be less likely to let her go if he finds out."

"Because she's made herself twice as valuable to me."

Barrett's smile became a sinister leer. "I'll have three for the price of two, and I'll have a novel twist added to my intimate plans."

Emmaline's stomach did an unexpected turn. John Barrett was truly a nauseating man. Were she another woman, she might actually feel sorry for the sisters who would soon be in his degenerate clutches.

But she was not another woman.

"I don't care what you do with them once you get them away from Derek . . . *if* you can get them away from Derek."

"I assure you, madam, I will prevail." Barrett's jaw locked with determination. "I would have preferred to wait until the captain's financial situation was so critical that he was either forced to sell the indentures back to me, or until everyone would indeed believe he did when I produced forged papers to prove the transaction. The law would've taken care of the problem then, and I would've been long on my way back to England before he could come after me. It is fortunate, however, that the *Sea Breeze* is in port and will be sailing for England next week. I've worked with the captain of that ship before and I'll have no difficulty booking passage for myself and *two* bond servants, with no questions asked." Barrett smiled. "Of course, I'll have to rush the forged papers through processing, but that will only be a matter of sweetening the price. Once I'm back in London, no one will question their validity."

"As for the Gibson fellow . . ." Barrett shook his head, "it saddens me that I'll be forced to turn his fate over into the hands of a rather bloodthirsty associate on the island, but I fear Gibson would prove more trouble than he's worth on the return voyage."

"You intend kidnapping the two women?" Emmaline attempted to ignore budding uneasiness. "If you think you'll easily accomplish that feat, you're dangerously underestimating Derek. He won't suffer a kidnapping without a fight."

"Madam . . ." Barrett was fast losing patience. "I repeat, I am not a fool. Captain Andrews won't discover it was a kidnapping until it's too late. A note from the Gillian bitch explaining she and her sister have run off with Gibson will keep him searching the island for them long enough for me to—"

"I thought you said you intended to dispose of Gibson."

Barrett's impatience intensified. "When the note is found and Gibson disappears at the same time as the two women, Captain Andrews will draw the obvious conclusion." Emmaline did not respond, allowing Barrett to continue. "In any case, by the time Captain Andrews starts to suspect what happened, the *Sea Breeze* will be well on her way back to England. He won't be able to follow because he won't be able to obtain a cargo and he's without sufficient funds to undertake such a voyage with an empty hold."

Barrett's thick lips twitched with enjoyment. "So . . . he'll be trapped into remaining in Jamaica indefinitely. That should suit your purpose, should it not, madam?"

"You are diabolical."

"Thank you." Barrett bowed. "I consider that a compliment coming from you."

Emmaline's eyes narrowed at his backhanded compliment. "Somehow I sense it is paramount at this point to warn you that all your plans will be for naught should Derek learn the woman is to bear his child. He's a stubborn sort, you know. He would never abandon the search then."

Barrett's heavy brows rose. "I fail to see the need for your concern, madam. Haven't you maintained that you need only separate him from the Haige woman and he'll be yours again?"

Emmaline's delicate jaw firmed. "Don't take me for a fool! I'm not as easily manipulated as you would like to believe. I know there's more to your plan than you have revealed."

"Bitch!" Barrett was suddenly enraged. "I've told you all I intend telling you!"

"Bastard! I'll find out anyway . . . and if I discover you've deceived me or you have any intentions beyond those you've already expressed, I'll see that you regret it."

"I would be careful about making threats if I were you."

Emmaline's narrow nostrils flared with indignation. "You don't frighten me."

"Perhaps it would be wiser if I did."

"My dear Mr. Barrett, perhaps I should also take this opportunity to warn you that you'll be making a drastic mistake if you underestimate *me*."

Barrett's face flamed. "The same might be said for myself, Madam Dorsett. I would say we're at stalemate."

"You flatter yourself!"

Emmaline turned toward the door, then turned back abruptly. Her fragile features were as hard as stone as she added in a measured tone, "It occurs to me that I would be remiss if I left without making myself perfectly clear to you, considering the consequences involved. So, the situation is this: Should you, or your machinations, become an impediment between Captain Andrews and myself, I will personally see to it that *you* are removed, along with the impediment."

"Bitch! You would threaten me in my own office?"

"I would threaten you wherever I choose! If you are wise, you will not forget it!"

Her warning still ringing behind her, Emmaline emerged

onto the street. Incensed, she climbed into her carriage. The bastard did not fool her. Nor did he intimidate her. If he were not cautious, he would find that the greatest mistake of his life would be in failing to realize that Emmaline Dorsett meant what she said!

Emmaline paused in her thoughts as the streets slipped past and Quaco turned onto the rough road out of town. But first she need take some steps of her own to dispense with the totally unexpected problem she had encountered earlier.

Emmaline's hand unconsciously slipped to her flat stomach. She would visit Dr. Clark tomorrow to confirm Dr. Phelps's assessment of her condition. If Dr. Phelps was correct, she would have Dr. Clark, who by reputation had no such qualms, take the necessary steps to eliminate the problem. She would use the day or so it took for recovery from the doctor's procedure to gather information through the usual channels. So armed, she would then attack the problem of Mr. John Barrett with renewed vigor. She—

Her thoughts jolted from mind as the carriage lurched into a deep groove in the road and her stomach began a familiar churning, Emmaline closed her eyes.

No.

Not again . . .

Emmaline swallowed thickly.

Yes.

Again.

John Barrett slipped temporarily from mind.

It was a conspiracy, all right . . .

Derek's strong features were knit into a frown as he strode along the dock toward the *Colonial Dawn*. It had been a damned difficult day! His mood had been foul after his furious exchange with Gillian that morning. His consequent, unscheduled interviews throughout the day with the commercial agents in port had not improved it. Determined, he had gone so far as to hire a carriage to take him to the inland homes of some of the estate owners, but the result had been the same. Smiles and denials—a conspiracy to keep him on the island until he was financially destroyed.

There was only one person with that kind of power in the port of Kingston!

Or, perhaps two . . .

Derek's frown darkened as the masts of his ship came into view. The long carriage ride to Master Tuit's estate had given him time to do considerable thinking about his abominable behavior that morning. He had finally admitted to himself that a throbbing head and a queasy stomach had changed him into a bonafide monster in his dealings with Gillian.

Derek's jaw ticked with annoyance. Gillian, of course, was not blameless. Had she had a lick of sense, she would have catered to his uncertain physical state instead of taunting him, instead of behaving like a shrew, instead of—

Derek halted the progression of his angry thoughts. It would do no good to rehash either Gillian's foolish behavior or his own. He did not doubt she had learned a valuable lesson and would not press him again for explanations that were not due her. She would be waiting just as she had been instructed to wait, and she would be eager for his forgiveness.

Gillian's exquisite face bright before his mind, Derek stepped up onto the gangplank. She would be almost as eager to be forgiven as he was to forgive her . . . to take her into his arms and—

Rapidly descending the staircase to the berth deck moments later, Derek turned toward his cabin. He came to an abrupt halt at the sound of voices in Adria's cabin. Gillian. He could not mistake her soft, feminine tone.

But there was another voice, deep and male, speaking softly to her in response.

Derek thrust the cabin door open.

Gibson . . . his arms around Gillian . . .

A flash of movement and the hard crack of Derek's fist against Gibson's jaw sounded in loudly in the cabin. The smaller man slammed backward against the rear wall, his expression dazed. Derek smiled menacingly as Gibson shook his head and took an aggressive step toward a confrontation from which there would be no return.

Slipping between them unexpectedly, Gillian halted Gibson's advance. Her back to Derek, she whispered softly to Gibson and Derek's jealousy soared.

"Get out of the way, Gillian!"

Gillian turned toward him with a snap. "No, I won't! I won't let you force Christopher into something he'll regret simply because he helped me to my feet!

"You're trying to tell me you fell and Gibson was helping you up?" Derek laughed, a harsh sound void of mirth. "If you think I'll believe that—"

"It's the truth!"

Derek looked at Gibson in direct challenge. "Is that true, Gibson?"

Gibson's gaze was pure ice for the long moments before he responded with a single word. "Yes."

"Coward."

Gibson's spontaneous advance was again halted by a sound from Gillian, and Derek's rage soared.

"Get out of this cabin, Gibson! And don't come back!"

Hesitating a fraction of a moment that silently voiced his

contempt, Gibson strode past Derek and disappeared into the passageway.

Derek turned back to Gillian. "I warned you . . ."

"Oh, yes, I forgot." Gillian's smile was frigid. "My *master* ordered that I shouldn't let another man touch me—for any reason. How marvelous to have the power to impose restrictions upon others when one imposes no restrictions at all upon oneself."

Bold, infuriating witch . . .

Turning sharply on his heel, Derek stormed from the cabin, leaving Gillian cold-eyed and resolute behind him. Slamming the door behind him as he entered his cabin, Derek stood in the reverberating silence, struggling with his rage.

The thought he had had the previous day returned unexpectedly to mind.

It had all begun that frigid day on a London dock long months ago when Gillian's glorious, haughty eyes had first met his.

The question remaining was, where it would end?

The babe's soft wailing continued. It echoed in the darkness, blending with the shrieking of the storm that beat Gillian backward as she struggled toward the sound.

The whistling wind battered her.

The icy rain flayed her face.

The muddy ground dragged at her feet.

The babe's wail weakened as whispers in the screeching wind grew louder.

She's gone, you'll never find her.

She'll never be yours.

The whistle of the wind became a howl.

The rain became a deluge.
She could not walk.
She could not see.
The babe wailed on . . .

Gillian awoke with a start. Her breathing labored, her anxiety intense, she glanced around her. She saw the interior of Adria's cabin, the pallet on which she lay. She heard the sound of her sister's even breathing. She raised her hand to her forehead to find it damp with perspiration, and she closed her eyes against the heavy pounding of her heart.

She had seen her babe's face in that dream . . . a beautiful little girl with light hair and eyes as black as night. Derek's eyes. She had seen the babe, but she had not been able to reach her.

The pain still lingered.

The small, airless cabin squeezing the breath from her lungs, Gillian threw back the coverlet and stood up abruptly. She reached for her clothes, slipping them on with trembling hands as she glanced at her sister again. Adria had had as much difficulty falling asleep as she after Derek had left. Adria suffered for her, but Gillian knew her sister could not possibly know the full extent of her tormented secret.

Unwilling to dwell on that agonizing thought, Gillian slipped her feet into her shoes and walked to the door. Stepping up onto the deck moments later, she breathed deeply of the fresh night air, realizing as the breeze fluttered the locks of pale, unbound hair on her shoulders that she was shuddering.

Gillian walked the few steps to the rail and grasped it tightly, then glanced back at the quarterdeck to see the shadowed figure on watch there. Linden—she could not mistake his brawny outline.

Turning her back on the seaman's speculation, Gillian stared out at the dark sea. The air was warm, the night breeze balmy, in sharp contrast with the morning which seemed so long ago when she had stepped down from a prison cart onto the cold London dock and had grasped Adria's trembling hand. She had been so confident then, so righteous and haughty, and so contemptuous of all connected in any way with the travesty of justice to which they had been subjected. She had held Adria and herself above them all, and she had been determined to survive—no, to emerge victorious from the demoralizing fray about to commence.

She had been a fool.

Gillian's throat tightened to pain. She had learned the hard lesson that there could be no true victory in an experience with human misery such as they had shared—that those subjected were changed forever in ways she had never imagined, and those who appeared victors were ultimately defeated by their own soul-numbing inhumanity.

Raising her gaze to the dark sky above her, Gillian was momentarily stunned by the beauty of the heavens. The silver moon glowed luminously, lightening the docks with the brightness of day as the stars glittered and winked in a breathtaking display unmatched by any she had seen before. Somehow the brilliant celestial beauty that contrasted so vividly with the darkness of her personal anguish paralleled the beauty and contrasting torment of lying in Derek's arms, as well as the sense of wonder and contrasting anxiety of knowing his babe grew within her.

Gillian slid her palm against her narrow waist, allowing it to rest gently there. Christopher had listed the options for her, but she had known immediately there could only be one. She could not end the life of Derek's unborn babe, because she loved it. Her true anguish lay, however, in the truth she had sought to deny—that she loved Derek, too.

Gillian searched her mind, seeking to identify the moment when that love had begun. Had it begun when she had first lain in Derek's arms, when he had made love to her with a passionate sensitivity and gentleness that had betrayed a part of him otherwise concealed? Had it grown with his increasing tenderness during the long nights of the voyage, and with the wonder she had sensed in him, matching her own, at the consuming scope of emotions between them? Had it begun to flower when he had stormed into Charles Higgins's house of ill repute and claimed her? Had it come into full bloom as he had fought and lost his battle with the depth of his emotions each time he had touched her since?

Uncertain, Gillian knew only that she loved Derek, that somehow he had become a part of her, and that in his arms, she was complete.

But Derek did not love her. He had made it painfully clear that his feelings for her stopped short of that mark.

Gillian turned to search the shadowed masts of ships docked along the harbor. The *Brighton Belle* was somewhere among them. Christopher knew that the captain of that ship was a man who despised the penal transportation system of enforced indentured servitude. Christopher was certain he could convince him to transport the three of them to the colonies in lieu of payment for his work as seaman. Most important of all, the *Brighton Belle* was scheduled to be loaded and ready to sail in a few days.

Christopher's plan to get her off the *Colonial Dawn* without Derek's knowledge was simple. Derek would not discover she was gone until it was too late and he would then—

"Gillian . . ."

Gillian turned with a gasp at the sound of a voice at her elbow. Her heart pounded as Derek continued softly. "What are you doing up here alone this time of night?"

Gillian stiffened. "I was restless. I couldn't sleep."

Derek's gaze searched hers. "Neither could I. I want to talk to you. Will you come for a walk with me, Gillian?"

Gillian paused a long moment before nodding.

The knot in Gillian's chest squeezed to pain as Derek slid his arm around her shoulders and drew her against his side, then called out to Linden. "We're going for a walk."

"Aye, sir."

Minutes later the sound of their footsteps was echoing along the dock.

"What's the matter, dear? Is something wrong?"

The enormous master bedroom of the Dorsett sugar estate was illuminated with silver moonlight as Emmaline turned toward the sound of Robert's voice. The deep lines in his full, jowled face were emphasized by the shadows as he lay beside her, but she saw only his obvious concern as he touched her cheek lightly.

"Aren't you feeling well?"

Emmaline did not smile. "I'm well enough."

Momentarily silent, Robert spoke again with the genuine warmth of tone so characteristic of all his dealings with her. "Is something bothering you? If it is, my dear, you know you can tell me."

Emmaline remained silent, her gaze traveling the scant gray hair on her husband's balding pate. Somehow, over the years she had become accustomed to the sheen where his hair had once been and had accepted it without thought.

Suddenly realizing Robert awaited her response, Emmaline replied, "I suppose I've just taken on too much of late with all my visits to Mrs. Lindham during her illness."

Emmaline glanced away, suddenly uncomfortable with the excuse she had used for her persistent traveling back and forth to town. She had made certain to visit the old woman several times as a precaution, but her visits had been short and timed to coincide with her more pressing interests. Her discomfort increased as Robert lowered his head to touch her lips with his.

"Do you know what I think, my dear? I think it might be time to take a holiday."

"A holiday?" Emmaline frowned at Robert's unexpected suggestion. She had no time to think about a holiday now. *Especially* not now, with her visit to Dr. Clark the next morning looming more darkly with each passing hour and John Barrett's threatening machinations hanging like a black cloud over her head.

Emmaline attempted a smile. "You're so busy with harvesting, and with putting in the new crop. Surely you have no time."

"You've always said you wanted to see England."

"England?"

"Or the colonies. Philadelphia, New York, Charleston, wherever appeals most to you."

Emmaline stared at Robert. His timing was almost ludicrous! With the weight of her future lying in the balance of the next few days, Robert had suddenly gotten it into his head to show her the world!

Emmaline managed a casual response. "Why would you want to travel now, dear?"

Robert hesitated. Emmaline saw the thought he put into his words as he replied, "Because you've been looking peaked of late. Beautiful as always, but peaked."

Emmaline stiffened. "I have?"

"Yes. I've begun thinking that perhaps I've been too ardent in my intimate attentions."

"Really, Robert!" Emmaline was somehow miffed. "Whatever put that thought into your head?"

"I'm glad, my dear, because I love making love to you. I hope you'll never tire of the intercourse between us."

Robert kissed her lingeringly. A familiar warmth expanded inside Emmaline despite her previous distraction, surprising her.

Damn! Why did Robert have to be so old and fat and homely?

"You see," Robert continued softly, "I know I'm old and fat and homely . . ."

Emmaline was momentarily taken aback.

"And I know you're young and beautiful, and filled with the normal desires of a young, beautiful woman."

"Robert . . ."

"But I want you to know that I want you to be happy, Emmaline. I want you to have everything I can possibly give you . . . everything you married me for."

"Robert!" Emmaline was truly distressed. "What's the matter with you? I married you because I love you!"

"Emmaline dear . . ."

Emmaline's throat tightened unexpectedly. "I won't have you talk like this, Robert!"

"You're so young and you had such a difficult beginning in life. I'm sure you must've had many dreams. I have a mirror, you know. I know I couldn't possibly fit the picture of the man you pictured in them."

"I'm not a child, Robert."

"I suppose you aren't . . ." Robert drew her closer. His

voice dropped to a whisper. "I'd be lost without you. You know that, don't you, my darling? You are my life."

The tightening in Emmaline's throat intensified as she slid her arm around her husband's broad waist. Suddenly uncertain of the source for her anger, she whispered, "How many times must I tell you that you'll never have to do without me? *Never!*"

Robert drew her closer in return, and Emmaline's throat constricted to the point of pain. Somehow Robert had sensed her feelings. She need be more careful about that in the future.

The unexpected warmth of tears heavy beneath her lids, Emmaline frowned. She would be herself again after her visit to Dr. Clark in the morning. In truth, she had not thought the impending deed would loom so darkly in the silence of the night, displacing all other thought and precluding sleep. She would be glad when it was over, and when it was, when Derek was finally hers, again, she would make certain Robert wouldn't suffer for the sharing of her time.

Yes, everything would all be all right after her trip to Dr. Clark was over and done . . . and after Derek was hers again.

That determination in mind, Emmaline settled against Robert's soft bulk and closed her eyes.

"What did you want to talk about, Derek?"

The moon's glowing rays lent a patina of silver to Derek's dark-eyed gaze as he stopped walking and looked down at Gillian, his expression solemn. They had left the dock area to take a nearby road that wound along a deserted beach. The ground had been suddenly soft underfoot as Derek had stepped down onto the narrow beach, drawing her along with him. Derek had maintained his silence as they had wandered farther, as Gillian's anticipation had heightened with each successive step.

The sea lapped softly against the shoreline as Gillian pressed again. "Derek?"

The night wind gusted unexpectedly, flaying Gillian with glimmering strands of hair that shone molten silver in the moonlight. Capturing the long, wayward locks in his hand, Derek curled them around his fist, studying them briefly.

"Your hair is like you, Gillian—unmatchable."

"That's not true. You've forgotten about Adria. She and I are almost identical."

"No, you're not."

"Yes, we are."

"No, that isn't true. You were distinctly different from each other to me from the start."

"In temperament, perhaps."

"In that way, too."

Gillian frowned, unwilling to pursue the discussion. "We didn't walk all this way to discuss the similarity between Adria and me, did we, Derek?"

"No." Derek released her hair abruptly. He grasped her shoulders, holding her immobile with the intensity of his gaze. "You're angry with me, aren't you?"

Gillian's response was sincere. "No, I'm not."

Derek gauged her response. "You were angry with me this morning."

"Yes."

"Why aren't you angry now?"

Gillian shrugged. "This morning was a long time ago."

"Meaning?"

"Meaning that I've done a lot of thinking since then, and I've realized—"

"Don't go any farther, Gillian. Just let me say the words I want to say."

Slipping his arms around her, Derek pulled her flush against him. She felt the heavy hammering of his heart against her breast as he held her tightly. "I'm sorry." His lips against her hair, he repeated, "I'm sorry. I was a damned bastard this morning. My head was pounding, my stomach was churning, and when I came into the cabin and saw you in your nightclothes with Christopher—"

Gillian stiffened. She attempted to draw back from his embrace but Derek allowed only enough distance so he might see her face. He saw the anger that flashed as Gillian rasped, "You don't really think that I—"

"No, I don't." Derek's eyes hardened unexpectedly. "But I do think that given the chance, Gibson would use it to his advantage."

"You're insane! Christopher is a friend! If he's fond of anyone in that way, it's Adria!"

"Gibson doesn't even see Adria! He sees only you."

"Derek, please—" Gillian shook her head. "I don't want to discuss Christopher."

"Neither do I. There are other things that need be said."

Derek paused. Gillian saw the torment in his eyes as he looked at her. She felt the need to stroke the tense lines from his face, to tell him it was all right, that her anger was gone because she had come to terms with what must be done, that he needn't concern himself as to where the future would take them from there, because he would soon be free of the unexpected burden she had become to him. But she did not.

Gillian sighed. "Please say what you want to say, Derek. I'm tired."

"Damn you, Gillian!" Derek was suddenly angry. "What's happened! You were angry this morning and this afternoon, but everything has suddenly changed. Don't you care anymore?"

Gillian's heart ached with Derek's distress. "Oh, I care."

"Then?"

"What good would it do for me to rant and rave, Derek? What's done is done. It can't be changed, and it can't be ignored."

"What are you talking about?"

"What happened last night . . ."

Derek stiffened. "I told you, I won't answer to you or anyone else about my whereabouts. I don't owe you any explanations. My time is my own. I've apologized for my treatment of you this morning. That's as far as I'll go."

"I know."

"Gillian, listen to me!" Derek's torment became her own as he rasped, "I can't make any promises about the future or how long these feelings between us will last. I only know that I want you now, more than I've ever wanted any other woman. And I can only tell you that I won't let you go, if you rage or rant or carry on, or even if you decide to remain cold, as you are to me right now."

"I'm not cold to you, Derek."

"No? How would you describe the way you're acting?"

"I've accepted the situation as you put it to me, that's all."

"You have . . ."

Gillian nodded.

"Suppose I told you I don't want you to 'accept' it this way? Suppose I told you I want you to—"

"Derek . . ." Tears rose unexpectedly to Gillian's eyes. They had so little time left to them—just a few days. She didn't want to spend it in anger. She wanted . . . she *needed*—for just this short time, to love Derek as she wanted to love him . . . enough to last the rest of her life. Her voice emerged as a rasping whisper. "Let's not talk anymore."

Unresponsive to her soft plea, Derek remained motionless as Gillian slid her arms around his neck . . . as she raised herself on tiptoe to memorize the shape of his lips with her tongue . . . as she tasted his mouth . . . as the tasting lingered and became a kiss.

Uncertain of the exact moment when Derek's arms snapped closed around her, when he joined the fervor of her kiss, when the kiss became longing and the longing became loving, Gillian felt the sand beneath her back and Derek's weight upon her. Reveling in the beauty, in the hunger, in the soul-shattering need that rose between them, Gillian surrendered the warm flesh of her breasts to his kiss. She raised herself to aid his trembling hands as he stripped away her undergarment to find the warm, moist nest awaiting him. She gasped as he entered her abruptly, claiming her, and then going still.

Breathless, she raised anxious eyes to Derek's to find his gaze fixed on her face. She heard his rasping whisper.

"Gillian . . . it's right and good between us. You know that, don't you, darling?"

. . . for as long as it lasts . . .

"Yes . . . I do, Derek."

"I've never felt about any woman the way I feel about you . . . you know that, too, don't you?"

. . . with no explanations due . . .

"Yes."

She felt Derek's throbbing within her, then his anguished murmur, "It's too soon . . ."

It came then, the cataclysm of ecstasy, jolting and shuddering through them in simultaneous waves as they clutched each other close, allowing their passion full measure.

Replete and sated upon her, Derek was motionless for long moments before he raised himself to look down at Gillian solemnly. Glancing around the dark, deserted beach abruptly, he withdrew himself from her and stood up. He drew her to her feet beside him, briefly adjusting his clothing before he brushed her trembling fingers from the buttons on the front of her dress and fastened them in her stead.

"This was a damned fool thing to do—out here." Derek paused, dipping his head to brush the last glimpse of her breasts with his kiss before he buttoned them from sight. His handsome face grew intensely sober. "We're going back to the ship, and when we get there, I'll make this moment worthwhile. I promise you that, Gillian, because the truth is that I've never, *never* wanted you more."

Derek's words rang in Gillian's mind as Derek slid his arm around her and turned her back in the direction from which they had come. They sustained her.

For a few days she would ignore reality. For a few days she would indulge joy without thought to tomorrow.

For just a few days more.

Sixteen

Adria turned, uncertain if she had heard someone in the passageway beyond her cabin door. Her heart pounding, she went suddenly still. It had been difficult falling asleep the previous night after Gillian, Christopher and she had made the dangerous decision to escape. The night had become even more trying after she had awakened midway to find Gillian's pallet empty. Her mind had raced as she had waited for Gillian to return.

First had come the thought that Gillian had gone down to the galley for something to calm her troubled stomach. When she did not return, she had thought Gillian might be up on deck. Afraid to go upstairs to check for fear of calling attention to Gillian's absence, she had continued waiting, her fears mounting—Gillian had run away . . . she was sick . . . she was alone in the dark somewhere.

Common sense had again prevailed, and her heart had ached at the thought that Gillian might be with the captain.

Then had come the thought that if she *wasn't* with the captain . . .

Her heart gave a nervous leap as the approaching step halted outside her door. She held her breath as it was thrust open abruptly.

Gasping with relief as Gillian entered, Adria pushed the cabin door closed behind her.

"Gillian, I was so worried! I awoke midway through the night and you were gone. I didn't know where you were! I was afraid to look for you for fear of alerting someone to your absence."

Gillian's brief smile was apologetic. "I'm sorry, Adria. It was thoughtless of me to leave without explanation, but I—I wasn't able to sleep. I went upstairs on deck for some air."

"But you were gone all night!"

"Derek was there."

Adria went suddenly still. A low, sober lament began in her heart at her sister's revealing expression.

Gillian . . . poor, dear Gillian . . .

"Derek and I talked. We went for a walk . . ."

Adria did not reply. No explanation was necessary.

"Are you disappointed in me, Adria?"

"Gillian, how could you even ask such a question?"

"You know the truth, don't you?" Gillian challenged her with her gaze. "I didn't realize it myself until last night— truly I didn't."

"Yes, I know." Adria's heart squeezed to pain at her sister's distress. "But you mustn't blame yourself for feelings you can't control. The captain has been kind to you in so many ways."

"And not so kind in others."

"He was fair. He kept to the letter of the agreement you struck with him during the voyage."

"As did I."

"He protected you from John Barrett."

"Because he despises the man."

"He obviously cares for you. He rescued you from Charles Higgins at great personal expense."

"It suited his purpose."

"Gillian, he rescued *me* from Charles Higgins when he rescued you, although he thinks very little of me."

Gillian's lips tightened. "His judgment of women is decidedly faulty."

"He bought my indenture because he knew you couldn't be happy if I remained behind in that place. He did that for you."

"Yes, he did that for me. That's when I started to believe that he—" Gillian halted abruptly, continuing more softly a moment later. "But whatever he feels for me made little difference when a woman ashore struck his fancy."

"Gillian, please don't torture yourself!"

"Adria," Gillian spoke with soft determination, "I'm merely facing a truth Derek doesn't deny. But I suppose the true shame of it is that I'm *not* torturing myself."

"You are!"

"No, I'm not." Gillian paused, her gaze riveted on her sister's face. "To my everlasting humiliation, I made the decision last night to strike it all from my mind so that the memory of the last few nights Derek and I will spend together might not be tarnished."

"Gillian, please . . ."

"I've shown myself to be totally lacking in pride, Adria, one area where I never thought to find myself deficient."

"You had no choice in doing what you did last night!"

"I did."

"Gillian dear . . ." Profound understanding shone in Adria's eyes. "You had no choice because you *love* him."

Gillian's eyes grew moist. "Oh, Adria, why did I doubt even for a moment that you would understand?"

"Where is the captain now?"

"He's on deck. I dressed and came here as soon as he left the cabin."

Adria took a short breath. "Do you still want to follow through with our plans?"

"Yes." When Adria remained silent, Gillian continued more softly. "Last night didn't make any true difference, Adria. Derek doesn't *love* me."

Gillian's pain her own, Adria rasped, "He cares for you, I know he does."

"Yes. I know he does, too. But not enough. He made it clear to me last night that he values his freedom above all, and the truth is that I could no more abide the possibility of Derek's continued straying than I could abide uncertainty as to the fate of the child I will bear."

"Are you sure, Gillian?"

Gillian paused. "Christopher will find out the details of the *Brighton Belle*'s sailing this morning?"

"Yes."

"Tell Christopher that no matter how it appears, I'll be ready whenever he says the time is right."

"He'll be here shortly to take me to the tavern. You can tell him yourself."

"I dare not stay. Should Derek find me in here with Christopher again so soon . . ."

Adria did not respond.

"Tell him for me, Adria."

A moment later, the door closed behind Gillian. Still staring at the door, uncertain how long Gillian had been gone, Adria jumped as another knock sounded. She opened the door, noting as she did that Christopher glanced past her into the cabin.

"Gillian's not here."

"Where is she?"

"In the captain's cabin."

Christopher stiffened.

"Gillian went up on deck last night when she couldn't sleep. He was there."

"So the bastard took her back down with him."

"Christopher . . ."

"He wants the dockside whores and he wants Gillian, too. He's too much of a fool to see that Gillian's worth a thousand of those women!"

"Christopher, please don't!" Grasping his arm, Adria stopped his heated tirade, continuing softly, "It's going to be all right. I know it is."

"Everything's changed, damn it!" Christopher's voice rose angrily. "He's got her again, and if he manages to convince her that he won't stray again, she—"

"No, she won't change her mind."

"How do you know that, Adria? How can you be sure?"

"Because Gillian said so. She said to tell you that last night changed nothing."

Christopher was suddenly silent. When he spoke again, his voice was softly apologetic. "I'm sorry, Adria."

"Christopher, please . . . Don't you think I realize what you're risking for Gillian and me?"

"I had no right to take my frustration out on you."

Adria's gaze lingered. The sight of Christopher—his compact, muscular build, his curly, sandy-colored hair and brown beard, the light dusting of freckles across the bridge of his nose, the direct, gray-eyed gaze that had brought her through long difficult days when death was so close—had become so dear to her that her heart ached at the sight of him. The pity of it was that he would never know how much she loved him.

Adria forced a smile. "Let's not look back, Christopher. It's time to look forward. Will you speak to the captain of the *Brighton Belle* this morning?"

"As soon as you're safely delivered to the tavern."

"Then there's no time to waste, is there?"

Adria reached behind her for her bag. Christopher was staring at her intently when she turned back. She was taken by surprise when he slipped his arms around her unexpectedly and hugged her close.

"I'm proud of you, Adria."

Adria's throat was still tight as she emerged from the cabin moments later, Christopher walking behind.

Seated on the shaky examination table, Emmaline scrutinized Dr. Clark's unsteady movements as he turned toward his instrument case, frowning. The thin, unkempt fellow's appearance was even more seedy than she had remembered and the smell of liquor on his abominable breath even stronger. His office was nothing more than a pigsty, and she was intensely aware that if circumstances had not been so dire, she would not have stepped one foot over the threshold.

Emmaline followed the doctor's fumbling movements, silently cursing. Somehow, within the course of the past twenty-four hours, her life had deteriorated into a shambles. Derek was slipping farther away from her with each passing day. She sensed that if she did not make her move to restore things between them quickly, he would be lost to her forever. John Barrett, the revolting fellow that he was, had revealed only too clearly that he could not be trusted. His desire for revenge on Derek was such that she was uncertain of the lengths he would go to achieve it.

And now this final, unexpected occurrence that had sent her temporarily reeling . . .

Emmaline breathed deeply in an attempt at control. Despite her attempts at denial, despite her amazement that a man of Robert's advanced age could father a child, she had known instinctively that Dr. Phelps was correct in his identification of her condition the previous day. She had contemplated the situation over and again through the long night past as Robert had held her comfortingly close against his bulk.

Against his *soft, flabby* bulk . . .

Emmaline frowned as Derek's dark, handsome image returned unexpectedly before her mind. All this because Derek believed she had truly betrayed him those long years ago.

Actually, it amazed her that Derek had not realized by now that her tryst with the British seaman that had so enraged him had been nothing more than the ploy of an immature young woman obsessed by the excitement of the power she wielded over her handsome, possessive young lover. She had not expected that the encounter would end in the seaman's death. That had not been a part of her plan. but she was certain she would never forget the sense of *ultimate omnipotence* she had experienced as she had met Derek's gaze over the seaman's lifeless body.

She had striven to recapture that sense of omnipotence ever since. Her preoccupation with Puckamenna, Obeah, and other island black magic was an extension of that desire. It had not taken her long to realize, however, that it was not only the power she wanted, but Derek as well.

Emmaline took a strengthening breath. She had sworn that she would get Derek back, and she had dedicated too great a portion of her life to that end to abandon it now.

Dr. Clark turned toward Emmaline and she inwardly winced. The man was truly a repulsive sight. He was unshaved, uncombed, and unclean, his features marked by the deterioration of drink. Emmaline's gaze dropped to the sharp instrument in his hand, then back up to his bloodshot eyes. A tremor moved down her spine even as her delicate jaw hardened.

"I tell you now, Dr. Clark, that I have reservations about your ability to complete this procedure safely."

Dr. Clark straightened up with an unexpected air of affront. "I assure you, madam, that I have performed this service for island women many times."

Emmaline's emerald eyes narrowed. "I am not an 'island woman,' Dr. Clark. I should hope you would recognize the distinction!"

Dr. Clark unexpectedly stood his ground. "Of course . . . but you must realize, also, that whatever the social status of my patient, the medical procedure is still the same."

Emmaline's narrowed gaze became slits of snapping anger. "The consequences for you would not be the same, however, should you err!"

"Madam . . ." Dr. Clark's expression was controlled, his voice cold. "Do you want me to terminate your condition or not?"

The ignoble bastard!

"Well?"

"Not only are you a degenerate, but you are also an uncompassionate, insensitive affront to the noble profession you practice!"

"I repeat, do you want me to terminate your condition or not?"

"Cold, unfeeling . . ."

"Yes or no, Mrs. Dorsett!"

Emmaline mumbled a few more choice words.

Dr. Clark remained unmoving. "I didn't hear you."

"Yes!" Emmaline exploded with fury. *"Yes, yes, yes, damn you! Get it done, quickly and with utmost care, because if you make any mistakes, you may rest assured that if my husband doesn't see that you pay a steep price, I will use my obeah to come back from the grave, if necessary, to* take care of the matter myself! Do you understand that, Dr. Clark?"

Dr. Clark nodded, surprisingly unaffected by her harangue as he started toward her. "Lie back on the table."

Abruptly in control once more, Emmaline instructed flatly, "Stop right there."

"Yes, Mrs. Dorsett?"

"Wash your hands."

"That isn't necessary."

"I said, *wash your hands!*"

Dr. Clark jumped with a start at Emmaline's unanticipated outburst. In her suddenly shaken state, Emmaline almost laughed aloud. She was not amused, however, when Dr. Clark turned back to her moments later and held out his unsteady hands for her scrutiny with unexpected sarcasm.

"So, you have managed to distinguish yourself from my other patients, after all, Mrs. Dorsett. Now, shall we begin?"

Her gaze fixed on Dr. Clark's face, Emmaline lay back slowly, reluctantly, against the table.

Emerging from Dr. Clark's office a short time later, her step unsteady, Emmaline approached her carriage.

Beside her in a moment, Quaco opened the door and took her arm. Seating her carefully, the old slave looked into her colorless face, noting the beads of perspiration that covered her pale skin and the weak fluttering of her eyelids as he mumbled, "Dat boogooyaga man . . ."

Emmaline leaned back weakly against the seat, Quaco's comment ringing in her mind as she replied in a frail voice totally unlike her own, "That filthy man, indeed. Take me home, Quaco."

Her eyes remaining closed as the carriage snapped into motion and clattered up the street, Emmaline spoke no more.

The *Brighton Belle* behind him, Christopher walked quickly along the dock, carefully scrutinizing the street around him. Seeing no one who would question his presence there at midmorning when he should be working at the tavern, he hastened his step. He was well aware that the ease with which he had been able to follow through with his plans so far was due to the good will Adria had established with the proprietors of the Royal Arms Tavern. Her ministrations to Mrs. Healy's burns had doubtless saved the woman's foot from the surgeon's knife. The old couple doted on her and had made it clear that they would do anything for her.

Christopher's jaw locked with determination as he reached the tavern and turned toward the back entrance. He paused briefly at the kitchen window as he glimpsed Adria working at the table. His brow furrowed. Difficult days would soon be upon them. He had at one time thought Adria would not be up to the test, but he no longer entertained such doubts.

Adria's delicate features drew into an expression of deep concentration as Christopher's gaze lingered. A new Adria had emerged since landing on the island, but the old Adria had not totally disappeared. He was suddenly intensely grateful that she had not, for surely no one was more sensitive to the distress of others as Adria . . . nor as totally selfless. Not even Gillian, with her matchless fortitude and generosity of spirit, possessed Adria's infinite gentleness.

Two beautiful women, almost identical in appearance yet totally unalike with the exception of the integrity so deeply ingrained in the characters of both . . . it occurred to Christopher in his moment of silent contemplation that he was privileged to know them both.

Adria looked up from her work, catching his eye. She froze as he moved quickly toward her. She waited expectantly for him to speak as he reached her side.

Uneasy with the lack of privacy in the busy kitchen, Christopher glanced uncomfortably around them. At a light touch on his arm, he turned to see Mrs. Healy beside him.

"It seems to me that the two of you might be needin' a few minutes to yourselves." She moved Adria gently aside and assumed her place at the floured board. "Take all the time you need. I'll have no trouble handlin' these biscuits until you're done."

Acknowledging Mrs. Healy's generous offer, Christopher drew Adria off into the alcove they had used before. Moments later, their brief discussion completed, he watched as Adria returned to her work, pale but determined, and his admiration grew.

With a critical eye, Robert surveyed the flat, endless fields of creole cane baking in the unrelenting sun. It had occurred to him as the morning had progressed that these fields that stretched out as far as his eye could see represented the total sum of his life's work. He recalled a time when he had devoted himself entirely to the fifteen-month cycle of planting and harvesting that began with the sound of the conch at dawn and continued until dusk—a time when he had believed nothing could bring him more happiness than the success of his sugar estate and the completion of a great house that was an island showplace.

Raising his broad-brimmed hat from his head, Robert

wiped his forehead dry of perspiration with the back of his arm, pausing as the breeze moved against his scalp . . . his *balding* scalp . . . and the ache inside him swelled. Somewhere along the line, the years had gotten away from him. He had not realized the true depth of that loss until he met Emmaline.

Robert's throat constricted painfully. He had been in the fields since early morning. He was determined to follow his usual routine so that—

The sound of horse's hooves behind him turned Robert abruptly toward the sound. His heart began a furious pounding as Lester drew his mount to a halt nearby and slid to the ground.

Robert felt the welling of tears. He loved Emmaline. He knew she did not love him, but he had hoped she would somehow discover love for the child she carried within her. He had held her in his arms last night, feeling her distress, knowing he loved her too much to stop her from doing what he knew she was contemplating, and hoping . . .

But morning had come, and nothing had changed.

Robert's voice emerged in a hoarse hiss as the massive Negro reached his side. "Is it done?"

Lester nodded nervously. "Missus back from doctor."

Something about Lester's expression . . ."Is the mistress all right?"

Robert's heart jolted as Lester shook his head. "Missus be sick. Jubba say bring massa."

Robert turned abruptly toward his horse. Mounted with a quickness that belied his rotundity, he turned the animal in the direction of the great house with growing panic. Strangely, in all his sufferings as the morning had progressed and he had contemplated the child he would never see, the child who would never take its first breath, the child he had loved with startling intensity from the moment he had learned of its conception, it had never occurred to him that in losing the child, he might lose Emmaline as well.

No . . . please, no . . .

The denial echoed over and again in Robert's mind as he spurred his horse to a mindless pace over the uneven ground. Racing up the staircase of the great house minutes later, breathless from his frantic pace, Robert turned toward the master bedroom. He paused outside the doorway in an attempt to rein his emotions under control. Entering, he halted abruptly, unconscious of Jubba's concerned expression or the uncertainty of the other servants milling nearby when he saw Emmaline lying pale and motionless on their bed. His rasping whisper was shaken.

"Emmaline?"

"Robert . . ."

Emmaline attempted to raise her head from her pillow. Her skin was blanched of color, her face streaked with tears. Beside her in a moment, he pressed a kiss to her damp cheek. Finding it cold as ice, he turned to shout, "Get Dr. Phelps, quickly!"

"No . . . please . . ."

"Emmaline, dear, you're ill."

"No . . ." Emmaline's emerald gaze met his. "Make them all go. I—I must talk to you." When Robert still hesitated, Emmaline begged, "Please . . ."

Robert turned toward the slaves still hovering. "Go. I'll call you when I need you."

Taking Emmaline's cold hands in his, Robert kissed them with growing despair. "Are you in pain, dear?"

"No."

Despising his pretended ignorance, Robert urged, "Jubba said you went to the doctor."

"Yes . . . I did."

"What's wrong?"

"Robert," Emmaline's eyes welled. "I did a terrible thing."

His heart aching, Robert paused. Dear Emmaline . . . penitent now, when it was too late.

"What did you do, dear?"

"I cannot believe I—"

"Tell me, Emmaline."

"Dr. Clark was such a filthy man! Dirt under his finger-nails . . ."

"Tell me, Emmaline."

"You're too old to have a child, Robert!"

"A child . . ."

"You're over fifty years old!"

"Emmaline, please . . ."

"You worked so hard to attain this land . . . this house. It wasn't fair to bring confusion and disorder to it!"

His anguish too difficult to bear, Robert gripped Emmaline's chin and held it gently in his grasp as he repeated with a sorrow that came from his soul, "What are you trying to tell me, Emmaline?"

"I-I . . ."

"Emmaline, please . . ."

Emmaline's emerald eyes met his. "I couldn't do it!"

Robert went momentarily still. "Couldn't do what?"

"I couldn't do it! I couldn't let that filthy man put an end to our child!"

Robert drew back, stunned as Emmaline held his gaze.

"You will have to learn to bear it, Robert!"

Robert parroted mindlessly, "Bear it?"

"Seeing me get fat and ugly, with a stomach that will precede me when I enter a room."

A slow glow began inside Robert. "You could never be ugly, Emmaline."

Emmaline's pale face was stiff. "I'll lose my waist"

"Not for long."

"My breasts will swell beyond proportion!"

"That's not entirely distasteful."

"The babe will cry all night."

"We'll have Jubba."

"The dirty linens will stink."

"Odors don't bother me."

"The babe will demand feedings at all hours!"

"We'll have a wet nurse."

Emmaline went momentarily silent. "A wet nurse?"

"And the babe will stay in the nursery where the nurse may tend to it without disturbing you."

Emmaline's eyes grew cold. *"My* child . . . suckling at another woman's breast?"

"Emmaline . . ."

"My child . . . kept apart from me?"

"Dear . . ."

"That will not do, Robert!" Emmaline's expression was suddenly unyielding. "My child will lie in a cradle beside our bed until it sleeps through the night!"

"Emm—"

"Until I'm certain it is well and thriving!"

"Emmaline!"

"I will have it no other way, Robert!"

"Emmaline, dear . . . the servants will be devoted to any child of ours."

Emmaline drew back, outraged. *"Never* as devoted as its *mother!"*

Robert shook his head.

Who was this woman in his bed?

Emmaline's pale lips twitched. "Are you angry with me, Robert?"

"Angry?"

"For having conceived a child when you're so *old?*"

The glow inside Robert expanded to the warmth of bliss. "Emmaline, don't you realize that you've made me the happiest man in the world?"

Emmaline did not immediately respond. Tears slipped unexpectedly from the corners of her eyes as she questioned hoarsely, "Then why haven't you kissed me?"

Not realizing his cheeks were damp as well, Robert leaned down to kiss Emmaline firmly, lingeringly. When he drew back, Emmaline reached up to smooth the wetness from his cheeks.

"You're crying."

"From happiness, dear."

Emmaline paused again, the moist green of her eyes intense. "Do you love me, Robert?"

Astounded by the question, Robert replied, "Emmaline dear, could there be any doubt?"

Emmaline continued her avid scrutiny and he frowned with increasing discomfort. "What are you looking at so intently, dear?"

"At you."

"Of course, but why so intently?"

"You didn't ask if I loved you."

"Should I have?"

"Yes."

"Do you?"

"Yes."

"I'm glad."

Emmaline's green eyes glittered into his. "I really do, Robert."

Robert paused to consider the continued intensity of Emmaline's gaze. He frowned, choosing his next words carefully.

"Was there something else you wanted, dear?"

"Yes."

"You know you can ask anything of me and if it's within my power, it will be done."

Emmaline's voice dropped to a whisper. "There *is* something that is very important to me . . ."

"Tomorrow?"

John Barrett's protruding eyes appeared ready to pop. Peters had entered his small Kingston office a few minutes earlier with a sly grin that had stood the hackles up on his spine. He knew that look. He did not return the odious fellow's smile as he pressed. "You're sure?"

"That's right. I 'eard it straight from the 'orse's mouth, I did."

"Don't try to be clever!" Barrett was not amused. "I can't believe—"

Peters's sly grin turned unexpectedly into a snarl. "The *Brighton Belle* sails tomorrow mornin' on the tide and Gibson will be signin' on as a member of the crew in order to pay for the bitches' passage. Believe what I tell you or not, I don't care! I'm tired of 'angin' out in that alley be'ind that tavern, anyways! Gibson almost caught me listenin' at the window when 'e came back from talkin' to the captain. There would've been 'ell to pay if he did. I would've 'ad to slit the bastard's throat to get 'im off me."

"No, not yet! You'll have your chance!" Barrett's frown deepened. "The *Brighton Belle* . . . William Morris is her captain, is he not?"

"That's right."

"I know him well. He's made his position on enforced indentured servitude well known." Saliva trailed unnoted from the corner of Barrett's lips as he mused. "Gibson will have no difficulty getting the sister off the ship in time to sail on the tide, but Andrews doesn't let his bitch out of his sight. Gibson must have worked out a plan to slip her away before Andrews realizes she's gone."

" 'E didn't say nothin' about no plan."

"Fool! You don't really expect that he'll take on the entire crew to get her out of that bastard's clutches, do you?"

Peters's snarl turned menacing. "I don't know, and I don't care."

"You'll care if it fills your pockets for you, won't you?" Barrett nodded as Peters's eyes narrowed. "Because that's what I'll do . . . fill them well . . . when those Haige women are mine." Barrett laughed aloud, the mirthless sound echoing even as he rasped, "Alert your 'friends' that they have more work to do for me, and have them ready at the crack of dawn. You may advise them that I'll fill their pockets, too, if they serve me well, because I tell you now that I'll spare no expense to have Gillian Harcourt Haige lying under me at last."

Barrett laughed again. The sound rebounded sharply as he raised a determined fist upward. "Just one more day!"

"Tomorrow?"

Gillian's throat clenched tight. She struggled to breathe past the sudden restriction as Adria's cabin momentarily spun around her. She felt Adria's supportive touch, saw Christopher step spontaneously toward her, as she forced a steady response she did not feel. "I'm all right. It's just that . . ." She swallowed and began again. "I thought we had a few days before the ship sailed."

"What difference does it make?" Gillian felt Christopher's intense scrutiny as he continued slowly. "Unless you've changed your mind."

"No . . . no, I haven't, but morning tide comes early. Derek will still be on deck. He'll never let me leave the ship without him."

Christopher took a step forward that brought him close enough for her to see the flecks of gold in his clear, light eyes. "Gillian . . ." His gaze grew pained. "Are you sure you want to do this?"

Long moments passed before Gillian managed a response. "I have no choice."

Relief flashing, Christopher slipped his arms around her unexpectedly and drew her comfortingly close. Gillian closed her eyes, allowing the sound of his voice to assuage the ache inside her as he whispered, "I'll take care of you and Adria, Gillian. On my life, I promise you."

Releasing her a moment later, Christopher stepped back. He stated flatly, "Here's the plan . . ."

There was no doubt about it . . . it was a conspiracy.

Derek moved restlessly on his bunk, his gaze drifting to the shaft of silver moonlight shining through the porthole. It occurred to him that he had watched the major portion of his life pass by that porthole, or one similar to it. The sea was his livelihood and the *Colonial Dawn* was his home. Both his livelihood and his home at risk while in England months previous, he had taken desperate measures. It seemed somehow ironic that desperate measures had merely acted to increase his desperation to the extent that not only was he still in danger

of losing his livelihood and his home, he was also in danger
of losing something he valued even more.

Derek glanced at Gillian as she lay silent and still beside
him. He could ill afford the monumental price Charles Higgins had demanded for Gillian and Adria's indentures. He had
known it was a foolish step to cut his finances so short, but
he had considered the risk minimal. The port of Kingston was
a gold mine of shipping. He had been certain he would have
a new cargo within twenty-four hours of completing the repairs on his ship.

He had never been more wrong.

Derek moved restlessly once more. He had no choice in
what he must now do. He would visit John Barrett's office
in the morning. Bastard that he was, Barrett would not hesitate to admit, for the pure satisfaction it would give him, if
he were the one responsible for the blacklisting of his ship
with the commercial agents in port. If Barrett was indeed
responsible, he would handle the man, with the power of
persuasion or with the power of his fists. Either way, *he*
would get his satisfaction, also.

If it was not Barrett, however . . .

Derek's jaw tightened. Emmaline, still beautiful and self-
absorbed, had never forgiven him for having refused her
when he had been released from prison. Indeed, he had come
to think she truly believed she could eventually wear down
his resistance with her foolish maneuverings. He had never
met Robert Dorsett, but he had heard the talk. Dorsett would
do anything to please his wife. He would soon find out just
how far the man might have gone.

Derek felt the nudge of panic and his jaw instinctively
firmed. His ship might slip into the hands of the receivers,
as might his scant personal possessions and the recently purchased indentures of two. The third indenture, however,

would remain his . . . indefinitely . . . until the term was completed . . . until—

Gillian moved. He sensed her wakefulness although he could not see her face clearly in the limited light. Sliding his arm around her, he drew her closer. He heard her soft sigh as he settled her against him and a familiar ache came alive deep within. He had never believed he could care for a woman as he cared for Gillian. She belonged to him . . . by law . . . to him alone. He would not lose her.

Curling his palm around Gillian's cheek, Derek turned her toward him, halting when he felt the dampness of tears.

"Gillian, are you crying?"

Her response was soft, indistinct. "No."

He caressed the moisture from her cheek. "Can't you tell me what's wrong?"

"Nothing's wrong."

Somehow unwilling to risk the response he might ultimately receive, Derek did not press her. Instead, he whispered, "The night was made for us, Gillian. It cushions feelings sometimes too sharp to bear in the full light of day. Let me make you forget your tears."

He took her then, with gentle, tumultuous loving. Clasping Gillian close when it was done, Derek allowed the joy of the intimate warmth of her to fill him, the sound of her even breathing to lull his mind.

His former cares somehow assuaged, inexplicably content, he then closed his eyes.

Derek's arms tight around her in the aftermath of their lovemaking, his breathing slow and even, Gillian did not stir. The bittersweet bliss of his embrace never stronger, she closed her eyes, wishing with all her heart that tomorrow would never come.

Seventeen

Tomorrow had come.

Peeking out through slitted lids, Gillian watched Derek, unaware of her scrutiny, dressing silently in the gray light before dawn. She followed his movements as he fastened his britches, noting the familiar way the garment hugged his muscular thighs and the firm curve of his buttocks. Turning, he reached for his shirt, allowing her a view of the heavily muscled chest that had cushioned her cheek hours earlier, the tight, lightly furred surface against which she had rested her palm through the long night. She felt a tug of sadness as he drew the garment closed, his action somehow symbolic of the conclusion of all intimacy between them.

Derek moved briefly into the light, preoccupied with his thoughts as his long fingers worked at the buttons of his shirt. Gillian's gaze lingered on the strength of his profile, etched against the pale light of the room, an image that had been engraved into her heart for the pure male beauty of it. The lay of his heavy dark hair against his neck and the broad stretch of his powerful shoulders called for her touch, stirring memories she fought to suppress.

Appearing to sense her scrutiny, Derek turned unexpectedly in her direction. She noted the intensity of his gaze as he stared toward her in the semidarkness, the thin scar that ran the length of his cheek tightening. She recalled a time when she had considered his appearance menacing for the sheer size and power of him and the potency of that gaze, but she no longer did. She had discovered the gentleness in that power, and the warmth that lay denied behind that dark stare. She knew the same voice that often spoke with a formidable authority that shook a lesser man, occasionally ringing with threat, was also capable of a husky, loving whisper that shook the soul.

Remaining silent, unmoving, Gillian felt Derek's gaze sharpen the moment before he walked slowly toward her.

"You're awake, aren't you, Gillian . . ."

Gillian did not respond. Derek stroked her cheek. She felt his relief as he whispered, "No more tears . . . I'm glad." He leaned down to brush her lips with his. "It's early. Go back to sleep. I have some business to take care of this morning. When I come back, we'll take a carriage ride." He kissed her again. He lingered, then stood abruptly. The door closed behind him and Gillian closed her eyes.

The beginning of the end . . . a new beginning . . . Gillian wasn't sure which the closing door signaled. The only thing she knew for certain was that she would never feel Derek's touch again.

Emerging on deck, Derek inhaled the clear morning air, his eyes drifting to a horizon glowing a brilliant gold with the rising of the sun. A Jamaican sunrise was almost as breathtaking as a Jamaican sunset. It had occurred to him as an afterthought of his one-sided conversation with Gillian a few minutes earlier that he had been selfish in his preoccupation with his financial difficulties over the past weeks. He had allowed Gillian no more than a cursory glimpse of an island unmatched in beauty. He was determined to correct that oversight before he sailed again.

Derek's strong features hardened. And he *would* sail again, on the *Colonial Dawn*. He had awakened determined to put uncertainties to rest without another day's delay. Once he had a scheduled sailing date, he would make his decision as to whether he would—

The sound of running footsteps on the gangplank turned Derek in its direction just as a slight young man stepped onto the deck, breathing heavily. Derek frowned at the shaggy-haired, carelessly dressed fellow, his gaze narrowing as he strained to recall where he had seen him before.

Gulping, the fellow snatched off his oversize hat and addressed him breathlessly, "I have a message from Mr. Healy at the Royal Arms Tavern, sir!"

Oh, yes, he remembered—the young fellow did odd chores at the tavern. His response was curt.

"What is it?"

"It's Mrs. Healy, sir. She fell and reinjured her foot. Mr. Healy said we'll be needin' Mistress Adria to come as soon as possible so's she can start the mornin' chores in the kitchen, and maybe tend to Mrs. Healy's foot like she did before." He paused. "Mrs. Healy won't let Dr. Clark touch her no more since Mistress Adria took over her care."

Derek frowned. So, the Haige women each had unexpected skills. He supposed he should not be surprised.

Stepping up onto the deck a short distance away, Cutter interjected, "I saw Gibson below a few minutes ago, Captain He's ready to leave. Mistress Adria and he should be up shortly."

The boy's expression became strained as he looked back at Derek. "Sir, Mr. Healy said he'd have my head if I didn't fetch them back quick."

Somehow annoyed, Derek considered the young fellow's obvious agitation. He snapped, "At the foot of the stairs— the second door to the right—and make sure you knock!"

"Yes, sir!"

Derek turned back to Cutter. He was relating his plans for that morning when footsteps sounded on the deck behind him. Turning, Derek met Gibson's cold-eyed stare. He glanced at Adria, walking silently beside Gibson, his mind unconsciously registering as it always did that despite their duplication of feature, Adria and Gillian were as distinguishable from each other to him as if they were not truly twins at all. He frowned as the young messenger stumbled in his haste to help Adria up onto the gangplank, almost tripping her.

"Be careful, you young fool!"

Noting Gibson barked a similar admonishment, Derek glared as the boy glanced back at him briefly, then lowered his head with embarrassment and followed Adria's hasty step down the gangplank. He was still staring at the young fellow when a word from Cutter drew him back to their conversation.

In a moment the three were forgotten.

"Gibson got the first sister off the ship, all right!"

Peters's voice held a note of glee as he turned to John Barrett, crouched beside him on the shadowed dock. He paused to glance at the two men similarly concealed in the shadows a few feet away. His mates were ready to go and eager for the coin that would be rattling in their pockets once this little chore was taken care of.

Peters's evil grin flashed. Nothin' like the smell of blood to bring the rats out of their holes . . .

Peters turned back to Barrett, noting that the fellow's swarthy face dripped with perspiration despite the brisk morning breeze. He spoke again.

"Shall I send my mates to snatch that one right now?" Peters motioned toward the three men moving quickly down the dock. "Just to make sure she don't get away?"

"And alert Gibson before he can get the real prize off that ship? You damned fool! We won't make a move until *Gillian* Haige is in our hands. Then Gibson is yours!"

Peters's leering smile dimmed. He was only too conscious of the bulge in Barrett's pocket, revealing the presence of a small pistol concealed there. He had never seen a bloke as obsessed as Barrett was with that one. Haige witch.

Noting that Barrett was obviously struggling with his thoughts, Peters remained silent until Barrett suddenly snapped, "On second thought, maybe your 'friends' should follow them. Tell them not to let either Gibson or the Haige woman out of their sight." Barrett paused. His jaw twitched nervously. "Gibson will have to get things moving within the hour . . . in time for high tide."

Peters hesitated.

"Do what I said, damn you!"

Peters snapped to his command. Within minutes, his cohorts were following the quick-moving trio down the dock.

Crouching beside Barrett again, Peters fixed his gaze back on the *Colonial Dawn* . . . waiting.

Walking rapidly, Christopher glanced toward the sea, gauging the slow swell of the tide against the dock, then back at the two walking alongside him. On one side, Adria returned his gaze apprehensively. On the other, identical blue eyes reflected physical distress that prompted his soft question.

"Are you all right, Gillian?"

"Yes." Her small white face overwhelmed by the ragged brown wig covering her fair hair, her slenderness enveloped in male attire indistinguishable from the young messenger's, Gillian stumbled again.

Silently cursing the oversize men's shoes Gillian wore as his hand snapped out to steady her, Christopher assessed Gillian silently. She attempted a smile. "It's the nausea . . ." Her throat worked convulsively. "It'll pass."

"We only have a little farther to go." Christopher noted the fine veil of perspiration that covered Gillian's face, the weak fluttering of her eyelids. She had to maintain her disguise just a little longer.

Breathing a sigh of relief as they reached the tavern, Christopher waited only until they had stepped out of sight on the path to the kitchen before sweeping Gillian up into his arms. He saw Mrs. Healy's look of concern as they entered the kitchen. He remained silent as he followed the old woman to a small room nearby and lay Gillian on the cot there.

His heart pounding, Christopher turned sharply as Adria moved worriedly to Gillian's side. "I'll take care of Gillian. Change your clothes. We don't have much time."

Hardly aware of Adria's presence as she slipped into the corner behind him and stripped off her dress to don the male clothing awaiting her, Christopher took Gillian's hands in his. They were so cold. He chafed them anxiously as he turned to Mrs. Healy.

"Some water, please."

"No. No water." Gillian's voice was gaining in strength. "I'll be all right. Let me sit up."

"No."

"Yes, Christopher. Please." Gillian's tone was anxious. "How much time do we have?"

"Less than an hour."

Gillian pushed his hand aside and sat up. A smile twitched unexpectedly at her lips as Adria approached them in her male garb. "You make an outrageous boy, Adria."

Surprising him, Adria returned Gillian's smile. "Yes, *we* do."

Gillian drew herself to her feet. Unsteady at first, she straightened her shoulders with determination. "I'm ready."

Christopher scrutinized Gillian's pinched face, the blue rings under her glorious eyes, the revealing, spastic working of her throat, and the slight, almost indiscernible, quiver of her lips. She looked frail and weak . . . and he had never loved her more.

Darting Mrs. Healy a brief, appreciative glance, Christopher turned back to the two awaiting his cue.

"Let's go."

"Something's wrong, I can feel it."

Withdrawing his watch from his pocket, Barrett checked it nervously, his voice a low growl. "It's getting late. Somebody should've come back for Gillian Haige by now."

Silent cursing the fact that the *Brighton Belle* was docked at the distant corner of the harbor where it could not be easily observed, Barrett shifted with obvious agitation. Something had slipped past him somehow . . . somewhere.

Making a snap decision, Barrett drew himself abruptly to his feet. He turned toward Peters. "Let's go."

Peters stood up, uncertain. "Where're we goin'?"

"Don't ask stupid questions! Just follow me!"

* * *

Derek walked swiftly down the gangplank of the *Colonial Dawn*. Glancing around him, he saw the dock was just beginning to surge with the traffic of the new day. There was nothing unusual there, nothing amiss, yet . . .

The uneasiness with which he had awakened that morning rapidly increasing for a reason he could not quite identify, Derek paused, automatically stepping behind a pile of crates where he might more closely scrutinize the surrounding area unobserved. It had been years since he had felt so strong a feeling of apprehension upon awakening, not since that day so many years ago that had altered the course of his life, the day when he had found Emmaline and—

The sound of rapidly approaching footsteps coming from the direction of the *Colonial Dawn* interrupted Derek's thoughts. They were rapid, light.

Derek drew back farther, waiting . . .

Stunned, Derek saw the young messenger from the tavern come into view.

Reaching out abruptly, Derek snatched the fellow from his feet and dragged him back behind the crates. Holding him helpless with one strong arm, Derek demanded, "What's going on here?"

The boy gasped with fear. "M-mistress Adria forgot somethin', is all! She sent me back to the ship to get it."

"You weren't going back to the ship. You were coming *from* it."

"No, I wasn't, I—!"

"Yes, you were!"

"I didn't do nothin', Captain!" The youth struggled to free himself from Derek's grip, his eyes bulging.

Derek's heart lurched as realization gradually dawned.

"You didn't leave the ship with Gibson and Adria, did you? You waited until I left so you could sneak off unseen."

"I didn't!"

"Somebody else left the ship dressed like you. It was Gillian, wasn't it!"

The boy began struggling again. "Let me go!"

Derek's jaw hardened to steel. "Who put you up to this?"

The boy struggled harder.

"Was it Gibson?"

The boy jerked himself free with a sudden thrust, his feet flying over the dock as he made his escape. Derek made no attempt to pursue him as painful reality registered sharply.

Gillian had run away.

Derek snapped into motion.

Emerging furious from a search of the ship minutes later, his suspicions confirmed, Derek struggled against the deadening ache within him.

"No, damn her! *No!*"

Back on the dock, Derek started off at a run.

"Where is she!"

The kitchen of the Royal Arms Tavern went silent as Mrs. Healy looked up at the raging specter before her, inwardly quaking. Eyes as black and hard as onyx snapped fire as Captain Andrews took a threatening step forward. As broad and tall as the man was, dressed totally in black, he had been a picture of menace she never seen matched before as he had appeared in the doorway minutes earlier, as he had searched the surrounding rooms, then returned to assault her with his furious question.

Her healed foot taking that moment to twinge in silent reminder of a debt not yet fully repaid, Mrs. Healy returned

the captain's stare, inwardly chafing at her husband's pecu-
liar timing in having left at that particular hour to busy himself at the dock warehouses blocks away.

"I told you, I don't know what you're talkin' about. Neither Christopher nor Adria came to work this mornin'."

"You're lying!"

"I am not!"

"Where's the boy . . . the one you sent to fetch Gibson
and Adria."

"I didn't send no boy."

"The young fellow who does odd chores . . ."

"I tell you I didn't send no boy to your ship!"

Captain Andrews's gaze grew suddenly cold. "I hope you
realize what you're risking here, Mrs. Healy. You know you
could go to prison for aiding in the escape of indentured
servants—and one of them a convict, at that!"

"Christopher is no more a convict than I am!"

"That may yet work out to be true."

Mrs. Healy flushed. "You don't scare me, Captain! I don't
know nothin' about where Adria and Christopher are! If
you're tryin' to find them, you're goin' to have to go somewhere else to get your information!"

Captain Andrews's chest began a slow heaving under the
dark shirt that she had no doubt was as black as his heart
itself. Mrs. Healy took a spontaneous step backward. Aye,
he was a formidable man. It was no wonder Adria's sister
had sought to escape him.

Captain Andrews's voice dropped a tone in menace. "I'll
give you one more chance before I call in the law."

"You don't have to go that far, darlin' . . ."

Mrs. Healy's eyes snapped toward Sadie as the plump
barmaid appeared in the kitchen doorway. The captain
turned toward her as well, and Mrs. Healy inwardly tensed.

It was no secret that Sadie had been pining for the captain's return since the night she had spent with him. She knew her promiscuous barmaid's appetites well. She would get her man with a smile, with a tickle, or any way she could. She had always considered that Sadie's business was her own, but she was determined that she would not let Sadie sacrifice the future of two decent young women for a rollicking roll in the hay.

"I'd watch what I say if I was you, Sadie!"

Turning toward the old woman with a viciousness not often employed, Sadie snapped, "I say what I like!" She forced a smile. "The captain here's an old friend . . . ain't you, Captain?"

Captain Andrews's expression remained stiff. "Do you have something to tell me, Sadie?"

Sadie's smile warmed as she sauntered to his side and placed the flat of her palm against his heaving chest. "You was real nice to me, Captain. You treated me like I was a lady." She winked. "And even though I didn't get the chance to prove to you that I ain't, I got the feelin' that I owe you somethin' for that."

"Be quiet, Sadie!"

Sadie turned sharply in Mrs. Healy's direction. "Save your breath! I told you I don't have to take your orders. I never did like that Chris Gibson, anyways . . . with them dirty looks he was always givin' me after me and the captain became friends." Sadie turned back to smile up at Derek. "I don't know where the women are, but I saw Chris Gibson walkin' down the dock a little while ago. He was with two young fellas I never seen before."

"Two young fel—" The captain's color rose as he pressed, "Do you know where they were going?"

Sadie nodded. "I heard one of them say somethin' about the *Brighton Belle* sailin' on the tide."

The captain's powerful frame went rigid. Squeezing Sadie's hand appreciatively, he snapped into motion, leaving Mrs. Healy staring at Sadie's pleased expression.

Mrs. Healy's hiss was harsh with fury.

"Do you realize what you've done!"

"Sure I do." Sadie shrugged. "All I can say is I hope the captain gets to that ship just a little too late to stop that woman of his, 'cause I wouldn't mind comfortin' him in his loss. I wouldn't mind at all." Her expression turning cold, Sadie concluded abruptly, "I'm goin' back to work."

Mrs. Healy did not bother to respond. Looking back out the doorway through which the furious captain had disappeared, she clung to the consolation that unless she had missed her guess, the tide was already high, and—

The *Brighton Belle* had sailed . . .

Standing on the dock, staring at the graceful silhouette of the vessel, its sails billowing against the clear horizon in the distance, its bow dipping as it turned fully out to sea, Derek was struck with a sense of loss so intense that it was almost debilitating.

It was too late.

Gillian was gone.

He had lost her.

"He's bleeding!"

Adria's frightened exclamation followed the sudden lapse of sound in the wake of the scuffle that had briefly ensued in John Barrett's congested, dockside office. Her eyes wide,

Gillian was frozen into immobility at the sight of Christopher crumpled on the floor in a motionless heap, blood streaming from the gash on the back of his head where he had been struck from behind.

John Barrett halted Adria's advance toward Christopher with a warning hiss.

"Stay away from him!"

Gun in hand, John Barrett turned his narrowed gaze toward Gillian. She felt the heat of his lascivious perusal, even as her mind reeled with the rapid, unexpected progress of events that had delivered her a prisoner to John Barrett's office.

Christopher's plan had seemed to be going so well. The young messenger from the tavern had arrived at dawn and had had little difficulty being allowed below on the *Colonial Dawn* with the excuse of an emergency at the tavern. Wearing the clothing Mrs. Healy had provided the previous day, along with the wig the old woman had secured from a troupe of penniless actors recently arrived on the island and eager for a profitable exchange, she had walked past Derek without suspicion, even after she had drawn his attention by stumbling in her oversize shoes.

With Adria similarly garbed after leaving the tavern, Christopher, Adria, and she had approached the *Brighton Belle* without attracting undue attention. Sailing had obviously been imminent and she had experienced a relief tempered with silent anguish when the gangplank had come into view.

Then it had happened, the sudden, unexpected thrust from nowhere that had knocked her against a wall of crates, momentarily stunning her. When she had regained her senses, she had been held immobile from behind with a knife at her throat. The hot, fetid breath of her unknown captor had brushed her cheek as he had halted Christopher's rush toward her with a growled warning.

"Another step and this one's done for!"

She was unclear about what happened after that except that she had been dragged through back alleys, stumbling with her arm twisted behind her and the knife pressed so sharply against her back as to steal her breath until they had arrived in the office where they now stood. John Barrett had been waiting. Desperate action from Christopher moments earlier had resulted in the vicious attack that had left him unconscious at her feet.

The silent tableau was ominous: John Barrett, his expression savage, the gun in his hand cocked and ready; three sinister henchmen who had already demonstrated a propensity for violence awaiting his command; Adria and she defenseless with Christopher lying bleeding and unconscious on the floor of a small, dingy office in a warehouse district where calls for help, and even the bark of gunfire, would most likely go either unheard or ignored.

Barrett's jowled face was flushed with triumph as he spoke.

"Ah, Mistress *Gillian Harcourt Haige,* do I sense a deeper respect now than you previously afforded me? Or is that fear I see in your eyes?"

Gillian did not immediately respond, allowing Barrett the opportunity to continue a shade more softly. "Or are you simply more conservative in your speech now that you must be concerned for more than *one* in guarding your physical safety . . ."

The significance of Barrett's words dawned gradually, leaving Gillian incredulous as Barrett laughed again. "Yes, your precious little secret is not a secret from me!"

Christopher stirred and Barrett's amusement faded as he

turned toward the thin, evil-looking fellow nearby. "Make sure those two watch Gibson closely and there'll be a few more coins in this for all of you when all is over and done."

Barrett turned back again to Gillian, his smile broadening. "You didn't really think you would escape me, did you, Mistress *Gillian Harcourt Haige?* I thought I had at least impressed you with my intelligence and determination, although you made it clear that you considered me odious and contemptible. But, you see, this odious, contemptible man now has control over your destiny—just as he promised you he eventually would."

"You vile beast!" Gillian's words emerged in a furious hiss. "Had you a decent bone in your body, you would allow my sister to tend to Christopher's wound instead of gloating while he is bleeding!"

"I never made claim to decency, Mistress Haige!" Barrett's jaw tightened. "Nor do I aspire to that status. Decency is merely an excuse the weak use for their inadequacies."

"I suppose I should not be surprised . . ." Gillian's lips curved with contempt, "that a man of your low caliber should be so totally ignorant of the true definition of the word."

"Low caliber . . . is that so, Mistress Haige? I suppose you consider your handsome lover, Captain Andrews, a man of higher caliber than I. I suppose that's the reason you were running away from him when you so conveniently ran right into my arms." Barrett's low laughter was harsh. "If so, I believe you're the one who should look to more closely at your definition of the word *decent.* At least *I'm* not a convicted murderer!"

Pausing to allow that thought to linger, Barrett continued moments later. "But since you're so obviously confused, I also advise you to dismiss any thoughts you might be entertaining that Captain Andrews will find you, because there's little chance of that. Gibson and you have done your work too well, you see. You have escaped your dear, *decent* captain without leaving any trail whatsoever—so well, in fact, that by the time he realizes what really happened, our little party will be on its way back to England."

"Back to England!"

"Yes, my dear, where we will reestablish and legally clarify the status of your indenture."

Gillian shook her head. "Legally clarify?"

"Stipulating that your sister and you are bound to *me* for the next four years . . . or more."

"No!"

"Oh, yes, Mistress Haige!"

"Never, I tell you!"

"I wouldn't say never, Mistress Haige . . ." Barrett's features drew into truly sinister lines, "Someone you hold dear might be caused to suffer badly should you decide against cooperating."

Gillian glanced at Adria, who had remained silent through the exchange, then down at Christopher who was beginning to stir.

Barrett's evil grin widened. "A strong young man such as Gibson here is extremely valuable in so many ways . . ."

"You are despicable!"

"Perhaps."

"You are unworthy of the manhood you claim!"

Barrett took a threatening step toward Gillian that raised Christopher abruptly to his knees. Struck again from behind, Christopher collapsed with a grunt of pain that started Adria toward him.

Enraged as much by the viciousness of the blow that again felled Christopher as she was by the rough, bruising hands that stopped Adria's surge toward him, Gillian rushed at Barrett, attacking him with unrestrained fury.

Unable to avoid Barrett's sudden, vicious blow to her face, Gillian staggered backward, her senses reeling. She clutched the nearby desk, slipping slowly to the floor just as the door snapped open with a splintering crack!

Angry shouts . . . a single, deafening report of a gun . . . a deep, familiar voice calling her name as the light faded and oblivion assumed control.

The splintering of the Barrett's office door . . . the crack of a gunshot echoing in the room . . . grunted orders from island policemen as they subdued the struggles of the human vermin seeking to escape them . . .

"Is she all right?"

Turning briefly toward the inquiry from the overweight, middle-aged man behind him, Derek lifted Gillian up into his arms with a curt response.

"I don't know."

"Take her outside to my carriage." Robert Dorsett's gray brows were knit with concern. "Quaco will drive you both directly to Dr. Phelps."

Derek hesitated, momentarily uncertain. He glanced toward the corner where Gibson was drawing himself unsteadily to his feet, Adria at his side; toward the small, weasellike fellow Barrett had addressed as Peters lying dead on the floor, felled by the single shot fired; toward Barrett, being dragged away with his two remaining cohorts by uniformed policemen unimpressed by his furious ravings; then back at Dorsett's solicitous expression.

Everything had happened too quickly that morning for him to be fully certain of Dorsett's intentions. He had heard little about Robert Dorsett during the years he had traded on the island, except for the fact that Dorsett was Emmaline's husband. The man was a complete mystery to him and he had no reason to trust him. He was intensely aware, however, that had Dorsett not purposely sought him out that morning and revealed Barrett's plans to kidnap Gillian, he might have continued believing Gillian had escaped on the *Brighton Belle* until it was too late to rescue her. He would be endlessly grateful to the man for that, but—

"You needn't be suspicious of my intervention, Captain." Robert Dorsett's small eyes met his gaze directly. "It isn't entirely selfless, you see. Mr. John Barrett made the mistake of believing he could intimidate my wife." Dorsett smiled. "You know Emmaline, of course. You and she are old . . . friends, but you don't know me, and because of that you don't understand that although I've allowed Emmaline her 'unique pursuits' in relation to you for as long as they have remained harmless, I will allow no man, most especially a man such as John Barrett, to believe he might threaten or have dominion over her in *any* way. He and his cohorts will go to jail for this unspeakable attempt to deprive you of your legally obtained indentures, and for acts even more heinous that have heretofore gone suspected but unproved. They *will* be proved now, I assure you, and he will suffer to the full extent of the law. I'm not without influence on the island, you see."

Still hesitant, Derek clasped Gillian more tightly against him. The revealing gesture did not go unnoted by Dorsett's sharp gaze as he continued. "In an effort to set your mind at rest, I'll say one thing more. My darling Emmaline and I had a long talk yesterday afternoon. Suffice it to say that when it was done, I was as incensed as she at the despicable machinations John Barrett intended putting into play. You see, Emmaline explained to me that your feelings for Mistress Haige obviously go quite deep. Her sometimes outrageous sense of self-esteem has convinced her that there could be no other explanation for your ability to resist her. Special 'personal' circumstances that have recently come into play, which I won't bother to explain now but which have affected Emmaline deeply, and have changed her outlook on many things. One of them is her attitude toward you."

Dorsett's small eyes took on an unexpected glow. "As difficult as it may be for you to believe at the moment, the truth is that in spite of her sometimes excessive behavior and surreptitious conduct, Emmaline is the woman I love. For that reason, I am here as her official representative with a message for John Barrett that has been converted into the action that has just taken place. To you, however, Emmaline has asked me to convey her warm regards . . . and true regrets for all that might have been and *will . . . never . . . be.*"

Derek blinked.

"Yes, truly . . . you may set your mind forever at rest. My dear Emmaline has been long in coming to this point in her life. She will not reverse herself." Dorsett took a short step back. "Enough said. Now to the carriage, please. Your young woman does not look well."

Derek looked down at Gillian, still unconscious in his arms. The knot of fear in his chest tightening, he turned silently toward the door.

Eighteen

"Why did you do it?"

The strained silence of the cabin was broken by Derek's tense question as he turned toward Gillian abruptly. Grasping her arms as she stood slight and vulnerable in the male attire she still wore although hours had passed since her attempted escape that morning, he held her as much a prisoner with his gaze as with his barely controlled restraint.

Gillian took a shaken breath. They had returned to Derek's cabin minutes earlier after a silent ride back from Dr. Phelps's office. She had refused Derek's hand in stepping down from the carriage and his jaw had tightened. She had felt his anger building as they boarded the ship to the scrutiny of his men and walked directly below. She had been waiting for him to break the silence between them, and now that he had—

"Answer me, damn it!" Derek's dark eyes pinned her. "Why did you run away?"

Her jaw still throbbing from Barrett's blow, Gillian responded stiffly, "The answer to that should be obvious."

"It isn't obvious to me." The planes of Derek's face tightened. "Last night, we—" He halted abruptly. His voice dropped a note in timbre as he continued. "I want you to tell me, Gillian. Was it all an act? Were you just pretending when you came to life in my arms, when you returned kiss for kiss, when you—"

"I don't want to talk about it."

"*I* do!" Derek's grip tightened as Gillian struggled to escape it. "Was it because of Gibson? Is that why you tried to run away. Do you love him? Is that it?"

"No, Christopher has nothing to do with any of this."

"Liar!"

"I'm not a liar!"

"Gibson is the only one who could have engineered the escape that was planned."

"How do you know that?"

"Don't take me for a fool! Only Gibson could have managed to convince the captain of the *Brighton Belle* to take you on. Only Gibson could have—"

"Christopher didn't convince me to do anything I didn't want to do!"

Derek again went silent. "Why?"

"Why what?"

"Why did you want to run away? I thought we had talked things over. I thought everything was settled."

"It was."

"I don't understand."

"No, you never did." Gillian steeled herself against what she knew she must say, raising her chin as she held Derek's gaze. "Look at me, Derek. You see before you a woman who belongs to you, by virtue of a barbaric, inhuman law. I approached you on the ship—as a result of that law. I struck an intimate agreement with you—as a result of that law. You purchased my life for the next four years as easily as you could common chattel—as a result of that law. And we have lain in each other's arms for countless nights—as a result of that law. *Everything* that passed between us has been *as a result of that law.*"

Pausing, her throat tightening, her pain increasing more

with each word she spoke, Gillian continued. "Don't you see? *Nothing* that passed between us was truly real! How could I truly give myself to anyone when all license over my own person had been taken from me? I had been sold to the highest bidder with all liberties suspended! I no longer had any right to thoughts that were my own . . . to feelings that were my own . . . to anything that was contradictory to the desires of whoever held my indenture. You, in your position of total freedom, could follow your feelings . . . your reactions . . . giving all that transpired between us full rein; while I, in a position of submission, could not. Do you know what that means, Derek? Do you know how the very thought of such submission gnawed at the core of me until I felt I was being consumed? Yes, I tried to escape! Although you cannot seem to comprehend it, the reason is rudimentary and so much a part of me that in your inability to understand, I realize you never truly knew me at all."

Gillian's eyes glittered with emotion. "In simple words, the reason I tried to escape you is this! No matter what that law decrees, I am not and never shall willfully be your, or any man's, 'possession.' "

His chest heaving, emotions held rigidly in check lending a new harshness to his gaze, Derek rasped, "You're telling me that last night, and all the others you spent in my arms, meant nothing to you at all . . ."

Silent for long moments, Gillian managed a shaken whisper.

"They did not mean enough to sacrifice my soul."

Derek released her with a suddenness that sent Gillian a staggering step backward. He stared at her in a silence that grew increasingly heavy until the burden of it was almost more than she could bear.

Mesmerized by his gaze, Gillian was aware of the exact moment when the fury in Derek's dark eyes went cold. It was the moment before he turned abruptly toward the door, leaving in his wake only the stark finality of sound as the door snapped closed behind him.

Uncertain how much time had elapsed since Derek had left the cabin, Gillian glanced out the porthole at the familiar patch of sky that was visible beyond. Night had fallen. She had scarcely moved from the spot where she had sat at the edge of Derek's bunk, her only relief from the turmoil in her mind the sound of Cutter's voice in the passageway sometime earlier, followed by Adria and Christopher's mumbled responses, signaling their return. Time had become somehow suspended, and she—

Gillian's heart jumped to an escalated beating at the sound of a step in the passageway outside the door. She stood as the door opened, the dark sobriety of Derek's expression as he walked inside filling her with sudden trepidation. The sober menace of him filled the room as he advanced stiffly toward her, as he halted, towering over her, then placed a folded sheet in her hand.

Derek's voice was flat, emotionless.

"It's your freedom—yours, Adria's, and Gibson's."

Suddenly breathless as a soft ringing began in her ears, Gillian did not respond.

"It's what you wanted, isn't it?"

Gillian's throat worked convulsively. She nodded.

"Then that's the end of it."

In a moment, he was gone.

* * *

Alone in the cabin once more, Gillian swallowed against the tight knot in her throat as she opened the folded sheet Derek had placed in her hand. She read it slowly, realizing with growing incredulity that it was as he had said. The indentures for Adria, Christopher, and herself had been certified paid in full.

The low, keening wail that started within Gillian increased in strength, growing to a sound that consumed all thought, all feeling.

Numb, unable to think beyond the placement of her own slow, measured steps, Gillian turned toward the door.

The balmy night breeze stirred, whipping a heavy, dark lock of Derek's hair from his forehead as he stood at the ship's rail. Agitation a hard knot inside him, he recalled a similar night when he and Gillian had stood at that same rail. He remembered that her scent had tantalized him and that the warmth of her gaze had touched his heart as they had walked and talked, and had then made love . . .

. . . As all the while, Gillian had longed to be free.

A rustle of movement behind him turned Derek abruptly.

Christopher emerged onto the main deck first, followed by one slender, pale-haired figure, and then another. The faces of all obscured by the limited light, Derek was able to see their expressions clearly for the first time only when they halted briefly directly opposite him. He saw the challenge in Gibson's stare as he paused. He saw Adria's uncertainty as she stepped up onto the gangplank.

Then he saw Gillian.

It occurred to him as the moment played out with excruciating slowness before his eyes, as Gillian stepped up onto the gangplank behind her sister, as she walked off the ship without looking back, as she finally disappeared into the darkness beyond and out of his life forever, that it was over and done . . . and that Gillian had not even bothered to say goodbye.

Nineteen

Morning activity at the Royal Arms Tavern was at its height as Mrs. Healy turned to scrutinize the work progressing around her. A roast in the great fireplace was already becoming a golden brown, the aroma tantalizing despite the early hour. The ovens in the yard beyond had already produced bread, biscuits, and the first meat pies of the day. Wood to feed the oven had been chopped and stacked, fresh vegetables delivered and peeled, fish from the fresh catch of the day meticulously deboned by Adria's practiced hand. Or had that been Gillian? Mrs. Healy's lined face twisted with disgust. Two weeks, and she was still unable to distinguish one twin sister from the other.

Looking at the slight, pale-haired young woman working diligently on the last of the baskets of vegetables, Mrs. Healy shook her head, confused. Adria. No, Gillian. No . . .

Mrs. Healy glanced up as Christopher Gibson entered the kitchen from the rear. She followed his glance, a perfect indication which of the sisters was which. She saw him look briefly at the sister working near the doorway, then at the other working with the vegetables. His gaze lingered on the second sister, watching as she sorted the potatoes into great piles on the table, then attempted to sweep one of the piles into her apron to carry them toward the bucket in the corner.

Christopher's frown—his immediate rush to her side as

he brushed aside her attempt, pushing the potatoes into another nearby basket before carrying them in her stead to the waiting bucket to be washed—the young woman's protest at his interference as they argued softly in the corner—all immediately identified the sister in her mind. It was Gillian.

Unconsciously glancing back toward the identical sister who observed all in silence, Mrs. Healy felt a nudge of pain. Poor Adria. She wondered if it was as clear to others as it was to her that Adria loved Christopher Gibson, but that Christopher loved Gillian and that Gillian did not love him.

Also clear to her was the reality that Adria not only suffered for herself, but for her sister's and Christopher's despair.

Adria, selfless as always . . .

Christopher Gibson was a fool.

Mrs. Healy shook her head and picked up the first of the eggs boiled earlier. She cracked it with a twist of the wrist and began peeling, recalling the night two weeks previous when the solemn trio had appeared at the door of the tavern just prior to closing. She remembered her shock, recalling the fiasco of their attempted escape that same morning and thinking for a moment that they were about to try it all over again.

But the aura of suspense . . . or fear—whatever it had been that had raised the hackles on her spine earlier that day as she had helped send them off to their rendezvous with the *Brighton Belle,* had been missing. Looking into Christopher's eyes, she had seen merely concern. In Adria's she had seen only lingering shadows of incredulity. In looking into Gillian's eyes she had been startled to read sadness and a resignation that wearied the soul.

She had put all three into the room off the kitchen for the remainder of the night. That room had become Adria and

Gillian's when she had hired them and Christopher to work
in the tavern kitchen the following morning. They had been
working inexhaustively at whatever task had been assigned
them in the time since.

It appeared to Mrs. Healy's knowledgeable eye, however—an eye she had developed over years of observing the
peculiarities of the human condition—that for all her attempts to maintain a cheerful facade in doing her work, Gillian Haige's heart was elsewhere.

Mrs. Healy sighed and cracked another egg. She glanced
at Mr. Healy as he walked back into the kitchen, his balding
head glistening with perspiration, his saggy face drawn into
lines of concentration. Perhaps it was better being old, knowing you had progressed beyond such torment, and knowing
that although the best years were behind you and the handsome husband of her youth was no longer so, you still had
each other.

Mr. Healy looked up, and Mrs. Healy smiled. Mr. Healy
frowned, and turned back to his work.

Mrs. Healy gave an annoyed snort. And then, perhaps it
wasn't.

"Please stop that, Christopher!"

Gillian glanced around her, then back up at Christopher
to continue in a voice spiced with irritation. "I was perfectly
capable of carrying those potatoes, as well as the buckets
of water you snatched away from me earlier, and the laundry
you took out of my hands yesterday."

"You shouldn't be carrying heavy things."

"Christopher, please! I don't want to go over and over
this!"

"We won't have to go over it if you'll use caution in—"

"Caution? You mean sit back as if I'm privileged and watch you and Adria work to earn the money for passage home? No, that'll never happen."

"No, I don't mean that, and you know it."

"I don't know it!" Glancing around her, Gillian noted Mrs. Healy's scrutiny. "Mrs. Healy is watching."

"I don't care about Mrs. Healy."

"I do!"

Christopher's face flushed. "I don't want to make you angry, Gillian."

"Oh, Christopher!" Regret surged. "I'm not angry. I could never be angry with you."

Christopher's young, bearded face grew suddenly solemn. "Will you step outside with me for a few minutes, Gillian?"

Gillian looked at Mrs. Healy again, then back at Christopher. "I can't, I—" And then at Christopher's intense expression, "All right, just a few minutes."

Gillian turned reluctantly toward the rear door. They had walked a few steps into the yard out of sight of the kitchen when Christopher took her hand. The morning sun glinted on his curly, sandy-colored hair and red-tinted beard as he looked down at her, his pale, sober eyes intense with feeling. It occurred to her that she had never truly considered how handsome and appealing Christopher was. He was also gentle and sincere, yet he was one of the most courageous men she had ever known. Any woman would be proud to have a man like Christopher love her.

"I can't bear to see you unhappy, Gillian."

Gillian attempted a smile. "I'm not unhappy."

"You don't have to pretend with me."

"I'm not pretending. This whole affair could have turned out far worse if John Barrett—"

"John Barrett won't be in a position to bother you or

anyone else for a long time to come. Robert Dorsett has taken care of that. You can dismiss him from your mind."

"I have. Please don't worry about me, Christopher."

"Gillian . . ."

Gillian searched Christopher's earnest face. No, easy words of reassurance would not be enough for this man. He had shared her life and her anguish too long to separate himself from it. Only the truth would suffice. She owed him that much.

Taking a deep breath, Gillian began slowly. "I don't know if I can make you understand. It's not really unhappiness that you see, Christopher. It's the weight of resignation."

"Resignation?"

Gillian's smile became strained. "You know how stubborn I am. It's so difficult for me to accede to helplessness."

Christopher's lips tightened. "You mean the child . . ."

"No." Gillian's hand slipped to a narrow waist that yet revealed no sign of her condition. "I'm not sorry—not about the child. The child is mine and it was conceived in love."

"In *love* . . ."

"Yes." The words torn from her heart, Gillian held Christopher's gaze with hers as she continued, "The only problem was that Derek didn't love me in return."

Gillian paused in an effort to draw her emotions under control. "I wanted him to love me, you know. I hoped desperately, right up to the last moment, that Derek would declare his love for me rather than lose me, but he did not. Instead, he set me free and walked away."

At Christopher's soft protest, Gillian shook her head. "No, I know. It wasn't that Derek didn't love me at all. It was just that he didn't love me *enough*." Gillian took a steadying breath. "The truth is that after the first shock wore off, I was furious that Derek had released my indenture so easily. I felt betrayed. I wanted to rant and rave and shriek my frustration, and while I felt that way, it was easier." Gillian paused again. "It isn't as easy anymore."

"Andrews is a fool."

Gillian gave a wry laugh. "Perhaps he's smarter than you think."

"No, he isn't, Gillian." Christopher slipped his arms around her unexpectedly. The warmth of him was both comfort and anguish as he held her close. Wishing fervently she dared to linger, Gillian heard the revealing catch in Christopher's voice as he whispered, "I suppose I know, better than anyone else how big a fool he really is, because I—"

Gillian drew back instinctively, the aching void inside her tightening to pain as she concluded in Christopher's stead, "Because you're my *friend*." She continued more softly. "You'll never know what it means to me to know you're my friend, Christopher . . . how much it will always mean."

Christopher's light eyes searched hers. She saw his throat work convulsively. "Your friend . . ."

Never closer to tears, Gillian whispered, "Yes, Christopher . . . my very dearest friend."

Looking at Christopher for a long moment, Gillian raised herself up to brush his cheek lightly with her lips. He did not speak as she slid her arm through his and, turning back toward the kitchen, drew him along with her.

Looking up at him as they reached the doorway, she saw his face draw into a frown.

"What you just said changes nothing, you know."

Suddenly immobile, Gillian did not respond.

"I don't care how angry you get or how much Mrs. Healy disapproves, I won't let you endanger yourself by lifting anything heavy."

Her sudden relief overwhelming, Gillian laughed aloud. "Christopher, you are the most determined man!"

Gillian's smile slowly faded as she entered the kitchen. Dear Christopher . . . Any woman would be happy to have him love her.

Any woman but she.

Adria's eyes clouded as she turned back to her kitchen chores. The image of Gillian's stiff smile and the pain behind it remained before her eyes, as did the sober acceptance in Christopher's expression as he returned to his work.

The torment lingered.

She could bear it no longer.

His eyes weary, his head aching from lack of sleep, Derek sat at his desk. It had been a difficult two weeks. Strangely, Robert Dorsett, who had remained anonymous and invisible during the years Emmaline had pursued him relentlessly, had suddenly become his ally. Dorsett had moved swiftly, using his influence on the island to have Barrett suitably confined in an island prison where he awaited trial on a number of charges for which he doubtless would have escaped punishment were it not for Dorsett. He was certain Dorsett was responsible for the contacts he had again begun receiving from commercial agents in port shortly afterward and the contract for cargo he had recently signed.

With a sailing date a day hence and the loading of cargo under way, his financial status was now stable, but that realization afforded him little of the satisfaction expected. Instead, a slender, pale-haired image that had given him little rest night or day continued to haunt him.

A silent lament began again inside Derek. How many times had he thought he had heard Gillian's step outside his door? How many times had he turned, expecting to see her? How many times had her scent, her smile, her quick wit returned to tease his mind? How many times had he stretched out his hand in the middle of the night searching the bunk beside him, hoping that somehow . . .

Derek briefly closed his eyes, his torment intense. He had only begun to realize how great a part of him Gillian had taken with her when she had left. It had been more difficult than he had ever imagined it could be to grant her the freedom she had risked so much to attain, but the echo of her words, ringing over again in his mind had left him no choice.

Don't you see? Nothing that passed between us was truly real! Do you know how submission gnawed at the core of me until I felt I was being consumed?

And at his brief question about the hours she has spent lying in his arms . .

They did not mean enough . . .

Pain slashed viciously at Derek's innards once more, sharper and more keenly than any blade. He was bleeding from the wounds inflicted, even as his arms longed to hold Gillian close, as his body strained for Gillian's remembered warmth, the war between his heart and his mind leaving him a scarred and bloody battlefield from which there was no escape.

Despairing, Derek rubbed his hand across his eyes. Somehow, he had never expected that *words* could so efficiently stand between Gillian and him, that they could leave him so ineffective, so without recourse, so—

A sound at his open cabin door raising his head, Derek turned in its direction. Gasping as the image which had dominated his thoughts materialized before him, he stood up abruptly, his chair slapping back against the floor with a startling crack of sound.

The vision remained motionless in the doorway, pale hair glistening in the limited light. He took a short step forward, then another, only to halt stiffly as his harsh question rang on the silence between them.

"What are you doing here?"

The tavern yard was silent except for the chirping of birds and the hissing sound of a nearby lizard as it spread its colorful throat fan in vain display. A gentle breeze lifted curling tendrils of hair that had escaped Gillian's topknot to lie against her perspired neck as she reached down into the soapy water in the washtub in front of her. The long line of laundry behind her flapped gently as she fished for the last remaining cloth. She turned abruptly at a sound behind her.

Derek!

Paralyzed into motionlessness as Derek advanced toward her, Gillian felt her heart begin a fierce pounding. Derek's broad frame was tense, his handsome features tightly drawn. He was angrier than she had ever seen him.

Halting, Derek towered over her, frigid fury in his gaze as he demanded with tenuous control, "Why didn't you tell me, Gillian?"

Anger mixed with pain.

"Answer me, Gillian."

It assailed her senses.

"Gillian . . ."

She could not respond.

"Answer me, damn you!"

Gillian forced a response. "Tell you what?"

"That you were going to have my child!"

Gillian caught her breath. "Who told you that I—"

"Does it really matter who told me?" Derek's eyes turned hard and cold as stone. "It's true, isn't it."

Gillian stiffened. "What difference does it make?"

Derek went suddenly still.

"Do you hate me that much, Gillian?"

"Hate you?"

"Do you hate me so much that you couldn't stand the thought of letting me raise my own child?"

"Your child?" A slow shuddering began inside Gillian. "This child is mine!"

"Gillian . . ."

"This child will bear *my* name, not yours!"

"It will not!"

Gillian's delicate features hardened. "You seem to have forgotten something, Derek. You're no longer the master here, and I'm no longer your servant. I'm a free woman."

"Do you think you would be a free woman now if I had known?" Derek took a short step forward that brought him breathlessly close. "Do you think I would have let you go?"

"Oh, you would have kept us both for the term of my indenture, is that it, Derek? How magnanimous of you! I don't know how I could've been such a fool not to realize you would make so noble a gesture!"

"Gillian . . . damn you . . . *I'm* the violated party here, not you! I was the one who was deceived and manipulated when I was never less than honest with you."

"Oh, yes, you were honest . . . painfully so. 'For as long as the feelings between us last' . . . Those were your words, weren't they, Derek? How long do you estimate that would be? A week. . a month . . . a year?"

Pausing, his voice dropping to a hoarse whisper, Derek rasped, "Is it so hard to understand how I felt, Gillian? You invaded my life without warning. I had no place in my life for a woman, but you taunted me with your anger and your arrogance from the first day, fixing your image so deeply on my mind that I couldn't escape it. When I thought things couldn't possibly get worse, you appeared in my cabin and offered yourself to me. I knew I was a fool to accept your offer, but I was powerless to refuse it. How was I to know that you would give yourself to me so completely that the moments you lay in my arms would surpass any I had ever known? How was I to know that you would instill in me a longing that would not wane, that you would break down the wall I had erected around my heart a little more each day, with each look, each touch, each kiss?"

"I resented the way you made me feel, but I told myself what I felt for you was a short-lived emotion that would soon fade. I wanted to believe that. I tried to *make* myself believe it. Then you ran away, and when all was said and done, I discovered that there was only one thing you really wanted from me . . . only one thing you had ever wanted— your freedom."

Derek's voice dropped to a broken whisper. "I gave you your freedom for only one reason, Gillian. Because I loved you, too much to deny you."

Derek took a shaken breath. "But the strangest part of all was that . . . in my heart . . . I didn't believe you'd really leave me."

Derek swallowed tightly, his dark eyes bright with pain. "I tried to stay away. I told myself I didn't want you any more than you wanted me—that I didn't need you any more than you needed me—but it was all a lie I couldn't quite make myself believe."

Derek paused, swallowing again. His grip on her arms tightened as his shaken tone took on a desperate note. "But that's in the past now, Gillian. We have a reason to start over that even you can't deny."

"Derek . . ."

"No, let me finish." Derek's gaze grew intense. "I want you to love me as I love you, Gillian. I want you to need me as I need you. I want to fulfill you, to make your life complete, to give you joy. I want to take care of you, to share my life with you, to keep you with me always . . . and I want our child to share in our love."

Derek's handsome face was tense, his eyes black pools of torment. "There are many things that will be hard for you to forget, but I'm asking you to give me a chance to prove to you that our tomorrows will be better than our yesterdays, in every way. I want you to give me a chance to prove my love." His voice cracking, Derek rasped, "Will you try, Gillian? Please, try."

Please . . . Gillian's heart was filled to bursting. The proud, autocratic Derek Andrews was pleading for her love. This hard, angry man loved her as she loved him, as she had *always* loved him . . .

"Gillian . . ."

With a soft cry, Gillian was in his arms. She felt Derek's shuddering as he crushed her against him. She heard his rasping, ardent words in her ear. She felt his mouth on hers, swallowing her response, the loving words he had engraved so deeply into her heart. She returned them with her kiss, promising, pledging to love . . .

Oh, yes, how truly she would love.

Epilogue

The tranquil Jamaican night was warm and silent. A light breeze blew through the bedroom window, lifting the blind as Gillian moved restlessly in her sleep. The fine batiste nightrail she wore lay lightly against her, allowing a faint outline of smooth flesh beneath.

Standing over Gillian, the powerful, naked length of him a pale shadow in the darkness, Derek allowed his eyes to dwell on the total beauty of the vision before him. He recalled the scent of her glowing hair as it had entwined him in his passion hours earlier, the silky texture of her skin as she had moved sensuously under his lips, the taste of her mouth as she had surrendered it willingly to his. He remembered the rapture in her short gasp as the moist inner heat of her had closed around him.

A soft sound in the darkness turned Derek toward the cradle nearby. The blind moved briefly once more, allowing a shaft of moonlight to shine briefly across the babe within. Derek's gaze lingered as the babe shifted and grunted in its sleep.

At three months, the beautiful little girl had wispy hair that shone silver-gold in the semilight. Her incredibly long dark lashes rested against her full, pink cheeks, concealing eyes as black as midnight beneath them.

Juliana . . . his daughter . . .

He had not believed he could feel so much love.

Turning as Gillian's delicate hand slid unexpectedly into his, Derek met a brilliant azure gaze that had grown all the more glorious for the glow of love reflected therein. He touched his mouth to hers, then drew back to whisper, "Are you happy, Gillian?"

Slipping into the curve of his arm and leaning warmly against him, Gillian nodded. Slender as a reed again, she had blossomed with motherhood, seeming to grow more beautiful each day.

"Say the words for me, Gillian."

Momentarily troubled at his need for confirmation, Gillian reached up to press her mouth again to his. "Yes, I'm happy."

A familiar warmth swelled within Derek. Curving his palm around her cheek, he brushed Gillian's clear brow with his lips, her heavily fringed lids, the curve of her cheek, her chin, her mouth . . . the joy growing deeper as he settled there more deeply than before.

Juliana grunted again, distracting them, and Derek gave a soft laugh. "She snores like you."

Gillian flashed a tart smile. "She has your temper."

Derek shook his head. "We'll have to let her know we won't stand for that."

"She has my tenacity."

Derek smiled. "So she does . . ."

Scooping Gillian up abruptly into his arms, Derek carried her back to their bed. Lying beside her, he slipped the strap of her nightrail from her shoulder and brushed the darkened crest of her breast with his lips. He had returned from a voyage to Charleston two days earlier, the weeks away longer than any he had ever spent. He had returned to Gillian's eager, loving reception; a babe who had grown far too quickly in his absence to have made him fully comfortable with the time he had spent away from her; *and* to the sight of Adria and Christopher walking hand and hand.

At last.

He would never forget the debt he owed Adria for coming to his ship the night before he had sailed those long months ago. It frightened him that he had come so close to losing Gillian. He was more grateful to Adria than he could ever express that the voyage that would have taken him away from Gillian, possibly forever, had instead been spent in celebration and marital bliss.

Derek drew Gillian closer. His life had begun to settle, without threat. John Barrett had been tried and found guilty of crimes too numerous to mention. He would spend the major portion of his life in a Jamaica prison. No one deserved it more.

As for Emmaline . . . the mystery of her sudden change of heart had been solved a few months after Gillian and he had been married . . . when Madam Dorsett was seen in town with an astoundingly distended stomach preceding her.

It was said that the night her time came, the Dorsett sugar estate had rung with the echoes of Emmaline's screeching—but he supposed he couldn't really blame her. Not one . . . not two . . . but *three* little red-haired babes.

Robert Dorsett had been enthralled with his new daughters. As for Emmaline . . .

Rumor had it that she didn't have much time for black magic anymore.

Rumor had it that she didn't have much time to venture off the estate, either.

And rumor had it that Emmaline was pregnant *again* . . .

Derek snickered.

His snicker faded as Gillian drew his mouth to hers. He

indulged the kiss, deepening it with warmth, searching the hollows of her mouth, incredulous that the wonder of Gillian could grow greater each time he held her in his arms.

Drawing back, he whispered the words that came from a font within him that bore only Gillian's name.

"I love you, Gillian."

Gillian's passionate response lighting a familiar flame within him, Derek slid her nightrail to her waist to cover the other waiting crest with his mouth.

Gillian was his . . . forever his. She had made him a husband and a father. She had given his days purpose, and his nights . . .

Derek slid Gillian's shift lower, following the trail with his lips as he recalled the frigid morning on a London dock when Gillian's gaze had first met his. She had been angry. She was angry no longer.

He tasted the sweet, moist core of her.

He heard her breathless rasp.

And he loved her.

WHAT'S LOVE GOT TO DO WITH IT?

Everything . . . Just ask Kathleen Drymon . . . and Zebra Books

CASTAWAY ANGEL	*(3569-1, $4.50/$5.50)*
GENTLE SAVAGE	*(3888-7, $4.50/$5.50)*
MIDNIGHT BRIDE	*(3265-X, $4.50/$5.50)*
VELVET SAVAGE	*(3886-0, $4.50/$5.50)*
TEXAS BLOSSOM	*(3887-9, $4.50/$5.50)*
WARRIOR OF THE SUN	*(3924-7, $4.99/$5.99)*